RAVE REVIEWS!

Debbie Macomber

"Debbie Macomber writes delightful, heartwarming romances that touch the emotions and leave the reader feeling good."
—Jayne Ann Krentz

"Debbie Macomber is one of our premier storytellers."
—Anne Stuart Ohlrogge

Linda Lael Miller
New York Times bestselling author

"One of the hottes̶ ̶ ̶ ̶ ̶ ̶ ̶ ̶ ̶ ̶ ̶ ̶ ̶ ̶ ̶ ̶"
— *Times*

"Linda Lael Mil̶ ̶ ̶ ̶ ̶ ̶ ̶ ̶ ̶ ̶ ̶ ̶ ̶an with the written word."
—*Affaire de Coeur*

Patricia Simpson
1993 Winner of the *Romantic Times* Reviewer's Choice Award

"Patricia Simpson continues to demonstrate why she is fast becoming one of the premier writers of supernatural romance."
—*Romantic Times*

PURRFECT LOVE

Debbie Macomber,

Linda Lael Miller,

Patricia Simpson

HarperPaperbacks
A Division of HarperCollins*Publishers*

HarperPaperbacks *A Division of* HarperCollins*Publishers*
10 East 53rd Street, New York, N.Y. 10022

"Family Affair" copyright © 1994 by Debbie Macomber
"Switch" copyright © 1994 by Linda Lael Miller
"Lord of the Nile" copyright © 1994 by Patricia Simpson
All rights reserved. No part of this book may be used or reproduced in any manner whatsoever without written permission of the publisher, except in the case of brief quotations embodied in critical articles and reviews. For information address HarperCollins*Publishers,*
10 East 53rd Street, New York, N.Y. 10022.

Cover illustration by Jim Griffin

First printing: May 1994

Printed in the United States of America

HarperPaperbacks, HarperMonogram, and colophon are trademarks of HarperCollins*Publishers*

❖ 10 9 8 7 6 5 4 3 2 1

CONTENTS

Debbie Macomber
FAMILY AFFAIR
1

Linda Lael Miller
SWITCH
87

Patricia Simpson
LORD OF THE NILE
181

FAMILY AFFAIR

~ *by* ~

Debbie Macomber

ONE

"I've got the backbone of a worm," Lacey Lancaster muttered as she let herself into her apartment. She tossed her mail onto an end table and glared at Cleo. "I didn't say a word to Mr. Sullivan, not a single word."

Cleo, her Abyssinian cat, affectionately wove her golden-brown body between Lacey's ankles. Her long tail coiled around Lacey's calf like a feather boa, soft, sleek, and soothing.

"I had the perfect opportunity to ask for a raise and did I do it?" Lacey demanded, kicking her feet so that her shoes sailed in opposite directions. "Oh, no, I let it pass by. And do you know why?"

Cleo apparently didn't. Lacey took off her bright green vinyl raincoat, opened the closet door, and shoved it inside. "Because I'm a coward, that's why."

Walking into the kitchen, she opened the refrigerator and stuck her head inside, rooting out some sorry-looking leftovers, two boxes of take-out Chinese, and the tulip bulbs she'd meant to plant in her balcony flower box last October.

"I'm starved." She opened the vegetable bin and took out a limp stalk of celery. "You know my problem, don't you?"

Cleo meowed and wove her way between Lacey's ankles once more.

"Oh, sorry. You're probably hungry too." Lacey reached inside the cupboard and pulled out a can of gourmet cat food. To her surprise, Cleo didn't show the least bit of interest. Instead, she raised her tail and stuck her rear end in the air.

"What's going on with you? Trust me, Cleo, this isn't the time to go all weird on me. I need to talk." Taking her celery stick with her, she moved into the living room and fell onto the love seat.

"I work and slave and put in all kinds of overtime— without pay, I might add—and for what? Mr. Sullivan doesn't appreciate me. Yet it's *my* decorating ideas he uses. The worst part is, he doesn't even bother to give me the credit." She chomped off the end of the celery and chewed with a vengeance. The stalk teetered from the attack and then slowly curved downward.

Lacey studied the celery. "This might as well be my backbone," she muttered. Unable to sit still any longer, she paced her compact living room. "I haven't had a raise in the whole year I've worked for him, and in that time I've taken on much more responsibility and completed projects Mr. Sullivan couldn't or wouldn't do. Good grief, if it weren't for me, Mr. Sullivan wouldn't know what was going on in his own business." By this time she was breathless and irate. "I do more work than he does, and he's the owner, for heaven's sake!"

Clearly Cleo agreed, because she let out a low, wailing moan. Lacey had never owned a cat before, but after a devastating divorce she'd needed someone. Or some thing. The thing had turned out to be Cleo.

She'd first spotted Cleo in a pet-shop window, looking forlorn. Cleo's brother and sister had been sold two weeks earlier, and Cleo was all alone. Abandoned, the half-grown kitten gazed, dejected and miserable, onto the world that passed her by.

Lacey had been suffering from the same emotions herself, and once they met the two had become fast friends. No fool, the pet-store owner knew a sale when he saw one. He'd made some fast soft-shoe moves to convince Lacey what a good investment Cleo would be. If she bred her and sold off the litter, within a year or so, he claimed, her original investment would be returned to her.

Lacey hadn't been so keen on the breeding aspect of the deal, but it had sounded like something she should try. She wanted companionship, and after her disastrous marriage she was through with men. A cat wouldn't lie or cheat or cause hurt. Peter had done all three with bone-cutting accuracy.

Good ol' Peter, Lacey mused. She should be grateful for all the lessons he'd taught her. Perhaps someday she would be able to look back on her marriage without the crushing pain she felt now. He'd vowed to love and cherish her but then calmly announced one Sunday afternoon, without warning, that he was leaving her for someone else.

Someone else was a tall blonde with baby blue eyes and a voluptuous figure. Lacey had sized up the competition, decided she didn't stand a chance, and signed the divorce papers. Oh, there'd been some haggling, but she'd left that to her attorney and stayed out of it as much as possible. As soon as her divorce was final, she'd uprooted herself, moved to San Francisco, located a job she loved, and started life all over again.

Sort of.

This time, she was playing it smart. Men were completely out of the picture. For the first time, she was supporting herself. For the first time, she didn't need anyone else. Because it could happen all over again. Another blonde with a *Playboy* figure could disrupt her life a second time. It was best to play it safe. Who needed that kind of grief? Not her!

Lacey wasn't discounting her assets. With her straight brown hair sculpted around her ears, and equally dark eyes, she resembled a lovable pixie. She was barely five feet tall, while her brother, who was five years older, was nearly six feet. Why nature had short-changed her in the height department, she would never understand.

After the divorce, Lacey had felt emotionally battered and lost. Bringing Cleo into her life had helped tremendously, so much that Lacey figured she could do without a man. Her cat provided all the companionship she needed.

"Okay, okay, you're right," Lacey said, glancing down at her fidgeting feline friend. "I couldn't agree with you more. I'm a gutless wonder. The real problem is I don't want to quit my job. All I'm looking for is to be paid what I'm worth, which is a whole lot more than I'm making now." She'd come out of the divorce with a hefty settlement; otherwise she'd be in dire financial straights.

Cleo concurred with a low wail, unlike any sound Lacey could ever remember her making.

Lacey studied her cat. "You all right, girl? You don't sound right."

Cleo thrust her hind end into the air again and shot across the room to attack her catnip mouse. Whatever was troubling her had passed. At least Lacey hoped it had.

Muttering to herself, Lacey returned to the kitchen and reexamined the contents of her refrigerator. There wasn't anything there she'd seriously consider eating. The leftover Chinese containers were filled with hard, dried-out rice and a thick red sauce with what had once been sweet-and-sour pork. The meat had long since disappeared, and the sauce resembled cherry gelatin. The only edible items were the tulip bulbs, not that she'd seriously consider dining on them.

She'd hoped to treat herself to something extravagant to celebrate her raise. Domino's Pizza was about as extravagant as she got. But she wasn't doing any celebrating this night. If she wanted dinner, she'd need to fix it herself.

Her cupboards weren't promising: a couple of cans of soup mingled with fifteen of gourmet cat food.

Soup.

Her life had deteriorated to a choice between cream of mushroom and vegetarian vegetable. Blindly she reached for a can and brought out the vegetable. The freezer held a loaf of bread. Her choice of sandwiches was limited to either peanut butter and jelly or grilled cheese.

"Sometimes I think I hate you!" The words came through the kitchen wall as clearly as if the person saying them were standing in the same room.

Lacey sighed. Her neighbor, Jack Walker, and his girlfriend were at it again. She hadn't formally met the man who lived next door, which was fine with her. The guy suffered from severe woman problems; from what she'd heard through the wall, it sounded as if the pair was badly in need of therapy. Lacey avoided Jack like the plague, despite his numerous attempts at striking up an acquaintance. She was polite but firm, even discouraging. She had to give him credit. He didn't accept *no* easily. Over the months, his methods had become increasingly imaginative. He'd tried flowers, tacked notes to her door, and had once attempted to lure her into his apartment with the offer of dinner. Of all his tactics, the promise of a meal had been the most tempting, but Lacey knew trouble when she saw it and resisted.

As far as she was concerned, dating Jack was out of the question, especially since he was already involved with someone else. Lacey had lost count of the times she'd heard him arguing with his girlfriend. Some nights she was forced to turn on her stereo to block out the noise.

But being the polite, don't-cause-problems sort of person she was, Lacey had never complained. She might as well throw herself down on the carpet and instruct people to walk all over her.

"I wasn't always a worm," she complained to Cleo. "It's only in the last year or so that I've lost my self-confidence. I'd like to blame Mr. Sullivan, but I can't. Not when I'm the one who's at fault. You'd think it'd be easy to ask for a little thing like a raise, wouldn't you? It isn't, yet I'm left feeling like Oliver Twist. At least he had the courage to ask for more.

"Mr. Sullivan should thank his lucky stars. I'm good at what I do, but does he notice? Oh, no. He just takes me for granted."

Having finished this tirade, she noticed that Cleo had disappeared. Even her cat had deserted her. She found Cleo on the windowsill, meowing pathetically.

Lacey lifted the cat in her arms and petted her. "Have I been so wrapped up in my own problems that I've ignored you?"

Cleo leaped out of the embrace and raced into the bedroom.

The arguing continued in the other apartment.

"Sarah, for the love of heaven, be reasonable!" Jack shouted.

"Give it to him with both barrels," Lacey said under her breath. "I bet you didn't know Jack was dating on the side, did you? Well, don't get down on yourself. I didn't know what a womanizer Peter was either."

Sarah apparently heeded her advice, because the shouting intensified. Jack, who generally remained the calmer of the two, was also losing it.

If she listened real hard, she might be able to figure out the cause of their dispute, but frankly Lacey wasn't that interested.

"I saw him with someone new just last week," she added, just for fun. Lacey had bumped into Jack at the mailbox. There'd been a woman with him and it wasn't Sarah. But it was always Sarah who came back. Always Sarah he quarreled with. The poor girl apparently cared deeply for him. More fool she.

"I'm having vegetarian vegetable soup," Lacey informed Cleo as she strolled into the room, thinking her pet would want to know. "It isn't anything that would interest you, unfortunately." Whatever had been troubling her cat earlier was under control for the moment.

Dinner complete, Lacey set her steaming bowl of soup and her grilled cheese sandwich on the table. She'd just sat down when something hit the wall in the apartment next door. Instinctively, she jumped.

Angry voices escalated. Jack was no longer calm and in control. In fact, it sounded as if he'd lost his cool completely. The two were shouting at each other, each trying to drown the other out.

Lacey sighed. Enough was enough. Setting her napkin aside, she went over to the kitchen wall and knocked politely. Either they didn't hear her or they chose to ignore her, something they did with increasing frequency.

She'd just sat down again when an explosion of noise nearly jerked her off the chair. One or the other of the disgruntled lovers had decided to turn on the radio. Full blast.

The radio was turned off as abruptly as it had been turned on, followed by a tirade from Jack.

The radio was switched back on.

Off.

Once again, ever so politely, Lacey tapped the wall.

They ignored her.

Then, for whatever reason, there was silence. Blissful silence. Whatever had plagued the two was settled.

Either that or they'd murdered one another. Whichever it was, the silence was bliss.

When Lacey had finished her dinner, she washed the few dishes she'd used. Cleo continued to weave her sleek body between Lacey's ankles, meowing and wailing all the while. "What's wrong with you, girl?" Lacey asked again.

Squatting down, she ran her hand over the cat's spine. Cleo arched her back and cried once more.

"You don't seem to be yourself," Lacey commented, concerned.

It hit her then, right between the eyes. "You're in heat! Oh, my goodness, you're in heat." How could she have been so obtuse?

Leaving the kitchen, she rooted through her personal telephone directory, searching for the name the pet-shop owner had given her. If she was going to breed Cleo, she needed to talk to this woman first.

"Poor, poor Cleo," Lacey said sympathetically. "Trust me, sweetie, men aren't worth all this trouble." She quickly located the phone number and punched it out.

"I'm Lacey Lancaster," she said hurriedly into the receiver. "The owner of Pet's World gave me your number. I bought an Abyssinian several months ago."

No sooner had she introduced herself when the arguing in the next-door apartment resumed.

"I'm sorry, dearie, but I can't understand you." The woman on the other end of the line spoke with a soft Irish accent.

"I said I purchased an Abyssinian cat—"

"It sounds like you've a party going on."

"There's no party." Lacey spoke louder, close to shouting herself.

"Perhaps you should call me back when your guests have left," came the soft Irish brogue. With that the line was disconnected.

Something snapped in Lacey. Her never-cause-a-scene

upbringing went down the drain faster than tap water. She slammed the phone down and clenched her fists.

"I've had it!" she shouted. And she had. With men who didn't know the meaning of the words "faithful" and "commitment." With employers who took advantage of their employees. With Neanderthal neighbors, who shuffled one woman after another through their apartments without a second thought.

Lacey walked out her door and down the hall, her strides eating up the distance in seconds. However, by the time she reached Jack's apartment the fire had died down. Her anger would solve nothing. She tapped politely and waited.

The arguing stopped abruptly and the door flew open. Lacey was so astonished that she leaped back. Sarah leaped back, too, and glared at her. It was apparent the other woman hadn't heard Lacey knock.

"Hello," Lacey said, her heartbeat roaring in her ears. "I was wondering if you two would mind holding it down just a little bit."

The woman, young and pretty, blinked back tears. "You don't need to worry. I was just leaving!"

Jack appeared then, looking suave and composed. He brightened when he saw it was her. "Lacey," he said, flashing her an easy grin. "This is a pleasant surprise."

"With all your fighting, I couldn't even make a phone call," she explained, not wanting to give him the wrong impression. This wasn't a social visit.

"I apologize." Jack glared at Sarah. "It won't happen again."

Sarah's chin shot into the air as she jerked her purse strap over her shoulder. "I . . . I don't believe we have anything more to say to each other." She hurried past Lacey toward the elevator.

"Sarah." Jack placed both his hands on Lacey's shoulders and edged his way past her. "I'm warning you . . . just don't do anything stupid."

"You mean, like listen to you?"

"Dammit to hell," Jack muttered. He stared at Lacey as if this were all her fault.

Lacey opened her mouth to tell him exactly what she thought of him and then abruptly changed her mind. Jack wouldn't listen. Men never did. Why waste her breath?

With nothing more to say, she returned to her apartment. To her surprise she realized she'd left the door open. Her immediate concern was for Cleo, and she rushed inside in a panic.

She stopped cold in her tracks at the sight that greeted her.

"Cleo!" Her cat was in the throes of passion with a long-haired feline she didn't recognize.

Placing her hands over her mouth, Lacey sagged against the wall. She wasn't going to need the Irish woman after all. Cleo had already found her mate.

TWO

"Stop!" Lacey demanded, already knowing it was too late. The two cats ignored her. So much for the thrill of being a cat owner.

Knowing only one thing to do, Lacey raced into the kitchen and filled a tall glass with water. She'd get the lovers' attention soon enough. Rushing back into the living room, she tripped on a throw rug and staggered a few steps in a desperate effort to maintain her balance. By the time she reached the cats, most of the liquid was down the front of her blouse and only a few drops landed on the passionate couple.

By then they were finished and the strange cat was looking for a way out of her apartment. Typical male! He'd gotten what he wanted and was ready to be on his merry way.

Lacey was about to open the sliding class door that led out to her balcony when someone rang her doorbell.

Frowning fiercely at the alley cat, Lacey traipsed across her living room and checked the peephole.

It was her Don Juan neighbor, fresh from his argument with Sarah. "Hello again." He flashed her an easy smile which, Lacey hated to admit, hit its mark. She didn't know what was in her personality profile that made her vulnerable to this type of man, but whatever it was, she sincerely wished it would go away.

"I don't suppose you've seen my cat?" he asked.

"You own a cat?"

"Actually, he allows me to live with him."

As if she'd planned it this way, Cleo strolled past, her tail in the air, giving the impression of royalty. The long-haired mixed breed followed closely behind, looking as if he'd rested enough for a second go-round.

"There's Dog," Jack said.

"Dog? You named your cat Dog?"

"Yeah," he said, walking past her. He reached for his cat affectionately and cradled him in his arms. "I wanted a dog, but I had to compromise."

"So you got yourself a cat named Dog." In light of how she'd met his faithful companion, Lacey wasn't amused.

"Exactly."

"Well, listen here, your Dog has stolen Cleo's virginity. What do you plan to do about it?"

Jack's eyes widened. Lacey swore the man looked downright pleased. "Dog? What do you have to say for yourself?"

"It's you I'm asking," Lacey said, squaring her shoulders. "As a responsible pet owner, you have an answer, I hope."

His dark eyes narrowed. "I can only apologize."

"Then I accept your apology," Lacey murmured. It seemed darn little in light of the possible consequences, but the less they had to say to each other the better. Lacey wanted as little to do with Jack as possible. The more she saw of him the more attracted she was, which made absolutely no sense. She was like someone on a strict diet, irresistibly drawn to a dessert tray.

"Listen, I was hoping for an opportunity to get to know you a little better," Jack said, as if he planned to stay awhile.

Lacey couldn't allow that to happen. She all but opened the door for him.

"We've been neighbors for the past several months. I think we must have gotten started on the wrong foot," he said, showing no signs of leaving. "I understand you aren't interested in dating, but we could be a bit more neighborly, don't you think?"

Lacey nodded politely, if reluctantly. It would help to have someone to feed her cat and collect her mail on occasion. She would be willing to do the same for him, but she wanted it firmly understood that this was the extent of what she was offering.

She told him so.

"Friends?" he asked, holding out his hand.

"Friends," she agreed. They exchanged handshakes. She found his grasp secure, but his fingers held hers far longer than necessary. She disliked the way her heart reacted. This man was dangerous in more ways than one. The less she had to do with him, the better.

He seemed to be waiting for her to invite him to stay for coffee and chitchat. The thought was tempting. It would be nice to have someone to be neighborly with, but the lesson she'd learned from Peter had sunk in.

"We do seem to share a love of cats," Jack added, as if this were grounds for a long-standing friendship.

"I like Cleo," she said pointedly. "Now if you'll excuse me." This time she held the door open for him.

"It was nice talking to you, Lacey," Jack said with a boyish grin that was potent enough to topple her resolve to limit their relationship. "I'm hoping we can become *good* friends."

Lacey didn't miss the emphasis on *good*. The last thing

she needed or wanted was friendship with a known Casanova. Not when her she'd been fool enough to marry one who'd ruthlessly left her for another.

Since she hadn't summoned the gumption to ask for a raise, she found it even more difficult to explain to her neighbor that she wasn't interested in a man who kept women on the side.

Jack left then, to Lacey's intense relief. She scooped Cleo up in her arms and held her tight, as if her beloved cat had had a narrow escape. Cleo, however, didn't take kindly to being pressed against a wet blouse and squirmed free, leaping onto the carpet. She made her way to the seat of the overstuffed chair, her favorite spot for a cat-nap, and curled up contentedly. It might have been Lacey's imagination, but Cleo seemed completely at ease and thoroughly satisfied.

Just as Lacey was about to turn on the television, the phone rang. It was probably her best friend, Jeanne Becker. Jeanne had been one of the first people to befriend Lacey after her move to San Francisco. She worked as a dental assistant and was single, like Lacey, but had been dating Dave steadily for nearly a year. However, neither seemed to be in any hurry to get engaged. With so many friends divorcing, they both wanted to be very sure they were taking the right step.

"Well?" Jeanne asked. "Did you ask for your raise?"

"No," Lacey confessed.

"Why not?" Jeanne demanded. "You promised you would. What's so difficult about talking to Mr. Sullivan?"

"I have no defense. I'm a worm."

"What are you so frightened of?" Jeanne asked after a thoughtful moment, as if there were something deep and dark hidden in Lacey's childhood that kept her from con-fronting her employer.

"I don't know," Lacey admitted. "It's just that Mr. Sullivan is so . . . so intimidating. He's got these beady eyes, and when I ask to talk to him, he looks at his watch as if he doesn't have any time for me and asks how long it will take. And by the time he goes through this little routine, I've lost my nerve."

"Don't you know the man's psyching you out?"

"Yeah, I suppose," Lacey murmured, disheartened. "But knowing that doesn't do any good. My talk with Mr. Sullivan isn't the only thing that went wrong," she added. "Cleo's in heat, and the neighbor's cat stole into my apartment, and I found them . . . together."

"Oh, dear, it sounds like you've had a full day."

"It gets better," Lacey said. "The guy who lives next to me suggested we be neighborly."

"You mean the hunk who's been asking you out for the last six months? I met him, remember?"

Lacey wasn't comfortable thinking of Jack in those terms, but she let her friend's comment pass. "Yeah. He owns Dog, the cat who had his way with Cleo. And before you ask, I did get the name of his cat right."

"I could like this guy," Jeanne said, laughing softly.

"You're welcome to him."

"Lacey! Honestly, when are you going to let bygones be bygones? Peter was a rat, but he's out of your life. The worst thing you can do is blame other men for what happened between you and your ex."

"I'm not blaming other men."

"You've been divorced for over a year now and you never date."

"I don't want another relationship."

"You were wise not to date right away," Jeanne said sympathetically, "but now it's time you got on with your life. If you want my advice, I think you should go out with Jack. He's adorable."

"Are you crazy?" Lacey insisted. "He was fighting with Sarah again. It's all I can do not to tell that sweet young girl what I know. He's playing her for a fool just the way Peter played me."

"You're jumping to conclusions."

"I don't think so," Lacey insisted. "They're constantly fighting. From bits of conversation I've heard, it sounds like Jack wants her to move in with him. Apparently she's on to him because she refuses. I wouldn't trust him either."

"You know what's happened, don't you?" Jeanne asked. "You've gotten to be a cynic. I don't think you realize how much Peter hurt you."

"Nonsense," was Lacey's immediate reply. "He didn't do anything more than teach me a valuable lesson."

Lacey didn't sleep well that night. It was little wonder, in light of how her day had gone. The unpleasant run-in with her neighbor continued to plague her. Jack was easygoing and friendly, the kind of man who put people at ease. Not her, though. Lacey's defenses went up whenever he was around her.

As luck would have it, they met in the hallway on their way to work the following morning.

"Off to the coal mines, I see," he said amicably as they made their way to the elevator. He was dressed in a dark three-piece suit, and the only word she could think to describe him was debonair. His smile was wide and charming. Too charming, Lacey decided. His eyes were friendly and warm, the type of eyes a woman remembers for a long time.

"Where do you work?" he asked conversationally as he summoned the elevator.

"Sullivan's Decorating," she answered, without elaborating. Encouraging conversation between them wouldn't be smart. It would be far too easy to be seduced by his magnetism.

"Really? I think that was the firm the bank hired last year when we redecorated."

"We've been involved in several bank renovations," she agreed evenly. So Jack was a bank executive?

Lacey didn't press for information, although she couldn't help being curious.

As if reading her thoughts, he reached inside his suit pocket and handed her a business card. "Come see me if you ever need a loan."

"I will, thank you."

"I'll look forward to having you apply." He smiled down on her and, even knowing what she did about him, her heart fluttered. She was cursed, Lacey mused, destined to be attracted to the wrong kind of men. There was probably some technical name for it, some term psychologists used for women like her. *Nutty* would do, she decided. Tangling her life with his would be downright disastrous.

"Have a good day," Jack said when the elevator opened.

"You too." Her voice was little more than a whisper.

"Say," Jack said, turning back abruptly, as if struck by inspiration. "I don't suppose you'd be free for dinner tomorrow night?"

Instinctively, Lacey stiffened. So he hadn't given up trying. "No . . . I'm sorry, I'm not free," she said. Apparently she conveyed her message because he didn't press her.

He glanced at his watch and frowned. "Perhaps another time."

"Perhaps."

Lacey wasn't making Jack Walker any promises. But she couldn't get the thought of Jack out of her mind all day.

The following evening, when Lacey was taking her trash to the chute at the end of the hallway, she ran into Jack a second time, just as he was going out his door.

Taken by surprise, they stopped and stared at each other. He was dressed formally as if for a fancy dinner date. Lacey didn't need to be reminded that he could have been wining and dining her. She'd declined his off-hand invitation, but she wished briefly that she'd accepted. Then she decided she was right to refuse. There were probably any number of other women who struck his fancy. Then, too, there was always Sarah. Ever loyal, ever faithful.

"Hello again," Jack said, with his electric smile.

"Hello." Her voice sounded awkward. Stilted.

"How's it going?"

"Fine." She didn't ask about him. The answer was obvious. He looked wonderful. Bank executives shouldn't be this good-looking or this friendly.

"Here, let me help." He took the plastic garbage can out of her hand.

"I can do that." Nevertheless, she was pleased he offered.

"I'm sure you can, but let me play the role of gentleman. It'd make my mama proud." The smile was back in place, potent enough to melt away the strongest of resolves. Hers, unfortunately, dissolved faster than most.

They went down the hallway together. Lacey took pains to avoid brushing shoulders with him. "Thanks for the help," she said, when they neared her apartment door.

"No problem. I was happy to do it."

She reached for the doorknob, intent on escaping. "Have a good time," she said, turning her back to him.

"I probably won't," he said softly, "especially since I won't be spending the evening with you. I'm destined to sit through a boring dinner meeting. I wish you could have seen your way clear to go with me."

"I—" She was so flustered by his sweet talk she could barely speak. "I'm sure you'll have an enjoyable evening. Will you be seeing Sarah?" she added, not knowing where the courage came from to ask the question. Sarah was the one he should have invited, not her.

"Not tonight," he said. "I'm afraid I'm stuck with my secretary."

First he'd invited her, and when she refused he'd asked his secretary. Suddenly Lacey was furious. That was exactly what she expected of someone like Jack. Someone like Peter.

Poor Sarah was destined for a broken heart.

THREE

"Cleo's pregnant," Lacey moaned as she slumped into the BART seat next to Jeanne two weeks later. "I took her to the vet yesterday afternoon and he confirmed her condition." Lacey was deeply dismayed that her purebred Abyssinian had mated with Jack's tomcat. And her dissatisfaction with her neighbor didn't stop there.

Sarah had stopped by over the past weekend, and the sounds of their argument had come through the walls again. Both had been furious. This time, however, they kept the intensity of their disagreement to a lower pitch, and their fight didn't last long. No more than ten minutes had elapsed before Lacey heard Jack's apartment door slam and Sarah's footsteps hurrying down the hall. Jack had stuck his head out and called after her, but to no avail.

"What are you going to do about Cleo?" Jeanne wanted to know.

"I . . . I haven't decided yet." Several options were

open to her, but one thing was certain: she was determined that Jack accept some responsibility.

That evening, after work, with her heart in her throat,
Lacey approached Jack's door and knocked three times in
hard, timed beats.

"Lacey, hello! This is a pleasant surprise."

"Hello," she said stiffly. "Would you mind if I came in
for a moment?"

"Not at all. I'd be honored." He stepped aside and let
her into the living room, which was more than double
the size of her own. "Can I get you something to drink?"
he asked.

"Nothing, thanks." She sat down on a white leather
sofa and took a small notebook from her purse. "I'm
afraid this isn't a social call."

Jack sank into a recliner opposite her. He perched
close to the edge of the seat cushion and braced his
elbows against his knees. "Is there a problem?"

"As a matter of fact, there is," Lacey answered. "Dog
got Cleo pregnant."

"I see."

"I thought you should know."

"Yes, of course." He looked as if he were entirely in
the dark as to what she wanted from him. "Is there something you needed?" he asked after an awkward moment.

How like a man! "Yes," she said, having trouble restraining her irritation. "I want you to do right by my cat."

"Do right? Are you suggesting they marry?"

"Don't be ridiculous!"

"Then what do you mean?"

"It's only fair that you share the expenses with me."
She hated the way her voice trembled. "Dr. Christman,
Cleo's vet, prescribed expensive vitamins and another
checkup. In addition, I'll expect you to find homes for
your half of the litter."

"My half."

"Yes. Please submit the names to me for approval."

Jack scratched the side of his head. "You're serious about this, aren't you?"

That he should question her motives told her everything she needed to know about him. "Yes, I'm serious. Dead serious." She stood and handed him a list of her expenses so far. "You can pay me whenever it's convenient." Holding her purse against her chest as though it offered her protection, she kept her back ramrod straight. "There are consequences in owning an alley cat, Mr. Walker. Even one named Dog." Lacey knew how pious she sounded. Lines of righteousness creased her face as she let herself out.

She didn't realize how badly she was shaking until she was inside her own apartment. Her knees felt as if they were about to buckle. She sat on the love seat and Cleo leaped into her lap, eager for attention.

Lacey ran her hand down the length of Cleo's back. "Well, girl, you're going to be a mother. What do you think about that?"

Cleo meowed.

"This is destined to be an interesting couple of months," she said. Dr. Christman had given Lacey several pamphlets about the reproduction of cats. Lacey had read them a number of times. She'd grown up with a gentle cocker spaniel named Sherlock, but he'd been a male so she'd never been through this sort of thing.

The following afternoon, Lacey's doorbell rang. Jack was on the other side, leaning against the doorjamb. He gave her a slow, easy, heart-stopping grin.

"How's Cleo doing?"

"Fine. She seems to need a bit more attention these days, but other than that she's behaving normally."

"I had Dog neutered. He's keeping a low profile these days."

Lacey was forced to pinch her lips together to keep from smiling. As far as she was concerned, it would do Dog good to have his carousing ways curtailed.

"May I come in?"

Lacey wasn't sure letting Jack into her apartment was such a good idea. "All right," she said reluctantly, stepping aside.

Then Lacey made the mistake of politely asking if he'd like something to drink, and Jack asked for coffee. Since she didn't have any ready, she was required to assemble a pot.

To her dismay, Jack was intent on helping her. She turned on the water and measured out the coffee grounds, all the while complaining inwardly about her compact kitchen. She couldn't move without touching Jack in some way. When she stood on tiptoe to lift down the mugs, he stepped behind her, the full length of his body pressing against hers.

She felt trapped and silly and unbearably uncomfortable. Worse, she was blushing, although she did everything she could to disguise the effect he had on her.

"It seems only fair if I'm going to share the expenses of Cleo's pregnancy that I have visitation rights," he said casually.

A chill washed over her. "Visitation rights?"

"Yes. I'd like to check on her every now and again to be sure she's doing well."

Lacey wasn't sure this was such a good idea, either, but she couldn't think of any good reason to protest.

"I can assure you Cleo will be well cared for."

"I'm confident she will be, but I'd like to check on her myself."

"All right," she agreed with ill grace.

The coffee finished brewing and she poured them each a cup. Jack took his black and strong, but he waited while Lacey diluted hers with milk before returning to the living room.

Cleo walked regally into the room and without a pause jumped into Jack's lap. Lacey was amazed. Her cat had never been fond of strangers.

"Cleo," Lacey chastised. "Get down."

The cat would have been a fool to do so. Jack was petting her back in long, smooth strokes that left Cleo purring with delight. It was probably like this with every woman he touched. Lacey attempted to scrounge up resentment toward him, and to her amazement found she couldn't.

Instead, the very opposite was happening. It was as if Jack's hands were on Lacey. A series of warm, dizzy sensations began to grow in her. Sexual feelings. Her breath came in little short puffs. She sipped at her coffee and forced herself to look away, anything that would make this feeling disappear. It was much too uncomfortable to remember that part of her nature, the one she'd buried after her divorce and conveniently ignored until Jack walked into her life.

Looking away didn't help. Nothing did.

"Cleo's a beautiful cat," he said in a low, sexy drawl that had Cleo purring and Lacey's heart racing.

"Thank you," she managed.

The tingling feeling spread slowly, inexorably, through her body, leaving her with a need she wouldn't have dared express to another human being. It had been well over a year since a man had held her. Not once in all those months had she missed a man's touch. Until now.

Now it was torture to sit and do nothing. To her dismay, Jack seemed relaxed and in no hurry to leave.

"Have you thought about homes for your half of the litter?" she asked, to make conversation.

"No."

"I . . . I think my friend Jeanne will take one." Her gaze followed the movement of his hand against Cleo's soft fur. The brush of his fingers was light, gentle. A lover's touch. He would be a tender lover, Lacey mused.

She shook her head, needing to clear her mind before it completed the picture of making love with him. Oh, dear heaven, this was more than she could bear.

"Lacey." The sexy drawl was back. "Come here."

"W-why?"

"I want you to feel Cleo's tummy."

"It's much too soon for the kittens," she protested and all but vaulted out of her chair. He knew exactly what he was doing to her and he enjoyed it. Lacey's cheeks flamed.

She hurried into the kitchen. Running the faucet, she filled a sponge and wiped down her spotless counter. If only Jack would leave! But that would be asking for a miracle. He had her on the run and wasn't about to give up.

He moved into the compact kitchen, and she closed her eyes, praying for strength.

"It was nice of you to stop by." She hoped he'd leave before she made a fool of herself.

"Why did you turn down my invitation to dinner?" he asked.

She swore he was only inches behind her, but she didn't dare turn around.

"Lacey?"

She opened the cupboard and brought down a can of cat food. "I don't think it's a good idea for us to become involved."

"Why not?"

"It's fine to be neighborly, but . . ."

"Not too friendly."

"Exactly." Her heart continued to beat at maximum speed, clamoring loudly in her ear. She didn't dare look at him. She couldn't, without his knowing that she wasn't any better off than Cleo was with Dog.

"Turn around and look at me," he instructed her gently, and when she didn't comply he placed his hands on her shoulders and slowly moved her to face him.

Then he ran his thumb along the edge of her jaw. "Look at me," he repeated.

Lacey closed her eyes and lowered her head. "I think you should leave."

Using his thumb, he lifted her chin. "Open your eyes."

She had no choice but to do as he asked. Reluctantly her eyes opened and slid effortlessly to his.

"I remember the day you moved in." He spoke softly, clearly. His gaze was as dark and intense as she'd ever seen. "I realized then how badly I wanted to get to know you. There was something vulnerable about you. Something that told me I would need to be patient, and so I've bided my time. It's been a year now and I'm still waiting, but I'm growing restless."

Lacey's throat felt dry, and she doubted she could have spoken even if she'd wanted to. Which she didn't. What could she say? That she'd once trusted someone who'd destroyed her faith in all men?

"Who hurt you?" he asked.

She shook her head, unwilling to answer him.

He took her in his arms then, drawing her into a protective circle, easing her into his embrace. His hold was loose, comforting, seductive.

Lacey wanted to resist, tried to make herself pull away, and found she couldn't.

"I want to kiss you," he whispered, as if he felt he needed to warn her of every move he made for fear she'd bolt and run like a frightened rabbit.

"No." She shook her head wildly from side to side. Somehow she found the resistance to brace her hands against his forearms and push herself away.

He let go of her instantly, but hesitantly. "Why not?" he asked. "I would never hurt you, Lacey. I'd never do anything you didn't want, weren't ready for."

"You must think me a fool," she said, her breasts heaving with the effort it had cost her to walk away from him.

"A fool?"

"You love Sarah."

"Of course I love Sarah."

At least he didn't deny it. "How many other women do you have on a string? Don't answer that; I don't want to know. Just understand one thing. I refuse to be one of them."

"Lacey."

"Please leave." She folded her arms and thrust out her chin defiantly.

"Not until you listen to me."

"You can't say anything that will change my mind."

His laugh mocked her. "Not even when I tell you Sarah's my sister?"

FOUR

"Your sister!" Lacey repeated, stunned. For a moment she wondered if she could trust Jack to tell her the truth but then decided she could. The intimacy between Jack and Sarch was what had struck her the first time she'd seen them together. It made sense that they were brother and sister.

"Who did you think she was?" Jack demanded. "You assumed Sarah and I were lovers? How could you possibly think something like that?"

"You're constantly fighting, and—"

"Of course we fight, we're siblings. Sarah's living with a man and I don't approve. I wish to hell she'd use the brains God gave her and get out."

"Do you disapprove of their living arrangement or of the young man?" Lacey wanted to know.

"Both. As far as I'm concerned, she's making the biggest mistake of her life. Mom and Dad don't know, and I refuse to hide it from them much longer."

"*That's* the reason you keep insisting she move in with you!" Lacey had caught the gist of their disagreement several times and cheered when Sarah flatly refused him. This new information put a different slant on Sarah's refusal.

"How do you know what we argue about?" he asked, regarding her quizzically.

"You honestly think I can't hear you two? Those walls are made of papier-mâché." Her head was reeling. If Sarah was Jack's sister, that answered a multitude of awkward questions.

Jack stuffed his hands in his pockets and strolled to the far side of the kitchen. His brow creased as if he were deep in thought. "I didn't realize we'd been quite so loud."

"You both certainly seem to have strong feelings on the subject."

"All this time you believed I was two-timing Sarah?"

"What else was I to think?" she asked defensively. "Besides, there were all those other women."

"What other women?"

"The one I saw you with the other day at the mailbox, for example."

"You mean Gloria?"

"I didn't hear her name. . . . Listen, none of this matters. You're free to date whomever you want. You don't owe me any explanations."

He didn't seem to hear her. "Gloria's a friend, nothing more. We did date a few years back, but it didn't develop into anything. She's seeing someone else now."

"What about your secretary?" Lacey asked, before she could censor the question.

"Mrs. Blake?" He laughed outright. "She's fifty and a grandmother."

Lacey wanted so badly to believe him. "Fifty?"

He nodded. "There's only one woman I've had my eye on for the last several months, and it's you."

"You talk a sweet line, Jack Walker, but I've heard it all before." More times than she cared to count. More times than she wanted to remember.

He raised an eyebrow as he advanced a couple of steps toward her. "If you let me kiss you, who knows? You just might change your mind."

The temptation was strong, stronger than Lacey wanted it to be. "Another time," she said, her heart roaring in her ears as she backed away from him.

Jack looked disappointed. "All right, Lacey, I've been patient this long. I can wait." He checked his watch and sighed. "I'd better get back to my place. I'll stop by later in the week to check on Cleo." He waited as if he half expected her to protest.

She didn't, although she probably should have. Life had taught her that men weren't to be trusted. Everything Jack said was well and good, but she refused to believe he'd been interested in her all these months. No man had that kind of patience. At least none she'd ever met.

Before he left, he took her by the shoulders and gently planted a kiss on her cheek.

"Are you going to go out with Jack?" Jeanne asked when they met the next morning. Lacey's arms were loaded down with several large books of carpet samples. She swore they weighed twenty pounds each. Her arms felt like they were about to come out of their sockets.

"I don't know."

Jeanne eyed her speculatively. "Lacey, you can't let an opportunity like this pass you by. As I said before, the guy's a hunk."

"Handsome isn't everything."

"True, but it's a good start. Besides, I *like* Jack."

"You only met him once."

"True, but I liked what I saw."

Lacey didn't have an answer for that. They rode in silence for several moments.

"I see you brought your work home with you again." Jeanne glanced disapprovingly in the direction of the samples.

"We're making a bid for an accountant's office, and I stopped off on my way home last night and let him look over the different carpets and colors."

"More overtime you're not getting paid for," Jeanne murmured. "Did you ever stop to think what Mr. Sullivan would do without you?"

Lacey had given that question ample consideration. Every time she worked up a quote or dealt with a moody customer because Mr. Sullivan was "out of the office at the moment," she had that very thought. "He'd probably find some other schmuck to take my place."

"Don't be ridiculous," Jeanne said. "The man needs you. He knows it, and so do you. What you should do, my friend, is use this to your advantage. We both know you should be making double what you make now."

"Double?"

"I don't know what Scrooge is paying you, but I do know it isn't enough. If you don't say something to him soon, I will."

"Jeanne!"

"Relax. I won't. But it makes me angry the way you let him take advantage of you. I don't know what it is about you that lets him get away with it. Do you enjoy being a victim?"

"No!"

Jeanne shrugged. "Then do something about it."

Her friend was right. More than right. She was acting like a victim. Lacey left the BART station filled with indignation. It lasted until she reached the office.

Unfortunately, the lone elevator was out of order. Lugging the carpet samples with her, Lacey huffed and puffed up three flights of stairs and literally staggered into the office.

Mr. Sullivan glanced up and gave her a look of concern. In his late forties, he was fast going bald, and his blue eyes had faded over the years. His suits were meticulously tailored, though, and he insisted they both maintain a crisp professional image.

Lacey pressed her hand over her heart and slumped into the first available chair.

"Lacey, are you all right?"

She shook her head. She hadn't realized how badly out of shape she was until she'd trekked up those stairs hauling two twenty-pound books of samples.

Mr. Sullivan walked over to the water cooler and drew her a cup of clear cold liquid. "Drink this and you'll feel better."

"Mr. Sullivan . . ."—she was so winded her voice could barely be heard—"we need . . . to talk . . . about my . . . position here."

"Of course. You've done a wonderful job. I owe you a debt of thanks. I realize I've left you with some of the more unpleasant tasks lately, and I hope you'll forgive me for that."

He was a kindly man, she realized. Dissatisfied with her wages, she'd built him up in her mind as an ogre with few redeeming qualities. Much as she'd pictured Jack . . . until recently.

"Overtime?" Her lungs hurt, otherwise she would have elaborated.

He frowned as if he didn't understand her. "Are you saying that over time you'd like to become a full-fledged decorator?"

She nodded, but it was more than that.

"You're wonderfully talented, Lacey. In a couple of years I feel strongly that you'll make it." Having said that, he lifted the heavy sample books, replaced them against the wall, and returned to his desk.

Mumbling under her breath, Lacey walked over to her own desk. No sooner had she removed her jacket than Mr. Sullivan announced he was leaving for the rest of the morning. He didn't tell her where he was headed, which was typical.

When Lacey returned to her apartment that evening, the first thing she did was soak in a hot tub. It felt wonderful.

Her day had been hectic. She certainly wasn't in the mood for company when there was a knock on her door. She jerked on a pair of sweats. "Oh, please, make this fast," she muttered as she went to answer it.

Jack stood with Sarah on the other side. "I thought it was time the two of you met," he said.

"I'm Sarah," the pretty brunette said, holding out her hand. Now that Lacey knew they were brother and sister, it was easy to see the family resemblance. Sarah shared Jack's deep chocolate-brown eyes and thick dark hair.

"Jack said there'd been a misunderstanding." Sarah grinned as if amused.

"Please make yourselves at home," Lacey said, gesturing toward the living room.

Jack needed no further invitation. He helped himself to the love seat, and Cleo immediately snuggled in his lap as if she'd been waiting for his return.

Lacey and Sarah sat down too.

"I'm sorry for all the commotion Jack and I make," Sarah said. "He's pretty stubborn, you know."

"Me?" Jack protested.

"All right, we both are. Since Mom and Dad moved to Flagstaff, he's the only family I have here in San Francisco. We fight a lot, but we're close too."

"We'd argue a lot less if it wasn't for Mark," Jack said with a frown, eyeing his sister.

Sarah's jaw went tight. "Jack, please, you promised not to bring him up. At any rate," she continued, "I wanted to clear up any misconceptions you might have about me. Jack really is my brother."

"I should have realized that. There's a strong family resemblance."

Sarah stood. "I really need to go—Mark's meeting me for dinner—but I wanted to stop by and introduce myself. Jack's mentioned you several times and—well, I hope everything works out—with Cleo." She squeezed the last two words together in her rush to clarify her meaning.

Sarah left, but Jack stayed exactly where he was—on her love seat with Cleo snoozing contentedly in his lap. "All right," he said, after Lacey had seen Sarah to the door. "What's wrong?"

"What do you mean?"

"Something's troubling you," he said evenly, studying her.

Uncomfortable under his scrutiny, she debated whether or not to tell him the truth. The hot bath hadn't helped to soothe her mind the way she had hoped, and she couldn't stop thinking about what Jeanne had said about her choosing to be a victim.

"I'm a worm," she confessed, slumping in her chair.

"A worm," Jack repeated slowly, as if he wasn't sure of the word's meaning. "In what way?"

She tossed her hands in the air, not wanting to discuss it. The more she complained, the worse she felt. If she was going to whine about her job, she should be doing it to Mr. Sullivan. So far he was the last person to know how she felt, and she had no one to blame but herself.

"All right, you're a worm," Jack said, "but even a worm needs to eat. How about dinner?"

"Out?"

"We can order in if you want, but I bet a night in Chinatown would do us both a world of good."

Lacey blinked back her surprise. Jack was asking her to dinner and she found that she longed to accept more than she had wanted anything for a long time. Before she could resurrect a long list of objections, she nodded.

His smile rivaled the northern lights. "Great." Gently he set Cleo aside. "You like Chinese food?"

"I love it. Hot and spicy and lots of it."

"Me too. The spicier the better."

"They can't make it too hot for me," she told him.

He cocked an eyebrow. "Wanna bet?"

Lacey didn't. Jack insisted on a taxi to save hunting for a parking space in crowded Chinatown. Lacey would have been comfortable riding BART. She didn't own a car and her only means of getting around was public transportation. Luckily the City by the Bay had an excellent metro system.

The taxi let them off on Grant Avenue. Lacey loved walking along the busy streets of Chinatown. Goods from the small shops spilled onto the sidewalk, displayed on long narrow tables. The smells tantalized her. Incense blended with simmering duck and mingled with the keen scent of spices that floated in the air. Chinese lanterns lit up the corners.

Jack guided her toward what he claimed was his favorite restaurant, his hand holding hers. Lacey enjoyed being linked with him, so much so that she was almost frightened by the sense of rightness she experienced.

When they approached a steep flight of stairs that looked like something the Maya had constructed deep in the interior of Mexico, Lacey balked.

"It isn't as bad as it looks." Jack placed an arm around her waist. Lacey could deal with the stairs far easier than she could this newfound intimacy. It didn't help that she'd been up and down three flights several times that day. She explained what had happened with the office elevator, and Jack was appropriately sympathetic.

Dinner started with hot and sour soup, followed by pot stickers in hot oil. Jack did the ordering, insisting she try Szechuan chicken, prawns with chili sauce, and hot pepper beef. Every now and again he'd look at her to be sure she approved of his choices.

"We'll never eat all that," she insisted, leaning toward him until her stomach was pressed against the side of the linen-covered table.

"I know," he said, unconcerned. "There'll be plenty of leftovers for later."

It amazed her that they had so much to talk about. He respected her privacy and didn't pry into subjects she didn't want to discuss. He listened and his laugh was easy, and before she knew it she was completely relaxed. Her problems seemed much less important.

Lacey even managed to sample each of the multiple dishes Jack ordered, none of which she'd tasted before. They were so good, it was hard to stop eating.

By the time they left the restaurant, carrying the leftovers, Lacey was full and content. They walked along the crowded streets, stopping now and again to investigate the wares of a souvenir shop. Jack bought her a bar of jasmine-scented soap and a catnip toy for Cleo.

"Tell her it's from Dog," he said.

She smiled up at him. "I will. It's the least he can do."

"The very least," Jack agreed.

She had trouble pulling her gaze away from his. It had been a long time since she'd had such a happy time with a man.

"We'd better head back," Jack said abruptly, waving to flag down a taxi.

"So soon?" she protested, not understanding the swift change in his mood. One moment they were enjoying each other's company, and the next Jack looked as if he couldn't get home fast enough. He turned and looked at her, his eyes burning into hers. "I don't want to leave either."

"Then why are we going?"

"Because I can't go another minute without kissing you, and doing it on the streets of Chinatown might embarrass you."

FIVE

Neither spoke on the ride back to the apartment building. Jack paid the driver, took hold of Lacey's hand, and led her into the lobby. The elevator was waiting with the door wide open, and the instant they were inside Jack reached for her.

The moment their lips met, Lacey realized she'd been half crazy with wanting him. His mouth was firm and needy, as needy as her own. Standing on the tips of her toes, she linked her arms around his neck.

When he lifted his mouth from hers, she buried her face in his shoulder. He held her close, rubbing his chin across the crown of her head. His touch was as gentle as she knew it would be. Cleo trusted this touch, savored it. Now it was her turn.

She wanted him to kiss her again, needed him to, so she'd know this was real. Reading her mind, he used his thumb to raise her chin. His eyes met and held her for a breath-stopping moment before he lowered his lips to hers. His mouth was wet and warm, coaxing. Lacey sighed as her emotions churned like the dense fog that swirls around the Golden Gate Bridge.

This was real, she decided. It didn't get any more real than this. One moment she was clinging to him, breathless with wonder, and the next she was battling tears.

"Lacey."

She didn't answer, but freed herself enough to push the button to their floor, to escape as quickly as possible. She didn't want to talk, to explain emotions she didn't understand herself. Shaking from the impact of his touch, she realized how terribly frightened she was.

After Peter had left, she'd been in shock. If she'd examined her pain then, she would have had to acknowledge how deeply he'd wounded her.

Now there was Jack, patient, gentle Jack, who evoked a wealth of sensation. But she couldn't accept this promise of joy without first dealing with the dull, throbbing pain of her past.

"Lacey," he whispered, keeping his arms loosely wrapped around her waist. "Can you tell me what's wrong?"

She shook her head. An explanation was beyond her. "I'm fine." It was a small white lie. She'd hadn't been fine from the moment she'd learned that Peter was involved with another woman. She felt broken and inadequate. She had never recovered from the crippling loss of the dream she'd carried with her since she was a child, playing love and marriage with paper dolls.

It wasn't supposed to happen like this. Marriage was forever. Love was supposed to last longer than a night, commitment longer than a few months.

All that Lacey had gotten out of her years with Peter was a bitterness buried so deep in her soul that it took the tenderness of another man, one she barely knew, to make her realize what she'd been doing for the past eighteen months.

Silently, Jack walked with her down the hall that led to her apartment. Pausing outside her door, he brushed a tendril of hair from her face, his touch light and non-threatening.

"Thank you," he whispered, gently pressing his lips to hers.

She blinked. Twice. "Why are you thanking me?"

A smile lifted the edges of his mouth. "You'll know soon enough."

Her hand trembled when she inserted the key. Cleo was there to greet her, clearly unhappy at having been left so long. It took several moments for Lacey to pull herself away from her thoughts.

Setting her purse aside, she wandered into the kitchen. She could hear Jack's movements on the other side, storing the leftovers in the refrigerator. She poured herself a glass of water and smiled when she heard a light tapping sound coming from the wall.

She reached over and knocked back, smiling at their silly game.

"Good night, Lacey," she heard him say.

"Good night, Jack," she whispered, and pressed her flattened palm against the wall, needing this small connection with him, yet fearing it. She was glad he couldn't see what she had done.

Lacey couldn't have been more surprised when Sarah Walker entered Sullivan's Decorating two days after her dinner date with Jack.

"Sarah, hello!" Lacey said, standing to greet Jack's sister.

"I hope you don't mind my stopping in unexpectedly like this." Sarah glanced nervously around the crowded shop. Every available bit of space was taken up by sample books, swatches of material, and catalogs.

"Of course not."

"I was wondering if we could meet for lunch one afternoon and talk?"

Lacey was pleased, although surprised. "I'd enjoy that very much."

They agreed on a time the following week, and Sarah chose a seafood restaurant on Fisherman's Wharf, one of Lacey's all-time favorites.

Lacey saw Jack almost every evening that week, never for very long. He had a long list of convenient excuses for dropping in unannounced, easing his way into her life bit by bit. Lacey knew what he was doing, but she didn't mind. He made no attempt to kiss her again and she was grateful, but she didn't expect his patience to last much longer.

"I was divorced over a year ago," she mentioned casually one evening, not looking at him. With Cleo in her lap, Lacey felt secure enough to touch upon the truth.

Jack sat composed and relaxed on her love seat, holding a mug of coffee, his ankle resting on his knee. "I guessed as much," he said. "Do you want to talk about it?"

"Not now. Do you mind?"

It took him awhile to answer; it seemed like the longest moment of Lacy's life. "No, but I do feel we should. Someday. The sooner the better."

She knew he was right. For the past few days, she had been rewriting her journal. It was the only way she had of sorting out her feelings. The habit of keeping a record of events in her life had started while she was still in school, and for years she had written a paragraph or two at the end of each day.

After Jack kissed her, she'd gone back to the daily journal she'd kept through those painful months before her divorce. What amazed her was the lack of emotion in those brief entries. It was as if she had jotted down the details of a police report. Just the facts, nothing more. Bits and pieces of useless information while her world blew up in her face.

She'd reread one day at a time, and then with raw courage she rewrote those trauma-filled weeks, reliving each day, refusing to dull the pain. What surprised her was the incredible amount of anger she experienced. Toward Peter. And toward Michelle, the woman he'd left her to marry.

The bitterness spilled out of her pen until her hand ached and her fingers throbbed, but still she couldn't stop. It was as if the pen insisted she get it all down as quickly as possible because only then would she be well, only then could she move forward with her life.

She was afraid she was going to explode. Even Cleo knew not to come near her. Holding a box of tissues, she'd weep and pace and weep some more. Then she'd wipe her eyes, blow her nose, and toss the damp tissue willy-nilly. In the morning, she discovered a trail that reached to every room of her apartment.

Sleep avoided her. It wasn't fair. She'd purged her soul, or so she thought. Yet it was well after midnight before she'd fall into a fitful sleep.

Lacey wasn't in the mood for company the next evening when Jack arrived, but she was pleased he'd stopped by. He was easy to be with, undemanding and supportive.

Cleo jumped down from her position in Lacey's lap and strolled into the bedroom, as if she hadn't a care in the world. When Cleo left, Jack stood and moved to Lacey. He stretched out his hand to her.

She looked up at him and blinked and then, without question, gave him her hand. He clasped it firmly in his own and then lifted her from her chair. Deftly he switched position, claiming her seat, and drew her into his lap.

"You look tired." His gaze was warm and concerned.

"I'm exhausted." As well she should be after the restless night she'd spent. No matter how hard she tried, she couldn't bury the past. It prickled her like stinging nettles.

He eased her head down to his shoulder. "Are you able to talk about your marriage yet?"

It took several moments for Lacey to answer, and when she did she found herself battling back tears. "He fell in love with someone else. He'd been having an affair for months. Oh, Jack, how could I have been so stupid not to have known, not to have realized what was happening? I was so blind, so incredibly naive."

Jack's hand was in her hair. "He was a fool, Lacey. You realize that, don't you?"

"I . . . all I know is that Peter's happy and I'm miserable. It isn't fair. I want to make him hurt the way he hurt me." She buried her face in his chest.

When her sobs subsided, Lacey realized Jack was making soft, comforting sounds. Wiping the moisture from her face, she raised her head and attempted a smile.

"Did you understand anything I said?"

"I heard your pain, and that was enough."

Appreciation filled her. She didn't know how to tell him all that was in her heart. How grateful she was for his friendship, for showing her that she'd anesthetized her life, blocked out any chance of another relationship. Little by little, he'd worn down her resistance. All she could think to do was thank him with a kiss.

It had been so very long since a man had held her like this. It had been ages since anyone had stirred up the fire deep within her. Their mouths met, shyly at first, then gaining in intensity. After only a few seconds, Lacey was drowning in a wealth of sensation. The fire flickered, then burst into a heat so powerful, she felt as if her nerve endings were seared.

A frightening kind of excitement took hold of her. It had been like this when Jack had kissed her that first time, but even more so now. She opened her lips to his probing tongue and sighed with surprise and delight when it swept her mouth. Her initial response was shy, but after she gained more confidence she participated in full measure.

When they broke off the kiss, Jack's breathing came fast and hard. "Lacey," he murmured, "you go to my head."

"Good," she said, drawing his mouth back to hers. Their mouths twisted and angled against each other, seeking a deeper contact, needing more and more of each other to be satisfied.

"We have to stop," he told her. His chest rose with a sharp intake of breath.

"Soon," she promised. She wasn't nearly ready. Not yet. She had a year of lost time to make up. She welcomed his tongue and took delight in teasing him with her own until their sighs of pleasure mingled.

His hands were busy opening her blouse. Lacey helped him and moaned when he freed her bra and lifted her full breasts into his hands.

They kissed until they were both panting with a need so white hot it threatened to burst into flame.

"Lacey," he groaned, and buried his face in the fullness of her breasts, "you tempt me beyond reason."

"I do?" She basked in the glow of his words. After Peter, she'd been convinced no man would ever find her desirable again.

"We have to stop now."

Lacey had never meant for their kissing to develop to this point, but now that it had, she had few regrets. "Thank you," she whispered and lightly kissed his lips as she refastened her blouse.

"You didn't tell me very much about your divorce," he said.

"But I did," she assured him. "I told you almost everything."

He frowned. "Was I a good listener?"

"The very best," she said, with a warm smile. "You made me feel desirable when I was convinced no man would ever want me again."

Jack closed his eyes as if attempting to fathom such a thing. "He must have been crazy."

"I . . . can't answer that."

"Do you still hate him?"

She lowered her eyes, not wanting him to read what was going on inside her. She had thought she did. Now she wasn't so sure. "I don't know. For a long time, I pretended the divorce didn't matter. I told myself I was lucky to have learned the kind of husband he was before we had children.

"It's only been since I met you that I realized how deeply I'd buried myself in denial. The divorce hurt, Jack. It was the most painful experience of my life." She wrapped her arms around his neck. "Every time I think about Peter, I feel incredibly sad."

"That's a beginning," Jack said softly, rubbing his chin against the side of her face. "A very good beginning."

SIX

"I'm so pleased we could meet," Sarah said when Lacey arrived at the seafood restaurant. Seagulls flew overhead, chasing crows. The crows retaliated, pursuing the gulls in a battle over fertile feeding territory. From their window seat, Lacey could watch a lazy harbor seal sunning himself on the long pier. The day was glorious, and she felt the beginnings of joy creep into her soul. It had been a long, dark period. Her life had been dry and barren since the day Peter announced he wanted a divorce.

"I wanted to talk to you about Jack," Sarah said, her gaze fixed on her menu.

This didn't surprise Lacey, and if the truth be known she'd agreed to have lunch with Sarah for the same reason. Her curiosity about Jack was keen. He was an attractive, successful banker. They were about the same age, she guessed, and she couldn't help wondering how he'd gotten to the ripe old age of twenty-eight without being married.

"I understand you and Jack are seeing each other quite a bit these days."

Lacey didn't know why the truth unsettled her so, but she found herself fiddling with her napkin, bunching it in her hands. "He comes over to visit Cleo."

Sarah's soft laugh revealed her amusement. "It isn't Cleo who interests him, and we both know it. He's had his eye on you for over a year. The problem is, my dear brother doesn't know how to be subtle."

Lacey disagreed. "He's been more than patient."

"True," Sarah agreed reluctantly. "He didn't want to scare you off. We talked about you several times. He wanted my advice on how to court you. I was the one who suggested he send you flowers. He was downright discouraged when you repeatedly turned him down. Who would have thought that silly tomcat would be the thing to bring you two together?"

Lacey smoothed the linen napkin across her lap. The time for being coy had long since passed. "I like your brother very much."

"He's pretty wonderful." Once again Sarah admitted this with reluctance. "He liked you from the moment he first saw you."

"But why?" When Lacey moved into the apartment building she'd been an emotional wreck. The divorce had been less than a month old. She hadn't realized it at the time, but she'd been one of the walking wounded.

Sarah's look was knowing. "Jack's like that. He knew you'd been badly hurt and that you needed someone, the same way Dog did. He found Dog in a back alley, half starved and so damn mad he wouldn't let anyone near him. It took several weeks before Dog recognized Jack as a friend." She paused, leaned forward, and braced her elbows against the table. "But Jack was patient. He's been patient with you too, and it's paid off. I can't remember the last time he was so happy."

"I'm not a stray cat," Lacey said defensively. She

wasn't keen on the comparison, but the similarity didn't escape her.

"Oh, no," Sarah said quickly. "I didn't mean to imply that. Jack would have my head for even suggesting such a thing. But you were hurting and Jack recognized it. If you want the truth, I think Jack should have been a doctor. It's just part of his nature to want to help others."

"I see." Lacey wasn't finding this conversation the least bit complimentary, but she couldn't deny what Sarah said. For the last year she'd been walking around in a shell. Only when Jack came into her life did she understand how important it was to deal with her divorce.

Sarah sighed and set the menu aside. "Jack's wonderful. That's why it's hard to understand why he's so unreasonable about me and Mark."

"I've never known Jack to be unreasonable."

"But he is," Sarah said, keeping her head lowered as if she was close to tears. "I love Mark; we want to be married someday. We just can't marry now, for a number of reasons. Sometimes I think Jack hates him."

"I'm sure that's not true." Lacey couldn't imagine Jack hating anyone, but she could easily understand his being overprotective.

"It's true," Sarah said heatedly. "Jack refuses to have anything to do with Mark, and do you know why?" Lacey wasn't given the opportunity to answer. "Because Jack thinks Mark's using me. Nothing I can say will convince him otherwise. It's the most ridiculous thing I've ever heard, and it's all because we're living together. As far as I can see, my brother needs to wake up and smell the coffee. This is the nineties, after all."

The waiter arrived with glasses of ice water and a basket filled with warm sourdough bread. Lacey smiled her appreciation, grateful for the interruption. The aroma of fresh bread was heavenly, but the conversation was becoming uncomfortable. She was not sure how to reply to Sarah. She was far more at ease having Sarah answer her questions about Jack than playing go-between for brother and sister. Jack might be overprotective, but she couldn't imagine his disliking Mark without cause.

"What I'd really like is for you to talk to Jack for me," Sarah said, her eyes wide and pleading. "He'll listen to you, because—"

"I can't do that, Sarah," Lacey interrupted.

"I was hoping you'd consider it. I thought if you met Mark yourself, you'd be able to see how marvelous he is, and then you could tell Jack. You don't mind if he joins us, do you?"

Once again, Lacey wasn't given an opportunity to choose one way or the other. Sarah half rose from her seat and waved.

A sophisticated young man moved away from the bar and walked toward them, carrying his drink. Lacey studied Mark, trying to keep an open mind. As far as looks went, he was an attractive man. He kissed Sarah's cheek, but his gaze moved smoothly to Lacey and lingered approvingly. They exchanged brief handshakes while Sarah made the introductions.

"I hope you don't mind if I join you," Mark said, pulling out a chair, "although every man here will think I'm greedy to be dining with the two most beautiful women in the room."

Mark didn't need to say another word for Lacey to understand Jack's disapproval. He was much too smooth. And she didn't like the way he looked at her—as if she were a slab of meat on a butcher's block. What she didn't understand was how Sarah could be so blind.

"Sarah and I are in a bit of a quandary." Mark reached for Sarah's hand and gripped it in his own.

"We need help in dealing with Jack," Sarah elaborated. "Mark suggested the two of us get together and talk to you about our problem. I'm not sure it's wise, but Mark seems to think that you—"

"Right," Mark cut in. "I feel you might say something

that would smooth the waters between Sarah and her
brother for me."

"You want me to talk to Jack on your behalf?" she
asked. Apparently Mark had no qualms about having her
do his speaking for him. What Sarah's lover failed to
understand was that Jack would react negatively to such
an arrangement. Whatever small respect he had for Mark
would be wiped out.

"Just mention that you've met Mark," Sarah coaxed.
"You don't need to make an issue of it. I'm sure he'd listen to you. You see, Jack's living in the Middle Ages.
Mark thinks Jack is jealous. My brother and I used to be
really close—there wasn't anything I couldn't tell him."
A wistful look clouded her pretty features. "It isn't like
that anymore. It hurts, the way we argue. I can't help
agreeing that it seems like jealousy."

Lacey wondered if that could possibly be true. "Jack's
met Mark?"

"Oh, yes, plenty of times. From the very first, Jack's
had a grudge against him."

"We started off on the wrong foot," Mark admitted
dryly.

"What happened?" Lacey asked.

"Nothing," Sarah said defensively. "Absolutely nothing. But I've never been serious about anyone before, and
Jack just can't deal with it."

Lacey didn't want to take sides, but she found herself
saying, "I don't know Jack all that well, but I can't see
him as the jealous sort."

"I know, but you see, I'm crazy about Mark and Jack
knows it, and the way Mark figures—and me too—my
brother needs to accept the fact that his little sister is all
grown up, and he refuses to do it." Absently, Sarah tore off
a piece of bread and held it between her hands, as if she
wasn't sure what to do with it. "Can you help us, Lacey?"

"I doubt it," she said, as forthrightly and honestly as
she could.

"Jack would listen to you," Sarah said.

Lacey smiled softly at the fervor of Sarah's belief that she had any influence on her brother. "I'm only his next-door neighbor."

"That's where you're wrong," she said, her voice raised with the strength of her conviction. "Jack really likes you. More than anyone in a good long while."

Lacey wasn't sure of that either, but she let it pass. "You want me to tell your brother that you're a mature woman capable of making her own decisions, whether he agrees with them or not."

"Exactly," Sarah said.

"That's what he needs to hear," Mark concurred.

"As an adult, you're free to love whomever you wish," Lacey said.

"Right again." Sarah's voice raised with the fervor of her conviction.

Mark smiled at Sarah and she smiled back. "We know what we're doing, isn't that right, baby?"

"I'm over twenty-one," Sarah announced.

"You're both competent judges of character," Lacey said.

"Of course." Sarah's grin widened. "I couldn't have said it better myself."

They were momentarily interrupted by the waiter, who returned for their order.

"Jack's not an unreasonable person," Lacey continued. "If that's the way you both feel, you don't need me to tell him. Do it yourselves, together."

"He won't listen," Sarah protested.

"Have you tried?"

Mark tore the roll in half and lowered his gaze. "Not exactly, but then it isn't like we've had much of an opportunity."

"Is it your living arrangement that's troubling Jack?" Lacey asked.

"That isn't permanent," Sarah told her.

"We'll be married someday," Mark said. "But not right away. We want to be married on our terms and not have them dictated by an older brother."

Lacey kept silent because she feared her own views on the subject wouldn't be welcome. Over the years several of her friends had opted for live-in arrangements. It might have been the luck of the draw, but they'd all come out of the relationships with regrets.

"Loving Mark isn't a mistake," Sarah insisted a bit too strongly. "We're perfect together."

The waiter delivered their salads, but by then Lacey had lost her appetite.

"And Sarah's perfect for me," Mark added, before reaching for his fork and digging into the plump shrimp that decorated the top of his huge salad.

"Mark loves me, and I love him," Sarah concluded. "As far as I'm concerned that's the most important thing."

Lacey saw that both Sarah and Mark felt they could change her mind. It was important to clear that up immediately. "I hope you can appreciate why I can't speak to Jack on your behalf."

"Yes," Sarah said sadly. "I just wish Jack wasn't so openly hostile."

"Sarah?" The husky male voice came from behind her. "Lacey? What are you two doing here?"

It was Jack.

SEVEN

"Hello, Jack," Sarah said, recovering first. She didn't look pleased. Lacey knew their relationship was strained and wished she could help, but she couldn't think of a way to lessen the tension between them. Jack ignored Mark completely. But then Mark didn't acknowledge him either.

"How are my two best girls?" Jack asked, disregarding Sarah's cool welcome. He slid out a chair and sat down without waiting for an invitation.

"Feel free to join us," Sarah muttered sarcastically.

"Hello, Jack," Lacey said, her heart reacting in a happy way despite Sarah and Mark's sour reception. She lowered her gaze abruptly when he focused his eyes on her. She didn't have any reason to feel guilty, but she did—a little. It wasn't like she was doing something behind his back.

"Lacey and I were just having a little chat," Sarah said, after an awkward moment. "That's what you want to know, isn't it?"

"I didn't ask, Sarah. What you and Lacey talk about is none of my business." Jack ordered a cup of coffee and turned toward Lacey and Sarah, presenting Mark with a view of his back.

"If you must know, we discussed Mark and me," Sarah said, far more defensively than necessary.

Jack sipped his coffee, giving no outward indication that the topic of conversation troubled him. "Let's change the subject, shall we?"

"I bet you were hoping Lacey would talk some sense into me," Sarah said stiffly. "Well, you're wrong."

Jack leveled his gaze on his sister, his look wide and disapproving.

"You don't need to worry," Sarah continued on the same touchy note. "Lacey has refused to talk to you on our behalf."

"Mark asked her to?"

"Of course," Sarah returned belligerently. "What else can he do since you flatly refuse to speak to him?"

"I don't appreciate your dragging Lacey into this." Jack said, not bothering to hide his disapproval.

"You don't need to worry," Sarah snapped back. "It won't happen again."

It upset Lacey to watch the two of them bicker, knowing how deeply they cared for each other. But she was helpless to do anything more than listen.

"How's Cleo?" Jack looked at Lacey in a clear effort to find a more pleasant topic.

Lacey reached for her coffee. "Getting fat."

"Good," he said absently.

"How can you ignore Mark like this?" Sarah demanded. "You act as if he isn't even here."

Jack remained stubbornly silent for a moment before asking, "Have you ever asked Mark why I behave toward him the way I do?" He sipped his coffee. "It would be very interesting if he admitted the truth."

"Let's get out of here." Mark stood abruptly and

reached for Sarah's hand. "We don't need him, Sarah, we never have. Let's just leave well enough alone."

"But, Mark—" Sarah looked from her lover to her brother, her eyes bright with indecision.

"Are you coming or not?" Mark demanded irritably, dropping her hand.

"You could try talking to Jack," Sarah suggested on a tentative note, sounding unsure and pitiful. Lacey's heart went out to her.

"Do what you want." Mark turned and started to walk away.

Sarah vacillated, torn with indecision, before sighing heavily. "Mark, wait," she called, obediently trotting after him.

The silence that followed Sarah's departure was heavy with tension. Jack's face darkened with what appeared to be regret before he looked once more to Lacey. It seemed, for an awkward moment, that he had forgotten she was there.

"Jack," she said softly, touching his hand.

"I'm sorry." He shook his head as if to clear it. "I hope Sarah and Mark didn't make pests of themselves."

"Not in the least," Lacey assured him. "She's a delightful young woman, if a bit confused." Although it wasn't any of Lacey's business, she wanted to know. "Why do you actively dislike Mark?"

"There are several reasons," he said pointedly, "but you don't need to worry about me and my sister. It's not your affair."

"I see," she answered. She couldn't help feeling hurt by his abrupt dismissal. "I shouldn't have asked."

Jack sighed. "I saw him with another girl soon after Sarah moved in with him. It was clear they were more than casual acquaintances, but when I mentioned it to Sarah she claimed I was lying in an effort to break them up. Naturally Mark denied everything. It's like my beautiful, intelligent sister has been hypnotized.

She can't seem to see what's right under her nose."

"It's probably the most difficult thing you can do, isn't it?"

"What?" Jack wanted to know.

Lacey gently squeezed his hand. "Watch her make a mistake and know there's no way to keep her from making it."

Jack studied her for a long moment and nodded. "It's hell. And the worst part is losing the closeness we once shared. I don't know how she can be so blind."

"Sarah can't see what she doesn't want to see." It had been the same way with Lacey. The evidence was there, but she'd refused to notice what was apparent to everyone else.

When Lacey returned to the office, her head was filled with Jack and his sister. She wished there were some way she could help but knew it was impossible.

Mr. Sullivan was waiting for her, impatiently pacing the cramped quarters. As she stepped inside, he glanced pointedly at his watch.

"You're late," he announced.

"Five minutes," she said calmly, sitting down at her desk. After all the times she'd come in early and stayed late, she certainly didn't feel guilty for going five minutes over her lunch hour.

"Were you aware Mrs. Baxter was due this afternoon to go over wallpaper samples?" he asked, with thinly disguised irritation.

"Yes," Lacey answered, not understanding why her employer was so flustered.

"Well, Mrs. Baxter was in town earlier than she anticipated and stopped in. You weren't here." Accusation rang in his voice as clear as church bells. "I was left to deal with her myself, and I don't mind telling you, Lacey, that woman unnerves me. You should have been here."

Lacey straightened in her chair, unwilling to accept his censure. "Mr. Sullivan," she said evenly, refusing to allow him to badger her, "I'm entitled to my lunch hour."

He pressed his lips together and walked over to his own desk. "You're the wallpaper expert," he returned flippantly.

"I am?" If he felt that way, he should pay her accordingly. There would never be a better time to point this out.

"Of course you are," he snapped. "Whenever customers are interested in wallpaper I refer them to you."

"How nice," Lacey said.

He was making this almost easy for her. To her surprise, she wasn't the least bit nervous.

"How long have I worked for you now, Mr. Sullivan?"

"Ah . . ." He picked up a pencil and figured some numbers on a pad as if her question required several algebraic calculations. "It must be a year or more."

"Exactly a year. Do you recall that when you hired me we made an agreement?"

"Yes, of course." He stiffened as if he knew what was coming.

"There was to be a salary evaluation after six months and another at one year. The months have slipped by, and I've taken on a good deal of the responsibility of running the business for you, and now you tell me I'm your wallpaper expert! I can assure you no *expert* makes the low wages I do. I believe, Mr. Sullivan, that you owe me a substantial raise, possibly two." Having said all this in one giant breath, she was winded when she finished.

She'd done it! After all the weeks of moaning and groaning, of complaining and berating herself, she'd actually asked for the raise she deserved. It hadn't even been hard! She watched her employer and waited for his response.

"I owe you a raise?" Mr. Sullivan sounded shocked, as if the thought had never occurred to him. "I'll have to check my records. You might very well be right. I'll look

into it and get back to you first thing in the morning."
Having said that, Mr. Sullivan promptly disappeared—
something he was doing more frequently of late, leaving
her with the burden of dealing with everything herself.

Lacey felt as though a great weight had been lifted
from her shoulders. It was as if whatever had bound her
had fallen away.

The first person she sought out that afternoon was Jack.
She went directly from the elevator to his apartment,
knocking several times, eager to share her news. To her
disappointment, he wasn't home. She realized how
important he'd become to her. It was as if none of this
were real until she'd shared it with her neighbor.

Letting herself inside her own apartment, she
promptly greeted Cleo and then reached for the phone.
Jeanne answered on the second ring.

"I asked Mr. Sullivan for a raise," she said without so
much as a hello. "Jeanne, I'm so happy, I could cry. It
just happened. He made some offhand comment about
me being his wallpaper expert, and I said if that was the
case I should be properly compensated."

"Hot damn, girl. Congratulations!"

Lacey knew Jeanne would be pleased for her, if for
nothing more than garnering the courage to ask.

"I owe you so much," Lacey said, the emotion bubbling
in her voice. "I really do. Not long ago you claimed if I
wanted to be a victim, you couldn't help me, and I realized you were right. And Jack too, he's been—" She
stopped, thinking how much Jack had helped her. Not in
the same way as Jeanne, but by his own gentle understanding, he'd encouraged her and helped her to find herself. She understood for the first time how confronting
Mr. Sullivan was tied in with her divorce. She'd come out
of her marriage emotionally crippled, carrying a load of
grief and insecurity that had burdened her whole life.

"You haven't mentioned Jack much lately," Jeanne commented. "How's it going with you two?"

"I haven't talked about Jack?" Lacey hedged. "It's going fine, just fine."

"*Fine* suggests it's going great."

Cleo wove her way around Lacey's feet, demanding attention. With the tip of her shoe, Lacey booted the catnip toy as a distraction. Cleo raced after it.

"Now," Jeanne said, heaving a giant breath, "tell me how much of a raise Mr. Sullivan's giving you."

"He didn't say . . . exactly. All he said was that he was going to think about it overnight."

"Don't let him weasel out of it," Jeanne warned.

"Don't worry," Lacey said. "He wouldn't dare." At the moment she felt invincible, capable of dealing with anything or anyone.

As soon as she was off the phone, Lacey gave Cleo the attention she demanded. "How are you doing, girl?" Lacey asked. "I bet you're anxious to have those kittens." She stroked her back and Cleo purred contentedly. "Jack and I will find good homes for your babies," Lacey assured her. "You don't have a thing to worry about."

Jack didn't get home until after six. The minute she heard movement on the other side of her kitchen wall, she hurried over to his apartment. She tapped out a staccato knock against his door and was cheered to hear him humming on the other side.

"Who is it?" he called out.

"Lacey."

The door flew open. The minute he appeared, she vaulted into his arms, spreading kisses over his face. He blinked as if he wasn't sure what was happening.

"Lacey?" His eyes were wide with surprise and delight. "What was that for?"

"A thank-you." She wove her arms around his neck and kissed him again. "I'm so happy."

"My guess is something happened after we met at lunch."

She rewarded his genius, taking more time, savoring the kiss. With every beat of her heart, she thanked God for sending Jack into her lonely, bleak life.

"I'm almost afraid to ask what this is all about. Whatever it is, don't let me stop you." He closed the door with his foot and carried her into the living room.

She hugged him tight. His shirt was unfastened. Either he was dressing or undressing, she couldn't tell which. Her trembling body moved against his.

He kissed her with such intensity that her nipples tightened and started to throb. "Are you going to tell me what we're celebrating?" he asked her breathlessly.

"A raise," she said. "And long overdue. You see, I had to ask for it, and doing that was a growing experience for me." She paused to rub her nose against his. "I realize this probably sounds silly, but I couldn't make myself ask, and it got to be this really big thing, like a monster, and then I was terrified."

"But you did it?"

"Yes. I owe it all to you—and to my friend Jeanne. Knowing you has helped me so much, Jack. You've given me my confidence back. I'm not sure how you managed it, but since we've been . . . neighborly, it seems everything's turned around for me."

"I couldn't be more pleased, and naturally I'll accept the credit," he said warmly.

"Mr. Sullivan's going to think about it overnight, but you see this isn't about the money. It's about me."

"You certainly didn't have any problem confronting me when Dog stole Cleo's virginity. As I recall you were ready with a tidy list of demands."

"That was different. I wasn't the one affected, it was Cleo. I didn't have the least bit of trouble sticking up for my cat."

"I'd like to complain, but I won't," Jack said. "I'm

more than pleased that Dog decided to call upon Cleo; otherwise I don't know how long it would have taken me to break through those barriers of yours."

He kissed her then, slowly, thoroughly, leaving her trembling when he'd finished.

"We'll celebrate. Dinner, dancing, a night on the town. We'll—" He stopped abruptly and closed his eyes. "Damn."

"What?"

"I've got another one of those stupid dinner meetings this evening."

"It doesn't matter." She was disappointed, but she understood. "This is rather short notice. We'll celebrate another time. It doesn't matter, truly it doesn't." Nothing could mar her happiness. "How soon do you have to leave?"

He glanced at his watch and frowned. "Ten minutes."

"I'd better go."

"No." He kissed her hungrily.

"Jack"—she managed a protest, weak at best—"you'll be late for your dinner."

"Yeah, I know."

"Jack!"

He kissed her nose. "Spoilsport. Remember, we're on for dinner on the town tomorrow night."

"I'll remember."

Lacey returned to her apartment in a daze. When she slumped onto the sofa, Cleo settled in her lap, and she slowly stroked the cat's back, thinking over her day. Lacey wasn't sure how long she sat there before someone knocked on her door. Checking the peephole, Lacey was shocked to see who it was.

"Sarah!" she said, unlocking her door.

Jack's sister took one look at her and burst into tears. "Oh, Lacey, I've been such a fool!"

EIGHT

"Sarah, what happened?" Lacey led Jack's sister into her apartment. Sarah slumped onto the love seat and covered her face with both hands. Several seconds passed before she was able to speak.

"I . . . found out Mark's involved with someone else. I found them together, in our bed. I thought I was going to be sick . . . I couldn't believe my own eyes. Dear God, how could I have been so stupid?"

"Oh, Sarah!" Lacey wrapped her arm around Sarah's shoulders. "I'm so sorry."

"Jack *told* me Mark was seeing someone else, but I didn't believe him. I loved Mark . . . I really loved him. How could I have been so stupid?" She buried her face in Lacey's shoulder.

The experience was nearly a mirror image of her own, so Lacey could appreciate the devastating sense of betrayal Sarah was feeling.

"I know what you're going through," Lacey said when

Sarah's sobbing had slowed. She brought her a hot cup of tea with plenty of sugar to help ward off the shock.

"How could you?" Sarah said. She looked up at Lacey, her face devoid of makeup, her eyes filled with a hollow, familiar pain. The afghan Lacey's mother had crocheted for a Christmas present was wrapped over the younger woman's shoulders as if she'd been chilled to the bone. Sarah looked as if she were six years old.

"It's like your whole world has been violently turned upside down. But it's much more than that. The sense of betrayal is the worst emotional pain there is."

"You too?"

Lacey nodded. "My husband—ex-husband, now—left me for another woman. Apparently they'd been lovers for months, but I didn't have a clue. When Peter asked for a divorce, I thought I'd die." Memories of that final confrontation filtered through Lacey's mind. She found, somewhat to her surprise, that although they saddened her, she didn't feel the crushing agony that had been with her for the last year and a half.

"What . . . what did you do afterward?"

Lacey reached for Sarah's hand and squeezed her fingers. "After the divorce was final, I packed everything I owned and moved to San Francisco."

"Then it must not have been very long ago."

"The divorce was final last year about this time."

Sarah sipped her tea. "I was blind to what was happening. I trusted Mark, really trusted him. I nearly allowed him to destroy my love for my brother."

"Don't blame yourself."

"But I do!" Sarah cried. "Looking back, I can't believe I sided against Jack. He's never lied to me, and yet I believed everything Mark was telling me about my brother being jealous and all that other garbage."

"I believed too," Lacey said, "but when you love someone, the trust is automatic. Why should we suspect a man of cheating when such behavior would never occur to us? The very thought of being unfaithful to Peter was repugnant to me."

Sarah cradled the mug between her palms. "Do you think you'll ever be able to trust a man again?"

"Yes," Lacey answered, after some length, "but not in the same blind way. I couldn't bear to live my life being constantly suspicious. The burden of that would ruin any future relationships. I'm not the same woman I was eighteen months ago. Peter's betrayal has marked ·me forever." She hesitated, unsure of how much she should admit about the changes knowing Jack had brought into her life. "It wasn't until recently that I felt I could say this, but I believe it changed me for the better."

"How do you mean?"

"It was a long, painful ordeal. Only in the last month have I come to terms with what happened. For a long time I thought I hated Peter, but that wasn't true. How could I hate him when I'd never stopped loving him?"

"What do you feel for him now?"

Lacey had to think over the question. "Mostly I don't feel anything. I've forgiven him."

"You? He should be the one to beg *your* forgiveness."

Lacey smiled, knowing Peter as she did. "I could wait until hell freezes over, and that would never happen. Peter believes *I* was the one who failed *him*, and perhaps I did in some way. He needed an excuse to rationalize what he was doing."

"Mark blamed me too. How could you forgive Peter? I don't understand."

"You'd be right to say he didn't ask for my forgiveness. But I didn't do it for *him*, I did it for *me*. Otherwise his betrayal would have destroyed me."

"I still don't understand."

"In the beginning," Lacey said, "I couldn't deal with the pain so I pretended I wasn't hurt. But in the last month, I've realized that I needed to let go of Peter and the failed marriage, and the only way to do it was to admit my own faults and forgive him. If I didn't, I might never have let go of my bitterness."

Fresh tears brimmed in Sarah's eyes. "I'll never be as wise as you are."

Lacey laughed. "Oh, Sarah, if only you knew how very long it took me to reconcile myself to this divorce. I have Jack to thank, and my friend Jeanne. Even Cleo played a role."

"Jack's wonderful," Sarah admitted and bit her lower lip. "I've treated him abominably."

"That's one thing about brothers, they're forgiving. At least we can trust that Jack is. He's a special man, Sarah, and I can't believe you'll have any more problems setting matters straight with him."

They sat and talked, and as the hours passed Lacey realized how much they had in common. It was nearly ten o'clock when the doorbell chimed. The two women looked at each other.

"You don't need to worry. I'm sure it's not Mark."

Lacey checked the peephole anyway. It was Jack. Unlatching the chain, she opened the door and was immediately brought into his arms. He kissed her as if it had been weeks instead of hours since they'd last seen each other.

"Jack." Sarah's voice cut into the sensual fog that surrounded Lacey.

Jack abruptly broke off the kiss but kept his arm around Lacey's waist. She watched his face as he discovered his sister sitting on the sofa, wrapped in Lacey's afghan. His gaze went from Sarah to Lacey and then back again.

"Sit down," Lacey said, easing her way out of his embrace. "Sarah has something to tell you." Then, because she knew how difficult it would be, she leaned close and whispered, "Be gentle with her."

*　　*　　*

"Lacey," Jack said irritably, "don't lift that, it's too heavy for you."

"I'm fine," she insisted, hauling the carton out of the back of the rented van. It was heavy, but nothing she couldn't handle. Sarah had found an apartment of her own, and Jack and Lacey were helping her move. It had been an eventful month. Sarah had temporarily moved in with Lacey and the two women had talked, often long into the night.

"That should do it," Sarah said, as Lacey set the carton on the kitchen countertop. She looked past Lacey and whispered, "What's wrong with Jack? He's been a real crab all morning, and he wasn't much better last night, either. Did you notice?"

Lacey had, but she hadn't wanted to say anything. "I don't know what's wrong." But something was.

"If anyone can get it out of him, it's you."

Lacey wondered if that was true. After the last month she felt as close to Sarah as they were really sisters. And in that time she'd come to another, more profound realization.

She was deeply in love with Jack.

For someone who was convinced she was constitutionally incapable of falling in love again, this was big news.

"I can't thank you two enough," Sarah said when Jack returned from the truck. "I don't know what I would have done these last weeks without you." She hugged them, then turned away in an effort to hide the tears that glistened in her dark eyes. "I'll be fine now. You two go and have fun. I don't want you to worry about me."

Jack hesitated. "You're sure?"

"Positive." Sarah made busywork around her compact kitchen, removing several items from the closest box and setting them on the counter. All the while her back was to them. "Please," she added.

Remembering her own experience, Lacey whispered, "She'll be fine. All she needs is time."

Together Lacey and Jack walked outside to where Jack had parked the moving van. He opened the passenger door and helped her inside.

Lacey removed her bandanna and shook her head to free the thick strands of dark hair that were plastered against her face. Jack climbed into the driver's seat. She noticed how his hands tightened around the steering wheel. For several seconds he just sat there. Then he started the engine and moved out into traffic. But he still seemed deep in thought. Something was wrong.

"Jack," she said softly, "what's troubling you?"

Her voice broke him out of his reverie, and he smiled as if he hadn't a care in the world. "Not a thing. How about sharing a hot fudge sundae with me after we take the truck back?"

It sounded wonderful, but Lacey had discovered in the last few weeks that almost every minute she spent in Jack's company was special. *He* was special.

"Are you worried about Sarah?" Lacey pried gently, wondering at his somber mood. Something was on his mind, but she couldn't force him to tell her. He would speak up when he was ready, she decided.

"Not as much now as when she was living with Mark. Although it's been hard on her, discovering exactly what kind of man he is was the best thing that could have happened."

"She'll be fine," Lacey said confidently.

"Thanks to you."

"Oh, hardly. Sarah will come away from this experience a little more mature and a whole lot smarter. I know I did with Peter. But it takes time. Rome wasn't built in a day."

"I'll say. Look how long it took me to get to know you."

"It was worth the effort, wasn't it?"

He took one hand from the wheel and patted her knee. They were sitting so close to each other that their hips touched. The morning was muggy, but neither of them moved, enjoying this small intimacy. "The wait was well worth the while," he agreed and then added, his eyes dark and serious, "I'm crazy about you, Lacey; I have been for months."

"I'm crazy about you too," she returned softly.

What was definitely crazy was that they should admit their feelings for each other in a moving van in the heavy flow of San Francisco traffic.

After having spoken so freely, both seemed a little embarrassed, a little relieved, and a whole lot in love. Lacey felt as if she were in college all over again. The years of her marriage and the aftermath of the divorce vanished, as if they'd never happened.

"I don't want any ice cream," she whispered, her heart in her throat. "I want you."

Jack's gaze whirled away from the street and his eyes held hers briefly but intently. She could see the pulse in his neck accelerate. For the last few weeks, anything physical between them had been curtailed by Sarah's presence. Now they were free and Lacey was impatient to reclaim this man she loved to the very breadth and depth of her soul.

He didn't answer her, at least not with words, but she noted that he drove faster. As they dropped off the moving van and collected Jack's car, they didn't speak, but she felt the urgency as profoundly as any words he might have said.

Leaving his car in the underground parking lot, they caught the elevator. The instant the door slid closed, Lacey was in Jack's arms. His mouth sought hers with the desperation of a man locked in a dark room, unable to find the exit. His arms half lifted her from the floor, giving her the perfect excuse to cling to him.

"I'm crazy about you," she said again between frantic kisses, weak with yearning. She felt drunk with her need, as if she'd spent the last few hours sitting in a bar instead of the last few moments in his arms.

His hands gripped her hips and pressed her softness against the solid strength of his arousal. Instinctively Lacey moved against him until he groaned.

He caught her face between his hands and kissed her, using his tongue to stroke and tease her until she trembled and whimpered. His hand cupped her breast, and he moaned as he fumbled with the buttons of her blouse.

"Jack." From somewhere deep inside she managed a weak protest. "We're still in the elevator."

He lifted his head and looked around. "We are?"

She wrapped her arms around his waist and tilted back her head to smile up at him. "I don't know about you, but I prefer to make love in a bed with a mattress, pillows, and sheets."

"Where's your sense of adventure?" he teased, kissing her nose. He reached over and pushed the button for the fourth floor.

"Trust me, it's in full swing." She'd only had one lover, and that had been Peter. Inviting a physical relationship with Jack had taken more courage than she knew she possessed.

Naturally Jack didn't understand or appreciate that. It didn't matter for now. All that mattered was the blaze of passion in his eyes.

This intense feeling of desire was new to her. If he didn't continue kissing her, loving her, touching her, Lacey thought she'd die. It was as if years of dammed-up longing had broken free deep inside of her, swamping her senses.

He kissed her again and she sagged against him just as the elevator delivered them to the fourth floor.

"Your place or mine?" he asked, and then made the decision for her. "Yours."

Her hand trembled when she gave him her keys, and she was gratified to see his fingers weren't any steadier. In that moment, she loved him so much she couldn't bear it a second longer. Her arms circled his middle and she kissed the underside of his jaw, teasing him with her tongue, running it down his neck to the hollow at the base of his throat and sucking gently.

"Lacey, for the love of heaven, stop," he protested.

"Do you mean that?" she whispered, lifting her face.

"No . . . never stop loving me." The door opened and they all but stumbled inside.

Jack closed the door, lifted her in his arms, and carried her into the bedroom. Gently he placed her in the middle of the mattress and stared down at her.

"Sweet heaven, you're beautiful!" he whispered, as reverently as if he were praying.

She smiled softly and lifted her arms to him.

It was then she heard Cleo's pitiful meow. Jack heard it too. He glanced over his shoulder and then turned his gaze back to her. His eyes were tightly shut.

"Cleo's having her kittens," he announced and moved away from her.

NINE

"Cleo's having her kittens *now!*"

Lacey leaped off the bed as if she were coming off a trampoline. Her feet landed on the floor with a loud thud.

"Oh, my goodness!" She pressed her hands over her mouth and stared into the closet, where Cleo had made herself a comfortable bed in a darkened corner.

The Abyssinian meowed pitifully.

"Oh, Cleo," Lacey whispered.

Cleo ignored her, rose from her nest, and walked over to Jack, weaving between his legs, her long tail sliding around his calf. Then moved back into the closet and cried again, softly, pleadingly.

"She seems to want you," Lacey murmured, unable to disguise her amazement. It didn't make sense that Cleo would be more comfortable with Jack. After all, Lacey was the one who fed and nurtured her.

"She wants *me?*"

"It wasn't me she was crying for just now." Didn't anyone understand the meaning of commitment anymore? Lacey wondered. Even her cat turned to someone else in her moment of need.

Cleo was up again, seeking Jack's attention. He squatted down in front of the open closet door and patted her gently while whispering reassurances.

"Should I boil water or something?" Lacey asked anxiously. The moment had finally arrived, but she hadn't a clue as to what her role should be. She'd assumed Cleo would calmly give birth to her kittens one day while Lacey was at work.

"Boil water?" Jack asked. "Whatever for?"

"I . . . don't know. Coffee, I guess." She paced the carpet behind Jack in short, quick steps. Seconds earlier they'd been wrapped in an impassioned embrace, and now lovemaking was the furthest thing from either of their minds.

"How's she doing?" Lacey asked, peeking over his shoulder.

"Great, so far. It looks as if the first kitten is about to be born."

"How's Cleo?" Lacey asked again, her fingertips pressed against her lips. "Is she afraid? I don't think I can bear to see her in pain."

Jack looked up at Lacey, reached for her hand, and kissed her knuckles. "She's fine. Stop worrying or you'll make yourself ill."

No sooner had he said the words than Lacey's stomach cramped. She wrapped her hands around her waist, sank onto the end of the mattress, and leaned forward. "Jack, I don't feel so good."

"Go make that coffee you were talking about earlier," he suggested. "At this point Cleo's doing better than you are."

Cleo cried out and Jack turned his attention back to the closet.

"She just delivered the first kitten," he announced, his pleasure keen. "Good girl, Cleo," he said excitedly. "My goodness, will you look at that! Cleo's kitten is the spitting image of Dog."

Lacey hurried off the bed to look. Her stomach didn't feel much better, but she understood the source of her discomfort. She was experiencing sympathetic labor pains. "He does look like Dog." She squatted down next to Jack and studied the ugly little creature. "I don't mind telling you, Jack, this unnerves me."

"I could go for a cup of coffee," he said. "Cleo and I are doing fine."

Lacey hurried into the kitchen. Once she was there, she decided there was no need to rush. As Jack had so eloquently told her, he had everything under control.

"How's it going?" she asked when she returned with their coffee.

"Great. I think Cleo's just about ready to deliver a second kitten."

Lacey wasn't interested in viewing the birthing process, so she sat on the bed and let Jack play midwife.

"Here it comes," he said after a few minutes, his voice elevated with excitement. "This one's just like Dog too." He turned with a proud smile as if he'd given birth himself.

Grumbling, Lacey sank onto the carpet next to Jack. Cleo was busy licking off her tiny offspring. As far as Lacey could tell the kittens were no bigger than fur balls and ugly as sin, but that didn't keep her heart from swelling with a flood of emotions.

"Do you think she's finished?"

"I don't know," Jack returned. "How long do these things usually take?"

Lacey laughed. "How would I know?"

"You intended to breed her, didn't you?"

"Yes, before Dog so rudely interrupted my plans."

Jack wiggled his eyebrows. "You're pleased he did, aren't you?"

Lacey wasn't willing to admit anything of the sort. "You'll note that once Dog had his fun with Cleo, he was on his merry way."

"Perhaps, but with Cleo having Dog's family—well, it sort of cemented our relationship, don't you think?"

She suppressed a smile. "I guess it did."

"You can breed her next time if you're really serious about it."

He was right; it would be foolish to claim otherwise. "I'll get the pamphlet Dr. Christman gave me. That should tell us how long this process takes." She left him momentarily and returned reading the material the vet had given her.

"I think Cleo might be finished," Jack announced when Lacey walked into the bedroom and sat on the end of the mattress. "She's lavishing attention on her kittens and not acting the way she was earlier."

"It says here the birthing process generally takes a couple of hours," she recited and glanced at her watch. It hadn't taken nearly that amount of time for Cleo.

Before she could say as much, Jack said, "We don't have any idea how long she was in labor before we arrived."

"Right. It could easily have been two hours." She felt a tremendous sense of relief that it was over. "She only had two kittens, but it says right here that Abyssinians generally have smaller litters and Siamese have larger ones. That's interesting."

"I guess we should thank our lucky stars Cleo only has the two."

"Speaking of which," Lacey said righteously, "you never gave me the name of the family taking your half of the litter."

"I'll give one to Sarah," Jack said confidently. "A pet will do her good. Besides, she owes me big-time."

"But does Sarah want a cat?" Lacey might think of Jack's sister as family, but she didn't want to foist an animal off on her if Sarah wasn't willing.

"Of course she wants one. Dog and Cleo's offspring are special. Besides, a kitten will keep her company while she gets over Mark." He frowned as if he found speaking the other man's name repulsive. "It shouldn't take long for her to forget that rat."

"Don't be so sure," Lacey told him. "I was married to a man who displayed many of the same characteristics. Be patient with her," she advised again, and then added with a gentle smile, "As patient as you were with me."

"You've spoken so little of your marriage."

"If you review what happened with Sarah and change the names in the appropriate places, the story's the same, with only a few differences," she amended. "The biggest difference is that I was married to Peter. A couple of months after I moved here, I heard from a well-meaning friend who thought I should know that he'd married his blond cupcake and they were expecting a baby."

"Some friend."

Her smile was sad. "That's what I thought. The news devastated me. Not because he'd remarried, but because he'd been adamant about us not having children when I wanted a family so badly."

Jack drank from his coffee and seemed to be mulling over the information. "You're over him now?"

Lacey wasn't entirely sure how to answer him. Her hesitation appeared to give Jack some concern. He leveled his gaze at her and frowned darkly.

"Yes, I'm over him, and no, I'm not."

The corner of Jack's mouth jerked upward. "That's about as clear as swamp water."

"I don't love him anymore, if that's what you're asking. The hardest part was having to let go of the dream of what our lives could have been like together."

"Have you?" The words were stark and issued without emotion.

"Yes." She wanted to thank him for the large part he'd played in the healing process, but he didn't seem receptive to it. Although he'd asked her about Peter and her marriage, he seemed to find it uncomfortable to listen to the sorry details of her life with her ex-husband.

Jack stood and wandered into the living room, taking his coffee with him. When she joined him, she found him standing in front of the small window that looked down over the street. He didn't turn around. It was almost as if he'd forgotten she was with him.

"Jack?"

He turned around and offered her a fleeting grin.

"Does it bother you to discuss my ex-husband?"

He shook his head, and set his mug aside. "Not in the least. I was the one who asked, remember?"

"Yes, but you seemed—I don't know, upset, I guess. Peter was a part of my life, an important part for several years.

"The divorce was difficult for me, but I learned from it. I matured. Blaming Peter isn't important any longer. I understand now that I played a part in the death of our marriage. I wasn't the perfect wife."

"You say you don't love him anymore?"

She gestured weakly. "Let me put it like this. I don't hate him. My happiness doesn't hinge on what's happening in his life. My happiness hinges on me and the choices I make, and I've decided to live a good life." She hoped it would be with Jack. With all her heart, she prayed he felt as strongly about her as she did him.

He smiled. Lacey swore she'd never seen anyone more beautiful. It was strange, she realized, to feel that way about a man. It wasn't so much his looks, although heaven knew he was handsome. What she found so appealing about Jack was who he was as a person. He was trustworthy and generous. He'd helped restore her faith in love and life. His love had been a precious gift for which she would always be thankful.

"Jack," she whispered, "what's wrong?" Something was still bothering him.

He walked over to Lacey and tenderly gathered her in his arms. He rested his chin against the top of her head, and she heard a sigh rumble through his chest.

"You got your raise from Mr. Sullivan?" he asked.

"Yes." Lacey was sure she'd told him, but they'd both been so wrapped up in helping Sarah that he must have forgotten. "A very healthy one."

"Good."

Lacey eased away from his chest and met his gaze. "Why are you asking about Mr. Sullivan?"

"You love your job, don't you? Especially now that you're getting the respect and the money you deserve?"

"Yes, but what does that have to do with us?"

He brought her back into his embrace. "I love my job too. I've worked for California Fidelity for nearly ten years. Last Thursday I was given a promotion. This is something I've worked toward for years, but I never dreamed it would happen so quickly. It took me completely by surprise."

"Jack, that's wonderful." Stepping up on her tiptoes, she kissed him, so proud she felt she would burst. "Why didn't you say something sooner? We could have celebrated."

"My promotion means something else, Lacey."

"I'm sure you'll have added responsibilities. Oh, Jack, I couldn't be more pleased for you."

"It means," he said, cupping her shoulders, "I have to move."

The blood rushed out of her face so fast, Lacey felt faint. "Move? Where?"

He sighed and looked away from her. "Seattle."

TEN

"Seattle," Lacey echoed, stunned. "When did you intend to tell me, before or after we made love?" Stepping away from him, she pushed the hair away from her head, leaving her hands there, elbows extended. "You're no better than Dog!"

"What's Dog got to do with this? You're being ridiculous."

"I'm not. You were going to make love to me and then casually mention you were being transferred?" It was all clear to her now. Rainwater clear. Just like the tomcat he called a pet, he was going to take what he wanted and walk out of her life.

"I didn't plan the lovemaking, Lacey, if that's what you're thinking. You don't have any reason to be so angry. Besides, nothing happened."

"Thanks to Cleo. And for your information, I . . . have every right to be angry." Her fragile voice wobbled with emotion but gained strength with each word. "It'd be best if you left."

"Not until we've talked this out." He planted his feet as if to suggest a bulldozer wouldn't budge him before he was good and ready.

She pointed her index finger at him while she gathered her thoughts together, which unfortunately had scattered like water-starved cattle toward a river. "I've heard about men like you."

"What?" He stared at her as if he needed to examine her more closely. "Lacey, for the love of heaven, stop right now before you say something you'll regret."

"I most certainly will say something." She walked over to the door and held it open for him. "You . . . you can't drop a bombshell like that and expect me not to react. As for regrets, trust me, Jack Walker, I've got plenty of those. It'll take years to sort through them all."

"All right, all right." He raised his hands in surrender. Actually he posed as if she held a six-shooter on him. "Please, close the door. Let's sit down and talk this over like two civilized people."

"Are you suggesting I'm not civilized? Because I'm telling you right now, I've had about as much as I can take."

"Sit down," he said calmly and gestured toward her sofa. "Please."

Lacey debated whether she should do as he asked or not. She crossed her arms under her breasts and glared at him. "I prefer to stand."

"Will you close the door?"

She hadn't realized her foot had continued to hold it open. "All right," she said stiffly, as if this were a large concession. Chin held high, she moved, and the door closed with a decidedly loud click.

"This is what I thought we'd do," Jack said, pacing in front of the window he'd been staring out only moments earlier.

"We?" she asked, wanting him to think she resented the way he automatically included her.

"Me," he amended, casting her a sour look. "I'm going

to accept the promotion, Lacey. I thought about it long and hard, and I can't let this opportunity pass. The timing could be better, but I can't change that. I worked hard for this, and just because—"

"Of me?" she finished for him. "You don't need to worry, Jack, I wasn't going to ask you to turn down such a wonderful opportunity." Despite the shock and the betrayal she felt, maintaining her outrage was becoming difficult. Her voice softened considerably. "I wouldn't ever ask such a thing of you."

"I thought I could fly down for a weekend once a month," he suggested.

Once a month, she mused, her heart so heavy it felt as if it had dropped all the way to her knees. After having made such an issue of standing, she felt the sudden need to sit down.

Slumping onto the edge of the love seat, she bit her lower lip. So this was what was to become of them. Once-a-month lovers. Lacey wasn't foolish enough to believe it would be otherwise. Long-distance relationships were difficult. They'd both start out with good intentions, but she noted he didn't say where these monthly meetings would lead.

Jack motioned with his hands. "Say something. Anything. I know it's not the ideal solution. It's going to be hell for me."

"Expensive, too," she said. Already she could see the handwriting on the wall. He'd fly down for visits the first couple of months, and then he'd skip a month and she wouldn't hear from him the following one.

"We can make this work, Lacey."

Blinking back the tears, she stood and walked over to stand in front of him. His features blurred as her tears brimmed. She pressed her hands against the sides of his face, leaned forward, and kissed him. The electricity between them all but crackled, and it was several moments before Lacey found the strength and the courage to pull away.

"I . . . asked Sarah why you wanted to date me." She found it almost impossible to speak normally. "She told me you've been like this all your life. You find someone hurting and broken, someone in need of a little tenderness, and then you lavish them with love. What she didn't say was that once they were strong again, you'd step back and wish them a fond farewell."

Jack's brow condensed with a thick frown. "We aren't talking about the same thing. If you must know, you did represent a certain challenge from the moment we met. Until you, I'd never had much of a problem getting a woman to agree to go out with me. As for this other business, you're way off base."

"What about Dog?"

The frown darkened considerably. "What about him?"

"The lost and lonely alley cat you found and loved."

A hint of a smile touched his lips. "I don't think Dog would appreciate that description. We more or less tolerated each other in the beginning. These days, we share a tentative friendship."

"You took him in, gave him a home, and—"

"Hold on just one minute," Jack said sternly. "You're not suggesting that my friendship with Dog has anything to do with us, are you?"

It was apparent he didn't understand or appreciate the similarities. It would be one of the most difficult things she'd ever do to say good-bye to Jack, but despite what she'd claimed, she'd do it without regrets. He'd given her far more than he'd ever know. With Jack's love and support, she had learned to let go of the past. His love had given her the courage to move forward.

"Thank you," she whispered. She dropped her hands and stepped away.

"What are you thanking me for?" he demanded. "And why does it sound like another way of saying good-bye?"

She didn't so much as blink. "Because it is."

He paled visibly. "You don't mean that," he murmured.

Lacey couldn't think of anything more to say. Arguments crowded her mind. It would be easy to pretend that nothing would change after he moved to Seattle, but she knew it would.

Within a few months, Lacey would become little more than a memory of someone he once cared for. As he said, he didn't have a problem finding women interested in going out with him.

With all this talk of get-togethers, Lacey noticed, he wasn't offering her any promises. But to be fair, he hadn't sought any from her either.

"So it's over, just like that?" he said stiffly. "It was nice knowing you, have a good life, and all that rot?"

It sounded cold and crass, but basically he had it right. Unable to look him in the eye, Lacey nodded and lowered her head.

"In other words, once I walk out that door, that's it?"

"It's better this way," she whispered, the words barely making it past the lump in her throat. She prayed he'd leave before she disgraced herself further by weeping openly.

"You can't mean that, Lacey. I refuse to believe the woman who invited me to her bed a few hours ago is ordering me out of her life. It doesn't make sense."

"Exactly what are you offering me, Jack?" she asked defiantly. "A weekend once a month . . . for how long? Two months, maybe three? It isn't going to last—"

"Why not? For your information I'm hoping it doesn't last more than a month or two myself."

His words stung as sharply as a slap across the face.

"Maybe by that time you'll be miserable enough to be willing to marry me—"

"Marry you?" Lacey wasn't sure she'd heard him correctly, and if ever things had to be crystal clear it was now. "Of course," he snapped. "You can't honestly believe I was planning on making this commute every month for the rest of our lives, did you?"

"Well, yes, that's exactly what I thought," she whispered.

"I figured it might take a couple of miserable months apart for you to realize you love me."

"I know I love you now, you idiot. Why else do you think I turned down a hot fudge sundae? I told you how I felt this very afternoon."

He glared at her suspiciously. "No, you didn't."

"Jack," she said impatiently, "you were driving the moving van back to the rental company, and I looked you right in the eye and said it."

"What you said was you were crazy about me. There's a world of difference between crazy and love. If you love me you're going to have to make it abundantly clear, otherwise there's going to be a problem. You already know I love you."

"No, I don't," she argued. "You've never once told me how you feel about me."

He shut his eyes as if he were seconds away from losing his patience. "A man doesn't say that sort of thing lightly, especially if the woman has only admitted to being crazy. Besides, you must know how I feel. A blind man on the street would know I've been in love with you from the moment you knocked on my door and demanded that Dog do right by Cleo."

"You . . . never said anything."

"How could I? You were as prickly as a cactus. It took me weeks to get you to agree to so much as a date. Just when I was beginning to think I was making some progress, along comes this promotion. What else am I supposed to do but pray you miss me so damn much you'll agree to marry me."

"I do," Lacey whispered.

Apparently Jack didn't hear her. "Another thing. You just got your raise, and I've never seen you so happy. You aren't going to want to uproot your life now, just when you've finally gotten what you wanted."

"I don't think you heard me, Jack. I said I do. Furthermore, if I've been happy lately, did it ever occur to you it might be because I'd fallen in love with you?"

"You do what?" he demanded impatiently.

"Agree to marry you. This minute. Tomorrow. Or two months down the road, whatever you want."

He squinted his eyes and stared at her as if he wasn't sure he should trust her. "What about your job?"

"I'll give two weeks' notice first thing in the morning."

"Your lease?"

"I'll sublet the place. Listen here, Jack Walker, if you think you're going to back down on your offer now, I've got a word or two for you."

He stood and walked all the way around her. "You're serious? You'd be willing to marry me just like that?"

Her grin widened, and she snapped her fingers. "Just like that. You don't honestly believe I'd let a wonderful man like you slip through my fingers, do you? I can't let you go, Jack." She threw her arms around his neck and spread happy, eager kisses all over his face.

Jack wrapped his arms around her waist and lifted her off the ground. Their kiss was slow, tender, and thorough. By the time they finished, Lacey was left weak and breathless.

"I'll never let you go, Jack Walker."

"That's more like it," he said with a dash of male arrogance, and pulled her tightly against him again.

It was exactly where she wanted to be. Close to his heart for all time.

Debbie Macomber, an award-winning author of more than seventy romances, lives in Port Orchard, Washington.

SWITCH

~ *by* ~

Linda Lael Miller

ONE

"You're crazy," Jamie Roberts told her twin sister, Sara Summerville, orchestrating the statement with a pair of chopsticks.

Some of the other patrons of Wong's House of Eggrolls turned to peer at them from booths upholstered in cheap red vinyl. Sara folded her hands on the Formica tabletop, leaned in, and lowered her voice. "Maybe I am," she admitted, "but I'm also desperate."

Jamie was moved, her better judgment notwithstanding, by the note of true despair in Sara's tone. "We don't even look alike anymore!" she argued, in a loud whisper.

Sara tilted her gilded head to one side, a thoughtful expression on her face. "Of course we do, we're identical. You'd have to get a decent haircut, that's all, and maybe go a shade or two lighter. If you wore my clothes and makeup, everyone would think—"

"Now just a minute," Jamie broke in, a little frantic

because she could feel herself being railroaded, just like in the old days. "It isn't that simple to take over somebody else's whole identity! Besides, if your life is so dull it's making you crazy, why would *I* want to live it?"

Sara's gold bangles twinkled in the dim light as she folded her arms. She was wearing a spectacular Armani pants suit, tailored to her trim figure.

Fate had been better to Sara than to Jamie, but then Sara had had a personal agenda since the age of twelve, and she'd taken a lot more risks between then and now. And stepped on a lot of toes, though Jamie preferred not to think about that, in the interest of establishing some sort of closeness with her sister.

"Dull?" Sara countered. "Jamie, Jamie, Jamie. I'm the widow of one of the richest men in the world. I live in Europe. I can do anything I want, go anywhere I want, buy anything I want. 'Dull' is the last word I'd use to describe the way I live."

Jamie thumped her nails on the table. Her blue jeans, worn sweatshirt, and sneakers offered a telling contrast to her sister's designer clothes. "Okay, then go do things and buy things and leave me out of it. Good grief, Sara. I manage a chain of tile stores for a living, and I inherited a lot of debts from my ex-husband. My Visa bill is bigger than the gross national product of Bolivia, and I haven't had a date in eight months. Believe me, you don't want this life."

"Who knows?" Sara speculated. "I might even improve on it a little. Come on, Jamie, this is important to me."

"Why?" Jamie was honestly puzzled.

"Because it is. Can't you just trust me for once?"

Jamie made a huffy sound. "The last time we switched, you flunked my Medieval Poetry class and came this close to enlisting in the Israeli army!"

Sara smiled wistfully at the memory and made no attempt to refute the charge. "That was in college," she said, after a few moments of reflective silence. "We're mature women now."

Now it was Jamie who sighed. "Almost thirty," she marveled, with a distracted nod. Willard Scott could announce their upcoming birthday on national television, along with all the other ancients.

Suddenly, Sara reached out, took Jamie's hand, and squeezed it hard. "Please, James, do this for me. For the way things used to be between us. It's April now; all I'm asking for is a few months. Be me until September first, and let me be you."

Sara's childhood nickname for her tugged at Jamie's heart. They'd once been so close. But problems had arisen between them when Sara dropped out of college in their senior year and set out on a cross-country car trip with Jamie's boyfriend. They'd been estranged ever since—the whole thing seemed silly in retrospect—and they'd had little contact, except for the occasional stiff letter or impersonal card. Still, they were sisters—twins, no less— and Jamie wanted desperately to mend fences, to rebuild the old bond that had once allowed them to touch each other's hearts and minds, regardless of distance.

Besides, she'd already started thinking about her sister's palatial home just off the coast of France, on the sunny island of Tovia. Jamie had never actually visited. Alan, her ex, had kept her perennially broke, and besides she hadn't known how Sara would receive her. But she'd seen pictures of the place. It was like a Greek palace, with statues and a pool and a full staff of servants.

Jamie pushed away her half-eaten dinner. "There's more to this than you're telling me," she insisted. "You live like royalty. I'm definitely of the peasant persuasion. I can't believe you really want to exchange your life for mine."

Sara gnawed on her glossy lower lip for a moment. "I don't—not forever. I guess what it all comes down to is that I'm looking for a change and a challenge. Things are too easy for me. I want to see if I can survive in the real world."

"I need to think about this."

Sara's pensive expression turned to one of exasperation. "Oh, for heaven's sake, Jamie, you can be such a curmudgeon! You've been divorced for five years, and I'll bet you're still sleeping strictly on your own side of the bed. Furthermore, I'll lay odds that you're watching Alan's favorite television programs, buying his brand of toothpaste, and sleeping in his T-shirts. Maybe you've even renewed his magazine subscriptions."

Jamie blushed. She *was* still sleeping on her own side of the bed, as if she expected Alan to reappear some night and crawl in beside her in his jockey shorts. "I have not renewed his subscriptions!" she blustered, deliberately failing to mention the TV shows, the toothpaste, and the T-shirts. "You make it sound as if I'm still in love with the man!"

"Are you?"

"Of course not!" She drew a deep breath. "Of course not," she repeated, more moderately. "Alan was, is, and always will be a jerk and you know it. I should never have married him in the first place."

Sara reached for her cocktail, forgotten until then, and twirled the tiny paper umbrella between two fingers. "That's exactly my point. You're still stuck in that awful part of your life, James. It's time to move on, shake things up, effect some healthy changes." She raised weary brown eyes—exact duplicates of Jamie's own except for the skillfully applied shadow, liner, and mascara—to her sister's face. "Now, if you don't mind, I'd like to go back to your place and get some sleep. I've got a major case of jet lag."

In spite of the thing with the Israeli army and a few similar experiences, Jamie felt real sympathy for her sister. It was going to work, she thought. They *would* be close again.

"Come on," she said, reaching for her purse. "I'll take the sofa bed, and you can crash in my room."

When Sara smiled, Jamie wanted more than ever to please her. "See? You're already warming to the idea of letting me be you."

"Don't push it," Jamie warned, but she smiled back at Sara as she said the words.

Fifteen minutes later, they were in Jamie's apartment, a two-bedroom with a view of downtown Seattle. While Sara languished in the shower, Jamie plucked Alan's old T-shirts out of the middle drawer of the bureau, hurried to the cleaning closet, and shoved them in the ragbag.

She was putting clean sheets on the bed when Sara came out of the bathroom, bundled in a short terry-cloth robe. Jamie was struck, in that moment, by the strange frailty she saw in her sister. There was a haunted look in Sara's eyes, and shadows tinged the delicate skin beneath them.

"You don't need to give up your room," Sara said, trying to smile, a pink towel covering her hair like a turban. "I'm not so fancy I can't sleep on a fold-out bed."

Jamie wanted to put her arms around Sara, but something in the set of her twin's shoulders warned against it. They'd parted on bitter terms, and it wouldn't be wise to push.

"Sara, are you in some kind of trouble? Is that what this is all about? If something's wrong, tell me. You know I'll do whatever I can to help."

Sara stood still in the bathroom doorway for a few moments, just looking at Jamie and saying nothing. Then she gave a nervous little laugh and tossed her head. "You're such a worrywart. Honestly, James, a few months of shameless self-indulgence is just what you need."

Jamie sighed and shoved splayed fingers through her tousled hair. The prospect was gaining appeal with every passing moment. She finished making the bed and sat down on the foot of the mattress. "Okay," she said, "suppose—just suppose—I agree to this wild scheme. I have to come back to my own life at some point, you know. What if I get here and find out you've messed it up?"

Sara looked around the small bedroom. All of a sudden, the place seemed as anonymous as a hotel room to Jamie, in spite of the familiar clutter.

"Anything would be an improvement, if you ask me," Sara commented, setting her hands on her hips. "James, you're in a monumental rut, in case you haven't noticed."

Jamie felt heat flare in her face again. Nobody had ever been able to get under her skin the way Sara did, not even Alan. "Maybe I am," she said irritably, "but it's *my* rut. At least I know my way around it!"

Sara gave a long-suffering sigh, but her eyes were snapping with challenge. "Wow," she replied, with a wry twist of her lips. "What an accomplishment."

Once again, Jamie felt herself losing ground, and in her panic, she cried, "Do you think just anybody can manage a chain of tile stores?"

With a small smile, Sara held out one hand and admired her manicure. Her nails were perfect ovals, the same peachy-pink color as the inside of a shell Jamie had bought at a garage sale when she was eleven. She'd told everyone at school the next fall that her father had taken her and Sara to the ocean over summer vacation. In truth, he hadn't so much as written during that time.

"I wasn't planning to manage anything," Sara answered, with calm amusement. "I don't need to work at all, remember? I have plenty of money."

Jamie caught her hands together behind her back, hoping Sara hadn't noticed her own unfiled and unpolished nails. "You're forgetting one thing," she pointed out, as reasonably as she could. "I don't *have* plenty of money. And even if I agreed to change places with you"— she held up one hand against the bright light that was dawning on Sara's face—"which I haven't, I'd need a job and a home to come back to in September."

Sara folded her arms and tilted her towel-turbaned head to one side, eyes narrowed in speculation. Inspiration struck her visibly, after a few moments of silence, and Jamie waited, with equal measures of dread and excitement, for the newborn idea to be unveiled.

"I should have thought of it before," she said, drumming graceful, tapered fingers lightly against her upper arm. "I'll *rent* your life. It's a perfect solution."

Jamie figured she ought to be insulted by the suggestion, but in truth she was intrigued. Sara was an original thinker; you had to give her that. "What kind of money are we talking about here?" she ventured.

Sara considered briefly, then smiled a broad and generous smile. "A hundred thousand," she said. "After taxes."

Having been seated on the end of the bed all this time, Jamie bolted to her feet on a surge of shock and just as quickly sat down again. For several seconds, she was too stunned to speak, and when she did manage to say something, the words came out as one long croak. "A hundred thousand—"

"Dollars," Sara said triumphantly. "I'll have my accounting firm transfer the funds to your bank on September first."

Jamie felt faint. A hundred thousand dollars! She could pay off all the bills she'd been stuck with, travel, and finally start her own business with that kind of money. A small antiques shop, for instance, specializing in old toys. . . .

"There's a catch here somewhere," she insisted, as her basically pragmatic nature reasserted itself.

Sara didn't challenge the accusation—didn't speak at all, in fact. She just stood there and smiled, knowing she'd won.

Jamie hurled herself backward on the bed, gazed up at the ceiling, and moaned with frustration. "All my life, I've comforted myself with the idea that, in spite of all my mistakes and failures, I was a person who couldn't be bought. But you've just met my price."

Sara was standing at the vanity table, looking into the mirror as she unwound the towel from her hair. "Everyone has a price," she said, in a distracted tone. "Don't be too hard on yourself, James. At least yours is higher than most people's."

Jamie wasn't comforted, and she still couldn't shake the feeling that she was standing at the edge of some kind of abyss. She *was* bored and lonely and tired of her life, however, and she couldn't remember the last time she'd taken a risk of any real significance. She was overdue for an adventure.

And she wanted Sara to be happy.

The next morning, Jamie awakened in her sofa bed and found Sara standing on her head in the doorway to the kitchenette.

"Yoga," Sara explained. "I do it every day."

"Great," Jamie replied, scrambling out of bed and stumbling into the bathroom. She was not a morning person, but Sara, she remembered with grim resignation, had always been full of energy from the moment her eyes flew open.

After showering and putting on jeans and a T-shirt— it was Tuesday, her day off from work—Jamie returned to the tiny living room to find that Sara had finished her yoga and exchanged her leotard and tights for a simple, expensive linen dress. The garment, probably just taken out of Sara's Gucci travel bag, was wrinkle-free.

"This is never going to work," Jamie said, jerking open the refrigerator door and burrowing among jars and bottles and bowls until she found a carton of cottage cheese with an expiration date she could live with. She found a spoon and swallowed two mouthfuls before going on. "We're too different."

Sara sniffed Jamie's breakfast, made a face, took a bagel from the bread box on the counter, and stuffed it into the toaster. "Of course it will work," she replied. "You want the money, don't you?"

Jamie couldn't deny that she did. She'd tossed and turned half the night, just thinking of the things she could do with such a staggering sum. "Yes," she said.

Sara took the cheese carton from her twin's hand and, nose wrinkled, dropped it into the trash. "Let's start with your eating habits," she said. "I would never touch this stuff. It isn't even the low-fat variety, for pete's sake."

After that, Jamie's refresher course in Being Sara began in earnest.

It started with the bagel, spread with a thin layer of jam but completely innocent of butter or cream cheese. Then there was a two-hour lesson in applying makeup in both day and evening versions. Following that was a session in a fancy salon, with an exclusive hairdresser who demanded references from his clients and accepted Jamie only because of Sara's platinum American Express card.

As she and Sara left the salon, Jamie caught a glimpse of their reflections in a shop window. It was like seeing a double image in a mirror.

Sara spent the afternoon drilling Jamie, teaching her the names of her servants, neighbors, and shopkeepers. Like Jamie, Sara didn't seem to have a lot of close friends, but that was probably a good thing under the circumstances. It would be very difficult to fool someone who knew Sara intimately.

"You'll have to be nice to the cat too," Sara said that evening, as they sat at Jamie's kitchen table with the contents of Sara's purse between them. "His name is Lazarus, and he belonged to my husband." She shuddered a little, her eyes on the credit cards, documents, and cosmetics that had tumbled from her bag moments before. "Reprehensible creature."

Jamie allowed herself a half smile. "Who, the husband or the cat?"

Sara didn't meet Jamie's eyes. "The cat, of course," she said breezily. "Henri absolutely adored him, though. He even went so far as to mention the damnable thing in his will. As long as he lives, Lazarus must have all the cream and fish his evil little heart desires and be given the run of the villa, if you can believe it."

Jamie loved cats but because both Aunt Erlene and Alan had hated them, she'd never gotten one. It embarrassed her to realize she'd been living by other people's scripts all this time—wearing Alan's T-shirts for nightgowns, keeping to her own side of the bed, denying herself a pet. Most of all, though, she regretted letting the feud with Sara go on for so long.

"Lazarus won't be a problem," she said.

At last Sara looked directly at her sister again, with an odd, tense expression flickering far back in her eyes. "It means so much to me, Jamie, this time away. I really need a new perspective."

Once again, Jamie felt vaguely uneasy. She was in for some surprises in Tovia, she sensed that, but it was too late to change her mind.

"So do I," she said. Then, silently and with some chagrin, she added, *And I need the money, too.*

A week later, after spending all her free time on intensive training in the mores and manners of the impossibly rich, Jamie boarded a plane, wearing Sara's clothes and carrying her bags and passport, sank, knees trembling, into a seat in the first-class cabin, and asked herself what the hell she thought she was doing.

Once the craft was airborne, a flight attendant made the rounds, passing out champagne in elegant crystal flutes. Jamie took delicate but rapid sips, and after her second glass some of her nervousness faded away. By the time she'd finished a third, she believed she could bring peace to the Middle East without even breaking into a sweat.

The flight was fourteen hours long, and they touched down twice, once in New York and again in Madrid, with a change of planes, before making a final landing in Tovia. By then, Jamie's feet and ankles were swollen and she was so tired she could hardly hold up her head. She fumbled through customs, feeling a fresh rush of guilt when the officer compared her face with the one in Sara's passport, wielded his trusty stamp, and allowed her to pass.

Not surprisingly, since there were only about a quarter of a million people in all of Tovia, the airport was small, with a single baggage carousel. Jamie stood beside it, among the other passengers, and watched Sara's fancy leather bags make several revolutions before remembering that the luggage was supposed to be hers.

Awkwardly, she made her way through the dwindling crush of people and wrestled the suitcases off the conveyor belt. Just as she turned to scan the terminal for a porter, she saw a man striding purposefully toward her. He was handsome, with dark hair and eyes of a deep, anxiety-producing blue, and he wore an Italian suit, pale gray and exquisitely tailored. His aristocratic face was grim, but when Jamie met his gaze, he flashed her a quick white smile.

The experience was, for Jamie, like being struck in the stomach with a battering ram, but at the same time strangely pleasant. As he reached her and grazed her cheek with a brotherly kiss, she struggled to remember him from Sara's intense briefings.

He frowned, as if he'd already guessed that something was amiss, and took her bags. "I'm sorry Julian couldn't meet you himself," he said, and there was a stiffness in his tone and manner as he started toward the nearest exit, evidently trusting Jamie to follow him. "He must have been detained in Paris."

Julian? Sara definitely hadn't mentioned that name. "I see," she said. She was doing a pretty good job of imitating her sister, she thought, considering how tired she was. Jamie was teetering on the edge of a headache. She groped in the dark corners of her mind for the identity of the well-dressed Greek-god type schlepping her suitcases until it came to her. This was Rowan Parrish, a former neighbor of Sara's and evidently a fairly close friend.

Once she'd determined that much, the rest tumbled after it. Parrish was thirty-five, divorced and, like everyone in Sara's social circle, stinking rich. Although he was a member of the local aristocracy, he'd earned his fortune trading in Chinese artifacts, and he was an authority on antiques.

Outside, a shimmering black Rolls-Royce awaited them. The chauffeur—Sara had called him Curran, though whether that was his first or last name Jamie didn't know—got out of the car, opened the trunk, and stowed the bags as Parrish moved to take Jamie's arm.

She drew back and reached for the handle of one of the rear doors, only to remember too late that Sara would have waited for her escort to help her into the car. She checked herself, but out of the corner of her eye she saw Parrish watching her, the faintest line of puzzlement creasing his tanned forehead.

There was a brief silence and then, mercifully, Mr. Parrish opened the door himself. Jamie slipped into the cool, sedately posh interior with a grateful sigh. Curran took the wheel, and the other man, pensive again, joined her in the rear of the car, settling into the seat across from hers. The windows were tinted, soft classical music surrounded them, and the Rolls engine made a soothing sound, like the companionable purr of a great sleek cat.

Jamie sighed again and closed her eyes. She dozed, then awakened with a start, having no idea whether she'd slept for a minute or an hour.

She felt the car slow and saw a hint of high iron gates through the dark window. It was on the tip of her tongue to ask if they were almost there, but she stopped herself in time. Sara, of course, wouldn't have to ask such an elementary question, since the villa was her home.

"You must be exhausted," Mr. Parrish said gently.

Jamie felt something warm and soft brush against her heart. She and Sara had lost their mother when they were ten, and their father, an unlucky gambler with good intentions and a drinking problem, had shipped them off to his sister to raise. Aunt Erlene, who managed a tavern in a small town south of Seattle and lived in a two bedroom trailer, had met their bus and driven them home in her smoking, chortling old boat of a car. They'd had enough to eat, and Erlene had seen that they studied, so they could get college scholarships and make something of themselves, but tenderness had been in short supply. Even after all that time, Jamie realized, she was still a sucker for a kind word and a little concern.

"I'll be all right," she said finally. They were following a driveway paved with white gravel, and in the distance Jamie could make out the crystalline sparkle of the Mediterranean. "How's Lazarus?" she asked, mostly to make conversation.

The blue eyes narrowed again, briefly, and then he dazzled Jamie with another unexpected smile. This one, however, had a slight edge. "Hale and hearty, I'm afraid, with all his nine lives still before him. He's well named, our Lazarus."

Jamie lowered her gaze to her hands, now knotted in her lap. Sara wasn't fond of the cat; she merely tolerated him. She had to remember that, if she was going to succeed with the masquerade and collect the hundred thousand dollars that would change her life.

"Reprehensible creature," she said, in the same tone she'd heard Sara use, and added an elegant little shiver for good measure.

By that time Mr. Parrish was gazing out the window, and he didn't offer a reply. Jamie yearned for the quiet of Sara's suite in the villa. All she needed to get back on track, she was sure, was a hot bath, something to eat, and about twelve hours of uninterrupted sleep.

The car came to a smooth stop and Curran appeared, momentarily, to open one of the rear doors and extend a gloved hand to Jamie. She let him help her out and stood still on the brick drive, gazing at the villa in pure amazement.

It was a great, sprawling place, made of some glittering white stone, with what seemed like hundreds of arched windows glistening in the sun. Although it was still winter in America, lush vegetation bloomed riotously on all sides here and the lawn was green and vast and rolling, like the golf course of some exclusive country club.

While Jamie hesitated, spellbound, a large black cat sashayed along a stone railing on the veranda, tail high and slightly bristled. He leaped onto one of the marble steps, landing with an audible thump because of his bulk, and approached the new arrival with an air of condescending charity.

"*Reow?*" he said inquiringly, haughty as a sultan encountering a slave in an unexpected place.

Jet-lagged and quite charmed, Jamie forgot herself and bent to pat his enormous silken head. "Hello, your highness," she said, with what surely seemed to him a fatuous and idiotic smile.

Lazarus purred, sounding like the engine of the Rolls, and wound himself around and between her ankles.

"Interesting," observed Mr. Parrish, from behind.

Jamie extricated herself from the cat, at the same time pretending she hadn't heard the remark, and proceeded into the villa at a brisk pace. She forced her tired mind to focus on the memory of Sara's sketches of the interior of the house.

The foyer was just as Sara had described it, a huge room with a black-and-white tile floor of the finest marble, a six-foot chandelier hanging from the domed and frescoed ceiling, a staircase fit for a grand hotel,

Louis XIV chairs and tables, and paintings any museum would have been happy to claim.

Jamie tried to look bored. Turning to face her escort, she held out one hand in a gesture of farewell. "Thank you for everything, Mr. Parrish. You've been very kind."

"Mr. Parrish?" he echoed, with anger catching fire in his eyes.

Jamie blushed, flustered. Another foolish slip. The man was Sara's friend, after all. She wouldn't have addressed him so formally. Putting one hand to her forehead, she managed a faltering smile, and the confusion in her manner was quite real. "I—I guess I'm more exhausted than I thought, Rowan," she said.

Just inside the front door, which still stood open, Lazarus sat grooming himself. He was possessed of a certain grand disinterest, ignoring both Jamie and Rowan. Jamie felt a profound hope that the animal would forgive her for snubbing him, after he'd offered such a generous greeting. Friends, she suspected, were going to be in short supply.

Rowan regarded her in a solemn and already familiar way. "Are you all right, Sara?" he asked.

The chauffeur came in before she had to answer, bringing the baggage, and a moment later, a maid hurried down the curved staircase, her color high.

"I'm so sorry I wasn't right on hand to greet you, Mrs. Summerville," the woman blurted, fairly choking on the words in her eagerness to get them said. "We've been busy making up your room, and of course now that Mr. Parrish is back from China, he'll be needing his regular suite—"

Jamie had expected to be addressed as Mrs. Summerville. It was the reference to Mr. Parrish's "regular suite" that threw her off-balance. Sara hadn't mentioned that he stayed at the villa.

"That's fine, Myrtle," Jamie said smoothly, starting up the staircase. Thank heaven, she knew the master suite was at the front of the house, with a terrace overlooking the ocean. "Please see that Mr. Parrish is comfortable."

"Yes, Mrs. Summerville," Myrtle replied. If she'd noticed anything different about her employer, it didn't show in her plump, ingenuous face. "I could bring a supper tray upstairs, if you're hungry. If I know you, you didn't touch a bite of that awful airline food."

Actually, Jamie had wolfed down every morsel the flight attendant had put before her, but her stomach was empty again. "I'd like that," she said. "Thank you."

Jamie turned, before continuing upstairs, to look back over one shoulder. Rowan Parrish was still standing in the center of the foyer, staring at her thoughtfully. She gave him a cool nod, as she thought Sara would have done, and headed for her room.

She was in the private bathroom, with its fireplace, sweeping view of the sea, and gold-plated fixtures, running water into the enormous pink marble tub, when something struck the door with a solid thump. Jamie's heart had stuffed itself into her throat and triggered the flight-or-fight response, when Lazarus strolled through the narrow opening and greeted her with a matter-of-fact meow.

Jamie laughed at his audacity, and when she spoke it was in a conspiratorial whisper. "You shouldn't be here. After all, we're not supposed to be friends."

Lazarus positioned himself on the closed lid of the toilet and began another bath. Glad of his company, Jamie stripped off Sara's clothes and slipped into the tub.

She'd been there for about fifteen minutes when she heard the suite's main door open.

"I've brought your tray, Mrs. Summerville," Myrtle called cheerfully. "Will you just listen to me! I can't seem to break the habit of calling you that. I'd better get used to your new name, now that you're remarried and everything."

Jamie sank to her chin, closed her eyes, and seriously considered drowning herself. Among the other things Sara had neglected to mention, it seemed, was a brand-new husband.

TWO

"I'll kill her," Jamie whispered, the rush of her breath making glittering, iridescent canyons in the blanket of bubbles brimming over the edges of the tub.

"*Reow*," said Lazarus, in what could only be interpreted as complete agreement, swishing his black tail back and forth and gazing at Jamie with unblinking yellow eyes.

"What was that, Mrs. Summ—Mrs. Castanello?" Myrtle called companionably, from somewhere beyond the bathroom door.

Jamie closed her eyes, fighting down a welter of emotions: panic, fear, and outrage that her own sister would set her up like this. "Nothing," she called back, in a high and slightly hysterical voice. *Just go away so I can think!* she added mentally.

When she heard the outer door close, Jamie sprang out of the tub like some sleek creature rising from the depths of the sea. Lazarus, startled by the noise and sudden motion, gave a meow of protest and fled.

After draping herself in a towel as big as a bedspread, Jamie padded into the suite and looked wildly around for the telephone. There were two, one on the vanity, one on the table beside the huge round bed.

Jamie had been intimidated by the bed in the first place; it looked like something out of a harem, covered in blue satin, as it was, and piled high with fussy pillows. Now that she knew a husband came as part of the package, her initial trepidation was rapidly turning to terror.

Reaching the vanity table, Jamie plunked down on the dainty bench and snatched up the receiver. She listened to make sure the line was clear, then punched out the correct overseas code, followed by her own number in Seattle.

"I'm sorry," responded a recorded voice, after two rings. "You have reached a number that has been disconnected or is no longer in service—"

She tried again, going through the sequence of numbers slowly, biting her lower lip. She'd misdialed the first time, she told herself. That was all.

The same recording twanged in her ear.

Numbly, Jamie replaced the receiver. Staring into the gilded oval mirror above the vanity, she saw Sara's face looking back at her, and a chill swiveled along her spine.

She'd known all along that Sara wasn't telling her the whole truth, but now it was beginning to dawn on Jamie that this wasn't just another of her sister's pranks. This wasn't high school or college. Sara had changed.

She, Jamie Roberts, had been had, and in a big way.

Even before she called the tile company where she'd been working for the last five years, Jamie knew what was coming. When her boss answered, though, she gave her name as Sara Summerville Castanello, Jamie's sister, and asked to speak to herself.

Fred Godwin sighed the heavy sigh of the long-suffering

and badly treated. He was a loquacious sort—Fred never knew a stranger, his wife always said—ever ready to talk to anyone about anything. It didn't surprise Jamie that he confided so readily in her now.

"I'm sorry, Mrs. Castanello," he said, "but Jamie's resigned and I don't have idea one where to find her. She just breezed in here, looking as if she'd spent the last month on some rich guy's yacht, and told me she was quitting. Wouldn't even wait for her paycheck. And after all I did for her, too."

Jamie closed her eyes, shaken, and leaned against the vanity, breathing deeply, willing herself not to lose it. "Did she say anything—anything at all?"

"No, ma'am," Fred said. "I couldn't get an explanation out of her, let alone two weeks' notice. I *will* say she seemed scared, and she was in a hurry too—why else would she leave without her money? And what about her pension plan? Am I supposed to roll that over into some new account or what?"

"I don't know," Jamie said, fighting back the urge to blurt out, *Fred, don't you recognize my voice? It's me, Jamie. The person you saw was Sara.*

"You sure sound like your sister," Fred told her, cheering up a little. "Listen, you hear from Jamie, you tell her there's no hard feelings on this end. She was a loyal employee for five years, and I don't know what we're going to do without her. I guess she must have had a good reason for bailing out the way she did."

Tears stung Jamie's eyes, and it was all she could do not to sniffle. Fred had never told her he appreciated her. "I'm going to give you my telephone number here in Tovia. Please call me immediately, at any time of day or night—reversing the charges, of course—if you hear from my sister."

Fred accepted the number, said he hoped everything was okay, and rang off.

Jamie folded her arms on the glass surface of the vanity table and laid her head down on them. The anger she'd felt toward Sara earlier had turned to sick fear. Fred had said her twin looked scared, and the fact that Sara hadn't stayed to collect her paycheck certainly proved his assertion that she'd been in a rush. Even Sara, coddled and spoiled by a rich husband, must know that no working person with bills to pay would commit such an oversight.

After a while, Jamie began to get a grip on her whirling emotions. Although her instinct was to rush back to the airport, fly home to Seattle, and turn the whole city upside down, if necessary, looking for Sara, she knew the plan wasn't a good one. She needed a couple of days to think, to get her emotional equilibrium. Dealing with Sara's disappearance would call upon every resource she possessed, and she would have to do it all on her own, so she had to marshal her forces, make a plan.

For the moment, she was simply too tired, too shocked, to think clearly or to go gallivanting back over the top of the world to her own country. Furthermore, she had no apartment to go to, unless she missed her guess, and certainly no job.

She went over to the harem bed, pushed all the pillows onto the floor, and crawled under the covers. Tomorrow, she told herself, Sara would call, laughing, and say it was all a grand joke. Fred had been in on it, and so had the phone company.

"Not funny," Jamie murmured, as Lazarus curled up next to her, warm and noisy. Her consciousness caved in on itself and faded quickly to black.

"Wake up, darling," a male voice drawled. "Your prince is home."

Jamie opened her eyes and sucked in her breath. A man was bending over her bed, a handsome one, with chestnut hair, an aquiline nose, and hard gray eyes. She opened her mouth to scream, then remembered that she was married.

Rowan's voice echoed in her mind. *I'm sorry Julian couldn't meet you himself*, he'd said, in the airport the day before; *he must have been detained in Paris*.

The room was bright with dappled, moving sunlight, the kind that is reflected off water. Jamie raised herself onto one elbow, veiling her panic, and squinted at the digital clock on the bedside table. Four-thirty-seven. Had she really slept almost twenty hours?

"How was France?" she asked, taking a chance.

"Paris never really changes," Julian said, turning away from the bed, to Jamie's vast relief. She hadn't decided whether or not to continue posing as Sara, but she knew damned well she wasn't going to sleep with this man to carry out the deception.

Julian was loosening his tie, and he kept his broad back turned to Jamie. His shoulders looked stiff under his expensive white shirt.

"What is Parrish doing back here?" he asked, in an undertone that revealed no emotion whatsoever.

Oddly, the mention of Rowan Parrish gave Jamie a degree of courage. She sat up in bed, well aware that she was clad in nothing but a twisted bath towel, and arranged the covers carefully. I wish I knew, she answered silently. "He's an old friend," she said, hoping the response was adequate.

Julian turned and looked at her with narrowed eyes. She would have sworn, just for that moment, that he despised her. It seemed strange, since they were, as far as she knew, newlyweds.

"An old lover, you mean," he replied, and each word struck Jamie like a small, smooth stone fired from a sling-shot.

She didn't trust herself to speak and wouldn't have known what to say if she had, though color surged into her face. All she was certain of was that her first impression had been right: this marriage between Sara and Julian Castanello was not exactly a match made in heaven.

Jamie settled back against the curved, velvet-upholstered headboard of the bed, her mind racing even as she did her best to appear calm. She folded her arms on top of the covers and glared at Julian, waiting.

He sighed and shoved a hand through his lustrous, somewhat shaggy hair. "I'm sorry, Sara," he muttered. "I shouldn't have said that."

"No," Jamie answered, feeling self-righteous and completely confused, as well as terror-stricken. "You shouldn't have. What happened between Rowan and me is in the past."

What happened between Rowan and me is in the past? What in hell had made her say something like that?

"I just get nervous when he's around, that's all," Julian confessed, moving to one of the tall, arched windows to stare out at the view. Reflected light flickered over his too-perfect face. "I can't help wondering how much he knows."

Jamie's heart was hammering, and she barely restrained herself from asking, *How much he knows about what?* It also occurred to her that she might be better off to confess the truth to Julian right then, to tell him she wasn't his wife Sara at all but Sara's identical twin sister. A nameless fear, one she couldn't explain even to herself, kept her from it. It didn't take a genius to figure out that something was very, very rotten in Tovia.

"Perhaps less than we think," she remarked.

Julian turned his cold, ruthless gaze on her. "Find out," he ordered, his voice low and yet sharp as a razor's edge. "Sleep with him if you have to, but *find out*."

Jamie averted her eyes and bit her lip, hoping Julian wouldn't see how revolted she was by this suggestion. "So much for the jealous bridegroom routine," she said, before she could stop herself.

He was on the bed beside her in the space of a heartbeat, kneeling on the mattress, his hand buried in her hair, wrenching at her scalp, his breath hot on her face and stale with the smell of wine. "Make no mistake, precious wife," he growled, his gaze alight with something that could scald, for all its coldness. "I haven't forgotten why we entered into this farce of a marriage, and neither will you, if you're as smart as you seem to think you are."

It was, incredibly, the depth of her fear that made Jamie brave. She was about to jam one knee into Julian's groin when he apparently read the intention in her eyes and withdrew. He leaped off the bed and turned, only to find himself confronted by a hissing Lazarus. The cat's ears were flat against his head, his teeth were bared, and the fur on his back and tail stood straight out.

Julian cursed and started to swing his foot at the animal, and Jamie cried, "Don't you dare hurt my cat!"

A profound stillness followed. Lazarus arranged himself, and Julian, straightening his tie and smoothing his hair, offered a strange parallel. After a long time, Julian looked at Jamie again, and it was as if he hadn't noticed her until then.

"*Your* cat? You've always hated that animal. What's going on here, Sara?" The low, even timbre of his voice was somehow more frightening than a shout.

"I've had a change of heart," she said coldly, trembling beneath the thin bedcovers. "Get out, Julian. I want to get dressed."

Another breath-stopping silence fell, during which Jamie feared she'd gone too far. Had she been too bold and inadvertently raised a challenge Julian's pride wouldn't let him ignore?

He looked at her with chilling contempt. "Wear something that will make Parrish want to confide in you—for old times' sake, if nothing else. I want to know what he's doing here."

Jamie didn't answer, or speak, or even nod. She just waited, and finally Julian went out, leaving her alone with Lazarus, her furry defender.

She bounded out of bed and dressed hastily in a black crepe jumpsuit from Sara's closet. She didn't dare defy Julian too openly when she didn't know what she was dealing with, and he'd already shown he could be violent.

Diamonds glittering at her ears and throat, Jamie was about to leave the suite when the phone made a polite but urgent jingling sound. She snatched up the receiver, knowing by that uncanny telepathy peculiar to certain twins that Sara was calling.

"Hello?" Jamie whispered, closing her eyes and holding her breath, praying no one had picked up an extension.

"I'm sorry about your job and your apartment," Sara blurted, half sobbing the words, "but I didn't have a choice. Don't forget your promise—if you do, we'll both die!"

It was over as quickly as that; before Jamie could say a word, the line went dead. Shaking, she lowered the receiver to its cradle and hugged herself, tears spoiling the eye makeup she'd applied so carefully.

By sheer force of will, Jamie pulled herself together. She repaired her mascara and eyeliner, squared her shoulders, and made herself leave the suite. It was a dubious comfort that Lazarus followed, his whiskers practically brushing her heels.

She found Rowan in the garden off the drawing room, quite by accident. He was standing next to a fountain, where a mossy statue poured water from a stone urn, gazing off into the distance as though he expected something, or someone, to appear on the horizon. Jamie could not guess whether he looked for salvation or destruction.

"Are you friend or foe, Rowan Parrish?" she asked, realizing only after the words were out that she'd spoken aloud.

He turned and regarded her, for the briefest of moments, with something that might have been tenderness. In the next instant, however, his face changed subtly. His expression was now closed, guarded.

"I might ask the same question of you," he said presently, raising his glass in an elegant salute. "To paraphrase, are you rich woman, poor woman, beggar woman—or thief?"

Jamie swallowed and looked away, injured by his words. The worst part was not understanding why the disdain of a stranger should hurt so much. "That was unkind," she ventured. His reply caught her by surprise.

"It was," he agreed gently. "I apologize. Which is not to say we won't lock horns again in five minutes. But then, ours was always a tempestuous alliance, wasn't it? Do you remember our picnic in that medieval ruin in the hills, Sara, when it rained and we got into a shouting match over whose responsibility it had been to check the weather forecast that morning?"

She didn't remember, of course, and Sara hadn't covered that particular part of her personal history. "Of course," she said, feeling an ache unfold in her heart because, even including the argument they'd evidently had, it would have been an inexplicably precious memory.

Rowan was silent, watching her again, in a way that made it seem that he'd already uncovered all her deepest secrets and was merely waiting for her to acknowledge them.

She almost told him who she was right then, almost blurted out that she and Sara had switched places, that something ominous was happening and she was afraid. In the end she stopped herself, because the odd, tender feelings Rowan Parrish stirred in her were, alas, no indication that he wasn't an enemy. It wouldn't be the first time, she thought cynically, that love had turned to hatred.

"Julian's back," she said, at long last, because she couldn't bear the silence and nothing else occurred to her.

"I know," Rowan replied, and the edge had returned to his voice. "Why are you standing in the garden with me, instead of welcoming your beloved husband back to hearth and home?"

Jamie shivered with the effort it took not to cross the small distance between them and slap the man with all the stinging force she could muster. She was fiercely glad she hadn't confided her secret.

"Why indeed?" inquired a third voice.

Jamie turned, startled, to see Julian striding toward her. He had exchanged his power clothes for slacks and a beige cashmere sweater, and he carried a cocktail in one hand and a wine goblet in the other.

Rowan said nothing, but simply toasted the new arrival with a somehow derisive lift of his glass. Jamie, flustered, feeling like the loser in some nightmare version of blindman's buff, snatched the wine from Julian's grasp. She had already swallowed a third of it before she took time to wonder if Sara would have chosen the cocktail.

"So nervous," Julian teased, stroking Jamie's back with fingertips that were still cold from the chilled goblet. "Do try to relax, darling."

Jamie took another gulp of the wine and stepped away from Sara's husband, just far enough to evade the touch of his hand. "I'm a little tired, that's all."

"Sara was in the States for a while," Julian commented to Rowan, with a sort of biting cordiality. Obviously, Sara was not the only one who had engendered Julian's dislike.

"I know," Rowan answered smoothly. "I met her at the airport."

Julian did not reply, but his gaze, as he glared at Rowan over the rim of his tumbler, was acidic.

"I don't believe you've mentioned what you were doing in the States," Rowan said. For the first time, Jamie noticed that he didn't have a recognizable accent, and neither did Julian. Either of them might have been from anywhere.

I don't believe you've explained why you're staying in

this house, Jamie countered silently, but she couldn't ask without betraying the fact that she wasn't Sara.

She took another sip of wine. "I was visiting family," she said. She wondered how well these two men knew Sara, whether or not they were even aware that she had a twin sister. At that point, virtually nothing would have surprised her.

"Oh, yes," Rowan responded dryly. "I remember now. You were staying with your brother, James."

Sara had been able to slip a husband past her, Jamie thought, as the wine rushed to her head, but by God she'd have noticed a brother. Since she was still feeling her way in the dark, not to mention being a little drunk and jet-lagged in the bargain, she simply said, "Right."

As twilight settled over the garden, a chilly mist, faintly salted by the sea, came with it. Julian slipped an arm around her waist and ushered her toward the gaping French doors leading into the house. "Come along, darling," he said. "I wouldn't want you to fall ill."

"Heaven forbid," Rowan commented, and Jamie saw an almost imperceptible twitch along his jawline.

There was another brief, lethal stare-down, and for a second Jamie was afraid the two men would actually come to blows. In the end, though, Julian simply gave her a little push toward the doors.

She resented the gesture heartily, but there was no graceful way to fight back, so she let it pass.

"I'd like to see that medieval ruin you mentioned," she said to Rowan, in a bright voice, when the three of them had gathered in the drawing room to await the call to dinner. "Again, I mean."

Julian was on the hearth, adding birch logs to the fire, and he didn't speak or turn around. Rowan refilled Jamie's wineglass from a decanter on one of the tables, laying his hand to bottle and glass without looking, as easily as if he'd been master of that house in some previous incarnation.

"Again," he repeated, with just the slightest note of mockery. "Fine. We'll go tomorrow." Rowan glanced toward the man standing near the fire, making no effort either to project or lower his voice. "If your husband approves, of course. Would you like to join us, Julian?"

At last, Julian turned. The look he gave Rowan was hot enough to ignite the wine in Jamie's glass, make it flare like a torch in her hand. She retreated a step, unconsciously.

Once again, however, Julian was gracious. "I have business to attend to in Rome," he said. "I'm afraid I must leave tonight, directly after dinner."

Jamie took a sip of wine, speculating. Julian hadn't intended to travel to Rome until the moment he mentioned the idea, she decided. He didn't seem like the type to put on casual clothes, however costly, when he was planning to leave on a trip right away. No, he was trying to give her time alone with Rowan, so she could get the information he wanted. She just wished she had a clue as to what she was supposed to find out.

Rowan made a *tsk-tsk* sound. "A pity," he said.

Julian set his jaw, then started to speak, but before he could, Myrtle waltzed in, black uniform crisp, to announce that dinner was served.

There wasn't much conversation during the meal. In fact, if it hadn't been for Lazarus, who lurked under the table to garner pieces of broiled lobster from Jamie's fingers, she would have thought she'd become invisible.

Julian seemed to be in no hurry, but before dessert was served he made his excuses and left the table. Jamie silently thanked a benevolent fate that she and her "husband" wouldn't be spending the night under the same roof and attacked her chocolate mousse with relish.

Rowan's low chuckle startled her, lifting her heart at dizzying speed and at the same time piercing it like an arrow. "Some things never change," he said. "I must say, that's a comfort."

Jamie lowered her spoon. The kindness in his tone

weakened her; she knew it was a trap, but she was drawn nevertheless. "Have so many things as all that changed, Rowan?" she asked cautiously, and with a gentleness she hadn't intended to reveal.

Again, his face hardened visibly. "Oh, yes," he answered gravely. "Everything has changed." With that, he pushed back his chair, rose, and left the dining room also, his dessert untouched.

The formal chamber seemed to yawn like some vast cavern when he was gone. Jamie's mousse lost its appeal, and she sagged back in her chair, despondent and so full of questions that she didn't know which to ask first.

Avoiding her room, where she might encounter Julian, Jamie found a lightweight jacket in one of the closets in a downstairs hall, slipped it on, and went out. Sara had warned her that the pathway leading down to the beach was steep, but the moon was almost full that night and Jamie could see clearly.

She walked along, hands plunged deep into the pockets of the borrowed jacket, to a small cove, framed on three sides with rugged, sharp-edged boulders.

Jamie sighed, feeling mist on her face as she stood watching the sea batter the mouth of the cove. The roar was deafening, and the force of the tide sent walls of spray high into the air.

Both she and Sara were in real danger, but Jamie had no idea how to save herself or her sister. She'd been forced into some deadly game, and no one had told her the rules. She didn't even know which side she was supposed to be on and she couldn't tell the good guys from the bad guys, if indeed there *were* any good guys.

Restless, yet somehow comforted by the churning, raging water, flinging itself into the little cove only to be trapped there, roiling like some devil's brew, Jamie climbed onto one of the boulders and looked down.

It was just the kind of thing the heroines of B-grade horror movies did, Jamie thought, even as two hands struck her hard from behind and she hurtled off the rocks and into the bubbling cauldron at her feet.

Being pushed was the first shock, and the icy temperature of the water was the second. Jamie flailed with terror as the current sucked her under, and a silent involuntary scream opened her mouth, stomach, and lungs to the furious sea.

She was going to die. That realization was the third shock, and the greatest by far. Jamie had never guessed, until then, just how badly she wanted to live.

She fought, but the water pounded her from above, and when she did manage to break the surface, the force of it slammed her against the rocks and she went under again. The scenario repeated itself as she struggled, over and over, to find air to breathe, but her strength was fading and after a while she couldn't tell which way was up and which was down.

Between one moment and the next, a delicious sense of warmth replaced the marrow-deep chill that had stiffened her muscles. The best thing to do, she decided, would be to fall asleep, to let the water take her. It was silly to keep fighting, wasn't it? She was so tired, and her lungs were bursting.

Something vaguely like a claw scraped her scalp, jarring her out of her dazed resignation, and then she felt fingers entangle themselves in her hair. A painful, blessed wrench followed, and Jamie's head was out of the water.

Air! She coughed and spat and sputtered and drew in great, greedy lungfuls of the stuff. Her rescuer—or her killer—gripped her by the shoulders and dragged her out of the freezing water.

"Don't kill me," she said, after throwing up salt water on the sand.

The light of the moon edged Rowan's face. "You're talking to the wrong man, love," he said, with a sort of gruff impatience.

When he was sure she was through emptying her

stomach, he hoisted her in his arms and started off into the darkness at a reassuringly brisk pace.

"What the hell were you doing out here in the dark?" he demanded, in a rasp underlaid with grudging concern. "Damn it, this place is dangerous enough in the daylight!"

"I was thinking," Jamie said, against the hard warmth of his shoulder.

"You couldn't prove that by me," Rowan retorted.

"Somebody pushed me. Was it you?"

"No," he said brusquely. "Didn't you see anyone?"

Jamie shook her wet head. She didn't want to trust Rowan, depend on him, care about him, and yet she felt herself leaning into his strength, taking comfort from it. "Just you," she replied. "It doesn't take a Perry Mason to theorize that you're the culprit."

They had reached a small stone cottage, on a bank overlooking the angry shore, and Rowan pushed the door open with one foot. Even though there was no fire and no light, Jamie felt warm. Even safe.

She had to be crazy.

"Here," Rowan said, setting her on a bed and shoving a blanket into her hands. "Get out of those clothes, and I'll build a fire."

Jamie peeled off the sodden jacket and once-glamorous jumpsuit with trembling hands. By the time she was finally able to wrap herself in the blanket, Rowan had a fire snapping on the hearth. She leaned toward the blaze, suddenly aware that she wasn't strong enough to walk, or even stand.

Rowan brought her whiskey in a disposable cup. "Here you are, little mermaid. Drink up."

"Was it you?" Jamie asked, her teeth chattering, as she raised the cup to her lips. "Did you try to kill me?"

"No," he said, and she believed him. There were 12-Step groups, she thought, for women like her. He sat down beside her on the cot, or bed, or whatever it was. "Think about it, Sara. If I wanted you dead, why would I have gone to all the trouble of pulling you out after pushing you in in the first place?"

Jamie was stumped. The whiskey was blending with her blood, warming it, flowing through her muscles and turning them to paste. "But you were there," she argued, clinging to the last shred of logic.

"I was following you."

"But you didn't see who attacked me?"

"No. There's a moon out, but there are clouds too. A couple of times, it was so dark I couldn't make out my own hand in front of my face. I wouldn't have seen you flailing about in the water, in fact, if I hadn't been up on the bank and looking in just the right direction."

Jamie's thoughts were muddled, and she yawned loudly. "Thanks," she said. "For being there when I needed you."

Rowan touched her hair, or she thought he did, at least. He withdrew his hand so quickly that she might have imagined the contact. "Rest," he told her. "I'm right here."

She sighed and sagged against his arm and shoulder. "I'm not sure that's a comfort," she answered. And then she fell asleep, and when she awakened, it was morning and she was buried in warm quilts. A fire blazed on the hearth and the smell of fresh coffee filled the air.

Memories of the night before made Jamie sit bolt upright on the narrow cot. "What is this place?"

"Just the old fishing cabin," Rowan replied. "You've been here a million times. How do you feel?"

"As if I nearly drowned," Jamie said, drawing the covers up under her chin. Mentally, she added the cabin and the deadly tide pool to the list of things Sara hadn't mentioned during her briefings. "I guess it made me forget a few things."

Rowan crossed the room and handed her a mug of coffee, but the expression on his face was anything but friendly. "Like what you did with the jade goddess, for instance?"

THREE

"What jade goddess?" Jamie asked, with an innocence born of pure truth, as she accepted the coffee. "I don't know what you're talking about."

Rowan uttered a sigh and turned away. "Forget it. I should have guessed I wouldn't get a straight answer from you."

Jamie breathed in the aroma and warmth of the brew, stalling. She'd wanted adventure in her life, and now she was caught in the middle of some huge and very dangerous mystery. She hadn't been issued a rule book, nor did she know who her opponents were. Her situation was proof, if ever she'd seen it, that the old adage about being careful what one wishes for was right on target.

"Tell me about the jade goddess," she said, after a restorative sip of the coffee. Every muscle in her body felt bruised, and her lungs ached. She tried to make some kind of contact with Sara—they had sometimes been able to touch mentally, if not actually communicate in words—but there was nothing but deep, troubling silence. A void.

Rowan, who had poured coffee of his own and settled in a chair at the rough-hewn table, raised an eyebrow and gave her an ironic look.

Jamie was stung by his cynicism, but she forged bravely on. If there was another viable option besides putting one figurative foot in front of the other, it hadn't occurred to her yet. "Indulge me, Rowan. It's the least you can do, isn't it, after carrying me off, keeping me overnight, and thereby ruining my reputation forever?"

His expression became downright sardonic. "Ruining your reputation, is it? Ah, Sara, my darling, you are indeed a piece of work. You are a living, breathing scandal, and you have been since you swept poor Henri off his feet and became the mistress of all you survey. Spending a night in the cabin with me won't even make a ripple in your legend."

Jamie averted her eyes, the coffee burning in her throat. Rowan made Sara sound like a heartless, social-climbing, gold-digging bitch. Jamie's strongest impulse was to defend her sister, to refute his accusations, but she couldn't bring herself to do it. Most likely, Sara had known exactly what she was doing when she'd traveled to Europe some six years before, serving as secretary and companion to a wealthy old woman. Sara had told Jamie when they were children, still playing with dolls, that she meant to find a man with money someday, preferably an aging one, and marry him.

"People change," she said weakly, after a long time.

"Not you," Rowan replied, in a flat tone.

She shrugged and took a big risk. "You were in love with me once."

"I was a fool," he said. "You threw me over, don't forget. Henri was the better choice for a husband, by your calculations, being nearly seventy at the time, rich as hell, and in questionable health. And then there was the problem of my being a younger son. The family title and most of the estates went to my elder brother."

Jamie didn't reply. She loved her twin unconditionally, though she was sure everything Rowan said was true. He couldn't be expected to understand—perhaps no one could, besides Jamie herself—how the early years of deprivation, uncertainty, and shame had marked Sara. Granted, that didn't excuse her behavior; lots of people had difficult childhoods without growing up to be manipulative, self-centered, and generally thoughtless. It was just that no one who really knew and understood Sara could hate her.

Could they?

"What a shock it must have been," Rowan went on quietly, cruelly, "when poor Michael was killed and it all came to me."

"I should think it would have been more of a shock to Michael," Jamie answered. She didn't mean to be flip or disrespectful of the dead, but she wasn't going to be bullied either. "Did you kill him to get his money?" The words were out of Jamie's mouth before she'd even tried them out in her mind.

Rowan looked, for one terrible moment, as though he might spring from his chair, stride across the room, and choke her to death on the spot. He contained himself, however, with a visible effort, and remained where he was. Fury had drained all color from his face, and his eyes were no warmer and no calmer than the currents that had closed over Jamie's head the night before. "I loved my brother," he said finally, "although I realize you probably have no concept of what it is to care for another human being simply because they exist. Furthermore, I had no need of his money, since I've made a fortune of my own in recent years."

Jamie clasped the mug with both hands, to keep from spilling the contents. She had never seen such anger, such restrained fury, in another person as she saw in

Rowan Parrish just then, and yet she sensed that he still cared for Sara in some deep and unwavering way.

"About the jade goddess," she prompted, wondering where this bold new side of her personality had been all these years. She could have used it when Alan was massacring her self-esteem, for instance, or when she'd been afraid to leave a job she'd hated.

Rowan put down his cup and folded his arms. A certain cold resignation had crept into his manner, and he sighed. "You know it all as well as I do, but we'll go through the charade if you insist. The goddess is a priceless piece of oriental art, dating back almost a thousand years." He spoke in the tone of someone reciting a trite and dog-eared story that didn't really bear repeating. "I believe you stole it—with the help of your adoring bridegroom, of course."

The accusation struck Jamie like a blow, making her already-troubled stomach ache with the same violence as her muscles and lungs. Sara was capable of a lot of things, but stealing? The idea was too difficult and too painful to accept, and yet she couldn't help thinking of her conversation with Julian the night before. Rowan knew something, according to him, and Julian was willing to throw his wife to the wolves to find out what it was.

"I would never steal anything," she replied finally.

"Not even if your fairy-tale life had turned to sawdust? If, for example, you could sell a piece of ancient statuary for upwards of five million dollars on the black market and make it all better? Think of it: no questions, no taxes."

Five million dollars! The sum made the hundred thousand Sara had promised for Jamie seem like small potatoes—dirty ones, full of worms.

"Oh, my God," she whispered, as the truth of what Sara had done dawned on her in all its shattering glory. Sara and Julian *had* stolen the goddess. Furthermore, there was no hundred thousand dollars, because if Sara chose to disappear, and it seemed she had done just that, there would be no Jamie Roberts to claim the money. "I've been such a fool!"

There was bitterness but no trace of compassion in Rowan's voice. "Spare me," he said. "Julian is a world-class dirtbag, but he isn't smart enough to pull off a heist on this scale. I'd bet my ticket to heaven that you came up with the original idea—and the plans for carrying it out."

"You don't understand," Jamie protested, realizing, as she started to her feet, that she was naked except for a blanket and she wasn't strong enough to stand. "I didn't—"

"Please," Rowan interrupted brusquely. "No protestations of innocence. I may be ill."

Jamie's frustration knew no bounds, and neither did her fury. If she told Rowan she wasn't Sara, and she still wasn't sure that would be a smart thing to do, he probably wouldn't believe her. He'd think she was just trying to get out of taking the fall for stealing his jade goddess!

"The hell with you," she said, and tried to get up again. The room spun, tilted at a crazy angle, and righted itself with a jerk. Jamie crumpled back to the bed, moaning softly.

Rowan opened a chest and produced a pair of gray sweatpants and a maroon fisherman's sweater with holes in it. Still looking grim, he tossed the garments to her. "I'll step outside while you put these on," he said. "When you're decent, I'll take you back to the villa and call a doctor."

"I don't need a doctor," Jamie said. There were tears in her eyes, and she kept her head down so Rowan wouldn't see. "Just get out and let me dress."

He left without another word, which was both a mercy and a disappointment to Jamie.

Putting on the clothes, which were musty and much too large, was an exhausting process, far more difficult than it should have been. She was trembling, every inch of her body glistening with perspiration, by the time she gasped out, "All right. I'm ready."

Rowan appeared in the doorway, a dark shape framed in daylight. "What's the matter with you, Sara?" he asked, in a tone Jamie hadn't heard him use before. "You're shaking, and you're pale as death."

"I nearly drowned last night," Jamie murmured. "Such experiences upset me, as a general rule."

"It's more than that," he insisted. "Are you pregnant?"

"I wish I were," Jamie said, and he didn't reply.

Rowan carried her back to the villa, where their arrival produced an embarrassing flurry. Jamie was already feeling much stronger, but she pretended to be weak, letting her head loll against Rowan's shoulder and keeping her eyes closed. The last thing she wanted to do was answer a lot of questions.

It was as if Rowan could read her mind. As he carried her up the main stairway, he called down to someone, "Get the police."

"Why did you say that?" Jamie hissed, furious. It was enough that she was lying to him, to Julian, and to all the servants, about her identity. She didn't want to lie to the police too.

"Don't worry, precious," Rowan replied acidly, a little breathless from the effort of carrying her across the landscape and up the stairs. "I haven't any solid proof against you yet, so you won't be arrested. Not today, at least."

"Or tomorrow, or next week," Jamie whispered angrily. "Because I didn't take your precious jade goddess!"

Reaching the door of the master suite, Rowan pushed it open with an unceremonious motion of one foot. "Coming from an inveterate liar like yourself," he said, flinging her onto the decadent bed and laying one hand to his heart, "I find that speech particularly moving."

"Is everything all right, sir?" It was Myrtle, standing in the doorway and wringing the hem of her apron between her hands. Jamie felt a flash of annoyance, since she was supposed to be mistress of the house.

"Everything is wonderful," she said, before Rowan could reply. "And Mr. Parrish was just leaving. Perhaps you wouldn't mind packing his bags for him?"

Myrtle turned crimson and flung a helpless, despairing glance at Rowan.

"Do as she says," he told the housekeeper quietly, without looking away from Jamie's face. "I'll stay at the cabin. In the meantime, call Mrs. Castanello's physician and ask him to stop by. I assume the police have already been contacted?"

"Yes, sir," Myrtle said. "They're on their way, and I'll ring Dr. Morrison right away." Having thus spoken, she departed, without a glance at Jamie.

It was a grueling day.

The police arrived first, and Jamie recounted her experience on the beach in minute detail. Yes, someone had pushed her into the water. No, she hadn't seen anybody—except for Rowan Parrish, of course. It seemed a little odd that he was right there, didn't it?

The local constabulary didn't agree that Rowan's presence on the beach was odd. He'd saved her life, after all.

After two interminable hours, the police were satisfied that this was going to be a tough case, and they left, promising to check the sand for footprints.

Jamie just rolled her eyes at that. If the killer had left that sort of evidence behind, it would have washed away with the tide by then.

The doctor came next. He was a nervous, plump little man with florid cheeks and a bald, age-spotted pate. He examined Jamie's bruises, told her to rest, gave her a shot of something that made her entire body go limp, and departed. Only Lazarus, who had been watching the proceedings from his perch on top of an antique bookcase opposite the fireplace, remained to keep her company.

"*Reow*," he said, jumping down from his vantage point, landing with a resounding thump, and padding over to leap up onto the bed. There, he draped himself across Jamie's feet.

He was only an animal, but Jamie was glad of his presence. He was, she thought glumly, the only friend she had left.

She settled back onto her pillows, with a sound that might have been either a sigh or a sob, and let the drug pull her under.

Jamie spent the rest of that day in bed, and all of the next, her arms, legs, and back so stiff she could barely move. On the third day, she got up, limped into the bathroom, and filled the tub with steaming-hot water. It was time to get back in action, though she had yet to decide what she would do.

The bath helped tremendously, and Jamie lingered for a long while, soaking away her aches and pains. Finally, she got out, dried off, and helped herself to lacy underwear, designer jeans, and a pink cashmere sweater from Sara's vast collection.

As she dressed, Jamie tried again to link herself with Sara, but there was only emptiness, and that frightened her more than anything that had happened since her arrival on the island. What could she do, call the Seattle police department and say, "I've lost telepathic contact with my sister"?

She left the bedroom, having purloined a lightweight leather bomber jacket from Sara's closet, and stepped out into the fresh April afternoon. A walk would clear her head, she decided. This time, though, she'd stay off the beach.

She was rounding the southwest corner of the house when Lazarus suddenly sprang out of a hydrangea bush to join her. He started down a path and Jamie followed, smiling a little. She would miss the cat when she went home.

The word *home* stopped her in the tracks of her borrowed sneakers. What if she couldn't go back ever? Suppose Sara, for whatever purpose, had made Jamie's life impossible to live? Just proving her true identity would be a challenge.

She might have cried, if she hadn't been so glad to be outside, in the fresh air and sunshine, and if Lazarus hadn't been capering along in front of her with an air of confidence.

The cat's path led through a thicket of weeds, but there was a good view of the sea, and the sky was that certain limpid shade of blue that always made Jamie want to take up painting. She was so enthralled with the scenery that she nearly tripped over Lazarus when he suddenly stopped and sat down.

"Most people walk dogs," commented a familiar voice. Rowan stood just ahead, an enigmatic smile curving his lips. Clad as he was, in boots, corduroy jeans, and a heavy gray sweater, he looked more like a fisherman than a nobleman and an expert on oriental art and antiques.

Jamie folded her arms and remained stubbornly silent. Rowan might have kept her from drowning, but he'd also made it clear that he believed she was a criminal. She wasn't about to get into another verbal sparring match.

"Feeling better?" He seemed determined to engage her in friendly conversation. It was a trap, she reminded herself.

"I think that's obvious," she said coolly.

Lazarus, the traitor, was looking up at Rowan and purring happily. It galled Jamie to realize that he actually liked this disturbing man.

"Has the conquering hero returned to the fold?"

"No." The question didn't trouble Jamie nearly so much as the prospect of having to deal with Julian again. Despite the alliance between Sara and him, he could definitely be listed in the Enemies column. In fact, Jamie had begun to think, darkly and in the very back of her mind, that it might have been Julian who pushed her into the tide pool. Of course, if she suggested her loving "husband" as a suspect, all the servants, and Rowan too, would probably testify that the master of the house had left for Rome right after dinner.

Lazarus made a squalling sound and darted into the underbrush, undoubtedly in pursuit of some small doomed creature. The sudden move startled Jamie and made her gasp.

Rowan immediately took a firm hold on her arm. "Take it easy, Sara. You look as though the devil just sprang out of the ground in a red mist."

Jamie was irritated by his assumption that he could touch her, and even more by the fact that she was enjoying even that small contact. She pulled free and started to walk around him.

He caught her by the wrist this time, and his grasp wasn't painful, but when she tried to yank her hand away, he held her fast.

"For God's sake, Sara," he rasped, "tell me the truth. Let me help you before something happens."

A shiver undulated through Sara's system and, though she tried, she was unable to hide it. She saw her fear reflected in Rowan's eyes.

She felt her resolve wavering, along with her courage, but inside her head a voice was chanting, *He's an enemy. He believes you're a liar and a thief. And even though he pulled you out of the water when you were ready to give up and die, he might have been the one who pushed you in. He could have staged the whole thing, in an effort to win your trust.*

"I can't," she said. "I can't tell you where the jade goddess is, because I don't know."

It was obvious, from the look on Rowan's face, that he didn't believe her. That was probably one of the reasons she was so surprised when he let go of her wrist and took a gentle grip on her hand.

"Come on," he said gruffly. "Let's go see how our ruins are holding up."

They climbed a grassy hillside with a spectacular view of the sea, moving ever closer to a stand of birch trees. Jamie's sore muscles protested the climb, but her heart was racing ahead on its own, like a spirited child hurrying toward a picnic.

Only there was nothing childlike about what was going on in Jamie's heart and in her body.

"Once," Rowan said, when they reached the tree line, "there was a Roman fortress on this site. The inhabitants would have been able to see for miles in every direction and bring the oil to a rolling boil in plenty of time to dump it onto the heads of any army foolish enough to attempt an invasion."

Grateful for the respite from Rowan's anger and mistrust, fascinated by the existence of anything so ancient, Jamie allowed her escort to pull her through the woods.

In a shady clearing, surrounded by trees and shadows, stood the remains of a stone structure. It had been a small building by modern standards, but virtually impregnable. Part of one wall still stood, dank and dark, with arrow slots high up, perhaps a dozen feet off the ground.

Jamie stopped, stricken by the odd, spooky magnificence of the place.

"Wow," she said.

"If I didn't know better," Rowan remarked, with neither affection nor rancor, "I'd think you'd never seen this place before."

Jamie stepped carefully through the rubble, needing to hide her face from him. "Let's pretend I'm a stranger," she said lightly. "Give me a guided tour."

He grabbed her, and wrenched her around to face him, and her breasts collided with his chest. "God help me," he muttered. "I'm sorry, Sara. I'm so sorry." Having made that cryptic statement and seen the shock in her face, he released her.

"You weren't going to hurt me, were you?" Jamie asked, though she knew the answer. The emotion emanating from Rowan a moment before had been passion, not anger. Even with her limited romantic experience, she sensed that much.

Rowan raked a hand through his dark hair. "No." He sighed. "I wanted to kiss you."

Jamie's pulse was hammering at the base of her throat. She took a step toward him. "Then do it," she said. She knew what she was doing was rash, but she didn't care. She yearned for Rowan's kiss as much as she dreaded what it would do to her emotions.

"Sara!" It was a protest, a plea. "You have a husband, remember?"

She stood close to him and put her arms around his neck. She was free to kiss any man she wanted, but there was no convincing Rowan of that. Not without a lot of complicated explanations and an album full of pictures to prove Sara had a twin, anyway.

"I'm not asking you to throw me down in the grass and make love to me," she teased. "I just want one kiss. For old times' sake, if you will."

Rowan glared down at her for a long moment, but he didn't pull out of her embrace, and finally, with a low groan, he lowered his mouth to hers in a crushing, hungry kiss.

For Jamie, it was another drowning, except that this time she was swamped by joy, not frigid pounding surf. She felt excitement, fear, and a rush of adrenaline unlike anything she'd ever experienced before.

She stumbled a little when Rowan suddenly set her away from him.

"*Damn* you!" he bit out. "It's bad enough that I've made an idiot of myself over you. I won't be an adulterer in the bargain!"

Jamie's eyes burned, and her vision blurred. She was starting to care for this man, against her will and her better judgment, and he plainly despised her.

"Rowan, listen to me," she began, faltering, reaching for him with one hand and dying a little when he stepped back out of reach. "Please, I'm not—"

He turned on his heel and stormed away.

It was too much for Jamie; she sat down on a stone, covered her face with both hands, and cried. She cried because she'd lost her sense of Sara's presence in the world, because Rowan hated her, because she'd wasted so much of her life back in Seattle working at a job she hated. She might have gone on crying until she died, like some princess in an obscure fairy tale, if she hadn't become aware of something small and soft butting against her arm.

With a sniffle, she looked down and saw Lazarus on the stone beside her. How long had he been trying to get her attention?

"You again," she said with affection, and lifted the cat onto her lap.

He allowed himself to be held and petted, and the interlude was comforting for Jamie. She began to regain her composure.

"It just goes to prove," Jamie said, burying her wet face in the silky fur on his back for a moment, "that not all males are fickle. Too bad you're not human, old buddy."

Lazarus meowed companionably, as if offering a comment, and Jamie laughed.

"Hey," she said. "What's your sign?"

Five minutes later, satisfied that he had saved his adopted mistress from mental collapse, Lazarus jumped down off Jamie's lap and disappeared into the woods. She followed, walking slowly back toward the villa, telling herself that if she'd gotten over Alan, she could surely put this hormonal infatuation with Rowan Parrish behind her as well.

Dinner was ready when she reached the house, and Jamie was surprised to discover that she had an appetite. She was about to carry her empty plate back to the kitchen when a telephone jingled somewhere. Her sixth sense, never well developed, lurched into maximum overdrive.

Sara.

She heard the housekeeper speaking to someone and stood stiffly, waiting. Afraid to move.

Myrtle appeared in the doorway of the dining room, her normally rosy complexion pale, her lower lip trembling. "It's for you, Mrs. Castanello, a man in Seattle who says he's calling about your sister."

Jamie knew what the caller would say before she made her way into the hall and picked up the receiver Myrtle had left lying on a table. The housekeeper scurried after her, prattling.

"I never knew you had a sister, Mrs. Castanello."

Jamie was shaking. She thought she would be sick, right there in the hall. "Please be quiet," she snapped, before speaking into the telephone. "Hello?"

"It's Fred Godwin, Mrs. Castanello," her former boss said. "I'm afraid I've got some terrible news. Your sister Jamie was found dead this morning. She was murdered."

Jamie's knees gave out; she sank to the floor, still clutching the receiver, her stomach twisting itself around her heart and her windpipe, smothering her. She'd already known, on some level, that Sara was gone, but consciously facing the reality was another matter.

"Mrs. Castanello?"

Jamie made herself speak, at the same time brushing off Myrtle's attempts to help her back to her feet. She wanted to kneel, to pray that it wasn't true, to bend over and touch her forehead to the cool floor and bleed from every pore because half of herself had just been ripped away. "I'm—I'm here," she said. "What happened to Sa—to Jamie?"

"Apparently she was jogging along a country road—funny, because I never knew her to exercise on purpose. Anyway, somebody strangled her and left her in a ditch. The police don't have any leads as yet."

"Thank you," Jamie managed to say, clutching the edge of the hall table with one hand, hauling herself awkwardly to her feet. "I'll want to have my sister's body sent here, to Tovia. Can you tell me where she was taken?" She wrote down the numbers of the King County morgue and the Seattle police, which Fred obligingly looked up for her, said her good-byes, and hung up. Then, without further ado, Jamie fell into a dead faint.

FOUR

Fortunately, Jamie's state of shock was short-lived. Once she'd absorbed the first blow—Myrtle and the gardener had revived her after her faint and taken her to the drawing room settee to lie down—a strange, icy calm descended. Within minutes, she was on her feet again, calling the Seattle police from the hall telephone. She was put through to a Detective Stan Reeger, in the homicide division.

"My name is Sara Castanello," she said. The lie came to her lips with disturbing ease. "I'm calling from Europe. My—my sister was Jamie Roberts. When I asked for the detective in charge of her murder case, the operator put me through to you."

"I'm very sorry about your sister, Ms. Castanello," Reeger said, with the kind of gruff grace one might expect from a seasoned cop. "That was a real shame."

Jamie closed her eyes for a moment, her mind flooded with garish images of Sara, strangled and tossed into a ditch, limbs askew. "Did she suffer?"

Reeger hesitated. "It was a fairly quick death," he said at length. "But she would have felt some pain, having her air cut off that way, and I won't try to tell you she wasn't afraid. Anybody would have been."

"Do you have any idea who might have done this?"

"No, ma'am. I was hoping you could offer a few possibilities."

To Jamie's way of thinking, Julian was the prime suspect, but she wasn't ready to explain the circuitous route she'd taken to reach that conclusion, especially in an international telephone call. Rowan was probably right in believing that Julian hadn't been the brains of the operation, but surely the man wasn't stupid enough, or clumsy enough, to strangle Sara with his own hands. He would have hired out a nasty job like that, and it was a safe bet that he had an alibi for his whereabouts over the last twenty-four hours.

"I'll have to give that some thought, Detective Reeger," she said. "My sister and I have been out of contact for the last five years or so, and frankly, I don't know a lot about her life. In any case, I'll fly to Seattle as soon as I can and make the necessary arrangements."

Reeger cleared his throat. "There wouldn't be much point in that, Ms. Castanello. The medical examiner always does an autopsy in cases like this one, and it may be some time before the—er—remains are released for burial."

Jamie fought down a wave of nausea, picturing her sister's body lying gray and cold on some lab table. "You'll get in touch with me if you find out anything, won't you? It's an international call, so please simply reverse the charges. . . ." Her voice faded away with the effort of trying to block out the terrible images in her mind.

The detective spoke gently. "I'll keep you posted," he said. "Just give me the number."

Jamie couldn't think what it was and she had to turn

to Myrtle, who was hovering nearby, for that simple information. She recited the number into the receiver as the housekeeper told it to her. "And don't worry about the time difference," she finished. "If you find out anything— anything at all—I want to know about it immediately."

"Yes, ma'am. And am I right in assuming you'd be willing to return to the States if we should need your help with the investigation?"

"Just call," Jamie answered. "I'll be on the first plane back."

She replaced the receiver and leaned against the table for a moment, composing herself, gathering her strength. At some point far in the future, she supposed, everything would catch up with her, but for now she couldn't afford to fall apart. She was sure that whoever had killed Sara, or ordered her murder, had known his victim's true identity, and that meant he knew Jamie herself was an impostor. She was in as much danger as Sara had been, maybe more.

Jamie was in the foyer, about to start up the stairs, where she intended to pack for an immediate departure to anywhere, when the front door flew open and Julian breezed in.

Just looking at him, suspecting what he might have done to Sara, whether directly or indirectly, she wanted to fling herself upon him, screeching and clawing, and rip off whatever parts of his anatomy she could get a grip on. "Stay away from me!" she said.

Julian's smile was practiced and quick, but she saw the the arrogance and greed in his eyes. "Is that any way to greet your long-lost husband?"

"You haven't been lost nearly long enough," Jamie replied, and proceeded up the stairs.

He caught up to her within a few strides, took her arm in a harsh grasp, and hustled her toward the second floor. She tried to pull free, but he was much stronger, and his fingers bit into the flesh of her elbow, bruising her, seeming to compress her bones.

Myrtle was still standing in the foyer, and Jamie called down to her in an even, reasonable tone, "Send someone for Mr. Parrish. Right away."

Julian half hurled, half dragged her along the upper hallway. Reaching the master suite, he shoved open the double doors and threw her inside.

"What the hell is going on here?"

Jamie supposed she should have been terrified, but her mind was calm, like the eye of some emotional storm. Grief and frustration and fear howled around her, but somehow she was keeping them at arm's length. "Sara's gone," she said. "Someone murdered her."

He closed the doors with an ominous click. "Since when do you speak of yourself in the third person?" he demanded. "If you're trying to convince me that you're cracking under the strain, forget it."

Jamie was grateful for his assumption, because she'd spoken without thinking. "I'm leaving," she said, opening a drawer and taking out a stack of designer jeans and tops and promptly laying them on top of the bureau. "This marriage is a charade and we both know it. I'm not willing to play the game anymore."

Julian didn't lay a hand on her, but she could feel the violence coiled within him, and if she hadn't been so numb over what had happened to Sara, she would have been mortally afraid. "Do you think you can back out so easily?" he hissed. "Because if you do, you really *are* losing it. You're in this as deep as I am, baby, and you're not going anywhere!"

"He knows," she said, taking a desperate gamble. "Rowan knows you and I took the jade goddess to sell on the black market."

Julian went white, even though he had to have considered the possibility before, and murmured a curse. "Did he tell you that?"

"You told me to find out what he knows, and I did."

"Why hasn't he told the police?"

"He has no proof," Jamie answered, still feeling nothing at all. She prayed the numbness would last until she was ready to deal with the permanent loss of Sara. "But he's working on it, Julian, and he means to nail us. The jig, as they say, is up."

She had to get away. Find a place to hide.

"You damn idiot," Julian breathed. "Parrish is trying to trick you into a confession, don't you see? It's guesswork, that's all."

Jamie nodded. "Yes," she agreed moderately, "but he guessed right, didn't he?"

Julian said nothing. He just turned and strode out of the suite, and Jamie went back to her packing. If only she could think of somewhere to go, she reflected, but no flash of genius came to her. She wouldn't be any safer on the other side of the world than Sara had been.

There was a polite rap at the door, and then Myrtle's trilling voice. "Mrs. Castanello? Mr. Parrish is downstairs."

"Thank you," Jamie replied, as the realization struck her that she'd just filled a whole suitcase with mismatched shoes and wire hangers. "Send him up, please."

Rowan arrived within a couple of minutes, not bothering to knock, his fine brow furrowed as he took in the suitcase and the crazy tangle of useless items inside it. "Sara—"

"I need to get away from here," she said matter-of-factly. "Please, Rowan, take me somewhere—anywhere—"

He crossed the room and gripped her shoulders. His touch, unlike Julian's, was gentle and lent her strength and a degree of comfort. "What's happened?"

"I'll explain everything, I promise. Just help me get out of this house."

Rowan released her. "All right," he said. He nodded toward the suitcase. "Dump that junk out, and put in some real clothes. While I'd love to see you running around the old family home in the altogether, it might shock the servants." With that, he went into Sara's closet, which was roughly the size of the suite of offices Jamie had worked in in Seattle, and came out with an armload of blouses, slacks, sweaters, and skirts.

"That's it?" Jamie asked, shock making her giddy. "Just like that, you're taking me to your house? No questions? No gibes about counting the silver and locking up the artwork?"

Rowan smiled and tossed the garments he carried onto the suitcase. "I'll take care of all that later," he said. "Questions included."

"Julian will try to stop us."

His smile broadened. "I've been looking for an excuse to knock your husband out of his boots. Bring him on."

Jamie folded the items Rowan had selected for her, added jeans and T-shirts, nightgowns and underwear, tucked everything into her bag, and snapped the catches closed before she dropped her bombshell. "Julian is not my husband. However, feel free to deck him."

"Don't worry, I do." Rowan took the suitcase from her when she would have hoisted it herself and led the way through the doors and into the hallway beyond. To Jamie's secret relief, they didn't encounter Julian at all. He'd been a tough guy with Jamie, but apparently he wasn't so eager to tangle with Rowan.

A sleek silver sports car waited in the driveway, and Rowan tossed Jamie's suitcase into the tiny trunk before opening the passenger door for her. He cast one last look toward the house, obviously still hoping Julian would show up, and then got behind the wheel and started the engine.

"Wait!" Jamie cried.

"What?" Rowan asked impatiently.

"I can't leave without Lazarus."

"You'll have to," Rowan pointed out, shifting the car into reverse. "The terms of Henri's will forbid anyone to take him off the grounds without a very good reason, remember?"

Jamie bit her lip. "I don't care. I want him."

Rowan turned the car around and headed down the drive. "We'll settle this argument another time," he replied. "But you might just trouble yourself to explain your sudden attachment to that animal. You always hated him, and now, all of a sudden, he's your best friend. And exactly what did you mean back there, when you said Julian isn't your husband?"

She sank back in the small leather seat, closed her eyes, and sighed. The reality of Sara's murder was nipping at her heels; she would be dragged down soon, into a mire of grief she might never escape. "I can't talk about it, Rowan. Not until we're away from here."

He accepted her reply, apparently, for he didn't say another word for almost twenty minutes. Jamie was silent too, feeling the fading sunlight on her skin, the salty wind ruffling her hair. Tovia might have been her own private paradise, she thought, if things had been different.

Finally, at dusk, Rowan brought the car to a stop at the side of the road. They were high above the villa; she could see the ruins in the woods and, of course, the sea. After turning off the engine, Rowan took her hand.

"Time to start explaining, my love. And leave out the lies."

Jamie sighed. There was a burning sensation behind her eyes, and her heart felt as heavy as a block of granite. She was beginning to mourn Sara—not the real one, of course, because she hadn't really known that woman after all, but the sister she'd invented for herself. The person she'd wanted Sara to be.

"You won't believe me. It's too fantastic."

"Convince me."

"I'm not married to Julian, because I'm not Sara. I'm her twin sister, Jamie."

"You're right, that's pretty wild. But go on. I'm listening."

"Think about it, Rowan. Sara hated the cat, and the feeling was probably mutual. But he and I took to each other right away."

"Stranger things have happened," Rowan said, but he spoke thoughtfully. Jamie knew he was taking in what she was saying, weighing the logic of it. She could sense that he wanted to believe her, whether he actually did or not.

"Sara's dead," Jamie said woodenly. "She was strangled sometime yesterday, on a rural road near Seattle. The police think her body is mine, because we traded lives."

Skepticism shadowed Rowan's face. "Convenient," he said. "If Jamie is dead, you can claim to be her and escape all the consequences of larceny on a truly grand scale."

Jamie hadn't anticipated that angle, and she was taken aback. When she finally replied, her voice was hollow. "Sara and I had the same blood type, and neither of us have ever been fingerprinted. But we didn't have the same teeth filled. I can prove I'm telling the truth. All I have to do is call my dentist."

"That's very good," Rowan admitted. "I suppose if I went to the trouble to check, though, I'd discover that your dentist's office burned down last month and all the records were lost."

She raised her wrist with a jerky motion and squinted at Sara's gold watch. "It's still morning in Seattle. Just get me to a telephone."

Rowan started the car, his jawline set tight, and pulled back onto the road. Within ten minutes, they passed between the towering brick gateposts of a sprawling country estate. He sped around the enormous circular driveway and brought the vehicle to an abrupt stop near the front step.

"I believe we have a telephone around somewhere," he said, shutting off the car.

Jamie got out without waiting for him to come around and open the door for her. "With your permission?"

Rowan had stopped to get her bag from the trunk, but he nodded toward the house. "My study is just off the foyer, on the left."

Jamie hurried inside. Her heart was still deadened, hollow and empty, but all of a sudden it was beating hard. She found the telephone on the corner of an exquisite antique cherrywood desk and immediately reached an overseas operator. Since she had to get her dentist's number from Information, the call was just going through when Rowan came in. He'd evidently left the suitcase in the foyer, and his hands were shoved into the pockets of his jacket.

It would be too awkward to explain who she was, given the fact that everyone she'd known in Seattle believed she was dead, so Jamie introduced herself as Sara and asked that her late sister's dental records be sent to her in Tovia immediately.

"Jamie Roberts," the nurse mused. "That's the poor woman who was murdered, isn't it? What a shame; she was so young. I'm sorry, Mrs. Castanello. It must have been a terrible shock to you."

Jamie was looking at Rowan and winding the cord round and round on her index finger. "It was. About the dental records."

"I'm afraid we don't have them anymore," the woman said. "The police came by and picked them up this morning."

Some of Jamie's numbness gave way to dread, and the pit of her stomach constricted painfully. "I see. I suppose it was Detective Reeger?"

There was a brief, pulsing silence. "I don't think that was the name. Just a second, let me check my log book."

The nurse put Jamie on hold, and canned music filled her ear. She wanted to look away from Rowan's face but found she couldn't.

After several minutes, the woman returned. "According to my notes, Mrs. Castanello, Ms. Roberts's chart was signed out to a Detective Alex Martinelli."

A headache began to pound beneath Jamie's temples, and anxiety stabbed through her vitals like a lance. It was routine for the police to examine a murder victim's dental records, she told herself, but that didn't change the awful premonition she had. "Thank you," she said. After several attempts to return the telephone receiver to its cradle, she succeeded and reached into the pocket of her jeans for the numbers she'd written down earlier, while talking to her former boss. In a few minutes, she'd reached the Seattle Police Department.

After a moment's hesitation, she asked to speak with Detective Alex Martinelli. Rowan was standing beside Jamie, now, and frowning. She could smell fresh air, and the scent of soap on his skin, and she wanted him to hold her very close and for a very long time.

The operator paused, then confirmed Jamie's worst fears. "I'm sorry, ma'am. There is no officer by that name. Perhaps Mr. Martinelli is with another police force?"

Jamie shook her head, too dazed to realize, until after the fact, that the woman on the other end of the phone line couldn't see the gesture. "I—I must be mistaken," she said. "Could you please put me through to Detective Reeger?"

There were more electronic sounds, and then a male voice came on the line. "Homicide. Goodrich here."

Jamie repeated her request.

"Let me get your number," Goodrich responded. "Reeger's out right now. He'll get back to you as soon as he can."

"That's all right," Jamie said, in a voice she barely recognized as her own. "I'll call later." She hung up, pushed her hand through her hair, and looked straight into Rowan's eyes. "Well, it wasn't a fire, like you said. Just a common, ordinary con job."

"What happened?"

"Somebody pretending to be a detective named Martinelli picked up my dental records. I think it's safe to say we'll never lay eyes on them."

Rowan sighed. "If what you say is true—and believing you, my darling, is a little like poking a hand into the fire after sustaining a third-degree burn—there would still be Sara's records. All we have to do is find out who her dentist was." He put a gentle, undemanding arm around her waist. "In the meantime, guilty or innocent, you're obviously at the end of your tether. I want you to lie down on that couch over there by the hearth. I'll get you some hot tea and then build a fire."

Jamie's defenses were weakening. "I'm not Sara," she said, because she needed him to believe her, to be on her side.

Rowan squeezed her hands, then raised one to his lips and brushed a light kiss over the knuckles. "Wouldn't it be wonderful if that were true," he said.

"Did you hate her so much? Sara, I mean?"

"Oh, it was much worse," Rowan said, with sorrow and irony in his eyes, even as his mouth shaped itself into a faint smile. "I loved Sara. And I must still be obsessed, or I would have left you with Julian. God knows, the two of you deserve each other."

Jamie turned away and moved slowly toward the couch he'd pointed out. It was no use trying to convince Rowan that she wasn't Sara, no use at all. Even if she did manage to produce dental records, her own or Sara's, he'd probably just think she'd tricked him somehow.

Something in the timbre of his voice stopped her, though she didn't turn around to meet his gaze.

"There *is* one thing that makes me think you might be an impostor," he said. "Remember that reference I made to our picnic at the ruins—when it rained and we argued because we each thought the other should have checked the forecast?"

"Yes," Jamie whispered. She still didn't face him, because she knew she couldn't endure the contempt and pity she expected to see in his eyes.

"It never happened."

Startled, she whirled. "Then why—"

"Strange as it sounds, when I first saw you, standing

there by the baggage carousel at the airport, I was struck by some difference in you that I couldn't quite put my finger on. I had the whimsical thought that you might be a stranger, maybe an actress who bore a strong resemblance to Sara, or even someone who had had cosmetic surgery for the purpose of looking like her. I tried to trip you up a couple of times, but I finally decided that my theories, while entertaining, were simply too farfetched. That's when I came to the conclusion that you were laying the groundwork—by acting vague and pretending to remember things that had never happened, I mean—to stage some kind of spectacular mental breakdown. Amnesia would be a bit of a stretch, outside a soap opera, but you always had a flair for the dramatic. Or Sara did, if you do indeed have the extreme good fortune to be someone else."

"What are you going to do with me?"

"For now, I plan to protect you." He pressed her gently onto the couch. "I'll be back in a few minutes."

Jamie couldn't have moved if all the draperies on all the windows in the room had burst simultaneously into flames. The inner resources that had sustained her up to now had ebbed away, like a low tide, and she wanted to curl into a fetal position and sleep for days.

She was staring into the empty hearth when Rowan returned, carrying a china tea service on a tray. He set everything down on a small table near the couch and went to build the promised fire.

"Sara wanted so much," she mused, speaking as much to herself as to Rowan. "That was the problem, you know. She wanted so much more than most of us do."

Rowan looked back at her over one broad shoulder, still crouched next to the fireplace. "What did Jamie want?" he asked.

Jamie's smile trembled on her mouth, fleeting and slippery. "A husband who loved her. Her own dusty little antiques shop. And a few babies."

"A nice dream," Rowan acknowledged.

"What about you? What do you want most in all the world?"

He considered, then said without rancor, "To turn the clock back to the day before I met you and head in the opposite direction."

Jamie would never know what made her ask the next question. Some defiant, self-destructive impulse, probably. "And to find the jade goddess? That's why you were staying at Sara's house when I arrived, isn't it? You were looking for it."

Rowan got to his feet and touched an empty space on the mantel. "Yes," he admitted. Then he sighed. "It's very unlikely that I'll ever see the goddess again," he went on, after a few moments of thoughtful silence. "I just want to prove that you and Julian stole the piece."

Somehow, without being aware of it, Jamie had poured herself a cup of tea. She lifted the drink from the tray with a small start of surprise. "This vendetta of yours is mostly about revenge, then," she said.

"It's about justice," Rowan retorted.

"You should have protected her better—the goddess, I mean."

A corner of Rowan's mouth lifted in a faint and sardonic semblance of a smile. "So now it's my fault she was taken, and not that of the thieves? Strange reasoning, Sara-Jamie."

She put down the cup and saucer with a clatter. "Don't call me that!"

Rowan looked as surprised as Jamie felt, though he didn't speak. The protest had risen without warning from some deep part of her unconscious mind, like a scaly dragon breathing fire.

"It's not as if Sara and I were the same person," Jamie said, foundering. She was frantic and afraid and desperately alone, and words she wouldn't have spoken under other circumstances tumbled from her lips. "Being a twin can be very difficult, you know. Sometimes, it was as though I didn't exist at all. There were moments when I honestly believed I was nothing more than a reflection of my sister. And you can stop thinking what you're thinking, Rowan Parrish, because I'm not crazy and I'm not trying to convince you that I am!" She tapped one temple with an index finger. "No extra personalities in here," she rushed on. "Just plain old plodding Jamie Roberts, who thought she wanted an adventure!"

"Stop," Rowan said gently.

She began to sob. "I loved my sister!" she cried, as Rowan sat down beside her and pulled her into his arms. "No matter what she was, or what she did, I loved her!"

He held her long after she'd fallen silent, long after the fire on the hearth had cooled to embers, long after twilight had sent long purple shadows creeping through the windows and across the floor.

"Come along," he said finally. "I'll tuck you in and we'll work things through in the morning."

She clung to him with both hands, something she'd sworn she'd never do again, with any man, after Alan had taught her the finer points of heartbreak. "Don't let me go," she pleaded hoarsely, no longer caring if he thought she'd lost her mind; maybe she had. Maybe she really was Sara Castanello. Maybe there had never been a Jamie Roberts at all. . . .

"All right," he assured her. "All right, love, I'm here. Don't be afraid."

Don't be afraid. Jamie might have laughed if she hadn't known how she would sound. Hysterical, at best. Stark raving mad at worst.

"Just hold me," she said. "Please." Hold me forever, keep me safe, change the world so nothing bad ever happens again.

"I will," Rowan answered, rising to his feet and pulling Jamie with him. He lifted her easily into his arms, the way he had done the night she'd almost drowned. "I will."

He carried her up a flight of stairs and into a large bedroom furnished in antiques. It was Rowan's room, Jamie knew. She was glad. She wanted to be close to him, for just this one night. She yearned to lie in his arms, whether he made love to her or not, and pretend it was she, Jamie, that he meant to hold, and not the memory of Sara.

Rowan laid her on the bed and dimmed the lights. He undressed her gently, without fumbling, as gracefully as if he'd done it a thousand times before. Then he took off his own clothes, crawled into bed, and drew Jamie back into his arms.

It was bliss, a quiet, magical time out of time. The jade goddess wasn't missing, and she'd never met Julian Castanello, and Sara wasn't dead. Best of all, Rowan cared for her, Jamie.

"Make love to me," she said.

She felt his lips, warm and soft, brush her forehead. "I'd like nothing better, but I'm afraid I'm not quite scoundrel enough to take advantage that way," he told her, with a rueful chuckle in his voice. "Wish I could summon up a little villainy, but there it is. I'm a knight who was never issued his shining armor, but a chivalrous fellow nonetheless."

Jamie smiled into his bare shoulder. "If you insist on being honorable, I suppose there's nothing I can do," she said, snuggling closer. And even though she still wanted him, a small, achy corner of her heart was warmed by the knowledge that he did not take loving a woman lightly. "Good night, Sir Rowan."

He laughed, and the sound was low and richly masculine. "Sleep well, milady," he replied.

FIVE

Already dressed when Jamie opened her eyes the next morning, Rowan sat beside the bed, legs outstretched, his aristocratic face solemn with contemplation. Seeing that she was awake, he gave her a brief, cryptic grin that was probably intended to serve as a "good morning."

There had been a similar scenario with Julian, right after her arrival in Tovia, and Jamie was tired of dealing with fully clothed males while she had only bedsheets to cover her. "Stop looking at me that way." Her suitcase was on a bench at the foot of the mattress, and she wriggled toward it on her knees, using the bedclothes for a shield.

"What way?" Rowan hadn't moved.

"Like we spent the night engaged in wild passion. We didn't."

"So I noticed," he said ruefully.

Jamie got tangled in the covers, lost her balance, and toppled forward, affording Rowan an embarrassing view of her bare backside. She righted herself as quickly as she could, face crimson, and narrowed her eyes, silently daring him to mock her.

He looked away for a moment, probably smoothing the amusement from his face. Then, finally, he rose to his feet. "I'll leave you to get dressed," he said. "After that, we'll figure out what to do about Julian."

Jamie gulped and her heart tripped, like a skater thrown off-balance, and went spinning. "About Julian? Does that mean—"

Rowan touched the tip of her nose, and though the gesture was innocuous, a surge of sweet well-being rushed through Jamie's spirit. "It means I believe you. You're not Sara."

"But, how—"

His pressed the same fingertip to her lips. "It was the way you lay in my arms last night, the way you breathed and moved, the way you fit against my side. Beyond that, I can't explain. Maybe it's just that I want so much for you to be real."

Tears burned in Jamie's eyes as she realized that the undeniable attraction between them was still about Sara. If Rowan wanted her, Jamie, it was because she had her sister's face and body. She bit her lip and nodded, since that was all she could manage, and he left the room.

Jamie washed her face in the adjoining bathroom, brushed her teeth with a new brush that had been laid out for her, and dressed quickly in black slacks, a gray-blue fisherman's sweater, heavy socks, and sneakers.

She didn't see any of Rowan's servants as she descended the stairs, and that was a relief. She'd spent the night in the master bedroom, and even though nothing had happened, Jamie was old-fashioned enough to be embarrassed by appearances. No one who knew she'd shared Rowan's bed—everyone in the house, probably—would believe the truth.

Jamie found the dining room by following the scent of

bacon. Rowan was already there, seated at the head of a beautifully carved table. "I've decided that Julian has no reason to kill me," she announced, going to the sideboard and helping herself to a plate. An appealing array of food had been set out in chafing dishes, including southern-fried potatoes, crêpes, biscuits, sausage, and bacon. There was fruit as well, along with yogurt and dry cereal.

Rowan rose from his chair, out of courtesy, and then sat down again. "Considering that he probably tried to drown you the other night, and that he either murdered Sara himself or ordered it done, that's a remarkable conclusion. Were you hurt when you jumped to it?"

Jamie summoned up part of a smile and joined him at the table. Her appetite was nonexistent, given all the shocks and traumas of recent days, but she needed to keep her strength up, so she nibbled. "We agree that Julian and Sara must have stolen the goddess. When I alluded to what they'd done yesterday, he didn't trouble to deny it. Still, if he had Sara killed—and I believe he did—he not only knows who I am, he can also be fairly certain that I don't know anything at all about the theft. So why should he worry about me?"

Rowan chewed and swallowed a bite of bacon before replying. "Because there's one thing he can't be sure of, Jamie. He's probably terrified that Sara told you the whole sordid story. He might even think you and Sara were trying to put something over on him, to cut him out of the deal somehow."

"But if they've already taken the statue, fenced it, and divided the money . . ."

"I've been thinking about this most of the night," Rowan said, when Jamie's words fell away for lack of momentum. "It occurred to me that maybe things never got that far. Something went wrong, I'm sure of it. Patience isn't Julian's long suit. If he had his half of the loot—the equivalent of roughly two-point-five million dollars—he'd have vanished by now."

"That would raise questions about Sara's murder. His disappearing, I mean."

"Would it? Don't forget. As far as the police are concerned, they found the body of Jamie Roberts, not Sara."

"Almost the perfect crime," Jamie mused. "If I'd drowned in that tide pool, people would have thought it was an accident. Julian, as Sara's husband, stood to inherit whatever she had."

Rowan shook his head, and Jamie thought she saw something like guilt flicker in his eyes. "Sara didn't have anything for him to inherit, really, besides the proceeds from selling the jade goddess to some crooked art broker. The villa itself belongs to Lazarus."

"The cat?" Jamie marveled. She'd known about the codicil in Sara's first husband's will, assuring Lazarus of a home and a constant supply of gourmet food, but she hadn't guessed that the animal might actually own property. "How is that possible? Lazarus is one smart kitty, but he can't manage an inheritance."

"He doesn't have to," Rowan said, clearing his throat. "Henri appointed me trustee before he died. I manage the whole shebang, as you Americans say."

Jamie sank back in her chair, momentarily surprised. Then she remembered how Myrtle had deferred to Rowan and called him sir, as though he were master of the house. His knowledge of the villa had struck her more than once, too. It was a vast place, with a complex layout.

"Is that why Sara came to Seattle?" she asked, with exaggerated calm. "Because you, as trustee, told her to leave the villa?"

Rowan looked patently annoyed. "Use your head, Jamie. Why would I have given Sara the boot and allowed Julian to stay?"

She didn't have an answer.

"In any case," he went on, with an effort to moderate his tone of voice, "Henri made a provision in his will that allowed Sara to live there as long as she wanted. She had an income most women, even in her social circles, would have considered more than adequate."

Jamie braced herself to learn something else about her sister that she hadn't known. "But?" she prompted.

Rowan sighed. "But she had a problem."

Jamie thought of her father, for the first time in a long while. She remembered his rare calls from Las Vegas or Reno, the lies and the promises that were never kept. Both Jamie and Sara had expected, against all reason, that he'd come home one day, land some kind of job, and make a home for them. It hadn't happened, of course.

"Sara was gambling."

Rowan nodded grimly. "She and Julian met in Monaco, a few months after Henri died. I suspect that was when Sara's pet vice became a slavering monster. It isn't too great a stretch to imagine that when her income was consumed by gambling debts she cooked up the scheme to steal the goddess. She knew it was here, that I was planning to take it to my gallery in Hong Kong. We'd talked about antiques and artifacts often when we were dating, and she even went on a few buying trips with me. She was well aware that the goddess was valuable."

Jamie felt a flash of jealousy, imagining Rowan and Sara traveling together, but she quelled it by reminding herself that she was supposed to be in mourning. She wondered if she would grieve, once the numbness passed, for the stranger who had been her sister.

"Why were you taking the goddess out of the country?"

"The piece was Chinese. I thought it belonged in the Orient."

"Were you and Sara having an affair? Is that why she was here and saw the statue?"

"Aren't we full of questions today?" Rowan responded, but his tone was good-natured and there was tenderness in his eyes. "The answer is no. Sara was married, and I do not sleep with other men's wives. Or at least if I do, I don't make love to them."

"It's that chivalry thing again," Jamie said. She was pleased by his reply and didn't try to hide it. "You are a very unusual man, Rowan Parrish."

"And you are a very lovely woman. Be forewarned, Jamie Roberts. When this is over—when I've dealt with Julian and you've had some time to get your emotional bearings—I intend to seduce you."

Jamie blushed because she wanted to surrender and she was sure it showed. Still, she wouldn't allow herself to think anything real or lasting could ever develop between the two of them. Rowan had loved Sara once, and Jamie didn't want to spend the rest of her life wondering if he was simply using her as a substitute. She had no desire to be a reasonable facsimile of someone else; her adventures in Tovia had taught her that, while she definitely wouldn't wish to change lives with anyone, there was no going back to her old ways of doing things. No more sleeping in her ex-husband's T-shirts and going around half-conscious, waiting for something to happen. When and if she got out of this confusing situation, Jamie promised herself, she would make her own magic.

Rowan pushed away his plate. "In the meantime, though, I have business in St. Rupertsburg, our capital city. I want you to come with me."

Jamie had no intention of turning down a viable opportunity to stay alive, but the idea of hiding out went against the grain. She'd spent her whole life as a coward, a hostage to her own fears about taking risks, but she had a different philosophy now. She meant to take an active role in everything that concerned her.

"All right," she said, somewhat primly, as if she'd been given a choice instead of a polite command. "I'll go, but I won't skulk about like some criminal." A plan was forming, in the dazed, shock-muddled recesses of her mind, but she wasn't ready to share it. "How can I solve my problems if I run away from them?"

"Sometimes flight is the only prudent course of action. To paraphrase, 'She who fights and runs away—'"

"She who fights and runs away," Jamie informed him, "loses the war."

"Not necessarily," he countered. "That isn't the way the saying goes, remember. You're overlooking the part about living to fight another day." Seeing that Jamie had pushed her plate away, he rose and came to stand beside her and offer his hand. "Come along, milady, and we'll see what we can do about keeping you alive."

Telling herself she was a fool, that when she could finally slough off Sara's identity and take back her own she would have to leave Tovia forever, Jamie gave Rowan her hand.

St. Rupertsburg was a small city, by most standards, but it was quaintly beautiful, full of stone buildings with tiled roofs, terraces, and courtyards, all poised at the edge of the sparkling sea like eager swimmers about to plunge in. Steep hillsides, thick with olive groves and vineyards, curved around the place like a mother's arm. A vast, rambling medieval keep loomed above it all, at once ominous and benevolent.

Jamie, riding in the passenger seat of Rowan's sports car, drew in a sharp breath.

"How could anyone ever leave such a place?" she whispered. "It's surely enchanted."

Rowan might not have heard her comment if the car's top had been down, but the afternoon sky was cloudy so he had left it in place. He chuckled, and there was a light in his eyes when he glanced at her. "It is beautiful, I'll grant you that, but there are no resident wizards and no dragon slayers. We're on our own, princess."

Jamie's unfeeling, frozen heart began to thaw in that

moment, and the process promised to be painful. "I'm scared," she confessed. Her idea had solidified a little on the three-hour drive along the coast to St. Rupertsburg, but the plan she'd formulated was a dangerous one, and she knew Rowan would reject it out of hand.

He reached across to squeeze her fingers firmly in his own. "Me too," he answered. "Let's make a bargain. I know you can't forget what happened to Sara, but for the rest of the day, let's put Julian and the jade goddess out of our minds and try to enjoy the city."

Jamie nodded, but she couldn't quite smile. "It's terrible, Rowan," she confided miserably, "but I don't feel any grief for Sara. I don't feel anything at all, except fear. It's as if she was only some woman I heard of once, or read about in a newspaper. A stranger."

Rowan didn't reply. They were entering the narrow brick-paved streets of the city, and he concentrated on his driving.

Jamie gazed at the buildings and the people. They appeared oddly dreamlike. She wondered if they were real, if she herself was real. Should she look into a mirror? Would the image she saw there be her own?

Rowan wove expertly through traffic that included every conceivable make and model of car and more than one donkey cart. At last they stopped in front of a spectacular old hotel with rows and rows of balconies overlooking the sea.

A cheerful parking attendant opened Jamie's car door and helped her out, and Rowan slipped from behind the wheel. A bellman appeared immediately to collect Jamie's suitcase, and that was when she noticed that Rowan hadn't brought any luggage.

He spoke to the two hotel employees in turn, handing each of them a bill, and then put his hand on the small of Jamie's back and steered her into the lobby. It was an elegant room, full of crystal and mahogany; priceless oriental rugs graced the floor.

Rowan didn't even glance toward the registration desk but headed straight for a bank of elevators on the far side. "I keep rooms here," he explained, in a teasing whisper, when Jamie gave him a questioning look.

An empty elevator arrived, and they stepped inside. "That's very aristocratic of you," Jamie replied. "Are we operating on the old hide-in-plain-sight theory? Julian must know about this place."

He waggled a finger at her. "Have you forgotten our agreement? We're not going to worry about Julian until tomorrow, remember?"

Jamie sighed. She had a headache and a strong hunch that her horoscope, should she work up the courage to read it, would say, Run like hell!

"Right," she grumbled. "Why should you turn a hair? It's *me* Julian wants to kill, after all."

Rowan cupped her chin in his hand and looked deep into her eyes. "And if he succeeded, I would die too. From the loss." He bent his head and kissed her lightly on the mouth. "I've fallen in love with you, Jamie Roberts."

No, Jamie thought despairingly. You may think you're free, but you're still under Sara's spell. You don't really want me, you want a reincarnation of her.

She shook her head. "Don't say that, Rowan. Please."

The elevator stopped and the doors opened, but Rowan didn't step off, nor did he allow Jamie to do so. He braced his hands against the wall of the cubicle, effectively trapping her between them. In the hall, an elderly couple looked at them curiously as the doors closed again.

"Why not?" he demanded. "Why can't I say I love you, Jamie? Tell me."

She swallowed hard and wrapped her arms tightly around herself. "Because you don't, not really."

Rowan reached out with one hand, never looking away from Jamie's face, and found the ornate STOP knob above the elevator buttons. She wondered distractedly if he had radar or something.

"What makes you say that?"

Jamie drew in a quick, deep breath, and let it out again in a mournful sigh. "We don't really know each other, Rowan. And things have been happening so fast that no one could begin to sort them out without a lot of time and effort." She hesitated, biting her lip. "When you look at me, you don't see me, Jamie Roberts. You see some fantasy version of Sara. As much as I care about you, I can't spend my life posing as someone else."

Rowan started to speak, then stopped. He released the STOP button and pressed the number for the top floor. His stride, as he stepped off the elevator and started down the hall, was rapid, but he didn't seem angry. To Jamie, he looked preoccupied.

She followed him to the white double doors of his suite and waited in silence while he produced a key from the pocket of his slacks and worked the lock. Beyond the threshold was a large living room, furnished in what appeared to be French antiques. There were lots of tables and mirrors, and colorful fresh flowers were everywhere, filling the air with a symphony of scent.

At last, Rowan spoke again. "I'll show you to your room," he said, and started across the lush white carpet toward another set of double doors. He pushed one open and gestured for Jamie to step through before him.

She found herself in a sumptuous bedroom with a white marble fireplace and a terrace overlooking the sea. Jamie felt a silken rope wind around her heart and squeeze tight. "It's beautiful, but—"

He silenced her with a light kiss on the mouth. "I'll take the other room, Jamie. I'm not going to pressure you; you must know that."

Jamie nodded. She couldn't quite make herself tell him that she not only wanted him to share her bed, to hold her and protect her as he had the night before, but to be her lover. Not after the speech he'd made about abstaining from sex until everything was settled and she'd gotten her emotions under control, and not after turning away his declaration of love.

"I know," she said, and she sounded disgustingly timid, even to herself. Realizing that she was wringing her hands, she wrenched them apart.

Rowan touched heer face gently, then withdrew. "I have some things to attend to," he said. "We'll have dinner when I get back and then go to the theater, if you feel like it."

She honestly tried to smile. "I could use a little entertainment," she said. "But I don't think I brought anything suitable to wear."

A corner of his mouth lifted, and some sad, gentle emotion moved in his eyes like a shadow. "No problem. There's a very good shop downstairs in the lobby. Buy whatever you want."

The idea of wearing a dress that she'd chosen herself appealed to Jamie, even though she would have to use one of Sara's credit cards to buy it. It would be a small step toward reestablishing her own identity. "I've been managing tile stores in Seattle for five years," she joked. "And I haven't had much leisure time. I'm a little out of practice when it comes to picking out dresses for dinner and the theater."

"You'll manage, I'm sure," Rowan replied, with tender humor. "Be careful, my love. If you leave the hotel, make sure you pay strict attention to everything that's going on around you."

She saluted. "Yes, sir," she said.

He laughed, kissed her again, more lingeringly this time, and then left her alone. His absence seemed to suck the oxygen out of the bedroom, and Jamie stood staring after him like a fool, warning herself not to fall in love with him.

The message wasn't getting through; she knew that by the ache in her heart and the weakness in her knees. Even if she managed to survive this extraordinary adventure, how would she ever survive losing Rowan?

She would, she insisted silently, the nails of her right hand digging into her left palm as she clasped her hands together in an unconscious gesture of entreaty. She had to become herself, in a way she had never been before. Only then could she find a man who loved her for being Jamie Roberts.

After some deep breathing and fast talking, Jamie freed herself from the attack of romantic paralysis and went into the echoing marble vault of a bath that adjoined the bedroom. There, she splashed water on her face, used one of the elegant little packaged toothbrushes waiting on the glistening cabinet housing the sink, and combed her hair with her fingers.

Without Sara's makeup and carefully arranged tresses, she thought, with a slight lift of her spirits, she was beginning to look like herself again. Now all she had to do was figure out who the hell she really was.

The suitcase full of her sister's clothes was delivered just as she was about to head downstairs, purse in hand, and explore the shop Rowan had mentioned. It suddenly seemed repulsive, the idea of wearing a dead person's garments, and she shuddered a little as she stepped onto the elevator.

The hotel's boutique was brimming with splendid things, and Jamie tried on several outfits before she selected a short dress of silk crepe. It was midnight blue and drop-dead sexy, with a scattering of tiny rhinestones across the bodice. After charging her purchase and having it sent to Rowan's suite—the clerk didn't bat an eye at this request, Jamie noted, but then it probably wasn't unusual for Mr. Parrish to entertain a woman—she went out into the late-afternoon sunshine.

It was late April, and a soft, balmy breeze fluffed her

hair and caressed her skin. Jamie was feeling better—she hadn't realized how it was getting her down, living in costume like an actress playing a part in a movie that never ended—and she wanted to buy fresh makeup and some casual clothes.

From the hotel she went to a nearby department store, where she bought some new things to wear and had a make-over at one of the cosmetic counters, buying new makeup instead of her old brand. She left just as the store was closing, her arms full of packages.

Jamie had entered the store by a different entrance, and for a few moments she stood on the sidewalk, bewildered. The sense of disorientation only lasted until she rounded the corner and saw the sea glittering in the late-day sunlight, and then she walked with a brisk step, thinking of the glamorous evening ahead. Just for that one night, she would take a vacation from her problems and indulge in the pretense that she and Rowan might actually have a future together.

When the limousine nearly struck her down in the crosswalk, Jamie thought at first she was only dealing with a careless driver. She was struggling to keep from dropping her bags and boxes, and muttering, when suddenly the rear door sprang open and a man leaped out—a man she remembered seeing inside the department store earlier. Before Jamie understood what was happening, he grabbed her by the arm and flung her into the car, leaving her purchases scattered on the pavement.

The inside of the vehicle was sumptuous and very dark, because of the tinted windows. The man shoved the barrel of a small handgun into Jamie's face and said, "Don't scream."

Bile rushed into the back of Jamie's throat, scalding, and she swallowed. It hadn't occurred to her to shout for help; she'd been thinking, ludicrously, that she would never have guessed it was so easy to kidnap someone. It had happened in the space of seconds, with no opportunity for struggle, and if anyone else had seen what was going on, nobody rushed to the rescue. Several horns had honked behind the limo, but that was probably only because the other drivers wanted the way cleared.

She straightened her clothes—Sara's clothes—and even though it was insane, under the circumstances, she felt a twinge of sorrow for the lost things in those bags and boxes. "Let me out of the car this instant," she said.

"Anything you say, lady," the stranger answered acidly.

"Who are you?" Jamie demanded.

"Nobody you know."

Fear was beginning to penetrate the haze of shock and general emotional befuddlement that had been plaguing Jamie since she learned of Sara's death. She tried the door handle, and her captor immediately shoved the pistol barrel hard into the side of her neck.

"I'd hate to mess up a nice car like this," he said, as though he were reprimanding her for parking in a private space or failing to return a library book on time, "but I'll shoot you if I have to. Don't make me prove it."

Jamie nodded. Carefully. "Just put that thing down," she said. "Please."

He lowered the gun to his ample lap. He was a dark-haired man, stocky but not obese, and well-dressed. Jamie sensed that he was strong as the proverbial bull, and her chances of getting away from him were nil.

"Is this what happened to Sara?" she asked, surprised by how calm she sounded. She'd thought she was screaming.

His answer was chillingly simple. "Yes."

"Oh, God," Jamie whispered, covering her face with her hands for a few seconds and fighting an onslaught of sheer hysteria. "You killed her—you personally killed my sister?"

"She wouldn't tell us where she put the jade goddess," he said, as though that were reason enough for any sort of reprisal, even something so brutal as murder.

"You would have killed her anyway," Jamie murmured, seething and shaken. She wondered if this monster would shoot her if she threw up all over his fancy car. "And you plan to do the same thing to me."

The man shrugged. "You'd talk too much afterward," he said. "We can't have that. So let's just get down to business. Your sister gave you the goddess when she landed in Seattle, and you hid it. I want to know where."

Jamie closed her eyes briefly and drew a deep breath. "Sara didn't confide in me. I've never seen that damn statue, and I wish I'd never heard of it, either."

"You've only just started wishing that," her companion said, settling back against the leather seat with a lusty sigh and gazing forlornly through the darkened window.

A chill tingled along Jamie's nerve endings. They were leaving the city behind, heading back along the coastline in the general direction of the villa. Rowan would learn she was missing soon enough, because the purse she'd dropped with her parcels contained a key to his room at the hotel, and he'd have a fair idea where to look for her too, she supposed.

"I suppose you work for Julian," she said evenly.

The man laughed. "Not exactly. He and the girlfriend owed me money. The girlfriend, she came to me and said she could get a certain piece of oriental art that I happened to want. We worked out a deal, and she and Julian lifted the statue from Rowan Parrish's house." The mirth drained from the round face, replaced by a look of cold fury that made Jamie's very bones seem to draw inward, shrinking from him. "I don't know why I'm telling you all this, when you already know what happened. They tried to put something over on me. I guess they planned to sell the goddess at a profit and buy me off with part of the proceeds. I didn't go for it."

"So you murdered Sara."

"She could have saved herself, but she spit in my face

when I asked her about the goddess. Nobody spits on Charlie Beech. Nobody."

Tears filled Jamie's eyes. Oh, Sara, she thought miserably, Sara.

"Sara didn't tell me where she put the statue," she said, after drying her cheeks with the back of one hand. The motion was quick and furtive. "Did you think to ask Julian, her partner in crime?"

"That slimebag? Yeah, I asked him. He said he didn't know, and then darned if he didn't meet with the damnedest boating accident you could imagine. It was right out of an Arnold Schwarzenegger movie."

Once again, nausea roiled in Jamie's stomach. She hadn't liked Julian, but she certainly wouldn't have wished him dead. It was a tragic irony that beautiful, privileged people, like him and like Sara, would actually commit crimes and endanger their own lives for the sake of greed.

"You sound proud of yourself," she said coldly.

"Oh, I am," Charlie answered. "I'm a master at what I do."

"A genuine hit man. Wow, I'm honored."

"You're a smart-ass," he countered wearily. "And you're also as good as dead."

SIX

Don't panic, Jamie warned herself silently, as the expensive car sped away from St. Rupertsburg. She tried hard to make contact with that mysterious part of her mind that had occasionally linked her, however tenuously, with Sara. It was as though the whereabouts of the jade goddess lay hidden somewhere in her unconscious, despite the fact that her twin had never mentioned the object or even hinted at its existence.

Not that it would do her any lasting good to find the statue, she reflected, staring thoughtfully at the back of the limousine driver's head. Charlie Beech meant to kill her, one way or the other; he'd already admitted that. Still, if she could turn the statue over to him, it might buy her some time. And the longer she could stay alive, she reasoned, the better her chances of escape.

"Where did your sister hide the jade goddess, Ms. Roberts?" Charlie asked at length, when they'd traveled quite a distance without speaking. His bored, desultory tone was terrifying for its lack of expression alone. "Tell me and save yourself a lot of suffering."

Jamie's stomach clenched as she imagined the ordeal that might lie ahead, but she was angry as well as frightened, and her anger sustained her. The icy coldness of the emotion kept her from being reckless.

"I don't know, but I have a theory."

Charlie turned his bulk, his silk suit making a whispery sound against the leather upholstery. "I'm warning you right now: no tricks. And no stalling tactics. I'm in deadly earnest here."

Jamie ran the tip of her tongue over her dry lips. "Do you want to hear my theory or not?" she asked evenly.

Charlie narrowed his eyes speculatively. "All right, spill it."

"There is an old fortress on one of the hills behind my sister's villa. She used to go there with someone she cared about, and I think it was a special place to her. It would have been like Sara to bury the goddess somewhere on the grounds or hide it in a hollow spot in the wall that nobody else knew about." Jamie's speculations stemmed from vague memorylike images flickering on the inside of her skull. The pictures became clearer with every passing moment. "Yes," she whispered, amazed. "Sara hid the statue somewhere in those ruins!"

Charlie leaned forward and tapped on the glass separating the back seat from the front, in order to get the driver's attention. The chauffeur lowered the barrier and turned his head. "Yes, sir?"

Jamie was stunned. It was Curran, Sara's driver, who, with Rowan, had met her at the airport the day she arrived in Tovia.

"The lady thinks we'll find what we're looking for in the ruins above the villa."

Curran nodded. "Very good, sir," he said. He met Jamie's eyes, squarely and with mild defiance, before turning his attention back to the road.

Charlie closed the divider with a press of a button on the armrest.

"Julian sneaked back and pushed me into the tide pool that night," Jamie muttered. "He must have suspected I wasn't Sara."

"See?" Charlie said, with a mocking smile. "You're just too smart for your own good."

Jamie didn't answer. She certainly didn't *feel* smart; nobody with half a brain would have gotten into such a mess in the first place. If she'd listened to her own instincts, she'd still be in Seattle, working for Fred Godwin and wishing something interesting would happen.

In which case she would never have met Rowan Parrish. She still didn't know whether falling in love with him had been a plus or a minus. No matter what happened when she and Charlie and Curran reached the ancient fortress, there was no happy ending on the horizon.

She settled back against the seat, closed her eyes, and tried to summon more images to her mind, but it was no use. All she could picture was Rowan's face—a face she might never see again.

Charlie was reading a paperback novel about space aliens when she finally stole another glance at him. He must have ice in his veins, she concluded, to sit there flipping pages and moving his lips, seemingly without a care in the world. No doubt kidnapping and murder were common notations on his To Do list.

It was dark by the time the villa came into view. Curran flipped off the headlights and steered the limo skillfully onto a tree-lined lane Jamie had never noticed before. The track was narrow and unpaved, and the big car jostled on its shock absorbers as they climbed.

The ruin was eerie in the light of the moon, and Jamie's legs trembled as she got out of the car. Unless she got very very lucky, very very soon, she was going to die in this dark place.

"How do you expect to find anything now?" she asked, hugging herself in an effort to ward off the evening chill and the fear.

Curran handed her a flashlight, but it was Charlie who spoke.

"*We're* not going to find anything. *You* are."

Jamie heard a faint rustling in the bushes, but her hope of salvation died a-borning. Just a rabbit or a squirrel, she thought. Then a whimsical voice made an announcement inside her head. *We regret to inform you that Sir Galahad won't be riding to the rescue tonight. He's otherwise occupied. You're on your own, kid.*

She pointed herself toward the ruins, sent a quick prayer heavenward, and stumbled forward. The beam of the flashlight wove crazily over the stones, caught on a pair of jewel-bright amber eyes. Lazarus!

Jamie took some comfort in the animal's presence, and she was glad that Curran and Charlie apparently hadn't noticed him. Too bad, she thought, with the whimsy of hysteria, that she couldn't borrow one of her feline friend's nine lives.

The ground was rough and uneven, scattered with stones both large and small. Jamie nearly fell several times, but each time she righted herself and forged on.

Sara, she pleaded silently, *help me.*

There was no blinding flash of light, no voice from the heavens. All of a sudden, though, Jamie knew where the goddess was hidden. The location of the cache was as clear in her mind as if she'd put the statue there with her own hands.

She went straight to the towering wall and pried at a loose stone, cursing when she broke a nail. "Help me, one of you," she snapped. "The statue is behind this piece of rock."

"This had better not be some kind of trick," Charlie warned.

Jamie stepped back as Charlie moved past her to the

wall, intent on his treasure. He worked the stone free with a pocket knife and had just reached inside the cache when Lazarus came hurtling down out of the darkness. The cat landed on Charlie's head and shoulders, screeching like a banshee, claws extended, all four paws working with a terrible, swift grace.

Charlie shrieked and fought his attacker in vain, and Jamie dropped the flashlight and fled into the shadows.

"Get him off me!" Charlie screamed.

Jamie crouched behind a rock and saw Curran take a small pistol from the pocket of his coat. At first she thought he meant to shoot Lazarus, and she cried out and started to bolt from her hiding place. Curran fired, Lazarus yowled shrilly and streaked off into the darkness, and Charlie crumpled to the ground.

Curran took the statue from his employer's limp hand and straightened. He looked lean and wolflike, framed in the great silvery circle of the moon, and Jamie held her breath. He seemed to be able to see her, even in the darkness.

"I don't kill women," he said. And then he turned and walked away, leaving Jamie crouched behind her stone and Charlie lying in a heap in the ruins. Curran got back into the limousine and simply drove away.

Jamie had been sustained and protected by a state of ongoing shock, but now that the worst had passed, leaving her alive in its wake, she fell apart. She slid down onto the ground and wept with great, violent, gulping sobs that made no sound at all. At some point, Lazarus returned and settled himself against her side, purring like a rotary engine.

A prickle at her nape alerted her, even before Lazarus stiffened beside her and shrieked like a panther. Jamie turned, horror pooling thick in the pit of her stomach, and looked up to see Charlie leaning against the rock she'd taken refuge behind. His leering face was torn and bleeding. He reached one awkward, crimson hand toward her, and she screamed and bolted off.

Charlie loomed there, like a well-stuffed scarecrow, illuminated by the moonlight. His eyes glittered, and he took a step toward Jamie, stumbled, and fell.

She ran blindly into the woods behind the fortress, her heart pounding in the back of her throat, afraid to go toward the villa in case Beech and Curran had posted an accomplice somewhere on the grounds. Gasping and whimpering in terror, she ran and ran—there were no other houses in sight—until her strength was gone, and then she collapsed onto the cold ground.

Rowan and the police found her just after dawn, sitting with her back to an old moss-covered gravestone that stood alone in the middle of a clearing.

Rowan knelt beside her in an instant, checking her for injuries, saying her name over and over again. Not Sara's, but her own. Then he wrenched her into his arms and embraced her fiercely. "It's over now," he said. "It's over."

Jamie luxuriated in being held, in being safe, with her lungs still drawing air and her heart still beating. Her mind was surprisingly clear.

"We found a body in the ruins," Rowan told her, after a long time, holding her gently by the shoulders and gazing deep into her eyes. "What happened?"

She gave him an abridged version of the story, from the moment she was snatched in the crosswalk in St. Rupertsburg to her frantic, mindless flight into the woods. One of the policemen made notes while she talked; another produced a blanket, which Rowan wrapped tightly around her.

"Curran took the goddess," she finished, getting to her feet with a lot of help from Rowan and clutching the blanket close like a cloak.

"I don't give a damn about that," Rowan said. "You're safe. That's all that matters."

A black, silken form brushed against Jamie's ankle, and she looked down to see Lazarus there, purring. "Here's the male of the hour," she said. "My hero."

Lazarus demurred. "*Reow,*" he said, with rare humility.

Jamie laughed and bent to sweep him up into her arms and then, leaning just a little on Rowan's strength, she walked down the hill to the sprawling villa overlooking the sea.

"I'm sorry you didn't recover the goddess," Jamie said, hours later, when the police were gone and she was ensconced in Rowan's house and bed, being shamefully pampered. She was wearing silk pajamas—his—and there had been a constant flow of tea, sympathy, and chicken soup all day long.

He touched her face. "Oh, but I did," he answered gruffly. "She's right here, wearing my pajamas."

Tears pooled along Jamie's lashes. "I love you," she whispered.

He kissed her. "And I love you."

Jamie drew back, albeit reluctantly. "I'm going to need some time."

"Before we make love, or before we get married?"

The thought of being Rowan's wife made her heart swell with a strange liquid warmth. "I want to make love now, today," she told him brokenly, slipping her arms around his neck, "but I can't marry you, Rowan. Not until we're both sure who I am."

Rowan's eyes were dark with tenderness and sorrow, but he nodded. "I know exactly who you are," he said. "But I can wait until you make the same discovery."

She kissed him and fell slowly back onto the pillows, and Rowan fell with her. The kiss intensified until Jamie's very soul seemed to burn, and she surrendered long before she'd been conquered.

Their lovemaking was bittersweet and violent, born of

joy, tinged with the shadow of the inevitable parting. Jamie writhed in Rowan's arms, arching her back when he opened the pajama top and laid claim to her breasts, first with his hands, then with his mouth.

The sensations were exquisite, and Jamie pitched beneath Rowan, wanting more, demanding more. She sobbed, when he finally thrust himself far inside her, and raised her hips high off the bed, trying to consume him, to draw him, body and soul, into her uttermost depths.

He groaned and kissed her, and the motions of their two bodies became more and more frantic with every passing moment. Finally, with a single hoarse cry that came not from one but from both of them, they entered into a fusion so complete, so elemental, that Jamie knew they would never really be separated again, no matter how many oceans might lie between them.

When it was over, and they lay still in each other's arms, breathless and exhausted, Jamie wanted to take back what she'd said about needing time. It would be so easy to stay, she thought, to marry Rowan, to bear his children and share his passion for antiques and art.

She couldn't. She owed herself, and Rowan, much more than a marriage of impulse. If she was going to wed this man, or any other, she wanted the relationship to last. The best way to ensure that was to wait and think, pray and heal.

They made love often, and with heart-wrenching urgency.

After a week, Jamie returned to Sara's villa alone, intending to say goodbye to Myrtle and the others and hoping for a few minutes with Lazarus. The cat didn't put in an appearance, though she searched all his favorite places in and around the house and even walked up to the ruin on the hill.

There was no sign of him anywhere. Sadly, Jamie gave up and returned to the villa, where a taxi was waiting. She'd refused to let Rowan drive her to the airport, knowing she wouldn't be able to bear telling him good-bye.

They'd parted with a kiss and a promise that morning, on Rowan's front walk, and Jamie had driven away without looking back.

She meant to keep going, keep searching, until she found the real Jamie, the best Jamie, the Jamie she was meant to be.

SEVEN

The gallery was exclusive, with an intimidating facade and real gold lettering on the leaded display windows. Through the glass, Jamie could see a lovely old harp, a china doll in an ornate wicker carriage, and a black cat bathing itself with an air of snooty decorum.

She smiled and tapped her fingers against the window, and the cat looked up at her with shining golden eyes.

Lazarus. She hadn't seen him in six months. What was he doing in Hong Kong?

A tiny silver bell tinkled overhead as Jamie opened the door and entered the antiques shop.

Lazarus hopped down from the window with a resounding thump and trotted over to her with a meow of greeting. She crouched, heedless of her white linen suit, to pet him and murmur the kinds of silly, senseless things cat lovers say to their favorite felines.

"May I help you?" someone asked.

Jamie looked up. At first, she thought the words had

come from a life-sized bronze statue of a Chinese warrior on display nearby, but a small birdlike woman with gray hair peered around it. She was exquisitely dressed, with the look of perpetual surprise that often comes with multiple face lifts.

Jamie raised herself, somewhat awkwardly, with Lazarus cradled in her arms like a fat, furry baby. "I'm looking for Rowan Parrish," she said, in a careful voice, not wanting to betray how important her errand was. "Is he in?"

"He's in the office, buried in paperwork," the woman said, offering a manicured hand. "I'm Doris Shaw, Mr. Parrish's assistant. If you'll just give me your name—?"

"Jamie Roberts," she replied, without a trace of the hesitation and doubt that had plagued her in Tovia.

Doris looked at the cat and made a *tsk-tsk* sound, but her manner and tone were benevolent and Jamie liked her. "You'll spoil your lovely suit, holding that old reprobate. Will you just look at him! You'd think it was his due to have the rest of us pay court to him!"

Jamie laughed and nuzzled Lazarus's head. "Lazarus is royalty," she said. "Naturally, he commands the proper respect."

Doris smiled, shook her sprayed and coiffed gray head, and excused herself. Jamie put the cat down gently and tried to brush the fur off her suit.

She didn't hear Rowan enter the room, didn't know he was there until he said her name. She lifted her eyes at the sound of his voice, found his beloved face, and felt her heart turn over. Her love for him had grown and ripened in the time they'd been apart.

"Hello, Rowan."

He was thinner, and his aristocratic features had taken on a cragginess that only added to his appeal. His eyes were full of wary hunger as he looked at her, but he made no move to come closer. "You look wonderful," he said hoarsely.

Jamie took one tentative step, lost her courage, and stopped. She'd done a lot of healing and growing in the past six months, and if Rowan rejected her, she knew she would recover. Still, it would be devastating to lose him and the life they might have together.

"Thank you," she said, her voice trembling a little, like her knees. She cleared her throat and blushed, running through a litany of motivational clichés in her mind: *Now or never . . . no guts, no glory. . . . no pain, no gain . . .* "Rowan—"

"Yes?" He still didn't move, damn him. He wasn't going to make it easy.

"I was wondering if you'd be interested in hiring an apprentice," she blurted out. "I've been working with antiques for months now, and studying on my own, and I think I could be an asset—"

"I'm not looking for an apprentice," Rowan broke in quietly, and for Jamie the world stopped turning. Then he smiled. "A partner would be nice, though."

Jamie stared at him, confounded, trying not to hope and already in over her head. "Are you saying—"

"I'm saying that I love you, Jamie Roberts. I want you to share my life, as well as my business."

With a soft cry, Jamie launched herself into his arms. "I accept!" she cried jubilantly, and Rowan spun her around in celebration, nearly overturning the bronze warrior. "Oh, Rowan, I love you, I love you, I love you!"

He laughed and kissed her hard.

"What is Lazarus doing here?" she asked, when she could catch her breath. "I thought he couldn't leave his estate."

Rowan smiled down at her, holding her close. "I'm afraid poor Lazarus fell on hard times. The villa had to be sold for debts and taxes, as it happened. Our friend here had to depend upon the kindness of his neighbors."

Seemingly unembarrassed by the mention of his reduced circumstances, Lazarus climbed back into the front window and began to bathe himself again.

Jamie laughed, completely happy. "I've been thinking about you ever since I left Tovia," she said.

"And I've been thinking about you," he replied. "Let me show you some of the scandalous things I imagined us doing together."

Warmth flooded through her. "How could I refuse an offer like that?"

Rowan smiled, took Jamie's hand, and led her toward a rear stairway, and she knew without being told that he lived upstairs and he was taking her to his bed. Somewhere in the back of the gallery, a door clicked as Doris let herself out.

Linda Lael Miller, the award-winning *New York Times* bestselling author of over twenty books, lives in Port Orchard, Washington, with her family.

LORD OF THE NILE

~ *by* ~

Patricia Simpson

To BB—
Bubbles are a girl's best friend

ONE

The bell on the shop door tinkled too soon. Surprised, Karissa Spencer looked up from the lioness she was sculpting. Had her partner already come back from his dinner run? She glanced over the railing of the loft to the gallery below. In the October dusk, the large room was bathed in shadows, and the lights on the sculptures and paintings were nearly swallowed by darkness. All was quiet, which wasn't at all like Josh Lambert, who usually blundered around and chattered constantly. Could he have forgotten to lock the door behind him, allowing a stranger to walk in after hours?

Ill at ease, Karissa picked up her sculpting knife and rose from her stool. "Who's there?" she asked.

She stepped to the railing and looked down. A slight movement caught her eye, and she glanced toward the pedestal that displayed a bronze of a panther. There in the shadows a pair of golden-brown eyes stared up at her, the same kind of eyes that had haunted her for more than a decade. Karissa felt a shiver of fear and excitement rush down her back. Sixteen years ago she had come face to face with an Egyptian panther and had been obsessed ever since by the animal's deadly velvet power. She had tried to capture its essence in clay, in bronze, in paint, and in marble, but the feral spirit of the cat had eluded her, and her sculptures seemed empty and lifeless.

No one else noticed. Her pieces were popular and afforded her a decent living. In fact, her studio and the gallery were going to be featured in an upcoming public television program called "Women Artists in America." But Karissa knew something was missing in her work. Never once had she re-created the raw power of the confident, dangerous animal she had seen in Egypt. Had her prodigious memory failed her, just as it had failed to fully record a terrible night long ago? Or was she not artistically gifted enough to capture the savage soul that smoldered in the eyes of the cat? Now here they were again, just as she had remembered, as if to remind her of her failure.

"Ebony," a voice declared in a soft sweep of baritone slightly tinged with a British accent.

"Pardon?" Karissa couldn't break away from the glowing eyes.

"If you would carve this in ebony, Miss Spencer, you would find satisfaction."

Ebony? She had never sculpted in wood. Ebony was dark brown, almost black, the perfect medium to accentuate the sinuous lines of a cat. Why hadn't she ever thought of trying ebony? Karissa placed both hands on the rail.

"You seem to know me, sir. Have we met?"

"A long time ago." His voice was smooth and rich, and she felt the tone vibrate somewhere deep inside her, as if to dislodge a memory long forgotten. But she did not remember this man.

"Oh?"

"Perhaps you will not recognize me as I am now." The man stepped away from the pedestal and into the light directed on a freestanding bronze of three cats. He was dressed entirely in black—black shoes, trousers, and overcoat. Even his hair was black, swept off his forehead from a widow's peak and falling in slight waves to his collar. He was undeniably handsome, a bit older than herself—probably in his mid-thirties—with a strong pointed chin and neat ears close to his head. She certainly should have remembered meeting such an attractive man.

Karissa never forgot a face, literally, because she possessed a photographic memory. According to her therapist, however, Karissa had unconsciously buried some of her Egyptian memories away because they were so painful. Until she brought them out and faced the truth, she would forever be missing one of the most important times of her life—the day her father disappeared.

Karissa cut off all thoughts of her therapist and her father and looked back at the man in the gallery. If he belonged to the missing part of her life, she wasn't about to admit it to him or spend any time searching her memory for his face.

"I'm sorry, but I don't recognize you," she replied.

"It was many years ago. In Egypt. I am called Mr. Asher." He bowed, almost imperceptibly.

"Mr. Asher." She inclined her head slightly in return. "How do you do?"

"May I come up?" he asked.

"I'll come down."

Karissa clutched the sculpting knife tightly and descended the stairs, highly conscious of his regard. Once she gained the lower level, she saw Mr. Asher was much taller than he first appeared. He stood half a foot above her, and she wasn't a short woman by any means.

He looked down at her and smiled, never once breaking eye contact, and slowly raised the corners of his sensual mouth, appearing charming and provocative at the same time. Not many men had the confidence or self-possession to meet a woman's eyes for such an extended length of time.

"Is there something I might help you with?" she asked, making a pretense of brushing something off a nearby bronze so she didn't have to continue to meet his intense gaze.

"Actually, yes." He stepped closer. "I have been looking for you for quite some time, Miss Spencer."

"Oh? Why?"

"You may be the only one in the world who can help me find something."

"Find what?"

"A tomb."

She gave a half laugh. "I'm afraid you have the wrong Spencer. My father was the archaeologist, not me."

"Your father is no longer available. You are. And I know you saw the lost sphinx."

The lost sphinx. Karissa felt something constrict her breathing as an overwhelming sensation of dread gripped her.

"No!" she blurted. She turned away, intending to run back up the stairs and continue her work, but his voice made her pause.

"I know you remember the sphinx, Miss Spencer. The evidence is all over this gallery." He swept the air with a wave of his hand. He wore black gloves. "You do remember, don't you?"

"The only thing I remember about the sphinx is what people tell me."

"And what have they told you?"

"That because of it a curse descended upon my family, which is why my mother sickened and died when I was twelve and my father apparently ran off, never to be heard from again. I don't see why anyone would try to find that sphinx."

"I have a personal interest in it."

She rolled the handle of the sculpting knife against

her palm, not really frightened of Mr. Asher but experiencing a great deal of disquiet. The topic of the sphinx was one she chose to avoid, she decided to ask him to leave. Before the words could come out of her mouth, however, Mr. Asher continued. "I have tried to locate you for many years, but you have made the task very difficult. You changed your name for a period of time."

"I got married."

"Yes." His glance swiftly took in the rest of her figure and darted across her right hand, which clutched the knife. "But you are married no longer."

"My husband died four years ago."

"Was your marriage a happy one?"

"Yes." She turned away so he couldn't see the uncertainty in her face. How dare he ask such a question? "I think you'd better leave."

"Have I offended you?" he asked softly, coming up behind her. "I was simply curious."

"My personal life is none of your business." She pivoted on her heel to head back to the stairs. "Good-bye, Mr. Asher."

"I will go as you request," he replied. "But first, spare a moment to hear my offer."

"What offer?"

"I will pay you a small fortune, Miss Spencer, if you will come to Egypt with me and help me locate the ruins of the sphinx where you saw the panther."

He knew about the panther! She felt even more uneasy. Slowly she turned to face him. "Sorry, but I can't help you. I don't remember anything about that part of my life."

"You have a photographic memory, do you not?"

Karissa paused and studied his handsome face, with its sharp elegant nose and wide lower lip. "How do you know that about me?"

"I know much about you. As I said, I have been trying to find you for years."

"What else do you know?"

"I know about the circumstances of your husband's death."

She felt the color fade from her face and her insides clench together. He couldn't possibly know about Thomas dying of a heart attack while in bed with an eighteen-year-old. Karissa forced the hard knot inside to dissipate and vowed once again to avoid thinking about her philandering husband.

"Mr. Asher, I have nothing more to discuss with you." She motioned toward the door. "Please leave."

He moved toward the door, and his footfalls were soundless on the oak parquet. Not many people could walk so quietly across the gallery floor. At the door he turned. "Will you not consider my offer? It is very important."

"I don't accept such offers from complete strangers."

"I could make you a rich woman."

"By robbing graves? No thanks."

He stood in silence for a moment, as if her words offended him. Then he put his hand on the doorknob. "My quest does not include stealing the possessions of the dead."

"What is your quest, then?"

"To find the mummy of a certain woman and thereby repay a debt."

"That sounds noble, Mr. Asher, but highly suspicious."

"I assure you, my intentions are purely honorable."

"I'll bet." Karissa walked up a few steps. "Listen, I lost my father and mother to that sphinx. I have no desire to risk my life just to help your credit rating."

"How can I change your mind?"

"You can't. Good night."

"You will find me persistent, Miss Spencer, for I must find the mummy as quickly as possible."

"If you harass me, Mr. Asher, you will find yourself arrested."

At that moment the door burst open, forcing Asher to

step aside, and Josh Lambert breezed in with a bag of Chinese food. "Dinner is served!" he announced. Then he noticed the dark visitor near the door. "Sorry! I didn't see you!"

In his haste, Josh bumped into the corner of a pedestal in back of him and nearly knocked over the marble sculpture that rested on the top. Only Mr. Asher's quick reflexes kept the piece from toppling to the floor. Karissa noticed that Josh's good-natured, absentminded clumsiness seemed worse than usual in comparison to the other man's elegant self-control.

"No harm done," Asher replied. He adjusted the statue until it was shown to its best advantage in the light. Karissa was impressed by his eye for the play of shadow and light on the marble.

Josh shot her a questioning glance.

Karissa paused, uncertain how to explain the visitor or his business. Not many people knew of her connection to Egypt, and she didn't intend to tell Josh about her troubled adolescence.

"If you will excuse me," Mr. Asher said, "I was just leaving."

He nodded slightly to both of them and, without making eye contact, walked through the doorway. She watched him disappear into the night, as silently as he had come.

Josh raised his eyebrows. "Who was that?" he asked.

"His name is Asher."

"Who's he?"

"I don't really know . . ." Her voice trailed off, and she found it difficult to concentrate on what Josh was saying as he trotted past her up the stairs.

"Karissa, did you hear me?"

"Pardon?"

"I said, do you want the Kung Pao chicken or the Mongolian beef?"

"Oh, I don't care, Josh. Let's just split them." As usual

he had bought twice as much food as they needed. His overindulgence was not limited to food but concerned every facet of their business, from decorating the gallery to buying the latest computer equipment. Josh called his extravagances "investments for the future." Karissa called them just plain extravagances and knew the gallery could not long sustain Josh's level of spending. The more pieces she sold, the more things he bought. She was tired of funding his spendthrift ways with her hard work. Josh had promised to cut back, but he was like a little boy in his lack of self-discipline.

Despairing, Karissa gained the top of the stairs, went over to her worktable, and gazed down at the clay lioness she had been working on for a week. Ebony. Perhaps that was the secret to capturing the spirit of the cat. She would buy some ebony and see what might come of it.

Two hours later Karissa and Josh closed up and left for the evening. Karissa lived in a brownstone on Montgomery Street less than half a mile from the gallery, and she was accustomed to walking back and forth alone. Tonight, however, Josh insisted on accompanying her. She always enjoyed the peaceful stroll along the avenues lined by sweeping hundred-year-old trees and stately old houses, but Josh was turning her evening walk into a noisy parade, full of jokes and anecdotes about their patrons and clients. At one time in her life she had needed jokes and laughter, and Josh had been a godsend. Her heart had been heavy and troubled then. Now she wanted more from a conversation than a good guffaw and more from a man than slapstick antics. But Josh had no other way of interacting with people. The worst part of it was, he seemed sure he was the man for her, and no matter how many times she gently turned him away, he always bounced back, more confident than ever that she would one day agree to a relationship.

More and more, Karissa found it impossible to work when Josh was around. She needed solitude, and Josh found it difficult to honor her requests for peace and quiet. She knew it was time to sever their partnership in the gallery, but in order to do that she would need money to buy him out. Most artists like herself did not make huge profits from their work; it was the ultimate sacrifice for having a career one truly enjoyed.

"As I was saying, Karissa—" Josh suddenly broke off and stopped in his tracks, half a block from her house.

Karissa stopped as well and glanced at him in surprise. "What's the matter?"

"Them." He nodded ahead to where three men in European-style business suits stood in front of a sedan that blocked the sidewalk.

Karissa surveyed the men in the light of the streetlamp. They were dark-skinned and had black hair and mustaches. Two of them were broad through the shoulders, while the third man was short and slight.

"They're watching us," Josh said out of the side of his mouth.

"Why would they do that?"

"Who knows? I doubt they're waiting to give us a sweepstakes check. They don't look the type."

"Let's cross the street," Karissa urged, "and see what they do."

Josh turned abruptly and Karissa hurried to catch up with him. She glanced over her shoulder at the men and saw one take a step toward them.

"They're coming!" she exclaimed.

Josh clutched her hand and set off at a quick walk. Karissa shot another glance backward and saw the two heavyset thugs trotting after them. Her heart pounded in alarm.

"Run!" she cried.

She and Josh dashed back toward the gallery, sprinting along the sidewalk. Josh turned into an unfamiliar street and pulled her up an alley. They ran along the narrow lane, dodging garbage cans and parked cars. But they couldn't run fast enough, and soon Karissa could hear the labored breathing of their pursuers close behind them. Adrenaline shot through her system, overriding the sharp pain in her chest as she sucked in gulps of air and forced her legs to go faster. Just as she thought she might outdistance the thugs, she tripped over a spade someone had left propped against a cement retaining wall. She landed on her shoulder and took the fall with a roll, but before she could scramble back up, one of the men grabbed her arm and wrenched her to her feet.

"Got you!" he shouted, panting. He had wide gaps between his teeth and wore a heavy cologne that reminded her of the bazaars of Cairo.

Karissa yanked her arm but he held fast. "Josh!" she screamed.

Josh skidded to a stop and turned around, just as the other man grabbed him.

The gap-toothed man squeezed Karissa's upper arm. "You are to come with us. If you cooperate, I will not have to hurt you."

"Cooperate?" Karissa glared at him. "Not on your life!" She stomped on his foot.

The thug gasped in pain but kept his grip on her arm.

"Let me go!" Karissa twisted and pulled.

He slapped her across the face. "I said cooperate!"

"Hey, now!" Josh exclaimed. "Don't go hitting her. I'm warning you—"

"Shut up, American!" The man pulled Karissa a few yards down the alley.

"What's it worth to you?" Josh demanded. "A couple hundred dollars? I can get you a couple hundred right now!"

"Shut him up, Shamir," the gap-toothed man ordered. Karissa held the side of her face, shocked by the man's brutal treatment. These men were dangerous. Were they connected to Mr. Asher? He said he was persistent. Would he resort to violence to get her back to Egypt?

The gap-toothed man dragged her toward the main street while Karissa struggled to see what Shamir would do to Josh. To her horror, she saw Shamir hit him over the head. Josh crumpled to the ground. Then Shamir picked him up, strode to the nearest Dumpster, heaved him inside, and dropped the cover with a loud clang.

Karissa hoped someone would hear all the noise and come to their assistance or at least call the police. But no one seemed to take notice of the action in the alley. She felt sick with dread.

"Let me go!" she yelled. Desperately, she dug her heels into the gravel of the lane and jerked her arm nearly out of her captor's grip. He clenched his hand around her forearm and drew a gun from his waistband.

"Shut up and quit struggling, or I'll do what Shamir did to your friend."

Karissa eyed the gun as it glinted in the darkness and then glanced down the alley where the big sedan waited for them.

"Let me go!" She twisted in his grip and ignored the flare of pain in her arm.

"Bitch!" He raised the gun to strike her.

Suddenly an unearthly snarl ripped through the night, a sound so foreign that all three of them stopped short.

"Abdullah!" Shamir gasped. His voice was pinched with terror. "It is Lord Azhur!"

"Shut up!" Abdullah ordered, but his tone was constricted as well.

Before anyone could act, a dark shape leaped from a high wall beside them and sailed through the air toward Abdullah, who clutched at Karissa's arm and nearly took her down with him. Karissa kept to her feet as she saw a streak of black soar past her and land in the alley. The streak took the form of a huge cat as the animal pinned Abdullah to the ground and then shook him by the nape of his neck until his spine snapped.

Terrified, Shamir staggered backward, holding his gun but shaking so badly he couldn't pull the trigger. In one magnificent movement, the cat leapt into the air, taking Shamir down by the throat. Karissa watched in horror as the panther opened the man's chest with one swipe of his huge paw. Shamir's cries gurgled to silence as his feet thrashed the ground. Sensing trouble, the driver of the car at the end of the alley sped away, abandoning the dead men. Then all was quiet. The cat turned around to face Karissa.

Her pounding heart lodged in her throat, choking her. Her knees shook with terror. The panther had saved her from the thugs, but for what reason? So she could become his victim as well? She met the unblinking gaze of the huge golden-brown eyes and was certain she would be the next to die.

Then a metallic noise rang out in the direction of the garbage Dumpster. The cat turned at the sound and growled deep in his throat. Karissa glanced up and saw Josh climbing out of the container.

"Josh, stop!" she cried.

Josh looked at her but didn't heed the warning. Perhaps he couldn't see the panther in the darkness. He slid down the side of the Dumpster and dropped to the ground, holding the side of his head where he had been struck. "Jesus!" he declared. "What the hell happened?"

He walked unsteadily toward her, still holding the side of his head.

"Josh, stop! There's a panther here!"

He paused when he caught sight of the shadowy form between him and Karissa. The big cat growled menacingly, lifting one side of its mouth to reveal sharp white teeth, and backed up closer to Karissa.

"My God!" Josh whispered. "What do I do?"

"Don't make any sudden moves. It just killed the two men who attacked us."

Josh glanced at the dead men and then back at the cat. He held up his hands as if to prove he meant no harm and took a step toward Karissa.

The panther growled again, more loudly this time, which convinced Josh to keep his distance.

"Okay, okay!" Josh sputtered. "I won't come any closer."

"Just stay there, Josh. Don't move. Cats are attracted by movement."

Josh stood as stiff as a statue, staring down his nose at the cat. The big panther slowly eased back until his long tail brushed against Karissa's shoes. The velvety tip of his tail flicked back and forth across her ankles, as if the cat were making sure she stayed put. She swallowed back a scream.

Minutes passed. Karissa felt a sheen of sweat between her skin and her silk shirt. Still the cat stood guard. Stood guard! Did he see Josh as a threat? Could the cat be protecting her? Karissa took a few steps backward. The cat paced sideways, positioning himself between her and Josh, but made no move to stop her. Heartened, she stepped backward again. The cat moved with her.

"He thinks he needs to protect me!" she exclaimed, dizzy with relief.

"Crazy animal! What do we do?"

"I'm going to try to move to the end of the alley. Just stay where you are, and let's see what he does."

"I wouldn't do it if I were you. Once you get far enough away from me, he'll jump you."

"I don't think so. He would have hurt me by now. I'm going to keep backing up, Josh. If you get the chance to make a run for it, call the police, okay?"

"Sure, but Karissa—"

"I can sense he isn't a danger to me, Josh. I can't explain how I know. I just do." Karissa gave him a brave smile, even though she felt anything but brave inside. "If

I get to the road, I'll try to make it to my house."

"Good luck."

Slowly Karissa began her journey to the end of the alley, talking softly to the cat the entire time. The panther snarled but didn't strike out at her. He seemed more intent on keeping his body between Karissa and Josh than impeding her progress.

Karissa heaved a sigh of relief as she reached the main road. Perhaps someone would see her and come to her assistance. Unfortunately the avenue was deserted. She waved to Josh to assure him that she was still all right, and he waved back. Then she turned around and headed for her house, trusting that the panther would not attack from behind. She looked over her shoulder and saw the dark shadow slink around the corner and pad soundlessly next to her at the base of the huge elm trees. By the time she reached the stone stairs of her entryway, she had begun to think of the cat as a shadowy companion instead of a threatening beast.

She fished her keys out of her pocket and slid them in the lock. The panther watched her while his tail flicked back and forth.

"I'm going in now," she declared. "You must go away."

The cat ignored her with regal indifference.

Karissa pushed open the door and stepped into her foyer. She flipped on the lights and looked back. The panther sat down on the step and lifted its paw. She watched in amazement as the huge animal began to preen himself. Did the cat intend to stay? She hoped not. She didn't want a mankiller sitting on her doorstep.

Even though her life had been saved by the big cat, she knew she had to alert the animal control center. The panther had killed two men and couldn't be allowed to roam the streets of Baltimore.

Karissa closed the door and hurried to her phone to call the police.

TWO

After the police left Karissa's house and she had talked Josh out of spending the night on her couch to protect her, she fell into bed, exhausted. Still, she couldn't sleep. The police had listened to her account of the panther attack and grudgingly admitted that the wounds on the dead men could have been inflicted by the claws and teeth of a big cat. But they couldn't find any other evidence to support her story. Until they finished their investigation they urged her not to say anything to her neighbors about the supposed panther. Such talk could start a city-wide panic. Karissa had agreed and watched them go, feeling as if they had only half believed her story.

Long past two in the morning she was still tossing and turning when she accidentally knocked the framed photograph of her grandmother onto the floor. Blearily she turned on her lamp, fumbled for the silver frame, and held the photo toward the light to look at the picture she loved so well. Her half-Egyptian grandmother, dressed in flapper clothes complete with cloche hat, sat listening to a Victrola while smoking on the deck of a ship sailing down the Nile. The photograph represented everything her American grandmother hated: the Egyptian blood that was considered a blight on the family tree, a woman smoking or doing anything even remotely unladylike, faddish clothes, and people who defied convention by marrying out of their class. Had Karissa been raised by her Egyptian grandmother, she might have had a happier childhood. But she had been taken in by her blue-blooded Baltimore grandmother after the sudden death of her mother, and Grandmother Petrie had tried to wring every last ounce of defiance and individuality from Karissa's character through punishment and ridicule.

Karissa sighed and set the silver frame on the night-stand. No matter how much she had been punished for her spirited character, no one could take away her physical resemblance to Menmet, her Egyptian grandmother. She had the same black hair and golden skin that had made her grandmother famous in her day. She even had the peculiar birthmark at the base of her skull, which she had been told was a trait peculiar to her Egyptian heritage. No one ever saw the red splotch, because it was hidden in her hairline, but Karissa often thought of the mark and was secretly pleased by this physical bond to her Egyptian roots.

Karissa lay back on her pillow. Now that her marriage was over and Thomas's death a faint memory, she was ready for something new, such as traveling to romantic lands and meeting people from different cultures. She wanted to pursue a life that truly fascinated her. Was her life here in Baltimore at the gallery the one she should be leading? More and more she didn't think so.

Karissa woke up at nine the next morning, only an hour before the gallery was due to open. She hurried through her shower and skipped her usual morning coffee. She threw on a pair of black leggings, a black scoop-necked body shirt, and a new blanket jacket in a planets- and-stars motif that she had bought to ward off the fall chill. She grabbed her purse, opened the door, and nearly stepped on a pigeon lying on the threshold.

Karissa stared down at the bird. It was dead, poor thing. Had it fallen from overhead? Karissa looked up at the gutter two stories above. How had the bird managed to fall at an angle so that it landed on her doormat? It didn't seem possible. Perhaps one of the neighbor cats had killed the pigeon and left it there. Karissa shrugged, went back inside for some newspaper, and rolled up the dead bird. Then she carried it to the rear of the house and carefully placed it in the garbage can.

She set off down the sidewalk toward the gallery, keeping alert for any signs of the sedan from last night. The police had tried to convince her that the attack was random, perhaps even a case of mistaken identity. But Karissa was convinced that the men had some connection to Mr. Asher.

The autumn morning was overcast and breezy, and leaves scuttled across the walk and over her shoes. Karissa hugged her jacket around her and increased her pace. At the corner she spied a man in black standing near a newspaper stand. Could it be Mr. Asher? Alarm shot through her, and she stepped off the curb to avoid him but noticed that he had begun to walk at an angle to intercept her. Karissa looked around frantically, thankful to see a handful of people on the street. She could call for help if he accosted her. Still, she kept her walk brisk and ignored his approach.

Asher spotted Karissa Spencer at the same instant she caught sight of him. If she had been surrounded by a hundred people he still would have recognized her in the

crowd, for she carried herself with a certain aloof pride—
a mark of nobility in his day. Karissa was also tall and
slender, which lent a fluid litheness to her movements.
And there was no mistaking her hair either, the luxuriant black veil that hung to her waist. Yesterday he had
almost reached out and stroked the shining ebony tresses.
He was glad he had controlled himself, because he was
quite certain that Karissa Spencer would have taken
offense at such a gesture. Perhaps she didn't let any man
stroke her. The possibility pleased him.

"Miss Spencer!" he called as she gained the other side
of the avenue. She acted as if she didn't hear him.

Karissa saw Asher cross the road and increased her pace.
Then he leapt from the curb to the sidewalk in an easy
spring that she couldn't help admiring. The man was
inordinately graceful.

"Miss Spencer!" He strode up to her and matched her
pace. "You should not be walking unescorted."

"I can take care of myself, Mr. Asher." She glared
straight ahead. She didn't like persistent people, especially attractive persistent men. Her husband had been
attractive, and she would forever regret the way she had
succumbed to him.

Nevertheless, Karissa glanced at the man beside her.

He wore his hair pulled back and tied at the nape of
his neck. Both earlobes were pierced but he sported no
earrings. The collar of a black silk shirt showed beneath
his expensive overcoat. Such dark clothing would make
most men look sallow and pale, but black only intensified the deep golden tones of Mr. Asher's complexion
and highlighted the flash of his teeth and eyes. She
couldn't imagine him wearing any other color, except for
white, which would produce the same effect.

Asher returned her look, and she was struck by the
warmth and intelligence in his golden-brown eyes. They

were bordered by long dark lashes and attractive laugh lines—definitely not the hard eyes of a criminal. He broke off the glance and looked straight ahead.

"I heard about your trouble last night."

"Oh? How?"

"There was an account in the morning paper."

"I'm surprised. The attack happened so late."

"True. It never ceases to amaze me how quickly news travels in this day and age, Miss Spencer."

"Or perhaps you know about it because you were there."

Asher stopped. "Do you think I had something to do with the attack?"

"Yes. Those men were Egyptians."

"They have no connection to me."

"I'll bet."

"They worked for a man named Mustofa. He is a dangerous man who, I am afraid, has followed me to your country."

"Why?"

"Come." He took her elbow before she realized he had even reached for her. "Let us keep walking while I explain. The sooner you get off the street, the better."

"Why? What is this all about?"

"The tomb I mentioned yesterday lies in a place called the Valley of the Damned. In the valley are many other tombs, most of which have probably gone undetected by grave robbers. There is a fortune to be found in the desert, Miss Spencer. Men like Mustofa will do anything to find those tombs, and they don't care who they torture, kidnap, or kill to meet their objective. I believe they are excavating in an area very close to the buried sphinx, and if they locate the tombs before I do, the mummy I seek will be lost to me forever."

"But how does this Mustofa character know about me?"

"His spies must have gained access to my files. But I am puzzled by how it could have happened. I have been extremely careful, especially where you are concerned."

She yanked her elbow out of his grip. "You have files on me?"

"Of course." He smiled slightly, showing a line of flawless white teeth. "I have been gathering information for years."

"Why?"

"As I said yesterday, you remain my only key to finding the tomb."

"And will you kidnap and torture me until I agree to help you?"

"My plan to elicit your aid is a nonviolent one, Miss Spencer. But as I have said, I shall be persistent."

"You're wasting your time." She strode forward, hoping to outdistance him, but he kept up with her effortlessly. "A television crew is going to be here next week to start filming a piece on my work. I have a million things to do before then."

"I see." Mr. Asher's tone was heavy with disappointment.

By that time, they had reached the gallery. She drew her keys out of her purse and unlocked the door as Asher stood by and watched her hands. Karissa opened the door, just enough to let herself in and prevent his passage, and then looked back at him. "Now, if you will excuse me, Mr. Asher, I have some work to do before the gallery opens."

He raised his glance and leveled it upon hers. Whenever she stared directly into his eyes, she felt as if her self-control slipped a notch, and found it very hard to look away. Even the soft low rumble of his voice was hypnotic. "I have a story to tell you that may change your mind, Miss Spencer."

"I doubt it."

"Nevertheless, allow me to take you to lunch this afternoon, and perhaps what I say will help you see this matter in a new light."

Karissa gripped the doorknob tightly. She hadn't eaten lunch with a man—other than Josh or a client—

for years, and never with one as mysterious and attractive as Mr. Asher. Not until this moment had she realized what a social recluse she'd become.

"Name the time," he said, "and I will call for you."

"Really, Mr. Asher. I—"

"Grant me an hour. That is all I ask."

She sighed and studied his face for signs of deceit but could see only sincerity. "Well, all right. Come back at two. If I can get away, I'll have lunch with you."

"Excellent!" He smiled again, this time with a slow sensual slant of his mouth. Karissa could imagine the strength and passion of that mouth and how his lips might feel upon hers, and her breasts tightened in a sharp twist of arousal. The sensation amazed her, not only because she was thinking of a man in sexual terms but because she was responding in such a way to a complete stranger.

When she looked back into his eyes, she saw a knowing glint there, as if he had read her mind. She should have been embarrassed to have a man share her thoughts, but with this man she didn't feel embarrassed at all. In fact, his smoldering gaze only made her ache for him more. She had the strongest urge to reach up and run her palm across his shining black hair, to stroke him, to kiss him—

"Until two, then." He inclined his head, and for a moment she thought he might ask to kiss her hand. Instead, he turned and walked noiselessly away.

Karissa sighed in relief and shut the door. Her interest in Mr. Asher was illogical and dangerous, and it was best to stay away from him. Before she took a step, however, she was grabbed from behind, her jacket was pulled halfway off, a hand was clamped over her mouth, and something jabbed her upper arm. Within seconds her world reeled into blackness.

*　　*　　*

When Karissa awoke, she found herself in a small room with plastered white walls and a peeling blue ceiling. The air in the room was so hot she found it hard to take a breath, and the white cotton shift she was draped in stuck to her in damp folds. Woozy and nauseated, Karissa struggled to sit up from the mat where she had been sleeping on the floor. At the movement, cockroaches scuttled across the tile and up the walls.

Karissa cried out in disgust and jumped to her feet, swaying as she fought for balance. Where was she? She blinked and looked down at the long white garment. Who had dressed her in an Egyptian *galabia*? And why was it so oppressively hot? She stumbled to the small barred window and stood on tiptoe to peer out. All she could see was an incredibly blue sky, with no hint of clouds, and the fringe of a palm leaf from a tree nearby. Karissa lowered herself from the window as a dark feeling of unease spread over her. There was no sky like the Egyptian sky. And no heat as dry and intense as the heat off the blowing Sahara Desert. Somehow, she must have been transported to the valley of the Nile. She sank against the wall, stunned that she had been so easily kidnapped and taken to a foreign country. But by whom?

The answer wasn't long in coming. Soon after she awakened, a thin man with a gun opened the door and ordered her out of the room. She tried to speak to him, but he seemed to know little English. Frustrated, Karissa stumbled through the door, still feeling groggy and clumsy. They must have given her an injection at the gallery and kept her drugged for days.

A wave of rage passed over her. Reluctantly she walked behind the man across a dusty courtyard with a broken fountain and then into a yellow house on the other side of the compound. Relieved to be out of the heat, but suffering a raging thirst, Karissa followed her guide and was shown into a small parlor off the main hall. A short, gaunt man with prominent brown eyes stood near the window, smoking a foul-smelling cigarette. He turned at her entrance and smiled, taking a long drag on the cigarette as he watched Karissa cross the floor toward him. He was balding and had a thin black mustache that traced the line of his full upper lip. His clothes appeared well made, but his white jacket and trousers were slightly out of date. He wore expensive crocodile shoes but smoked cheap tobacco, by the smell of it. The smoke nauseated her.

"Ah, Miss Spencer," he said.

"Mr. Mustofa, I presume?" She was so angry she could barely force out the words.

He smiled as if pleased that she knew his name and nodded as he held his hands up, palms together, in front of his face. Though the gesture was one of respect, it lost considerable effect because of the cigarette poking through two fingers on his right hand.

"Who do you think you are? Drugging me and taking me halfway across the world!"

"Had you not resisted, I would not have had to resort to such tactics, Miss Spencer."

He stepped to a side table and lifted an earthenware pitcher. With great deliberation he poured a glass of water. "I would expect that you are thirsty?"

She answered him with a haughty glare. She wanted to snatch the glass from his hand but stood where she was, unwilling to be manipulated. Mr. Mustofa smiled and took a long appreciative drink. Her entire attention focused on the sparkling glass and the slow bob of his Adam's apple.

When he finished, he let out a sigh of satisfaction. "You may have all the water you like, Miss Spencer. And it is bottled water, by the way. But first you must promise to help me." He set the glass down on a nearby table. She followed the movement with burning eyes.

"Help you do what?"

Mustofa came around the table. "I want you to show

me where a certain valley is, one you stumbled upon as a young woman."

"You expect me to help you, after you treat me like this?"

"You have no choice." Mustofa pointed the cigarette at her to emphasize his words. "You are my prisoner, Miss Spencer. And until you show me where the ruins of the lost sphinx are located, you will not have anything to eat or drink. Do you understand?"

"And if I can't remember?"

"I will know you are lying, because"—he tapped two fingertips on the side of his balding head—"I have been informed that you have a prodigious memory."

"If you think I can remember everything, you're a bigger fool than you look!"

Mustofa's black brows came together in a scowl. Abruptly, he turned. "Walaal!" he barked.

The door burst open and the thin man with the gun hurried into the room.

"Get this slut out of my sight. I do not want to see her until morning."

"Yes, Mr. Mustofa." Walaal grabbed Karissa's left arm but she jerked away.

"Keep your hands off me!" she said, realizing the guard had deceived her about not knowing English. He understood every word Mustofa had said.

"And do not let her talk you into giving her food or water. She will have nothing until she learns better manners."

"Yes, Mr. Mustofa."

"Starving me will get you nowhere," Karissa retorted. "I am worth nothing to you dead."

He turned around, his bony face flushed with anger. "You are worth even less if your memory is faulty. So use the coming hours to think, Miss Spencer. I am sure if you try, you can dredge up many childhood memories."

Karissa swept out of the room, shoulders straight and

head held high. She was not about to cooperate with a bully like Mustofa, even if she ever did remember the lost sphinx. She would have to find some way of escape.

Asher hailed a taxi at the airport and jumped in the back. Though the car was air-conditioned, he felt a sheen of sweat beneath his suit. Already the sun hung low in the sky, which meant he didn't have much time in which to find Karissa Spencer. Because of his worry for the American woman, he had made risky travel arrangements and had prayed the plane would touch down at the Luxor airport before the sun sank behind the western cliffs. Now he was praying Karissa was being held at Mustofa's compound, because he could probably reach the place before sunset. Still, to Asher, the traffic seemed to crawl through town.

The taxi rolled to a stop in front of a small yellow house behind a high wall. Asher dropped a large pound note in the driver's hand and slipped out of the cab.

"Keep the change," Asher said, not wanting to take the time to haggle over the fare.

"And your bags, sir?"

His bags. In his haste, Asher had completely forgotten about the three leather suitcases in the trunk of the taxi. "Take them to this address, will you?" He slipped his hand in his pocket and drew out a business card, then dipped into his wallet for another bill. "Here. This should cover it."

"Yes, sir."

The taxi pulled away from the cracked sidewalk just as a ringing began in Asher's ears—the first sign that the sun had melted into the horizon. Then all the noises around him roared to life as a more primal, acute hearing kicked in.

*   *   *

In Karissa's prison cell the hours dragged on, interrupted only by the scuttling cockroaches and the call to prayer by the Islamic muezzin at sunset and then again as the shadows of night crept into her small chamber. Cool air off the Nile drifted in through her window, bringing with it the aroma of street vendor food and the sounds of people taking their evening strolls, laughing and talking in the distance, too far away to hear the muffled scream of a woman imprisoned on the outskirts of town. Karissa knew it would be useless to cry out and she would probably get punished by the guard if she tried. Hopeless and frustrated, she stretched out on the mat and drifted in and out of sleep, feverish with thirst and weak from hunger.

Sometime during the night, Karissa awoke to the sound of voices. Her guard was talking with someone. She sat up and listened, trying to remember the Arab phrases she had learned as a child, but couldn't make sense of the conversation. Soon, however, she deduced that Walaal was being relieved by a new guard, whose voice was much raspier.

Karissa waited until Walaal left and then knocked on the door. "Sir?" she called. She heard a rustling sound and a metallic clink.

"Yes?" came a raspy reply in English.

"Please, may I have a drink of water? I am so thirsty."

"Well . . ."

She heard the lock turn over and stepped back as the door was pulled open. Standing in the moonlight was a burly man with a grizzled face and a dirty rag wrapped around his head. At the sight of her, he grinned and his eyes lit up.

"Well, well, well!"

Instantly, she regretted her request. The guard took a step toward her but she held her ground.

"A drink, eh?" He chuckled. "That could be arranged, my little flower blossom—for a price."

"I have no money."

"I am willing to barter. It is the way we do things here in Luxor." His grin widened, displaying teeth stained by nicotine. Karissa blinked back her disgust. She calculated the distance between his large body and the open door. If she could entice him farther into the chamber and switch places with him, she might be able to escape. But did she have the strength to run?

Still, this might be her only chance to get away. She brushed back a strand of hair and lowered her voice seductively. "What did you care to exchange?"

"What do you think?" The guard's eyebrows raised in delight as he ambled forward. "A taste of you for a taste of water."

She ducked away and turned, so that her back was to the door and he was no longer between her and the outside world. He laughed, obviously enjoying the game.

"First, my drink."

"Oh, you are hard ones, you American girls."

She nodded and kept her distance as he chuckled and went back outside. He returned with an old plastic bleach container. The thought of putting her lips to the discolored rim of the bottle nearly made her retch, but her thirst overrode her disgust.

"There you go, my flower." The guard held out the bottle.

She tipped it to her lips and let the tepid water fill her parched mouth. In great gulps she drank, forgetting to take it easy, until the guard pulled away the bottle, laughing.

"Do not drink too much! You will be sick." He capped the bottle. "I do not want you puking all over me when I am—" He made a lewd thrust with his hips. Karissa wiped her mouth with the back of her hand and watched him warily. He leaned over to set the bottle on the floor and reached for his gun to lay it on the tile as well, and at that moment Karissa lunged for the door.

The water and fear gave her the strength to run. She dashed through the door and across the courtyard, hunting for a gate in the high wall. The guard pounded behind her. Within seconds, Karissa knew her starved body was quickly losing power and she would never outdistance him. Frantically she ran along the base of the wall, praying she wouldn't step on a scorpion or snake in the darkness.

Suddenly the guard grabbed her from behind. She tumbled to the sandy ground on hands and knees. The guard pushed her hard in the small of her back, shoving her facedown in the dirt

"Get off me, you lout!"

"You are going to like this." He chuckled and fumbled with his pants. "American men are sissies. But we Egyptians are men, real men."

He grabbed her elbow and wrenched her over onto her back. He grinned. "We take what we want and our women love it!"

"Like hell!" Karissa glared at him and kicked wildly, trying to hurt him.

He only laughed and clamped a dirty hand over her mouth. She pummeled him with her fists, but her blows seemed to have no effect on him.

Suddenly a menacing growl rolled out of the shadows. The guard grunted in surprise and raised his head.

The growl came again, louder this time.

"Who is there!" the guard demanded.

A dark shape materialized from behind a clump of mimosa trees, and a huge black cat came toward them with measured footfalls. The panther was in no hurry, as if he was certain his prey was incapable of escape. He padded closer, his shoulder blades flowing up and down like the well-oiled pistons of a killing machine, and his eyes were uncompromisingly cold.

"Lord Azhur!" the guard gasped. He lumbered to his feet. "Please, Lord—"

The panther bunched his muscles and leapt upward.

THREE

Karissa scrambled to her feet as the big cat lunged at the guard. It looked like the same black panther that had saved her life in Baltimore. If so, how had he traveled to Egypt from the United States? Perhaps it wasn't a real cat at all. She half expected to wake up from a nightmare and find herself at home in Baltimore.

Yet the scrapes on her knees and the sand in her hair were very real, as was the body being dragged into the clump of mimosas near the wall.

Despite what had happened, Karissa realized her first concern had to be getting out of the compound. She glanced up at the high wall rising three feet above her head and knew she could never scale it. She would have to find a gate. Fighting a ringing in her ears and a shakiness in her legs, she stumbled forward.

Within moments, she felt a presence behind her and glanced backward to see the panther loping to her side. Instead of walking alongside her, the panther guided her to a small portal. Karissa opened the wooden door and stepped into a lane that led to a littered alley bordered by tall apartments and shops strung together with clotheslines and electrical wires. She paused, having no idea what to do or which way to go, especially in the middle of the night with no money and no identification. The cat seemed to have an agenda of his own, however, and padded ahead, stopping to look back at her. He blinked and his tail flicked back and forth as he waited.

Karissa decided to follow his lead. After all, the cat had now saved her life on two occasions. She walked after him. As he moved stealthily through the quiet Luxor streets, past sleepy houses, darkened apartment buildings, closed bazaars, and ghostly mosques, she struggled to keep up with him. Other than following the cat, she had no alternative but to throw herself on the mercy of the U.S. Embassy, which she decided to do in the morning, should the panther lead her astray.

The city stretched endlessly along the river. Soon her steps were dragging. She was still thirsty and hungry. She had used her reserves to fight off the guard, and now she was operating purely on determination and pride. But how many more steps could she will herself to take?

As if the cat read her mind, he stopped at a shadowed alcove and sat on his haunches, waiting for her to catch up. Karissa could hear the musical tinkle of water and her spirits rose. The panther had led her to a small fountain attached to the side of a building. She could see the stream of water, glinting in the moonlight. Karissa almost cried out in gratitude as she thrust her hands into the water and cupped mouthful after mouthful to her lips. Her mother's frequent warning not to drink unbottled water ran through her thoughts, but in her desperation Karissa ignored the voice and chanced illness.

Feeling much better after quenching her thirst, Karissa again trailed after the cat. Soon the panther turned down a tree-lined street that took them south of town. The city became a sprawl, with the houses farther apart, and here and there an irrigated field bordered the road. The cat veered to the right and padded down a smaller lane that headed toward the Nile, which gleamed in the distance. Karissa stumbled after him, sure she would last only a few more minutes. She had never felt so weak.

They passed between two pillars and continued down an avenue toward a two-story house surrounded by the graceful trunks and drooping fronds of date palms. She followed the panther to the front of the house, up the wide granite steps, and onto the veranda. The cat took her to the front door and then sat down.

Karissa glanced at the panther. "Now what?" she asked, unsure why they were at this residence. Did he expect her to knock on the door?

Before Karissa could decide what to do, she felt a swirling sensation in her head and her vision sparkled and tipped. She staggered sideways and then crumpled to the cool granite slab of the porch.

When she woke up, she was lying in a clean bed that was draped in a festoon of mosquito netting. Startled to be in unfamiliar surroundings, Karissa lurched to a sitting position and glanced around. She was in a large room tastefully decorated in brass and wood and potted plants. A half-empty glass of water stood on the bedside table. She couldn't remember getting into the bed, much less drinking the water. Had someone helped her do both things? Rays of morning sunlight slanted through the open doors of the balcony and poured across the blue oriental carpet. She must have been sleeping for hours.

Karissa slipped out of the bed and teetered for a moment, light-headed with hunger, and caught a glimpse of something white just beyond the French doors of the balcony. Holding her head, she walked across the thick carpet and looked down to see a dead ibis on the pale tile. She turned away in dismay that another dead creature had been left on her doorstep. But hunger and curiosity concerning her whereabouts soon overtook all thought of the bird. She was desperate for food and drink and hoped the master who ruled this house would be more accommodating than Mr. Mustofa.

Just as she decided to crawl back into the bed, she heard a light rap on the bedroom door.

"Miss Spencer?" A heavily accented female voice spoke from the other side.

"Yes?"

"Would you like some breakfast?"

Would she? Her salivary glands leaped into action at the mere mention of food.

"Yes!" She hurried to open the door. In the hall stood a small pudgy woman with black hair plaited in a braid that hung to her hips. She was probably in her fifties and had huge dark-brown eyes that glistened with kindness. But what caught Karissa's attention and held it was the tray of food the woman carried into the room.

"I am Eisha, the housekeeper."

"You know who I am?"

Eisha nodded and moved across the room to a small table. "My master has told me of you."

"Your master? And who might he be?"

"My master will wish to tell you himself. But he does not rise until midday. While you wait, you must eat and bathe and rest."

Karissa didn't appreciate the mystery surrounding her host and didn't admire a man who slept late, but she kept her views to herself. For now she would take advantage of his hospitality, if only to fortify herself for another escape. She stared ravenously at the plates of food Eisha uncovered: cold meats, pickles, savory *ful* beans and bread, and a mound of steaming scrambled eggs. Out of a silver coffee carafe drifted the wonderful aroma of strong

Egyptian coffee, flavored with cloves. The smell nearly made her swoon.

"I am not accustomed to American breakfasts," Eisha said, setting a place at the table. "Is this satisfactory?"

"It looks wonderful!" Karissa smiled shakily.

Eisha straightened. "When you are done, just ring the little bell." She gestured to a brass bell on the tray. "I will prepare a nice bath for you."

"Thank you." She pulled off a piece of bread and consumed it without chewing it more than three times. Next came a pickle and a forkful of egg. While Karissa ate, Eisha carefully poured her a cup of coffee. Karissa tried the spicy beans and washed them down with a long sip of fragrant coffee. In only moments she felt the empowering effect of the food. She turned to the housekeeper.

"Eisha, I need to get back to the United States. Is there a phone somewhere that I could use?"

"Yes. But eat first and then you may make your arrangements. I am sure my master wants you to stay until he has a chance to speak with you."

Karissa wondered if she had merely exchanged her miserably hot cell in the middle of Luxor for a more luxurious one. But she decided to finish the meal and ask questions later.

At half-past noon, Karissa walked down the hall toward the garden, where the master of the house awaited. Eisha had helped her make arrangements for money to be wired to a hotel in Luxor. Then Karissa had phoned Josh to tell him where she was and give him the phone number and address of the house in which she was staying. But Josh wasn't at home or at the gallery, and she was forced to leave a message on the answering machine. When she was done, she decided to wait for the master of the house to stir before she thanked him and went on her way.

Since her Western clothes had been stripped away by Mustofa, Karissa had been given a linen dress by Eisha to replace the dirty *galabia*. The garment was a lovely wrap of the finest gossamer, more filmy and feminine than anything she had ever worn. It was pleated in a way that concealed her while at the same time affording the barest covering in the heat. Instead of feeling awkward in the foreign attire, Karissa experienced a strange sensation of déjà vu, as if she had worn such a dress before, though she knew very well that she had not.

She walked toward that door which opened onto the garden. Near the door was a bird cage filled with chattering finches. A few steps away, another cage contained two falcons. More cages were scattered throughout the garden, all filled with birds native to Egypt, from hoopoe birds to swallows. Karissa's heart went out to the creatures. Though they lived in a beautiful garden and were obviously well cared for, they were still prisoners, just as she was. Beyond a tinkling fountain, she could barely make out the figure of a man through the leaves of the trees. She stepped toward him, intending to offer her thanks and then leave immediately.

Asher heard a light step behind him, turned around, and was struck speechless by the sight of Karissa Spencer in the linen gown. She walked toward him and he was lost. All he could see was the woman he had loved thousands of years ago: Senefret. Through the branches of the sycamore figs came a mirage from his past—a tall, fine-boned, exquisitely beautiful woman dressed in purest white. He stared as his heart leapt in his chest. Ah, beautiful Senefret! She was even more lovely than his memory of her.

For a long moment he let himself succumb to the vision and slipped into the past, where he had known the woman he had loved with all his heart. But as Karissa drew closer, he pushed the vision from his thoughts. It was unfair to himself and to Karissa to invest the American woman with the persona of an Egyptian beauty long since dead.

Long since dead but not forgotten, Asher's heart reminded him. Until that moment he had been able to ignore the anguish buried inside him, but one look at Karissa and the heartache roared up like the hot blinding sandstorm of the Sahara—the *khamsin*. The pain in his chest nearly sent him to his knees.

When Karissa drew closer and recognized him, her expression changed from open interest to dark suspicion, and the mirage vanished.

"Mr. Asher!" she exclaimed in disgust, stopping at the fountain a few feet away. "I should have known!"

"Miss Spencer," he replied, ignoring her angry remark. "Good afternoon." His tongue tripped over the English words, which never came naturally to him, no matter how many years he spoke the choppy language.

Karissa's scowl deepened, shadowing her luminous dark-brown eyes and wrinkling the flesh above her delicate pointed nose. He had the wildest urge to press his lips to the wrinkle and smooth it with a kiss, but he knew such a gesture would only infuriate her.

"You had this planned all along!" she continued, stepping forward in anger. "The thugs, the kidnapping, the rescue by your trained panther—"

"Trained panther?"

"Yes! The cat that kills people and leaves gifts at my doorstep. You could be arrested for manslaughter, you know, owning a dangerous pet like that."

"I have no such pet, Miss Spencer, I assure you."

"Then what brought me here last night?"

"Whatever it was, it was no pet."

"It seemed to know where you live."

He shrugged off the insinuation and smiled, mesmerized by the soft sloping curve between her nose and lip. Her mouth moved enticingly whenever she spoke, drawing down the tip of her nose. He wanted to touch that nose with his, to feel her lips upon his skin, to discover the taste of her neck. His loins stirred, almost painfully. In the sixteen years he had been in Luxor, he had never encountered a woman who could make his blood race like this one. He forced himself to glance away.

"Are you rested?" he asked, changing the subject. "Did you get enough to eat?"

"Yes, but don't think you can buy my cooperation with the bed-and-breakfast routine. I appreciate the hospitality, Mr. Asher, but I've made arrangements to leave. Tonight."

He sighed. "Even so, can I not interest you in lunch? You agreed to meet me for lunch in Baltimore and to hear what I have to say. Will you not honor that agreement in Luxor?"

"Why? It's useless." She swept away from him, turning her back.

"Useless? In what way?" Asher's gaze traveled down the shapely curves of her hips and legs as he imagined how it would feel to press against her slender length. His loins quickened again and he breathed in sharply.

"Nothing you say could bring back my lost memory. Half a dozen doctors have done everything they know to induce me to remember. But I just can't."

"You can't or you won't, Miss Spencer?"

She turned slowly to face him, and her expression was as cold as marble. "What are you implying?"

"That you don't want to face the truth. That there is something about the sphinx you don't want to remember."

"Well, it's easy to see why, isn't it? My mother died from the curse of the sphinx, and my father mysteriously disappeared."

"Oh?" Asher crossed his arms and tilted his head. "Did your father really disappear, Miss Spencer?"

He studied her face, searching for the truth in her reaction. She stared at him, her eyes wide. For an instant a tense silence hung between them, and then she whirled around and stomped to the fountain. Asher followed her, determined to help her remember. He would have reached for her bare shoulders, but she turned and glared at him.

"Leave me alone, Mr. Asher!"

"I want to help you."

"So I can help you find the sphinx. What a sterling motive, sir!" In disdain, she presented her back to him again.

"I may be the only one who can help you remember, Miss Spencer."

"And why are you so special?"

"Because." He leaned forward, closed his eyes, and breathed in the perfume of her hair. Every particle of his body wanted to experience the woman standing so tantalizingly nearby. "I was there that night."

He saw her entire body go rigid.

"Yes," he went on, "I was there. And I think I can guess what happened to your father."

"You are wrong," she finally replied in a thick tone. "No one else was there. Just me and then later my mother."

"Perhaps you were not aware of my presence."

"No!" Karissa shook her head vehemently. "I saw nothing! No one!"

"Some things are not what they appear to be, especially when seen through the eyes of a child."

"I wasn't a child. I was twelve years old!"

"A child nevertheless." He softened his tone. "You were a little girl who saw something she could not fit into the world she knew. So you chose not to define it or examine it ever again."

"I don't know what you're talking about!" She glared at him and he realized she was about to bolt. He grabbed her wrist to stop her.

"Let me go!" she shouted.

"Not until you look at the truth. You know what happened at the sphinx, Miss Spencer. Admit it to yourself! Take back that missing part of your life."

"No!" She yanked her arm, but he held her tightly.

His heart ached to see the pain in her face, but he pressed on, determined to finish what he had begun. "You saw something you cannot face."

"No!"

"Yes, Miss Spencer."

She shook her head and then covered her face with her free hand. Huge sobs heaved in her chest and she hunched over, miserable. Was the truth finally reaching her?

"You have it all wrong—"

"How was it, then?" he inquired gently. "Tell me."

"I can't. I can't!" Tears streamed down her cheeks. He released her wrist, and she covered her face with both hands as if ashamed to be seen crying.

An overwhelming surge of compassion washed over Asher. He couldn't let her stand there alone, suffering, so he reached out and surrounded her in a gentle embrace, tucking her against his chest until her tears subsided. To his amazement, she let herself be drawn to him. Asher sank his hand into the thick mass of her raven hair and urged her to lean her head against his chest while he slowly stroked her back. His body sang to her surrender as she placed her small palms on his torso and let her weight sink into him. He breathed in her scent and slowly increased the pressure of his embrace. He couldn't help himself. Though his aim was to offer her comfort, he couldn't deny his need for her.

Isis, how he longed to kiss her! He lowered his head and brushed the tip of his nose across the hair at her temple. At the movement, she turned her head and his jaw grazed her cheek. Asher's breath caught in his throat as her smooth skin passed over his. For a heart-thudding instant, she allowed her cheek to linger against his, and a tiny sigh escaped her lips.

"Karissa!" he said, his voice rough with passion. He pulled back to look at her. She glanced up at him in surprise, with tears clustered on her black lashes.

For a moment he stared down at her. He had no wish to denigrate her grief and remembrance by initiating intimate physical contact between them. And he had no intention of forcing himself on a woman who wasn't interested in his attentions. But for an instant he saw the light of desire flicker in her glance and knew he had not misinterpreted her sigh.

With a low moan born of loneliness and hunger, he gathered her up in his arms and bent to her tear-streaked face.

FOUR

The kiss began as a gentle press of his lips upon hers, but when he tasted the lushness of her mouth he couldn't stop. Karissa's lips were like a perfectly ripe plum—dark, luscious, soft, and wonderfully sweet. As he pulled her even closer, he heard her sigh again. The wistful sound set him on fire. Asher pushed his hand into her hair, reveling in the way the silky strands slipped between his fingers. The women he had known in the ancient days had worn ornate braided wigs, perfumed by cones made of animal fat that were placed on the tops of their heads. A man could not caress such coifs with the freedom afforded by Karissa's naturally luxuriant hair. He cradled her head with his palm as she leaned back to accept him. Then he slanted an intense kiss upon her, using his tongue to stroke the line between her lips until she allowed him entrance to her warm mouth.

It was Asher's turn to sigh this time, and the raggedness of the sound shocked him. What kind of hold did this American woman have on him, that he was so eager to give himself to her? He wanted her more than he had ever wanted a woman, even more than—

Asher broke off the thought and slipped his tongue into Karissa's mouth. He felt her exploring him, tentatively at first and then with a boldness that inflamed him. The kiss grew harder, hotter, wilder. Karissa's hands released their grip on his white cotton shirt and slid up his torso. She curved her arms around his neck and hugged him fiercely, grinding against his mouth as if she had hungered for him for thousands of years. Her passion took him completely by surprise. And yet, one night long ago Senefret had reacted to his kiss in just this way.

Karissa's breasts pressed against his chest, and he could feel the hard buds of her nipples. The thought that she was already aroused made him grow as hard as granite. He closed his eyes and the line blurred between this woman and the woman from his past, as he let his body surge to life for the first time in over a decade. Then he slowly slipped his hands down the graceful slope of her back and cupped her rump, pulling her against him and leaving no doubt as to his desire for her. She swayed in to him, perfectly formed to fit against him, which only made him ache for her more. Karissa sighed in his ear, driving him mad with her sweet warm breath, until he couldn't resist lifting her up slightly, just enough to ease her over his burgeoning flesh. He sucked in a long and tortured breath and fought the urge to make love to her right there in the garden. He had no right to ask that of her. In fact he had no right at all to kiss her and hold her like this.

Sighing, he let her slide back to the ground. He pulled away from her mouth and gazed down at her, surprised that he could have reacted so strongly. After a moment, she released his neck and let her hands slip down the front of his shirt as she glanced up. The plum of her mouth looked delightfully crushed.

Off in the distance someone called to him, but the summons barely registered. Asher drew his hands away from her back and lightly grasped her elbows, denying himself the pleasure of kissing her again. If he tasted her mouth once more, he knew it would be impossible to let her go.

"Are you all right?" he asked softly, not sure whether he referred to her emotional outburst—which seemed to have occurred hours ago—or to the passion that had just flared between them.

Karissa nodded and blushed and stepped away from him. "Isn't that Eisha calling you, Mr. Asher?" she asked in an endearingly uneven voice.

Asher glanced at the garden entrance where his housekeeper stood, holding a tray of food, and then returned his attention to Karissa. He ran the pad of his thumb along her cheekbone in a gentle caress.

"To you my name is Asheris." He put the accent on the middle syllable, which made a sound like the wind in the desert.

"A-*share*-iss." She let the name slip softly through her teeth.

He smiled quietly, pleased to hear his real name on her lips. "Come," he said, guiding her forward with a light touch on her lower back. "Take the midday meal with me so that we may talk."

Karissa strolled beside him to a secluded table near the fountain. There she spent the late luncheon in a strange state of disquiet, worried that by kissing Mr. Asher—Asheris—she had lost her objectivity in regard to him. She was also concerned that he would bring up the lost sphinx again, and she couldn't bear to think about that. He had taken her dangerously close to the edge of remembrance, and she wasn't ready to advance any further. Compounding the other two concerns was the fact that though she was physically and mentally distracted by the man sitting across the table from her, she could not afford to waste her time gawking at him. She intended to listen to his story and go back to Baltimore.

Karissa ate sparingly, too keyed up to be hungry for food. As she nibbled, she couldn't help recalling the passion she had just experienced in Asheris's arms. But what emotion could be in a man's heart for a woman he had known for mere hours? She had learned to be wary of men who displayed deep passion for no apparent reason, and had vowed never to fall for a charmer again. It seemed to be a family weakness to succumb to handsome men, and she was determined to break the chain.

She peeled a pomegranate with deft fingers as she worried about her feelings for the graceful, elegant Egyptian across from her. There was more than shallow attraction for him in her heart, so much more that she experienced a sudden swell of tenderness whenever she glanced at him. The undeniable attraction was intensified by a curious feeling of familiarity—that she already knew Asheris as an old friend, that she was accustomed to the width of his shoulders, the intelligent tilt of his head, and the slow sensual slant of his smile. Yet it was silly to think she already knew him. Such thoughts were for foolish romantics who believed in love at first sight.

As if he could read her thoughts, Asheris looked up from his plate and gazed at her, his eyes full of warmth. She returned the gaze, wondering why she wasn't nervous when staring at a man for minutes on end. She had never understood the words "falling into someone's eyes," but now she knew precisely what the phrase meant, for she felt herself plunging into Asheris's soul and had no power to hold herself back.

"I am supposed to be convincing you to help me," he declared at last, breaking a piece of flat bread apart and giving half to her.

She accepted it. "Yes. You mentioned something about a story."

"Indeed." His smile faded as he tore off a piece of bread and chewed it slowly. For a long moment he stared at a grove of acacia trees in his garden, but she could tell that his eyes weren't seeing the trees at all. He was contemplating the telling of his story as if to choose the right words, and from the look in his eyes the story was not a happy one. Perhaps nothing connected to the lost sphinx was pleasant.

"Is it a true story?" she asked.

"Yes. From long ago." He set down the bread. "It concerns my—ancestors."

The pause made her wonder if the story was connected to something or someone much closer than Asheris's ancestors. But she said nothing and waited for him to begin.

He sighed and raised his incredible eyes to meet hers. "A long time ago there was a beautiful young priestess named Senefret. She had been raised by the worshipers of Sekhmet, the lion goddess, to become the great royal wife of the king, but she did not want to marry him. He was an ugly misshapen man given to bouts of insanity, which, I have learned from modern science, was probably the result of intermarriage. You know, do you not, that Egyptian kings often wedded their sisters?"

"Yes, I've heard that."

"Unfortunately, the practice weakened the stock in many cases. So it was for the king. And Senefret did not want to spend her life married to such a monster, even though it would bring her glory and wealth."

"Sometimes glory and wealth aren't worth the sacrifice," Karissa noted, thinking of Grandmother Petrie and her sterile life.

"Agreed." Asheris chewed another bite of bread and went on. "So Senefret decided to take her fate into her own hands. She was a brave woman with a bold spirit, and she ran off to the northeastern border, where her older brother, who was a general in the Egyptian army, was fighting nomadic invaders. She was certain her brother would help her escape her marriage, but when she got to the border, she found him suffering from a mortal wound, and he died in her arms. Grief-stricken and knowing she had lost her only supporter, Senefret decided to die fighting. The following morning she donned the general's battle gear and, masquerading as her brother, rode to war next to the commander in chief of the army, who was half brother to the king and a great favorite of the people. During the course of the battle, she saved the commander in chief's life, and he, in turn, snatched her out of danger just as she was about to receive a fatal arrow. They rode back to camp together in the commander's chariot. A bath was drawn and wine poured, and the commander insisted that the young general join him in a toast while he bathed. The commander stripped, unknowingly revealing his well-conditioned soldier's body to the virginal priestess. Instead of turning away, Senefret decided to find out what it would be like to have a real man before she died in battle or was shipped back to Thebes. She removed her man's clothing and offered herself to him.

"The commander did not know who she was or where she had come from, and she refused to tell him. She asked that he kiss her, not question her, and the commander willingly granted her request, for she was a beautiful woman and her bravery on the field had impressed him mightily. For an entire night they made love. Then, before the camp awakened, Senefret slipped out of his tent to return to the tent of her dead brother. On the way she was captured by an agent of the temple of Sekhmet, who had sent a spy to follow her."

Karissa stared at him, mesmerized by the story and completely forgetting about the pomegranate on her plate. The tale seemed familiar. Had her father told her the story long ago when he used to tuck her into bed?

"Then what happened?" Karissa asked.

"Senefret was dragged back to Thebes. There it was discovered that she had been deflowered and was no longer fit for the king. This was an abomination to the gods. She was executed and entombed in the Valley of the Damned, forever barred from entering the afterworld."

"That's horrible!"

"Yes. And Senefret's body"—he paused and for a moment he seemed to have difficulty in speaking—"her body is the one I must recover and reinter, so she may find peace in the Fields of Iaru where she belongs."

"Fields of Iaru?"

"The equivalent of your heaven."

Karissa studied Asheris's face. While telling the tale of Senefret, he had expressed genuine emotion. Either he was a good actor or he was connected to the characters in the story on a personal level.

"How does this story pertain to your—ancestors?" she inquired.

"My family is related to the commander in the story."

"Oh." She felt let down by the easy explanation.

"But there is more to tell of the commander." Asheris poured a glass of wine and offered it to her. "The story is not yet finished."

"Then please continue." She took the glass and savored the brush of his warm fingers against hers. "Thank you."

"My pleasure." He poured a goblet for himself and slowly took a sip. "The commander had fallen madly in love with the mysterious Senefret. But he was caught up in his dreams of personal glory and bound by duty to finish the campaign in the north before he pursued a woman and declared his feelings. A year later, the commander returned to Thebes as a war hero. When he made inquiries about Senefret, it was discovered that he was the man responsible for deflowering the priestess meant for the king. The high priestess of the temple of

Sekhmet accused him of the crime. In those days priests and priestesses were very powerful, almost as powerful as the king himself. When they demanded the life of a mortal they usually got it, especially if that mortal had offended the king or committed a sin. On the day of his death, the commander was told of the fate of his beloved, and he was devastated. Then, for that one night with Senefret, the commander's life was forfeited—but not, I might add, in a conventional way."

"What did they do to him?"

"They mummified him alive."

Karissa froze in disbelief with the wine goblet pressed against her lips. She lowered the glass. "They *what*?"

"They mummified him alive. It was a practice known to them, a secret now lost."

"Mummified alive? I can't believe it. How?"

Asheris took a long draught of wine. "Many of the secret rites have been lost over the centuries. But the fact remains that the commander was buried alive and cursed by the temple of Sekhmet to be a living mummy until released by a woman who loved him. The priestesses were certain the curse would hold forever, because they knew the only woman who loved the commander was Senefret, and she was already dead."

He heaved a sigh and pressed on, his eyes dark and troubled.

"And because the commander was still alive in his tomb, his spirit, or *ka*, could never leave the earth and go to the afterworld where it belonged. The lioness cult therefore damned him to eternal hell, just as they had damned Senefret."

Karissa reached out and slipped her hand over Asheris's right wrist in a gesture of compassion. "This story is very sad."

"Yes." Asheris nodded and covered her hand with his left. "But Osiris, the god of the underworld, took pity on the lovers. He knew what it was like to be forever damned to remain in one world. So he lifted the curse, as much as was in his power to do so. Since he was lord of the underworld and ruler of the night, he released the commander's *ka* by allowing it to wander free, but only during the night hours. And only in the form of a cat."

"A cat?" Karissa felt a shiver race down her back. "A panther?"

Asheris nodded and silently regarded her as if waiting for her to draw more conclusions.

"Not the panther I saw at the lost sphinx!"

He raised his eyebrows as if to encourage her to reconsider.

"But that panther would have to be thousands of years old! How could he live that long?"

"He is no ordinary beast." He squeezed her hand and then reached for his wine. "He is the spirit of a damned man."

Karissa sat back, trying to take in all he had said, and fingered the stem of her glass. If what he said were true, she had been saved twice by a mythical panther. If the cat was supernatural, its unearthliness would certainly explain how it had traveled from Baltimore to Luxor. She glanced at Asheris.

"So the panther spirit was the cat who saved my life?"

"Quite likely."

"But why? Why me?"

"Because you are very important to him."

"Because I know the location of the lost sphinx? What has that to do with the mummified commander and the panther?"

"The man was locked inside the sphinx, Karissa. You let him out."

She paled. "When the sphinx collapsed?"

"Yes." Asheris finished his wine. "The sphinx guarded the entrance of the Valley of the Damned. But as everyone knows, the Valley of the Damned is in a barren desert that is constantly altered by wind and sand. No one knows for sure where the ruined sphinx lies buried. No one but you, Karissa. You are the single living soul who holds the key to finding Senefret's body."

"But I can't remember!"

"I think you can." He reached for her hand again and surrounded it with the warmth of his. "If you are willing to relive that night, Karissa, to face whatever troubles you about it, you could redeem the soul of a woman whose only sin was to choose personal freedom."

"I can't," Karissa replied in a low voice. She couldn't bear to think of two people trapped forever because of her. Yet the pain of examining the night at the sphinx would be even more acute. Besides that, she had no time to get caught up in Asheris's fantasy. She had her own problems and her own schedule to consider. She jumped to her feet, knocking back the chair. "I can't! I simply can't remember!"

In contrast, he rose to his feet with elegant gracefulness. "But will you try?" he asked softly.

She stared at him, wanting to run far away from him and into his arms at the same time. Was she losing her mind?

He placed his napkin on the table. "Will you at least agree to drive out to the desert with me and take a look? I will make it worth your while."

Karissa raised her chin and studied him. Money would enable her to buy out Josh and break away from his disruptive presence. That in itself would mean a welcome amount of peace of mind, perhaps enough to make up for the craziness of arriving in Baltimore a day or two behind schedule.

"How much money are you willing to pay me if I decide to go with you?" she asked after a long pause.

"Thirty thousand in U.S. funds, plus expenses."

The sum staggered her, but she didn't show her surprise. "I already made a plane reservation for eight o'clock this evening, though."

"I will buy a new ticket for you."

She swept back her hair and noticed that his eyes followed the movement. For thirty thousand dollars, she could be persuaded to spend one more day in Egypt. "All right—Asheris. Let's go."

FIVE

Asheris drove his Land Rover through the outskirts of Luxor, effortlessly dodging trucks piled with grain and easily passing overloaded buses. Karissa wondered if he did everything with such quiet competence. She glanced at him, appreciating the way he looked in his dark glasses, with his hair pulled back to the nape of his neck. Her gaze traveled across his sharp jawline, accentuated by the white collar of his shirt, and down his sinewy arms, where rolled-up sleeves revealed his tanned forearms. She liked the way the fine black hair lightly shaded his arms and could imagine his chest was similarly shadowed.

Asheris shifted into a lower gear and swerved around three camels while Karissa's gaze dropped to his lean thighs draped in a pair of khaki pants. He had long, well-formed legs and narrow aristocratic feet that manipulated the pedals with authority. She could imagine that Asheris did everything with authority. A vision of him moving over her in bed—making love to her with a maddening amount of self-control—flashed through her thoughts. Where had that vision come from?

To get her mind off the image of Asheris in bed with her, she stared out her window. She had been here only a short while and already was falling in love again with the lush green valley and the stark golden cliffs that bordered it. She loved the contrasts of Egypt, a place where skyscrapers rose beside pyramids, where British cruise ships sailed past feluccas used by fishermen since ancient times, where camel caravans loitered in the parking lots of gas stations. The delightful mixture of the sights and sounds of her childhood came rushing back, filling her heart with a joy so sharp she sighed out loud.

"What is wrong?" Asheris asked, slanting a sidelong glance at her.

"Nothing." She smiled. "It's just good to be back, that's all."

She looked at him and saw the corner of his mouth rise in that slow lopsided smile of his. The sight made her heart do a crazy flipflop. What was it about this man that could make her react so strongly just to his smile? Whatever it was, she was in danger of falling under the spell of Egypt again, but in an entirely new way.

Within forty-five minutes they had climbed through a steep pass in the cliffs, winding up an arid canyon until they reached the desert above. Instantly the Land Rover was hit by a blast of gritty wind. They rolled up the windows and Asheris dropped into a low gear as the road dwindled to a sandy track. Karissa surveyed the expanse of dun-colored sand dunes but saw nothing she recognized. Asheris continued the drive, and after another hour they passed through a vaguely familiar outcropping of sandstone.

"I think I remember that," she declared, nodding at the banded plateau. Her tongue, suddenly dry, stuck to the roof of her mouth.

"What do you remember about it?"

"The sphinx was near here. To the left, I think. Over there." She pointed to a sheltered cleft in the rock. Asheris steered the four-wheel-drive Land Rover to the cleft but found the passage barred by a boulder the size of a small sedan, as if someone had purposely blocked the path. He turned off the engine and put his right hand on the door.

The sudden silence closed in on Karissa, allowing the haunting wail of the desert wind to seep into her soul, reminding her of the night so long ago when her whole world had fallen apart. She suddenly regretted coming with Asheris.

"Shall we get out and look?" he asked.

"I can't."

"You can, Karissa."

"I'd be an idiot to go near the sphinx again. What about the curse?"

Asheris sighed. "The only real curse was invoked by the high priestess of Sekhmet and involved the commander in chief of the army. No one else."

"But what about my mother's death?"

"A coincidence, surely."

"And my father?"

"You must tell me."

"How can I when I can't remember?" She passed the back of her hand across her damp forehead.

Asheris turned to her. "Is there anything you recall about the sphinx? Anything at all?"

"It was night. That's all I remember."

"That is all?"

Karissa glanced at him. "Didn't you mention that you were there too? Don't you remember anything about the sphinx's location?"

"No. I was"—he glanced away as his voice trailed off in a vagueness that wasn't in keeping with his usual definite manner—"I was not myself at the time."

"What do you mean? Were you ill or something?"

"I wasn't myself, that is all." He sent her a hard look that warned her not to press the issue. She glanced away, perplexed, and decided to ask him later what he meant.

He reached for her arm. "Please, Karissa, you must trust me when I tell you there is no curse. If you will only walk awhile and look around, something might spark your memory. It is important that we find the lost sphinx as quickly as possible."

She pulled her arm away. "Can't you get it into your head that I don't *want* to remember?" Her voice was sharp with anger.

He paused, as if he possessed infinite patience even after such an outburst, and stared into her eyes for a long moment. "To remember is to start to recapture yourself. To heal."

She glared at him. Would the man never give up?

"If you cannot do it for yourself, do it for Senefret."

Her resolve to stay in the Land Rover faltered. Why did he have to remind her of the tragic priestess? Protecting her sanity was one thing. Refusing to help a stranded soul was quite another. She let out an exasperated breath.

"All right! But I can't guarantee anything." Karissa snatched her hat from the back seat, opened the door, and jumped out, prepared for the unforgettable searing heat of the sand. Though Asheris was maddeningly persistent, at least he had sent his manservant to purchase hiking boots, hat, and cotton clothing for her before they left Luxor, to make sure she had protection against the inhospitable desert. She plopped the hat on her head and looked up to find Asheris studying her.

He smiled at her as he slipped the keys in his pocket, obviously approving of the way she looked in her khakis. Trying not to think of his magnetic eyes or the way he had just twisted her around his finger, she stomped off toward the narrow cleft in the rocks. He walked beside her without making a sound.

Karissa plodded through the sand, squinting in the bright sun, and hoped she would see something familiar so she wouldn't have to review the events that took place when the sphinx collapsed. But the longer she stared at the rock outcropping and the dunes beyond, the less certain she became that she had ever set foot in the area. At the edge of the outcropping, where strewn rock gave way to the endless desert sand, Karissa stopped and pushed back her hat.

"Are those backhoes over there?" she asked, pointing to the outlines of yellow machinery about half a mile away.

"Yes. Mustofa has brought equipment out here to search. And should he find the entrance to the Valley of the Damned before we do, he will take everything without regard to ownership and sell it on the black market to the highest bidder."

"Maybe Mustofa knows something we don't, and that's why he's digging over there."

"No. I am fairly certain Mustofa knows very little. He has just made a good guess."

"Well, I don't recognize anything," she declared, looking back out to the dunes.

"Nothing?"

"Nothing." She turned and was surprised to find Asheris directly behind her. Was he trying to block her return to the Land Rover? Karissa glared at him. "Excuse me," she announced, taking a step as if to plow through.

"Wait." He reached for her shoulders and enclosed them in a gently restraining hold. "Just for a moment."

"It's almost four o'clock. I could still catch my plane."

"You can get a flight in the morning."

"Maybe I want to leave now."

"After you have come so far? Come into the shade and talk to me for a moment. Over here." He urged her to walk toward a shady crevice in the rock. Karissa spied a metallic glint at the base. Could there be water? She would love to dip her hands in some water.

"All right." She followed him. "But just for a moment."

There was indeed a small pool at the base of the rock and a patch of grass. Karissa hunkered down, untied the scarf from her neck, and dipped it in the water. She used the wet cotton to wipe her face and neck.

Asheris sat on a nearby rock and watched her. "Tell me of your mother," he said.

She glanced up in surprise. "My mother?"

"Yes. Was she sick for a long time before her death?"

"No. She died unexpectedly from a strange fever that baffled the doctors."

"Were your parents happy with each other?"

"My mother hated Egypt. She gave my dad a hard time about having to come here. They argued about it a lot."

"Did your father love your mother?"

"Yes . . . oh, I don't know." The question made her nervous. She had asked herself the same thing a hundred times and wondered why she could never bring herself to examine her memory for an answer.

"Did your mother love him?"

"It was hard to tell. Grandmother Petrie often said that my mother rushed into marriage because of my father's good looks and charm and warned me never to repeat the mistake."

"Marry in haste, repent at leisure, as they say?" Asheris remarked.

"Perhaps." She suddenly wondered if she were in danger of doing exactly what her mother had done by falling precipitously in love with the attractive, confident man who sat near the edge of the water.

Asheris picked up a pebble and tossed it into the pool, creating a series of rings that drifted away to nothing. "Did you ever think that your father might have had a lot in common with his associate, Dr. Raeburn?"

"Her?" Karissa pulled at the brim of her hat, mostly to hide her pinched expression. She didn't like discussing her parents' relationship. "Gracie Raeburn was plain and dowdy. Why would my father be interested in her when he had someone like my mother? My mother was a beauty, you know."

"It may have been that your father valued Dr. Raeburn's mind and not her face. Your father may have enjoyed talking about his work with a woman who shared his love of archaeology."

"Why are you bringing this up?"

"So that you will consider what was going on between your parents and Dr. Raeburn when you were twelve years old."

"What are you implying?"

"I imply nothing. Perhaps if you think about your parents and Dr. Raeburn, you will begin to remember."

"There's nothing to remember!"

Asheris took off his dark glasses and slipped them in the pocket of his shirt and turned his intense gaze upon her. She wondered if he intended to use his hypnotic eyes as a weapon.

"Karissa, you are fooling no one but yourself. There is a reason why you have let that night slip into blackness. I believe you saw something that highly disturbed you."

"I saw nothing!" She jumped to her feet as she pushed away a flashback, like a strobe light blinking on the sight of two people embracing and then blinking off again. "I remember nothing! Don't try to put ideas in my head!"

She glared at him over her shoulder. The vision of the embrace in the sphinx flashed into her mind again, this time more slowly, giving her enough time to see the expression on her father's face. She heard the echo of her own voice screaming. *No-o-o-o!* She saw her father glance in her direction, saw Gracie Raeburn twist in his arms. And then Karissa heard the ominous thud above their heads. Her heart twisted in her chest. She slammed her hat on her head and cut off the memory before it could rush to its horrifying climax.

Karissa dashed out of the tiny oasis, trying to outrun the memory. Just the notion that she might relive the moments inside the sphinx made her desperate with fear. She couldn't endure seeing it all again, couldn't bear to think that she had been responsible for—

She broke off the thought and ran through the slipping sand. Her hat flew off, but she didn't care. All she could do was run blindly into the desert, hoping that if she went far enough and fast enough she might outdistance the truth.

But she couldn't outdistance Asheris. He loped behind her, easily catching up with her, and grabbed at her arm to stop her. The movement knocked her off-balance and she fell, which sent her rolling down the slope of a dune. She slid to a stop at the bottom, but before she could scramble to her feet she was pinned to the ground by Asheris, who forced both wrists to the sides of her head as he straddled her legs.

She struggled to get away, but he held her firmly. After a few moments she surrendered and glared up at him. Only then did she realize her face was caked with tears and dust.

"Stop running, Karissa." His voice was much softer than the grip on her wrists. "It is time to see things for what they are."

"No!"

"Your father did not run off with Gracie Raeburn."

"Yes he did. They were having an affair!"

"Who told you that?"

"My mother. She suspected it for years."

"And you believed her?"

"Yes." Karissa stared into his golden eyes. Damn those eyes. How could she escape the power of those eyes and the way they could pull her thoughts right out of her mouth? Her heart pounded in her chest, her neck, and her temples as the truth welled up inside her. She ran the tip of her tongue over her parched lips and saw Asheris watch the movement.

He bent down.

"No," Karissa began to whimper but his mouth closed over hers and cut off her protest.

"I am here now for you," he said against her lips. "Open your soul to me." Then he kissed her in a lingering, thorough manner that set her heart racing all over again. Slowly he lowered himself until he sank down upon her, his firm chest to her breasts, his hard abdomen to her soft, trim torso, and his lean legs stretched alongside hers. The weight of him made her body flare into full arousal, and the sheer size of him made her wonder if he might cover and consume her like a dark falcon. And his tongue! His tongue drove her mad. The surface of his tongue was quite raspy, which heightened the erotic sensation of every stroke. No man had ever done to her with his tongue what Asheris could do.

Karissa melted into the sand as Asheris moved over her in the first step of the sinuous dance between a man and a woman. She could feel the mark of his arousal, and when he surged against her and groaned, she felt her woman's blossom open, spreading its nectar deep inside her, preparing for the seed it ached to receive. She wanted to respond to him, wanted to wrap her arms around his muscular shoulders and pull him down to her lips. But he held her wrists above her head, and all she could do was gasp and moan—as he bit her breasts gently through the cotton fabric of her shirt and bra—and arch upward as he kissed her throat and ears.

Open her soul to him? What did he mean? Did he want her to trust him enough to tell him everything she could remember so he could drag even more memories to the surface? Or did he want her to open to him physically and let him make love to her, here on the desert sand? How could she do either? She had known Asheris for less than a week. How could she succumb to a man with such certainty? Yet she knew she could trust him. And she knew she wanted him. There was no doubt in her mind that she wanted him—in her arms, in her thoughts, and in the deepest place inside of her. This need of him was elemental, undeniable, like breathing or eating. She had never felt so certain, not even with her own husband.

"Tell me now," he said, his voice husky.

"Tell you what?" She closed her eyes as he kissed her brow.

"Why you cannot face what happened that night."

An image as sharp as a knife blade sliced through her desire for Asheris. In the vision she saw her father look up, saw Gracie Raeburn slowly pull her arms from her father's shoulders.

"No!" she gasped.

"Tell me," he urged, rising to his knees. "What are you seeing?"

"Them together!"

"Who, your father and Dr. Raeburn?"

"Yes." She felt tears burning in her eyes. "I see them embracing. I see the look on my father's face."

"What kind of look?"

"It is—" She glanced at him and felt the corners of her mouth pulling down uncontrollably. She didn't want to break down, couldn't break down. Not in all her therapy sessions had she come this close to cracking.

"It is *what?*"

Karissa blinked through her tears and knew she was losing control. Something about Asheris's eyes induced her to spill her guts, to bare her soul. She sighed raggedly and then whispered, "It is ecstasy."

Asheris's grip eased on her wrists. "Ecstasy because of Dr. Raeburn?"

"Why else?" Her voice was flat.

"There are joys other than that between a man and woman," he said gently. "There is the joy of discovery."

"Joy of discovery?" She had never once considered her father might have been embracing Gracie Raeburn for reasons other than sexual intimacy, especially after hearing her mother's views on the subject. Could she have been mistaken? Could she have seen ecstasy on her father's face and attributed it to love or lust, when all the time it had been out of the sheer joy of finding a grave site intact after years of searching? Oh, God—

"What else do you remember?" Asheris asked, leaning closer. "Keep going!"

The vision came again, like a wave of nausea. She saw her father look up again, saw Gracie Raeburn once more slowly pull her arms from her father's shoulders as the sound of thunder filled the burial chamber, as the thunder filled Karissa's mind, choking out the hammering of her heart. She couldn't look anymore, couldn't bear to hear the screams.

"No!"

"What do you see, Karissa? What is happening?"

"I screamed. I couldn't believe he would betray Mother like that. So I started to yell." She sank back, exhausted, as the words died on her lips.

"What did he do then?"

"Nothing. There wasn't time." She closed her eyes, and tears dropped down her temples and into her hair. "If I hadn't yelled, they might have had time. They might have been able to save themselves."

"From what?"

"From the block, the granite block that came down. Oh, God!" She turned her head and wept openly, unmindful of Asheris. She longed to cover her face, but he kept her wrists trapped.

"Karissa." He kissed her left temple. "It was not your fault," he said. "You must know it was not your fault."

"It was! If I hadn't yelled, if I hadn't distracted them—"

"Many burial chambers were booby-trapped. Surely you knew that."

"But if I hadn't yelled, they might have had time to get away!"

She shut her eyes, trying to blot out the image of the huge granite block, as big as a boxcar, which had come roaring out of the darkness. But this time there was no stopping the sight or the sound. This time she heard the horrified shattering scream as the block of granite crushed her father and Dr. Raeburn and then set the entire disintegration of the sphinx in motion. Karissa watched it all again and realized she was screaming and screaming and screaming.

Then she was lifted to her feet and surrounded in the warmth of a loving embrace. She let her head be held against a strong shoulder, let her waist be supported by the link of a powerful arm, for she could neither stand nor speak nor stop the flood of tears that poured from her eyes. Then that someone enfolded her to a human heart and murmured the words no one had ever said to her— words she had desperately needed to hear when she was twelve years old and had just witnessed the gruesome death of her father.

"Karissa, let it go. It was not your fault. You could not have known. It would have happened anyway. There was nothing you could have done to stop it. You are not to blame. Karissa, my sweet, let this darkness out of your heart. Let it go."

For sixteen years she had believed that she had been responsible for the death of her father in the sphinx. For sixteen years she had lived with a guilt so awful she couldn't even look at it. And for sixteen years she had hung in an emotional limbo, frozen by the brand upon her child's heart that had damned her to a lifetime of unworthiness and guilt. No one had been able to see the brand, but she had known it was there, every day, and the invisible scar had crippled her in many ways.

But with each moment in these strong arms that held her, she felt the scar dissolving, each jagged edge smoothing out and uncoiling, while all the pain and anguish drained out of her as she wept. No one had ever held her or comforted her like this. Her grandmother had never even guessed she had a dark secret and had been too uninterested or afraid to examine the source of Karissa's rebellious tirades and black silences. So who held her now? Who cared enough about her to hold her like this? She glanced up through her tears, half surprised to find herself not in her grandmother's house in Baltimore but in the arms of an Egyptian man on the edge of the Eastern Desert.

He gazed down at her, his golden-brown eyes full of compassion, his expression intent with concern. And suddenly she heard his words again in her mind. He had called her his sweet. No one had ever murmured an endearment to her like that and truly meant it. And even if they had, she wouldn't have felt worthy enough to accept it. Now, however, she could. Asheris had helped her see she was not to blame for the tragedy so long ago. Her heart swelled with an almost painful surge of gratefulness.

"It has gone, the darkness?" he asked gently.

She gazed at him, stunned that Asheris could have walked into her life and started her on the road to healing just like that. She tried to smile, but the expression only reached her eyes. Wordlessly, she wrapped her arms around his torso and clutched him with all her strength. He had given her what no one else had offered. He had shown her the way to look at the past and forgive herself. New tears came, tears of release and relief this time, and he held her until the sobs subsided.

"Karissa?" he asked at last, pulling away to take a look at her face. "You are all right?"

She reached up and stroked his cheek with her right hand, cherishing the man who had just guided her through the gates of her trauma and beyond. "I think so."

He turned his head and kissed her palm.

"Who are you?" she asked in wonder, reaching up with her other hand. Her eyelids felt hard and scratchy from crying. "How did you ever find me?"

"It was you who found me," he replied. "But that story is for another time."

"Why not now?"

"The light is fading. I must get you back to Luxor before nightfall."

"But what about the sphinx?"

"We will have to look for it another day." He stepped away. "Come. We must hurry." He held out his hand to help her back up the slope.

Karissa reached for him and took a step, but dragged her feet because she was in no hurry to leave. Why was he suddenly so pressed for time? There was plenty of light to search for more clues. They might end up arriving in Luxor after dark, but why would that matter? His behavior was at odds with his insistence that they find the sphinx as soon as possible, and she didn't quite know what to make of it. With her second step, her boot hit something hard in the sand and she looked down. The corner of a piece of red granite stuck out of the dune.

"Wait!" she exclaimed. Karissa drew him back down the slope and then knelt on the sand. "Asheris, look!"

SIX

Asheris dropped to his knees beside her and brushed away the sand to expose a block of pink granite. Nearby, Karissa toed through the sand, searching for another block and quickly finding one. She glanced up and met Asheris's gleaming eyes.

"Could this be the lost sphinx?" she gasped.

"It might be! I am going to establish the bearings of the location." He scrambled up the dune and pulled a compass out of his pants pocket. Keeping the rise of the rock formation directly behind him, he held out the compass and noted the direction of the exposed granite blocks. Karissa joined him at the top of the dune and reached down for her discarded hat. The wind was harsher at the top of the dune, and she hoped they would leave soon.

"I will bring men out here to dig tomorrow," he declared. "And we will see if the blocks are truly part of the sphinx."

"And if so, then what?"

"Then we will find the underground corridor that leads from the sphinx to the necropolis of the Valley of the Damned."

"The necropolis is underground?"

"Yes. The sphinx was built to guard it."

Karissa smiled. Though she was emotionally drained, she was still highly aware of Asheris's excitement. "That would be something, if we've really come across the lost sphinx just like that, by accident."

"Not by accident." He smiled down at her and dropped the compass in the pocket of his pants. "You brought us here."

"You had a hand in it too," she countered. "If not for you, Asheris, I would still be running out in the desert. You helped me find the part of me that was lost and, in so doing, found these blocks."

"That part of you was there all along." He reached for her elbow and the gentleness in his voice turned to briskness. "Come. It grows late, Karissa. And I must be back before nightfall."

"Why?"

"I have business to attend to. And much to arrange."

"What do you do for a living, anyway?" she asked as they hurried toward the Land Rover. It was easier to talk of his life and interests than let her mind drift back to the night the sphinx collapsed.

"I am an antiquities dealer. I also lecture at the university here in Luxor and in Cairo, as well as in Europe." He pulled open the door of the vehicle and held it for her.

She got in and glanced at him. "As an expert in Egyptian artifacts?"

"Partly. I am considered an authority on the history of the New Kingdom." He closed her door and walked around to the other side of the Land Rover.

"My father would have enjoyed talking with you."

"And I would have enjoyed talking with him." He backed up the four-wheel-drive and made a wide turn to head out to the main road. "I would have asked him what naughty things you did when you were a little girl."

"Me?" She smiled, feeling lighter than she had in years. "Naughty?"

"Yes, you." He cocked an eyebrow and looked over the top of his sunglasses at her. "You kiss like a naughty girl."

"Oh, really?" She tried to repress an outright grin.

"Like you know what you want from a man."

"That isn't being naughty, Mr. Asher, that's being honest."

"Oh? And what truths do your kisses tell?"

"I think you know, because *you* kiss like a wicked little boy."

"Ah." He smiled his slow smile when he realized she had thrown his taunting words right back at him. The smile broadened as he turned his attention to the road. His teeth were very white against his skin.

Something warm and wonderful twisted inside her. Karissa gazed out the window, emotionally depleted but aware of a tantalizing prospect of happiness lurking at the edge of her exhaustion. Perhaps tonight, after she had rested and he had concluded his business, she could spend some time with Asheris before she left for Baltimore the next day. She could suggest celebrating the discovery of the lost sphinx and let the evening develop from there. She couldn't imagine leaving Luxor without telling him how much it meant to her when he had held her in his arms and given her comfort—without spending her last few hours in Egypt with him.

The only lover she had known had been her husband, and to define his perfunctory rituals in bed as lovemaking was to defile the very essence of the word. Though older than her by ten years, Thomas had been an indefatigable partner, determined to last as long as humanly possible before reaching a climax. But in his obsession with his own performance, he forgot the importance of touching, of exchanging whispered words of love, of conveying rich emotion through kisses of exquisite tenderness—the kind of kisses Asheris had already given her. Instinctively, Karissa had known there should be much more between a man and woman than the mechanical coupling she had experienced with Thomas, but until meeting Asheris she had never desired to explore her theory. Now she thought she would wither away in abject desperation if she missed the chance to make love with the man beside her. With Asheris, it truly would be making love, because her feelings for him grew deeper and broader with every kindness he showed her, every way in which he touched her, every time he kissed her. She felt herself opening to him simply at the rumble of his voice or the lift of his smile. Surely he must be falling in love just as quickly, the way he held her and looked at her with such warmth in his eyes. A person couldn't hide the truth that shone in his eyes. No one could fake such a genuine expression.

She sighed and crossed her arms over her chest. Was she a fool for falling for a man who lived a world away from her home in Baltimore? Was she crazy to think a man from another culture would be a good choice for her? Did she have a choice? Her heart knew no boundaries, geographically or culturally, and it was begging her to have faith in Asheris. She had spent a lifetime ignoring her inner voice. Perhaps it was time to listen.

Soon after they arrived back at Asheris's walled estate, he left to tend to his business. Karissa called Josh to tell him of her postponed travel plans, but once again was forced to leave a message on his answering machine. Wasn't the man ever home? She hung up the phone, realizing she hadn't given a definite date for her return.

Was she secretly hoping Asheris would ask her to stay for a few more days? She really couldn't linger, no matter how badly she wanted to get to know Asheris. She had spent the last sixteen years totally devoted to her sculpture. She couldn't throw it all away by being unprepared for the PBS special, even though she suspected that her life was quickly taking on a new dimension because of Asheris and that never again would she be completely satisfied with just her work.

Now that she thought about it, she felt even more driven to spend the last few hours with Asheris. To pass the time, Karissa took a long bath, luxuriating in the large sunken tub and savoring the foreign sensation of well-being that had begun to flicker in the center of her soul. She closed her eyes and sang an old torch song, never more aware of the words now that Asheris had come into her life. In the vaulted chamber her voice sounded pure and strong. Afterward she emerged from her bath, dressed in another of the delicate linen dresses Eisha had laid out for her, and slipped on the armbands and necklace that had been placed there as well. The jewelry seemed to be very old, crafted of gold-colored metal and colorful gems, probably paste imitations of carnelians and emeralds and real pieces of lapis lazuli. The wide, colorful collar suited the dress and set off her complexion. Karissa glanced at herself in the mirror and was slightly shocked to see how closely she resembled the female figures she had seen painted on the walls of tombs. Her Egyptian blood had never been as obvious as now, when she was dressed in the garments of another age.

Karissa continued to stare. Why did this garment feel so right on her skin? Why did the jewelry drape perfectly across her shoulders and breast? Why did she wear her cloud of black hair in a blunt style, just like the hair of the ladies she had seen in her father's books? Sekhmet, Senefret, Asheris, Osiris. Why did the unusual names

ring with such poignant familiarity? Was it because her
father had been an Egyptologist and she had grown up on
stories of the ancient world? Or did the familiarity spring
from some fountain much deeper than her childhood?
And why had Asheris provided her with these items of
clothing? Was it for her pleasure or for his? And if his,
whose image did he see when he looked at her?

Perhaps Asheris was obsessed with a vision from the
past. He didn't seem like the type of man to be possessed
by a fantasy, but why else would he want her to dress in
ancient clothing? She'd lay odds the image from the past
was Senefret. But why such an obsession for a person
long dead? Couldn't he be satisfied with a real flesh-and-
blood woman? Karissa slipped off one armband and was
infused with a strange mélange of hurt and resentment
for his failure to see her for herself. But she refused to let
the hurt eat away at her. She would demand the truth
from Asheris as soon as he came back for the evening.

Shaken and angry, she stumbled to the table near the
door, picked up the brass bell, and rang it sharply.
"Eisha!" she called.

Moments later, Eisha bustled through the open door.
"Yes, Miss Spencer?"

"Where are my clothes?" she asked.

"What clothes?"

"The *galabia* I was wearing when I came here the
other night."

"That?" A confused expression passed through Eisha's
dark brown eyes. "But that was just a rag."

"What did you do with it?"

"I threw it away, Miss Spencer." She glanced at the
linen dress Karissa wore. "Do you not wish to wear the
dress?"

"No. What about those khaki pants I had on this
afternoon?"

"They are dirty. They must be laundered."

Karissa frowned.

"Is there something wrong with the gown?" Eisha asked, tilting her head.

"Yes. I feel as if I'm dressing in someone else's wardrobe. Who does this belong to?"

"I don't know." Eisha wrung her hands, obviously worried that Karissa was upset. "Mr. Asher selected it from his collection for you to wear."

"What collection?"

"His artifact collection."

"Is the collection in the house?"

"Yes." Eisha looked over her shoulder as if afraid of being overheard.

"Would you take me to see it?"

"Mr. Asher likes to show the collection to guests personally."

"I don't think Mr. Asher will have enough time. And I would really like to see it before I leave tomorrow."

Eisha glanced at her and then sighed. "All right, Miss Spencer. Follow me."

Eisha led her along a corridor, into a darkened wing of the house on the other side of the garden, and down a few steps. She selected a large key and turned a decorative lock. Then she opened the door, flipped on the subdued lighting, and held the door open.

Karissa stepped into the room, awestruck. In pools of light, much like the arrangement of her gallery, she saw polished statues of granite, tables of ebony and ivory, boxes of all shapes, chairs with lion's feet for legs, alabaster chalices, and ancient instruments that looked like simple harps. But what caught her attention most strongly was a glass case at the end of the room in which a life-size figure of a woman stood bathed in light. Karissa moved closer, with Eisha at her heels. When she was near enough to make out the features of the woman, she stopped abruptly, shocked by the resemblance between the figure and her own appearance. The woman had long black hair, a slender face with wide dark eyes, a delicate nose, and full lips. She wore a dress identical to the one in which Karissa was attired.

"Who is this?" Karissa inquired, her voice hushed.

"She is an ancient one," Eisha replied. "The master had her statue carved by a French sculptor years ago."

"But who is she?"

"She was known as Senefret, a priestess of the temple of Sekhmet."

Karissa stared up at the beautiful haughty face of the priestess. Asheris *was* obsessed with the woman, and the only reason he was attracted to her was because of her similarity to Senefret. Her heart wrenched painfully. Karissa glanced down at her clothing and then back up to the housekeeper. "I am dressed exactly like her."

"You look much like her," Eisha observed. "Strikingly so."

"Is this dress something she might have worn?"

"Yes. As I said, it came from this collection."

"So I'm wearing a priceless artifact?"

"Yes."

She held up her arm and stared at the golden band. "And what of this? Is the armband real, too?"

"Yes, Miss Spencer."

Karissa felt a chill pass over her, even though the evening was still balmy. "This jewelry is probably solid gold!"

Eisha nodded.

"This is crazy!" Karissa slipped the golden ring down her arm and off her hand. "Do you have something practical to wear, Eisha? I don't care if it's one of Mr. Asher's shirts. Please, just get me something to put on until the khakis are laundered."

"As you wish. This will not make Mr. Asher happy, however."

"Mr. Asher won't be happy if I ruin these, either."

She reached for the strings of the necklace where they were tied together at the nape of her neck. The sooner she got out of the ancient garments, the better. She wasn't certain why she was driven by the need to take off the clothing, whether because of Asheris's peculiar devotion to Senefret or the odd way the ancient dress and jewelry made her feel. She looked up to find Eisha staring at her.

"I'm going back to my room," Karissa said. "Please find me something else to wear and bring it there."

"Certainly. At once." Eisha ducked out of the room to do Karissa's bidding.

Karissa found her way back to her chamber and waited until Eisha came back with a shirt and a light cotton robe, both masculine attire. Then she left, allowing Karissa to dress, and returned a few minutes later with the evening meal and a babble of apologies.

"I thought you might like to eat in here," she explained, carrying the food to the table, "since you don't have the proper attire."

"Thanks." Karissa saw the single plate on the tray and wished she didn't have to eat alone, even though her sentiments regarding Asheris had taken a sudden turn. "Isn't Mr. Asher dining at home this evening?"

"No. Mr. Asher is never home in the evening."

"Oh." Karissa felt a deep sense of deflation. She quickly replaced her disappointment with anger, however, for it was a much less vulnerable way to deal with a man like Asheris. "Does he usually stay out late?"

"Quite late."

So much for her plans to ask him about the clothes. Perhaps it was all for the best. She fell under his spell in his presence. Resigned to spending the hours alone, Karissa sat down at the table. She had dressed in the clothing Eisha had brought her, which smelled faintly of Asheris. She tried to ignore the light musky fragrance, but his scent made her pause for a moment and think of his arms and his kiss. Then Eisha put an aromatic plate of rice, lamb, and vegetables in front of her, and the smell of food brought her back to her senses. A folded newspaper lay on the tray.

"Would you like to see the paper?" Eisha asked, holding it out.

"Yes. Thank you."

"I sent the house boy to get a copy of the *Egyptian Gazette*."

"Thank you, Eisha." Karissa took the paper, which was published in English for diplomats and foreign residents. "That was kind of you."

"I heard you singing, Miss Spencer," Eisha put in, "when you were bathing."

"You did?" Karissa blushed. "I hope I didn't bother anyone."

"On the contrary. It sounded lovely. You have a remarkable voice."

"Why, thank you," Karissa said. Eisha smiled and nodded and left Karissa to her paper.

A minor headline at the bottom of the page caught her eye: *Man mauled by cat*. She scanned the article and realized she was reading an account of the panther attack on the guard who had tried to rape her. The succulent lamb caught in her throat as she continued to read. The article mentioned the name Lord Azhur, partially attributing the death to him. Who was this mysterious lord and what did he have to do with the panther?

Karissa glanced up from the paper to find Eisha carefully folding the linen dress near the bed.

"Eisha," Karissa began, "tell me, do you know anything about a person named Lord Azhur?"

"Lord Azhur?" Eisha's hands paused for a moment, but she didn't look up from her task.

"Yes. I've heard that name twice now, and here it is in the paper. Who is Lord Azhur?"

Eisha picked up the golden armband. "He is a character in our folklore."

"In your folklore? But when someone sees the man-killing panther why would they call out, 'Lord Azhur'?"

"Because Lord Azhur is said to be half man and half panther. And that is who they believe is attacking them."

"That sounds farfetched."

"Not to an Egyptian. Many of our ancient gods had the bodies of men and the heads of birds or animals. Perhaps they were half man and half beast as well."

"But we're not speaking of ancient gods, here, Eisha. We're talking about a panther attack in modern day."

"I know." Eisha nodded. "It has been rumored that Lord Azhur walks the earth again as he did thousands of years ago. There have been reports such as that one in the paper for many years now."

"And no one has caught the cat?"

"No." Eisha took the dress and jewelry to the door. "But no one has tried very hard to capture him, Miss Spencer, for it seems those who are killed by Lord Azhur are all unsavory characters, criminals, evil men."

Karissa chewed thoughtfully.

Eisha continued. "Lord Azhur does what our police sometimes fail to achieve."

"But isn't anyone curious to find out who or what this Lord Azhur really is?"

"He is a spirit, Miss Spencer, doomed to walk the earth for eternity. The Arabs named him when they first came across him in the desert. They soon learned to fear him. There are places that no man will go after sunset in the Eastern Desert."

"Why?"

"Because Lord Azhur haunts the desert there. Some say he guards the ancient tombs and will kill all who venture close to the valley where the tombs are said to be."

"But he is the one who brought me here. It must have been him. A panther saved my life and led me to this house."

"A panther?"

"Yes. I followed him for miles. He was in the United

States too, I'm sure of it. And he never once threatened me."

"I do not know how to explain it."

Karissa stirred her rice with her fork. She recalled the story Asheris had told her of the commander who had been cursed by the high priestess of Sekhmet, mummified alive, and then partially redeemed by Osiris. If the panther was more than just a simple creature, he might be the same cat Asheris had mentioned in his tale. And if the cat was the wandering spirit of the man buried alive, of course he would have wanted to protect the single human being who knew about the lost sphinx. And he would have brought her to the house of the modern man who was intent on finding the sphinx as well. It all made sense. The only part that wasn't easily explained was Asheris's connection to the sphinx and his uncommon loyalty to a woman long dead.

Karissa decided not to brood upon the subject. She would ask Asheris point-blank about it in the morning.

The next day she rose and padded across the carpet to the balcony. Just as before, she looked down to find a dead bird, this time a hoopoe bird. Karissa glanced around the sunny garden, even though she was certain she would see no sign of the cat that had left her the gift. She assumed the panther had brought the bird to her, just like the other times. Cats often gave their owners presents such as this as a symbol of love and respect. Did the panther have such feelings for her? She hoped not. She wasn't too crazy about the possibility that a man-killing cat considered her part of his "family." Karissa turned away and went back into the bedchamber.

Eisha came in a few minutes later with her clean khaki pants and cotton shirt and a promise to send someone out to buy her more suitable apparel later that morning.

Karissa took her breakfast in the garden, surrounded

by the caged birds, who were all singing and chattering. The air was still and warm, and Karissa savored the moment. Mornings and evenings were her favorite times of the day in Egypt, both far different from any she had enjoyed in the States. She felt a wave of homesickness, not for Baltimore but for her days in Luxor, when she had been a child. How she had loved it here! And how she would hate to leave.

At ten o'clock, Eisha came back to clear away the breakfast dishes. She chatted brightly about the garden as she put the plates on a tray, and Karissa listened, half amused. She wondered if Eisha had been longing for female company, for she was never in any hurry to break off their conversations. She didn't mind, though, because she had to wait two hours until Asheris emerged from his chamber, and those two hours seemed days away.

Suddenly, however, Eisha cocked her head. "The doorbell," she declared. "Mr. Asher must have a visitor. Excuse me."

Karissa nodded and looked at her watch as Eisha hurried out of the room. Ten-fifteen. Who could be visiting Mr. Asher at this early hour?

She finished her coffee just as Eisha returned.

"Miss Spencer," she said, "there's a gentleman to see you."

SEVEN

"A gentleman?" Karissa repeated, rising to her feet. Would Mustofa have the audacity to come here? "Did he give his name?"

"He said his name was Lambert."

Josh? Karissa couldn't believe Josh had come all the way from Baltimore after receiving her first message. He must have been traveling nonstop ever since, and paid a premium for tickets in the process. She was relieved that her visitor was Josh and not Mustofa, but she wasn't too pleased that Josh had dropped everything to fly to Egypt when it wasn't necessary.

"Shall I show him in?" Eisha added.

"Yes. And bring some coffee, please." Karissa motioned toward the empty carafe. "I'm sure Mr. Lambert will be in need of refreshments."

"Certainly." Eisha hurried off and returned with a slightly disheveled, stubble-cheeked Josh.

As soon as he caught sight of Karissa, he strode

forward in haste, swiping palm fronds out of his way and tripping once on the uneven tile of the old garden.

"Josh," she said. "What are you doing here?"

"I was worried." He grabbed both her hands and held her out in front of him. "Are you all right?"

"Yes." In fact, she was better than she had been in a long while but decided not to mention it. She slipped her hands out of his grasp. "I'm fine."

"So what happened? Did that Mr. Asher snatch you out of the gallery?"

"No. I told you on the answering machine that a man named Mustofa kidnapped me. Mr. Asher has been very accommodating."

"But why? Why were you kidnapped?"

Karissa briefly explained about the lost sphinx and the buried tombs, carefully omitting any reference to Asheris's story about Senefret.

"So how did you get away from Mustofa?"

"Believe it or not, a black panther rescued me."

"A black panther? You mean like the one we saw in Baltimore?"

Karissa nodded. Eisha swept forward with a tray of coffee, dates, and sweet breads. Karissa introduced Josh to the housekeeper and then motioned for him to sit down.

"The locals believe the cat is part of Egyptian folklore, a half-man half-panther creature named Lord Azhur."

"So what was he doing in Baltimore—vacationing?" Josh popped a date in his mouth.

Karissa glanced at him, wanting more than anything to bounce what she was feeling and what she had learned about Asheris off someone who knew her, someone she could trust. But though Josh was a longtime friend, he wasn't the type of person she could confide in. While Karissa knew he could be endearing, she still wished he would be less like a basset hound, tripping on his own droopy ears, and more like a man of thirty-two. So she sighed and decided to keep her own counsel. Besides, she should trust her own judgment.

"Everyone thinks I can remember the location of the lost sphinx," she explained, "including Lord Azhur. That's why he protected me, I assume."

"Hmmm." Josh took a long swig of coffee, and looked doubtful. "So what are you planning to do?"

"I was planning to fly back to Baltimore, either today or tomorrow."

"Oh."

"There really wasn't any need for you to come all this way."

"I was worried about you." He reached across the table and put his hand over hers. She let her hand remain but didn't enjoy his touch. "I couldn't sleep, thinking my favorite sculptress was in danger."

"I appreciate it, Josh, but I'm in no danger. And you shouldn't have gone to so much expense on my account."

"There are times when money is no object."

He gazed at her, with a crazy smile that made him look like a lovesick puppy. Karissa slipped her hand away, tempted to ask him if money was ever the object with him but didn't wish to hurt his feelings. That would be too nasty after all the hours he had spent traveling to her side.

She was about to suggest that Josh freshen up and take a nap when she saw his smile freeze and his gaze travel upward to somewhere above her head.

Karissa turned, just as she felt two elegant hands slip around the corners of the back of her chair. Asheris had come up behind her, but she hadn't heard the slightest sound of his approach. She glanced up at him, struck by his dark handsomeness and bemused by the way he stood behind her, as if laying claim to the space between her and Josh.

"I thought I heard a stranger's voice in my garden," Asheris said.

"This is my business partner, Josh Lambert," Karissa remarked, turning back to the table. "Josh, this is Mr. Asher, whom you may remember from the gallery."

"Sure." Josh pushed to his feet, forgetting his napkin, which fell to the ground. Flustered, he reached down, picked it up, and then offered his hand to Asheris, realizing too late that he still held the linen. Blushing and grinning, he transferred it to his other hand.

"How do you do?" Josh asked.

Asheris didn't move from his stance behind Karissa, which forced Josh to step forward and lean into the handshake. The subtle power play was not lost on Karissa. She sat back, allowing her weight to sink against Asheris's left hand. His long slender fingers pressed into her shoulder.

"Mr. Lambert." Asheris paused as if judging Josh in some way. "What brings you to my country?"

"Karissa, actually."

"Oh?" Asheris returned his right hand to the back of her chair.

"I was worried about her. I wanted to make sure she was all right."

"It is my hope that Karissa finds herself well taken care of."

"I do," she put in. A warm flood passed over her. She *was* being taken care of, better than anyone had cared for her in her entire life. Though she had never lacked for anything in Grandmother Petrie's home, she had never been given understanding and compassion, both of which Asheris offered in abundance.

"Even so"—Josh put his napkin on the table—"I still want to accompany you back home, Karissa, to make sure that Mustofa character doesn't threaten you again."

"Until she leaves, you are welcome to stay here as my guest, Mr. Lambert."

"Really? That would be great."

"In fact, you must be tired after your long journey.

Would you care to rest for a few hours and refresh yourself?"

"As a matter of fact, I would. I'm dog tired!"

Asheris slipped his hands free and clapped them. Eisha appeared. "Please show Mr. Lambert to a guest room, Eisha," he said. "He will be staying with us temporarily."

"Very good, Mr. Asher." Eisha turned to Josh. "Would you follow me, sir?"

"I'll catch you later, Karissa," Josh said, taking another date from the tray. "And thanks, Asher."

Asheris nodded slightly.

Josh strode after Eisha while Asheris lowered his hands, but this time his palms came to rest on the tops of her shoulders. Karissa thrilled to his touch. Before she could say anything, however, he lowered his head and pressed a tender kiss near her ear.

"You are unquestionably," he said, "the loveliest creature in my garden."

She flushed with pleasure at his words. "Thank you," she murmured.

"It was nice to awaken to the sound of your voice." He brushed back her hair and kissed her neck, and she couldn't resist inclining her head to allow him room for more kisses. His lips ventured across her neck as his hands slid down the front of her cotton shirt to caress her breasts. A sigh escaped her, and she tipped her head back against his shoulder as he hovered over her.

"Asheris." She gasped. "You're up early, aren't you?"

"Yes, I am up," he murmured in her ear. "Very much so."

She flushed again, wishing the back of the chair was not there to separate them.

"Was I talking too loudly?" she asked, trying not to succumb to his mouth but having little success. She was about to melt against the chair. "Did I wake you?"

"Exquisitely." He eased a warm hand into the opening of her shirt, slipped his fingers into her lacy bra, and pinched her nipple, which gave her a delightful spiral of sensation. "And do I not awaken you as well?"

"Yes!" She couldn't bear the one-sided embrace for another instant. Twisting around, she stood up and rose into his arms, and he took her in a fluid motion.

Hungrily their mouths came together as her arms went around his neck. He slid his hands down her back and pulled her hips to his. In a moment they were fused, her breath coming fast and hard as he crushed her against his straining body. Their kisses turned into a frenzy of tongues and lips, passionate nips, and ragged sighs. Karissa wanted him so fiercely she didn't care if they sank to the tile and made love right then and there, in broad daylight. She longed to consume him and be consumed in return, and the sharp need for him made her moan out loud.

"Karissa," he murmured. "I ache for you."

She half opened her eyes, nearly overcome by the need to join her body and soul to his. But she could not forget the clothes and the doubt that nagged her, making her wonder about Asheris's motives. She couldn't give herself freely as long as that doubt held her back.

"Is it me you ache for," she murmured, "or another?"

He pulled away from her mouth and she felt his body tense.

She glanced up, anxious to read his expression before he could hide his initial reaction. Asheris's face was full of surprise and then wariness. His wariness was all she needed to answer her question and cool the flames of her desire.

"I *do* remind you of someone," she said, her voice breaking. "It isn't me you want, is it?"

"Yes, it is!" He tried to pull her closer, but she pushed against his chest.

"Let me go," she demanded miserably. "Please, Asheris."

"Karissa, do not pull away from me!"

"I have to!" She stepped back, and he reluctantly

loosened his hold on her. "I knew by those dresses you gave me to wear that I reminded you of someone else. But I'm not playing second fiddle to anyone again. Not ever!"

"You are not playing second fiddle, Karissa. I do not know how to explain it, but there is something about you—"

"That reminds you of that priestess, right?" Karissa wrenched out of his grip. "That's why you came on to me so strongly, so quickly!"

"It is much more than that. You must believe me."

"Why should I? You're just like my husband, looking at me and wishing you were with another woman. Maybe all men are like that. Who knows? And who gives a good goddamn!" She broke into a sob and whirled away, stumbling blindly through the garden. Men could go to hell. Thomas, Josh, and Asheris—all of them.

He came up behind her. "Karissa, please, you must listen to reason."

"Go to hell!" she cried. "I'm leaving!"

"Do not do this. You must not leave me like this!"

"Why not?" She turned at the door. "I have better things to do with my life than serve as a stand-in for other women. How do you think that makes me feel?"

He paused, struggling for something to say to convince her to stay. The look on his face was so desperate that for a moment she almost believed he truly cared about her. Then logic and pride brought her back to her senses.

"I thank you for your hospitality," she said. "But I'm taking the first flight out of Luxor. If the blocks turn out to be the lost sphinx, you can mail me a check. I assume you have my address in your files."

Asheris sighed. "There are reasons for my conduct," he said. "I am not able to tell you everything about my life. I only ask that you have faith in my actions and trust what you feel for me."

"I've been fooled before, Mr. Asher, and it just isn't worth it."

"I am not trying to fool you, Karissa. What I feel for you is unbelievably real, unbelievably good. Surely you can see that."

"No. Sorry."

"Then you are lying to yourself again."

"Who has been lying to whom!" She glared at him, her emotions roiling, unable to trust her feelings or the motives of this handsome man.

"You cannot go!" Asher reached for her arm just as Josh appeared in the doorway.

"Keep your hands off her!" Josh demanded, lunging for the Egyptian. He would have knocked Asheris to the ground but for the Egyptian's finely honed reflexes. Asheris quickly stepped to the side and out of Josh's path. Josh stumbled through thin air but didn't lose his balance. He spun around, angry and breathing hard.

"I knew there was something funny going on around here!"

"Josh!" Karissa exclaimed. She didn't want him getting involved in her personal affairs with Asheris and hated to see the Egyptian have the chance to make a fool out of her partner. She dashed to Josh's side and took his arm. "It's okay!"

"No, it isn't okay! This asshole thinks he can push you around, and I don't like it."

"Karissa has done nothing against her will," Asheris put in calmly.

"I'll bet. I saw the way you just grabbed her and heard what you said. She doesn't have to stay here another minute. She can damn well leave whenever she pleases!"

"Yes." Karissa raised her chin.

The best solution was to leave Asheris's house and go to a hotel downtown. From there she could make travel arrangements, leave Asheris and Egypt far behind, and get back to her own life—which she should have done long before succumbing like a little fool to Asheris's charm.

"Get your bags, Josh. I'll call a cab." She turned to Asheris. "If I may be permitted the use of your phone?"

"Of course." His eyes glittered at her. "You know I can refuse you nothing."

For a moment their eyes locked and held and Karissa had her first glimpse of Asheris's wrath. The warmth she was accustomed to seeing had vanished. In its place was a cloud of stormy topaz, so cold and unemotional that she shuddered.

Without another word, he brushed past her and strode into the house.

As impossible as it seemed, Karissa couldn't get a flight out of Luxor that day and was forced to make reservations for the next afternoon. She and Josh got rooms at the Blue Palace Hotel and spent the rest of the day cruising the bazaars. When the merchants took their afternoon break, Karissa retired to her room to work on her interview presentation. She didn't emerge until dinner, which she and Josh had agreed to share at the hotel restaurant at eight o'clock. Josh didn't show up until eight-fifteen, leaving Karissa to while away the minutes drinking a glass of wine and gazing across the glistening expanse of the Nile. She sat in the outdoor section, which was built of white stone overlooking the river. A balmy breeze drifted through her hair and ruffled the gauzy skirt she had purchased at a market stall. The evening air was a perfect temperature, the view was gorgeous, and the spicy smells of lamb and chicken coming from the kitchen were heavenly. Even though she brooded over Asheris, she still enjoyed the ambience.

"Sorry I'm late!" Josh declared as he strode up to the table, startling her out of her thoughts. "I had an important errand to run." He wiggled his eyebrows and opened his suit jacket, just enough to permit her a quick view of a handgun stuck in his waistband.

Karissa watched in concern as he rebuttoned the jacket. "Why did you get that?"

"I have a feeling we aren't through with your Egyptian friend yet. And the next time I confront him, I'm going to have a little firepower to back me up." Josh plopped down in his chair. "You wouldn't believe how easy it was to get the sucker. And how cheap it was!"

"I don't like guns, Josh."

"Well, neither do I. But I feel a whole lot safer with it." He picked up the menu. "Have you ordered?"

"No. I was waiting for you."

They ate dinner and chatted about the upcoming PBS special. Karissa couldn't help thinking about the lunch she had shared with Asheris, and how he had captivated her with his story. All Josh could do was crack jokes about flight attendants and complain about airline food, claiming he had been served a roll that was hard as a dog biscuit. When Josh got up to pay for dinner, Karissa wandered over to the edge of the balcony and leaned on the warm stone, remembering the way Asheris had touched her and kissed her. She had almost been fooled into thinking he really cared for her.

Josh wanted to check out the nightlife in Luxor, but Karissa declined, worried that she might be seen by Mustofa or Asheris. She wanted to turn in early anyway, because of the big travel day ahead of them, so she returned to her room and got ready for bed. She slipped on the khaki shirt, making it do double duty as a nightshirt. Then she made sure the door connecting her room with Josh's was locked, tucked her room key into the pocket of the shirt, and slipped between the cool sheets. The bed smelled of heavy cologne, pine-scented air freshener, and cigarette smoke, a far cry from the clean smell of the bed linen at Asheris's home. The two days she had spent in that luxurious environment had spoiled her. She sighed and lay back, wanting to forget the man but knowing it would take a long time before her mind would be clear of him.

Karissa drifted off to sleep and didn't awaken until close to dawn, when a strange clicking sound brought her back to consciousness. She rose to her elbows, listening for the unfamiliar noise, and then saw the dark shape of a man outlined against the open doors of her balcony. Someone had come into her room by way of the French doors.

"Josh!" Karissa yelled.

At the sound of her voice, the dark shape bolted toward her. She scrambled out of bed, tripping on the sheets, but caught herself to keep from falling to her hands and knees.

"Josh!" she screamed.

The man grabbed for her. She glanced at his dark face beneath a mop of black hair and a huge mustache but didn't recognize him. Was he another of Mustofa's thugs? Whoever he was, now that she had seen him, she was probably in serious trouble. For a moment she hesitated, unsure of where to go or what to do. The intruder's stocky body blocked her way to the main hallway, so she dashed toward the balcony, praying that Josh had heard her.

Dressed only in the khaki shirt and her panties, she grabbed a hotel robe from the bed and raced through the French doors. She flung a leg over the side of the baluster and looked down at the one-story drop below. She would have to jump over the side and into a garden area that bordered the outdoor pool. With luck, however, she might run into someone to help her down below. Without much thought to personal injury, Karissa sat on the rail of the baluster and pushed off, just as the intruder burst onto the balcony. She landed with a hard thump in the sandy earth below, and felt as if her knees had just jammed into her thighs.

She yanked on the robe and limped off, headed for the shadows along the side of the hotel. Behind her she heard a thud and a gasp as the man with the mustache hit the ground. She had only seconds left to go around to the front of the hotel, find the lobby, and ask for help.

Just then Josh hollered from above. The man with the mustache stopped and looked up, which gave Karissa time to race down the gravel path toward the front of the hotel. Then, in the dawning light, she saw the locked gate in the wall. It made sense, since the path led to the pool, that the gate would be closed and locked to prevent accidents in the water. Karissa's heart sank. The wall was too high for her to scale. And now the intruder had turned and was running toward her. She backed against the wall, trapped in a veritable box canyon.

Her heart leapt in her throat as the man ran up, a cruel triumphant smile on his face.

"Nowhere to run, American?" he asked.

She refused to answer him and wished she were wearing more clothing. If this man was anything like the last thug with whom she had dealt, he might attempt to assault her.

Karissa crossed the robe over her body, as if to protect herself, just as a black shape sailed through the air.

The black panther had come to her rescue again.

The cat hit the intruder dead center in the chest and knocked him to the ground. The man yelled and struggled with the big cat. He even managed to lumber to his feet and stumble into the bushes, with the panther at his heels.

Josh careened around the corner, brandishing his handgun. "What's going on?" he cried.

"Lord Azhur went after the intruder!" Karissa pointed in the direction of the tangled undergrowth. Josh peered into the bushes, which were still quite shadowed even though light was slowly climbing in the east. In a few minutes the sun would show above the cliffs of the Eastern Desert.

"Stop!" Josh yelled. Still the man crashed through the shrubbery, sniveling in terror at being chased by a huge animal. A bloodcurdling snarl rent the air and the man broke free, mere feet from Josh.

Josh reacted without thinking and squeezed off a shot. The bullet buried itself in the man's leg and sent him toppling to the ground. Over the top of the fallen man soared the panther, leaping through the air. Aghast, Josh staggered away and took another shot, hitting the cat in the shoulder before he fell backward into the sand.

The panther plunged to the ground and collapsed in the sand, panting heavily and trying in vain to regain his footing. Karissa watched him struggle and was filled with compassion for the beautiful animal that had saved her life on three occasions.

"Josh!" she cried, appalled that he had hurt the panther. She ran toward the cat.

"Watch out," Josh warned. "It might be dangerous!"

"You shouldn't have shot him!" she exclaimed, sinking to her knees beside the animal. "How could you?"

"It was an accident."

By that time, two men from the hotel came running around from the back. Karissa recognized the bellboy who had been on duty that evening and another man she had never seen, probably the night manager.

"What is going on?" the manager asked.

"I caught this guy breaking into my friend's room," Josh explained, training his gun on the man with the mustache. "He needs to be turned over to the police."

"I will call them," the bellboy said, turning on his heel to return to the hotel.

"Bring him inside," the manager said, pointing to the bleeding man. Then he caught a glimpse of the dark shape in the shrubbery behind Karissa. "Is there someone else over there?" He stepped closer.

"No." Karissa shielded the panther from view. "Just my garment bag," she lied. "The thief tried to steal my things."

The manager stroked each side of his mustache with the curl of his right index finger, as if deciding whether the disturbance could be covered over easily, thereby restoring the decorum of his hotel. "Very well." Then he reached down and yanked the intruder to his feet. "Come along, you," he demanded. "You have much to explain."

Josh kept his gun trained on the intruder and guided him toward the back of the hotel, leaving Karissa to deal with the cat for the moment.

She glanced up to watch Josh disappear around the corner of the building and felt the first rays of sunlight on the back of her shirt and the calves of her bare legs. What could she do about the panther—call a vet? And what would the veterinarian do once he discovered his patient was none other than the man-killer, Lord Azhur? Would he demand that the panther be put to sleep? She couldn't take the chance. And yet who else could dig a slug out of a panther's shoulder?

Struggling with the dilemma of what she should do, Karissa pushed back the branches of a shrub so she could take a good look at the cat, only to find that the panther had vanished. In its place was a tall slender man lying face down, his black hair tumbling over the crook of his arm, his long, lean legs splayed in the sand, and his left shoulder a bleeding mess.

Then he moaned and turned to face her. For a moment Karissa couldn't speak, so great was her shock at seeing the familiar features.

EIGHT

"Asheris!" she exclaimed.

His eyelids fluttered. Then his eyes opened and found hers. "Karissa."

"It can't be! You—" She broke off, too shocked to complete the improbable thought. "You and the panther are—"

"A tale for later," he gasped. "Please, help me."

She jerked back to reality, back to the sight of the blood on his arm and in the sand and the ashen tint to his skin. Now was not the time to ask him about the panther and what she thought had transpired a few moments ago. There was a flesh-and-blood man on the ground in front of her who needed medical attention.

"Can you get up?" she asked.

"With your assistance."

She got to her feet and reached for his uninjured arm, leaning backward to pull him up. Slowly and shakily Asheris rose. As he stepped from under the shrubs and out of the shadows she realized with another shock that he was completely naked. Karissa was worried about his condition but couldn't help noticing the sculpted beauty of his torso and hips, and the dark hair that feathered from his belly and then spread out at his loins. He was uncircumcised. She had never seen a natural man before.

She flushed at the sight of him and stripped off the white hotel robe she was wearing. She was dressed only in her shirt and panties, but the long shirttails were sufficient covering.

"Here," she said. "Put this on." She eased the robe over him, taking care not to hurt his injured shoulder. He put his right arm through the sleeve, and she tied the belt around him.

"Thank you," he said.

"Come up to my room and I'll call a doctor."

He reached for her forearm. "No doctor."

"The police, then."

"No police. Just you."

"But you've been shot!"

"I will be all right." He closed his eyes for an instant, fighting off a wave of pain.

"Come on, then." She slipped her arm around his waist. "The back door must be open."

He draped his right arm over her shoulders and leaned heavily upon her, as if most of his strength had drained away with his blood. She staggered for a moment, until she found a rhythm in the way they walked together, and then guided him toward the back of the hotel. She prayed they wouldn't run into Josh, because she didn't want to have to explain Asheris's presence or the possibility that the Egyptian had transformed from a panther into a man.

They slipped in the back and headed for the elevators. From across the lobby Karissa glimpsed Josh and a policeman walking into a room, accompanied by the manager. Relieved that Josh was occupied at least for a while, she pushed the button for the elevator. Perhaps she could get Asheris out of the hotel before Josh found out he had been there at all. She felt compelled to protect Asheris's secrets from everyone.

Asheris was silent all the way to the room. Luckily Karissa had put her room key in the shirt pocket the night before. She pulled out the key while Asheris stood beside her, pale and quiet.

"You need a brandy," she remarked, pushing the door open.

"Yes."

She shut the door and led him to the bed. He sank down on the mattress.

"Lie down and I'll have a look at your shoulder," she said.

Asheris lay back, his raven hair stark against the white pillow. Karissa loosened the robe and gently drew back the left side.

She grimaced. "I'll have to clean the wound before I can see anything. But I'll get you that drink first." She rose and hurried to the bar near the television where small bottles of liquor were lined up. She unscrewed the cap on a bottle of Courvoisier and poured it into a glass. Then she returned to the bed.

"Here." She handed the drink to him. Asheris took the glass in his left hand and rose up just enough to sip the brandy.

"Thank you," he murmured.

"I'll get some soap and water." She headed for the bathroom, glad to have something important to do, because the sight of Asheris wounded was highly disturbing.

When she returned to the bedside, she could see the brandy had already affected him. His cheeks had more color in them and his eyes were open and clear. She flipped on the lamp and sat down beside him, acutely conscious of the nearness of his body and the slightly spicy scent of his skin, as if he had dusted himself with coriander.

Carefully, she dabbed his shoulder with a wet washcloth until the ragged edges of the wound were visible. Asheris had been shot at such close range that there were powder stains on his shoulder.

"You're lucky," Karissa observed. "It looks as if the bullet just grazed you."

"Good. Just wrap my shoulder."

Karissa made a dressing with a clean folded washcloth and tied it in place with strips of a torn pillowcase.

"Good," Asheris said again when she finished.

"Now what?" she asked. "Do you want to go home?"

"Yes. And I want you to come with me."

"I told you, Asheris, I have to go back to Baltimore."

"I must show you what was found yesterday." He looked into her eyes, and she felt the familiar hypnotic sensation melting away her resolve. She broke away from his gaze and stood up, determined to resist him, but his rich voice followed her. "Karissa, please come back with me."

"I'm not going anywhere with you until you explain some things first."

"Such as?"

"Such as who you really are."

Asheris sighed and lay back against the pillows that she had piled in back of him. The robe fell open above the belt to reveal the taut suppleness of his abdomen. Karissa glanced away from his body and looked into his eyes.

"So?"

"So," he repeated tiredly. "Surely you must have guessed who I am."

"I think I have, but it's too outrageous to consider."

"Why?"

"Eisha told me about a legendary man who could change back and forth into an animal. But it's just a folk tale. It isn't possible!"

"How do you know?"

"I've never seen it happen! No one has!"

"No one has seen your God, yet many believe in him."

Karissa stared at Asheris, unable to refute his reasoning. He reached out and gently drew her back down beside him. She acquiesced and sat near his hip with her hand still in his.

"Karissa, there are powers possessed by some people that would astound you, especially in the days long ago when the mind of man was more open to possibilities than now. In my day, man was obsessed by the unknown and the fantastic. In this day, man is obsessed by facts and data." He paused and closed his eyes for a moment, as if gathering his strength, and then continued. "Unfortunately, while looking for proof and applying human rules to the universe, man has become rigid in his thinking and has lost more knowledge than he has gained over the centuries, believe me."

"You're saying we are more backward now than we used to be?"

"In some respects, yes."

"And you're saying that a few thousand years ago, people knew how to change other people into animals?"

"Yes. Modern man holds himself apart from the animals, but in truth we are not that far from being beasts, you know."

"Then you *are* Lord Azhur."

He nodded.

"What were you doing here at the hotel?"

"Following Mustofa's man."

"Well, if you are Lord Azhur, you are also the man in the story you told me, the commander of the Egyptian army who loved the priestess Senefret."

"Yes. But you must tell no one."

She couldn't believe it. She was sitting on a bed talking with a man who had been mummified alive three thousand years ago, a man who had been searching for centuries for the woman he loved. Preposterous!

Unbelievable. When she tried to pull her hand away, however, he clasped it firmly and drew it to his chest.

"I know you find my tale hard to believe, Karissa. But you must realize that I am telling you the truth."

"Why should I believe you?" she retorted. "How could you appear as a real man to me now if you'd been mummified alive?"

"I have been partially freed of my curse," he replied gently.

"How?"

"By you. When you came to the sphinx and shouted 'No!' you released me from my tomb but not from the curse of being a panther."

"How could I do that?"

"I am not certain. I think it had something to do with the particular resonance of your voice and the single word you spoke."

"You mean I set up some sort of vibration in the sphinx?"

"Perhaps. I also believe you are somehow connected to my past, though in what capacity I am not sure."

"But if you are the panther, why couldn't you find the sphinx yourself? You saw where it was after it collapsed."

"I have no memory of the time I spend as a panther."

"You don't know what you do when you're the cat?"

"No."

"You are a killer."

"I have heard that and read accounts of it, but I have no memory of it."

Karissa stared at him, wondering what it would be like to lead the life allotted to Asheris, in which he lost every night to the ruthless nature of a big cat.

"That is why I tried to locate you for so many years, Karissa. I believe you are the key to finding Senefret and ending this accursed life of mine."

The mention of Senefret brought back her heartache in full force. She looked down to hide the hurt in her eyes from him.

"You should have told me the truth right from the start," she remarked. It required great effort to keep her voice from cracking in anguish.

"I felt that you would not have understood. You would have been afraid of me." He kissed the tips of her fingers. "But you are not afraid of me now, are you?"

She shook her head, knowing things would be simpler if he wouldn't treat her with such warmth and kindness. It broke her heart to think that he had pledged his love to someone else.

"But it wasn't fair of you to lead me on."

"Lead you on?"

"Yes." She glanced up at him, knowing her gaze was full of recrimination. "You led me to believe you cared for me, when all along you saw Senefret every time you looked at me."

"That is not true."

"Then why did you give me her dresses to wear, her jewelry to put around my neck?"

"Because when I look at you, Karissa, you are everything I remember from the days I was a whole man. The modern world falls away when I am with you. I can forget the centuries of loneliness when you are in my arms. There is something about you that calls to me, deep inside, in a place that has no voice—no words to explain—only feelings that cry out to be heard. Yes, you remind me of Senefret, but that is only the barest beginning of what I see in you."

"I don't believe you!" She jerked her hand away and rose to her feet. She realized she was crying. His words had moved her but she still couldn't trust him. Karissa swiped at her wet cheeks. "You are obsessed with her!"

"I search for her out of love and honor, Karissa. I must assure Senefret a proper journey to her afterlife. I could have done much more for her had I gone back to Thebes in time. I might have saved her life. But I chased after my own glory. And I soon discovered that glory was meaningless, empty, nothing!" He sighed bitterly. "I had to learn my lesson about the importance of love by losing the only woman I had ever cared for."

"And you still love her, don't you?"

"Yes, I love her—the memory of her. When you truly love someone, it is forever."

"I see." Karissa reached for her cotton pants and pulled them on, stuffing the khaki shirt in the waistband. She felt as if she would shatter into a thousand pieces of despair if he said anything else about his priestess. The sooner she got him out of the hotel and into a cab, the sooner she could get him out of her life and begin the long battle to forget him.

He stepped up behind her. "Why must you be upset?" he asked.

"I'm not upset. I'm simply in a hurry. We don't want anyone coming up here and asking questions, do we?"

"No."

"So hang on and I'll get you something to wear."

Asheris regarded her for a long moment, as if he wanted to say more, but then seemed to think better of it. He reached for the brandy glass. Karissa hurried to the door that connected her room with Josh's and slid back the dead bolt. She turned the knob, hoping that Josh hadn't bolted the door from his side. He hadn't. The latch clicked open and she swept into the room.

Asheris was taller and more slender than Josh, but Josh's clothes would do in a pinch. She grabbed a pair of jeans, sandals, and a shirt out of his messy suitcase and returned to the room.

"Here," she said, handing them to Asheris, "I'll tell Josh we borrowed these."

"I do not think you understand all that I have said," he put in.

"Oh, I understand." She brushed back her hair in a brisk gesture, trying to affect a casual air. "I respect you for keeping your vows, I really do. But from now on, just leave me out of your obsessions, okay?"

He frowned slightly and then sighed, as if he had abandoned the effort to explain himself to her. Then he untied the robe. It fell to the floor before Karissa could turn around. Didn't he care that she would see him naked?

She headed for the door while he pulled on the clothes. "Hurry, Asheris. Josh is bound to return any minute." She turned to see if he were dressed.

"I am ready." He looked up.

For a moment Karissa gazed at him dressed in Josh's blue-and-white striped shirt tucked into a pair of blue jeans. Asheris's lean frame lent the clothes a neatly tailored look, completely different from the way Josh appeared in them. Asheris would look well groomed in anything. It had more to do with the carriage of the man inside the clothing than the clothing itself.

They took the elevator to the lobby. On the way down, Asheris sank against the back of the car and closed his eyes.

"Are you all right?" Karissa asked, watching the color fade from his face.

"I feel light-headed," he replied.

"You lost a lot of blood out there in the garden," she said. "Here, put your arm around me. I'll help you stay on your feet until you get to the cab."

Asheris seemed grateful to drape his arm around her shoulders. "If I use you as a support, will not people think there is something amiss?" he asked.

"No. They'll probably think we're just crazy about each other."

"And are we not, Karissa?" he asked quietly, looking down at her with his smoldering golden eyes. "Do you not understand what it is I feel for you?"

She shook her head slowly, mesmerized by the heat in his eyes.

"You are a part of me," he said. "Your eyes speak to my heart."

Before she could say anything, he bent down to kiss her, his breath faintly laced with brandy. His lips and his words drove a shaft deep into the very core of her and pierced through the armor she had been wearing as protection against his charm and kindness. In the face of his confession, her armor fell away, leaving her emotions more raw than ever. She reached up to touch his cheek as her heart surged in her chest and the elevator dipped to a stop. Only the sound of the elevator doors sliding open kept her from turning in his arms and revealing how she felt about him.

She was yanked back to reality by the sound of a familiar voice.

"Karissa! What in the world—"

Karissa pulled away from Asheris to see Josh standing in the lobby with a stunned look on his face. She straightened and Asheris let his arm slide away.

Josh stared at them, from one to the other, as Karissa and Asheris stepped out of the elevator.

"Karissa?" he asked, his voice cracking. "What's going on? What's Asher doing here?"

"Mr. Asher has something to show me," she said. "We're going to his house for a couple of hours."

"But—what about our flight?"

"I don't know, Josh."

"But"—Josh moved to the side as Karissa brushed past him—"wait a minute, he's wearing my clothes!"

"I'll bring them back."

"You'll bring them back?" Josh exclaimed. "What in the hell is going on?"

Karissa saw a few hotel patrons and the desk clerk turn their heads and look at them. "Please, Josh, keep your voice down."

"Okay, but"—Josh sputtered as he followed them toward the front door of the lobby—"but Karissa, you can't go like this. We're flying home together in a few hours. And I came all this way just for you!"

"I know, and I appreciate it, Josh, but I can't go back right now."

"What about the PBS interview?"

"I'll be there in time."

"But I thought you and I—" He broke off and glanced at Asheris and then back to her. "I always thought we— aw, the heck with it!"

He came to a complete stop at the door of the hotel, as if the truth had suddenly dawned on him. Karissa glanced at him and could hardly bear to look at the crest-fallen expression on his face.

"It would really be best if you went back to Baltimore," she said gently.

"Karissa is safe with me," Asheris put in kindly. "Though you cannot see it now."

"I can't believe it, Karissa. You've always given the cold shoulder to every man you've ever met. Why not this guy? What's so darn special about him?"

"I'll explain when I get back," Karissa said, pushing open the door. "But right now we've got to run. Goodbye, Josh."

"See you in Baltimore," he replied in a resigned tone.

Relieved that Josh had accepted the situation, she followed Asheris through the doorway and out to the sidewalk, where a taxi waited at the curb.

By the time they tended to Asheris's wound, ate a light meal, and drove out to the site of the sphinx, the afternoon sun was already well on its way toward the horizon and the desert was an inferno. Karissa drove the Land Rover to spare Asheris the pain of shifting, and he seemed to be recovering quickly from his loss of blood. By the time they reached the rock formation, he claimed to feel much better, except for the soreness in his shoulder.

They got out of the truck and Asheris led her to the site, where laborers had cleared away an impressive amount of sand to reveal a jumble of pink granite blocks. In the pile was a dark hole as tall as a man. Karissa shaded her eyes and peered in the direction of the opening.

"A passageway," Asheris remarked. "Come, I will show you."

They hurried toward the twenty or so men who were streaming in and out of the passage, carrying buckets of sand and dumping them a few yards away. A single man in long flowing robes and turban stood near the entry with a rifle cradled in his arms. When he caught sight of Asheris, he strode up to them.

"Mr. Asher," he said with a huge grin and then flashed an interested glance at Karissa. "We have found something."

"What, Jamal?"

"A sealed room! We have been waiting for hours for you to come and see."

"I was detained." Asheris took Karissa's elbow. "Let us have a look."

"We cannot show you now."

"Why not?"

"It is too late." Jamal glanced around fearfully. "You know that the men will not stay here after sundown because of Lord Azhur."

"I told you not to worry about Lord Azhur. He is only a character in a legend."

"The men will not agree to stay. No matter what you pay them, they will not stay."

Karissa glanced at Asheris, wondering what he would do. Already the men had stopped working. Some were piling their tools in a rusted, battered old lorry while others climbed in the back.

He squeezed Karissa's elbow. "We'll find the room ourselves. Is there a lantern in the sphinx?"

"Assuredly. Five of them, sir. And other tools. Keep to

the corridor and go to the right. You will find the sealed room. No problem."

"Thank you." Asheris frowned. "Has there been any trouble with Mustofa or his men?"

"No, Mr. Asher. They do not see us working on this side of the dune. We are discreet, as you have instructed."

"Good. Then I will see you tomorrow."

"Tomorrow, sir, at dawn, as you wish." Jamal gave a quick bow and then hurried toward the truck, which was already idling. The men motioned for him to hurry.

"Come," Asheris said. "Let's see what we can find."

Karissa surveyed the jumble of blocks, remembering in vivid detail the way the sphinx had collapsed upon itself many years ago. "Is it safe?"

"Once we get in the corridor, we will be out of danger." Asheris led her forward.

By the time they turned right and into the long corridor, Asheris's heart was thudding in his chest, not from the effort of walking but from anticipation. After centuries of separation and grief, he might be meters away from Senefret. He held the lantern aloft and grimaced from the pain that shot through his left shoulder.

"There's the sealed doorway," he said, almost in a whisper.

Karissa clutched his upper arm and drew close to him. Even though he realized she was frightened, he loved the way she clung to him in the dark, as if she depended upon him to keep her safe. He would give his life to protect her and only wished she would believe it.

"What do the seals say?" she asked, releasing his arm to reach out and touch the ancient plaster that had changed little in the arid subterranean chamber.

Asheris stepped forward and craned his neck to see the hieroglyphs stamped in the plaster. His heart skipped a beat as he saw the familiar group of pictures surrounded by an oval line that made up the cartouche, or symbols, of Senefret's name.

"It is her name. She is here!" he said. The raspy sound of his voice echoed in the darkness. "This is Senefret's tomb!"

Karissa squeezed his arm, happy to share his excitement.

Then Asheris noticed the way the plaster was roughly applied and the crooked placement of some of the seals. He bent down and inspected the wall.

"What's the matter?" Karissa asked, noticing his disquiet.

"This door has been sealed twice, Karissa. Someone entered the tomb after the burial and sealed it up again." He touched a crooked seal.

"Do you think grave robbers might have plundered the tomb already?"

"Thieves would not take the time to replace seals." He put the lantern on the dusty floor. "Give me the crowbar and I will begin."

Feverishly, Asheris chipped away each seal until a rectangular line showed the entrance to the tomb. Why had someone gone into the tomb after the burial? Would someone have burned Senefret's mummified body, thus eliminating the possibility of an afterlife? He couldn't bear the thought. Like a madman he hacked away at the blocks, pulverizing the old plaster and limestone. He had to know. He had to find her. With every stroke he prayed to the gods that he would find Senefret's mummy unmolested. He didn't care about the treasures with which she might have been buried. His only concern was to find her body.

After what seemed like hours, he loosened one block enough to push it into the chamber. The air of the room drifted past them, still fragrant with myrrh and cedar. Karissa stood near him, holding the lantern up to help him see his progress. Shortly afterward he knocked another block free. After that there was a quick succession of loose blocks, which afforded an opening big enough to crawl through on hands and knees. His shoulder burned and throbbed from the exertion, but he refused to give in to the pain.

"Come!" he exclaimed, too excited to remember proper English. "The lantern to me, please!"

Karissa relinquished the light and crawled after him into the chamber.

Asheris rose to his feet and grabbed her elbow to help her stand. They both took in the sight of the tomb as they stood hand in hand in a pool of light.

In the center of the small room stood a stone sarcophagus covered with hieroglyphics, on top of which was a small cedar box.

"Where are all her things?" Karissa asked. "Her furniture, her belongings?"

Asheris looked around at the bare floor, strewn with dried flower blossoms and wreaths.

"She died in disgrace. Perhaps the priestesses forbade them to bury her with anything that might help her in the afterlife."

"Could grave robbers have taken everything?"

Asheris considered the question and then shook his head. "No. The flowers have remain undisturbed except for that single path from the sarcophagus to the door. As you can see, no one has walked anywhere else in the chamber."

"So what's in the little box?"

"We shall see," Asheris replied, stepping toward the sarcophagus. "And then we will find out if Senefret is here with us."

He picked up the cedar box just as running footsteps echoed in the corridor outside. Karissa grabbed his arm in alarm. Asheris reached for the crowbar and thrust the box into her hand just as a gun and a man's arm appeared in the opening of the tomb.

NINE

"I will kill whoever moves first," said a voice in the darkness. Karissa surreptitiously slipped the cedar box inside her shirt. Asheris held the crowbar in the air, ready to strike, although they both knew it would be little defense against a gun.

The armed man motioned for someone to crawl forward. Two other men came into the chamber. Asheris made a move to accost them, but the man with the gun shouted, "I will shoot Miss Spencer if you so much as touch one of my men."

Karissa recognized the voice of Mustofa.

With an exasperated sigh, Asheris stepped back to protect Karissa, while Mustofa crawled into the chamber and got to his feet. The lantern threw shadows on his gaunt face, accentuating the hollows of his cheeks and his cold deep-set eyes. He smiled.

"This tomb seems rather barren," Mustofa continued, sweeping the air with his hand. "But I am sure there are others, are there not?"

"The others should not be disturbed, Mustofa," Asheris warned. "There is a reason this place is called the Valley of the Damned."

"A ruse, surely," Mustofa sneered, "to deter those of us who seek the treasure buried here."

"It is no ruse."

"Then what are you doing here?"

"It is a matter that involves personal honor, something I do not expect you to understand."

Mustofa narrowed his eyes. For a moment he studied Asheris, and then his regard landed on Karissa. She kept her expression as blank as possible, all the while praying he wouldn't notice the box inside her shirt. His sneer pulled his mouth to one side.

"Tie them up, Rashad," he ordered. "Ali, get the lid off this coffin."

A short squat man strode forward, slipping a coil of rope off his shoulder.

"No tricks, Asher," warned Mustofa. "Or Miss Spencer will be punished. Do you understand?"

"I understand."

"Then put down the crowbar," Mustofa said.

Asheris dropped the tool. Rashad kicked it across the room, well out of reach. Then Rashad stepped behind them and ruthlessly pulled Karissa's arms behind her. The cedar box dug into the tender flesh of her belly but she made no sound. He lashed a rough rope around her wrists and pushed her down on the floor, where he tied her ankles as well. He did the same to Asheris.

Meanwhile Mustofa and Ali had managed to slide away the heavy stone lid of the outer sarcophagus and lean it against the wall. Mustofa stepped closer to see inside the coffin. He picked up the lantern and held it near his head.

Karissa watched him, knowing from her father's lessons that Mustofa was probably looking at a wooden sarcophagus. Many nobles and kings were buried within three sarcophagi: stone, wood, and solid gold. She found herself holding her breath as the other men gaped at the contents of the coffin.

"Let us get the second lid off and we will see if this is worth our trouble." Mustofa held the lantern high as his man pried off the lid of the second wooden coffin. Once he got it loose, he heaved it over the side as if it had no value, even though it was covered with intricate paintings and inlaid with semiprecious stones. She knew what they were interested in—the gold coffin.

Mustofa looked upon the treasure of the innermost sarcophagus, and his eyes lit up in delight and greed.

"Ah, look at that beauty!" he exclaimed. "We are rich!"

Karissa exchanged a look of frustration with Asheris. He yanked at the ropes that bound him but couldn't pull free.

Mustofa looked down at him. "You might as well accept your fate, Mr. Asher. You are not going anywhere. I cannot allow you to get in my way, not when a fortune is involved."

"Do not disturb the evil ones buried here, Mustofa!" Asheris warned. "You will unleash those better left entombed."

"Superstition and lies, Asher. I do not believe you for a moment! You want it all for your precious museums!"

Asheris scowled and glared at the flower-strewn floor of the tomb. There was no use arguing with a greedy man like Mustofa.

"Rashad," Mustofa ordered, "you will remain outside the tomb to make sure Mr. Asher and Miss Spencer stay where they are. Ali, you come with me. We must go back to Luxor for crates and weapons before Asher's men return in the morning."

"We will be back at dawn, Asher," Mustofa commented, stuffing his pistol in his belt. "Sleep well."

Then, with a dry laugh, Mustofa took the lantern and left them tied up in complete darkness.

The gloom was so intense that Karissa couldn't see her feet in front of her. A sheen of sweat broke out on the surface of her skin. She was deep in the earth near the ruins of the haunted sphinx, very close to the place where her own father lay crushed beneath a rock. How could she survive the coming hours without going crazy with fear? Would she perish in the same place as her father, but with no one knowing what had happened to her?

"Asheris?" she called through the blackness. Her voice quavered. She scooted closer to him but stopped in alarm when she heard the low growl of a panther.

"Asheris?" she called again. Had he transformed in the darkness and freed himself from the rope? She couldn't see a thing!

Then something soft and velvety brushed her cheek. His tail? Karissa held herself stiff, wondering what the panther would do. She felt a warm shoulder rub gently against hers, and then the cat stretched out along the side of her leg. In the stillness of the tomb, she heard the quiet thrum of his purr and felt the rise and fall of his powerful rib cage against her knee. For a long while she held her breath, not daring to move, until she realized the panther was simply guarding her. Gradually her tense muscles relaxed and she resigned herself to spending the night in the bowels of the earth with her strange, otherworldly companion.

Hours later she awakened to the sound of a man's terrified scream. Karissa jerked to attention, unable to tell what time of day it was or what was happening. All was still completely black, and she knew only that the cat was no longer lying beside her. Desperately she peered into the blackness, trying to make out something—anything—in the gloom. She heard a slow dragging sound go past the doorway of the tomb, and then all was quiet

again. She struggled against her bonds to sit up, grimacing in pain at the cramps in her hips and shoulders, and
waited in the oppressive silence for Lord Azhur to
return.

After what seemed like hours, she saw a light pass by
the tomb entrance, and then the light came through the
opening in the bricks. Karissa watched anxiously and was
relieved to see Asheris duck into the chamber. He
glanced at her and slid the lantern toward her.

"Are you all right?" he asked.

"Yes." She tried to focus on his face, because he was
completely naked again and it was a shock to see him
unclothed. "What about the guard, Rashad?"

"He's dead."

She didn't ask anything more about Rashad's death.
She didn't want to know.

Asheris stepped behind her and knelt down to untie
her bonds. When he was finished, he pressed a quick kiss
just below her left ear. "We must hurry," he said. "Dawn
has come, and Mustofa and his men will be back any
moment."

Karissa slowly got up and rolled her shoulders as
Asheris slipped into his clothes. She stumbled on stiff
legs to the sarcophagus and looked into the stone coffin.
Inside was the golden inner coffin, still as gleamingly
bright as the day Senefret had been interred. The funer-
ary mask showed a lovely face with large eyes and a sensitive mouth. If the mask bore a likeness to the young
priestess, she must have been very beautiful. No wonder
Asheris had fallen in love with her.

Asheris came up behind her. "Help me lift the lid," he
said, striding to the foot of the coffin.

Karissa reached down and felt with her fingertips for
the lip of the cover. After a few minutes of prying and
swearing, they managed to free the top. Though the
cover was a thin shell, it was astoundingly heavy.

"It's too heavy!" Karissa gasped.

"Slide it your way, then," Asheris said, straining with the effort of supporting most of the weight. Karissa staggered back a few steps, just enough to tilt the golden lid against the edge of the thick wall of the outer stone sarcophagus.

"Good," Asheris panted, carefully lowering his end. "I can reach inside. That is all that matters."

He stooped and grabbed the lantern, bending closer for a better look. Karissa moved to his elbow and peered in. She could see a linen-wrapped figure. A sweet musky smell rose up from the mummy. Dried flowers littered the body and the inside of the coffin.

For a moment Asheris stood· there, simply staring down at the mummy, as if caught in his dreams. Gently Karissa touched his elbow.

"Is it Senefret?" she asked.

"It is her face on the coffin."

"She was very beautiful."

"Yes." He turned and held out the lantern. "Take the lantern and turn the wooden lid flat on the floor. We will use it to carry Senefret out of her tomb."

Karissa hurried to do his bidding and didn't question his directions, for she knew it would be impossible for them to drag the golden coffin out of the chamber, no matter how precious it was to Senefret's afterlife.

Reverently, Asheris lifted the mummy out of the half-open coffin and carried it to the wooden lid. Gently he deposited the figure onto the lid and then looked up.

"We will slide it out to the hallway. Then we can pick it up. It should not be too heavy."

"Okay." Karissa wiped her palms on her cotton pants. The notion of walking around in the dark with a dead person's body made her break into a sweat all over again. "What will we do if Mustofa comes before we get out of the sphinx?"

"We will try to find a place of concealment along the way. Give the lantern to me and I will hang it on my arm."

She held the light out to him and then squatted down to push the lid along the floor. The small cedar box scraped against her ribs. In all the excitement, she had forgotten about it. It would have to wait until they were out of danger.

The scraping sound of lid against limestone echoed through the corridor and made Karissa even more nervous. She was certain that someone or something would hear the racket. Ages seemed to pass before they hoisted the lid into the air and carried it down the darkened passage. Karissa took up the rear because it was easier walking forward than backward. The only drawback to the rear position was the feeling that her back was vulnerable to the unholy inhabitants of the Valley of the Damned. Her heart thudded in her chest, making her light-headed and short of breath, and she kept her eyes and thoughts focused on the faint patch of light she could barely discern in the distance.

Just as they passed through the jumbled blocks of the demolished sphinx, Asheris lurched to a stop.

"What?" Karissa whispered.

"I heard an engine," he replied. "Someone is coming!"

Asheris glanced around quickly to locate a place to hide. Then he propped the edge of the coffin lid on one knee and used his right hand to turn off the lantern. She felt a tug on the wood as he guided her around a pile of blocks and into a closet-sized opening. Karissa scraped her shoulder on a piece of granite but stifled the cry that formed in her throat.

They watched in heart-stopping dread as Mustofa and his men tramped through the ruins carrying shovels, picks, and crates, ready to plunder as much as they could before Asher's crew arrived for the day. Then they'd most likely kill Jamal and his men or run them off. As soon as the others had turned the corner toward Senefret's tomb, Asheris moved out of their hiding spot, and they went on toward the opening in the sphinx. Karissa worried with every step that the mummy would bounce off its unseemly bier.

The cold light of morning nearly blinded her. Her eyes watered and she sneezed as they stumbled onto the sand. Walking up the slope of the dune became a strenuous exercise as the sand gave way with each step they took. Karissa glanced over her shoulder, praying that Mustofa's men would not come after them. She couldn't remember feeling as desperate in her entire life.

Just as they reached the Land Rover, Karissa heard a sharp metallic sound from deep in the earth, and then a resounding thud. Even from a distance the noise was quite loud. Memories from the past came rushing back in a hot flood as she heard the horrible yet familiar sound of a giant block of stone sliding down a track.

She whipped around to say something, but Asheris held up his hand to stop her, his head cocked as he listened intently.

Then from deep inside the sphinx came a sound like the collision of two locomotives. Blocks of granite rolled out of the sand and bounced down to the bottom of the dune. The entrance to the sphinx disappeared in a shower of granite and sand. Someone screamed and the cry pierced through the thunder of the cave-in and then was gone. As if to answer the dead man, a sharp wind came whistling across the dune, blasting sand into Karissa's face.

She hunched away from the biting wind. "The sphinx is falling apart!" she cried.

"We must hurry! The whole area might give way."

Asheris threw open the back doors of the Land Rover and motioned for her to jump in. Then he hoisted the lid and the mummy into the back of the vehicle, slammed the doors, and ran around to the driver's side. Karissa secured the mummy, pulled the cedar box out of her shirt and put it on the floor beside Senefret's body, and then climbed over the back seat just as Asheris pulled away from the rock formation and headed for the road.

Karissa fell into the passenger seat and looked back to see the dune sliding into a huge pit. Blocks of granite rolled into the pit, bouncing end over end as if sucked into a whirlpool of sand. Soon the wind became so fierce and full of sand that she couldn't see beyond the rock formation.

Pale and stricken, she turned to Asheris. "What do you think happened?" she asked, brushing the gritty hair out of her eyes.

"Mustofa must have tried to carry the golden sarcophagus out of the tomb, and his greed outweighed his caution."

"He set off a booby trap?"

"Very likely."

"Why didn't we set it off?"

"Some traps are fashioned to spring when a certain weight passes across a portion of the floor. We took nothing but the body of a woman—feather-light after her long sleep."

"Do you think they're all dead?"

"Yes."

Karissa regarded Asheris's sharp profile and the sad turn to his sensual mouth. He had found his long-lost love and was about to give her over to the afterlife. He had nearly completed his task. Why wasn't he pleased?

"What's wrong, Asheris?" she asked.

He reached over and placed his hand on her thigh. "I must think for a while, my sweet." Then he slid his hand away and glanced at her, but the usual warmth in his eyes was gone. In its place was a weariness and concern she had never seen before. She longed to ease his trouble but realized she would help him most by honoring his request for time. She sat back and closed her eyes, bone weary herself.

Six hours later, Karissa stood in a private guest cabin aboard the freighter *Victoria*, in quarters Asheris had booked for a trip down the Nile. Outside a windstorm raged, as though the gale had followed Senefret's body from the tomb to the river.

Karissa rubbed her arms and thought about Asheris while the ship rocked beneath her. He had gone below to make sure Senefret's crate was stowed securely. He was due back any moment. She wondered what she should say in regard to her feelings for him. She couldn't imagine going back to Baltimore without telling him how much she cared for him. And yet if she did disclose her feelings, what good could come of it? She and Asheris were soon to return to their former lives. Revealing her feelings would only complicate a smooth reentry. And yet she longed for him to open his soul to her as she had once done for him.

Asheris had spent the morning procuring a coffin and a crate for the transport of Senefret's body, and making arrangements for this ship to take them down the Nile to a suitable burial site with which he was acquainted. He had convinced Karissa that it would be safer for her to accompany him and then be escorted to the airport the next day. Mustofa might have miraculously survived the cave-in and decided to come after them to keep them quiet about the treasure trove in the Valley of the Damned.

Karissa had agreed to his plan. If she flew out by tomorrow, she could still make the PBS interview, although once she got to Baltimore she would hardly have time to take a breath before the film crew arrived at her studio. But she knew she didn't want to leave Asheris until the last moment. She might never see him again, and every minute between now and tomorrow morning would be precious, even though Asheris had lapsed into a contemplative mood she didn't understand.

She heard the key in the lock and slowly turned to face him.

He came in, glanced at her and smiled, and then carefully shut the door.

"Is everything all right?" she asked.

"Yes." He ran both hands through his hair. "Now we can relax for a few hours."

He let his arms fall to his sides and walked to the couch, where he sank down and stretched his arms along the back of the cushions. He was dressed in tan cotton pants and a tan-and-white striped shirt with the sleeves folded up on his forearms. Yet when she looked at him, all she could see was his naked torso and the light dusting of black hair on his chest. She blinked away the vision and turned her gaze to his face. He was studying her.

"How is your shoulder?" she asked.

"It will heal in time."

"Time." She sighed and sat in a chair next to the couch. "Everything has to do with time, doesn't it? I feel like a slave to it, especially now."

"I have been thinking about time all day," he said, "and how fickle it can be."

"And why is that?"

"Because of you."

She flushed with the pleasure at hearing him echo her own thoughts. "Because my time in Egypt is almost gone?"

"It is more complicated than that."

Karissa looked down at her hands. Why did she think he was going to talk about Senefret again? If he mentioned her once more, she'd have to leave the room because she wouldn't be able to hold back her tears. She longed to be the woman foremost in his heart and mind—in fact, the only woman in his life. When he spoke of loving Senefret, he unknowingly caused her great pain.

Then she felt him reach out for her hand. Asheris's rich voice rumbled softly. "In all the years I spent searching for a lost part of my life, I felt adrift. I believed I felt adrift because I was separated from Senefret."

That damned Senefret. Karissa felt a lump forming in her throat and tried to pull away, but he wouldn't release her. She jumped to her feet.

"Let me go," she said, pulling her hand from his. "I can't bear to talk of Senefret!"

"Wait, Karissa." He stood up and took her shoulders. "You must hear me out this time."

She swallowed her anguish and stood there, loving the way his hands felt on her shoulders. He looked down, and his dark lashes swept his cheeks. "You are not aware of all the feelings I possess. Senefret is with me now, on her way to her rightful resting place. I should spend the day praying for her soul, her *ka*. And yet"—he paused and raised his glance to look at her—"the hours with you, Karissa, are quickly coming to an end."

Was he saying that he might choose a real woman over an ancient memory wrapped in gauze?

"I have been struggling with this for days," he added. "My head keeps reminding me of my duty to Senefret, but my heart is telling me to consider something entirely different."

"And what is that?" she asked, praying he would say the words she longed to hear, that he loved her and she was more important to him than anything or anyone. "What is your heart saying?"

"That I should spend these hours with you."

She touched his cheek. "What would be so wrong with that?"

"It would show disrespect for Senefret. And unfairness to you. I do not even know where my own heart lies, Karissa, and yet I wish for you to give yourself to me."

"And if I give myself freely? No strings attached?"

"Still, it would be unfair. I am not a whole man, Karissa, neither in heart nor in body, as you well know. I can offer only a part of myself."

"Then I will accept whatever you give me," she replied.

The pressure of his hands increased. "How can that be enough for you?"

"Because you will be more special to me than any other man."

"How can you be sure?"

"Because"—she stroked his temple and pushed her fingertips into his lustrous black hair—"because I love you, Asheris." The words she thought would be difficult to say came out with surprising ease and warmth born of the truth in her heart. "Even if you don't love me in return, it still won't change the way I feel. I have fallen in love with you. I can't deny it."

He stared at her, a strange light in his eyes, as if her words had paralyzed him. Then she raised up on tiptoe and pressed her lips against his. The instant their mouths met, she felt a melting sensation, a surrender in her body as well as his. With a low moan, Asheris's hands slid down to her elbows as he bent to the kiss, and her hands slid up the front of his shirt and around his neck. The fragrance of his shampoo, his clean shirt, and his faint scent of coriander filled her senses as his tongue slipped into her mouth. She closed her eyes tightly, embracing him with all her heart as his hands moved up and down her back and into her hair. For a long lingering moment, the only sound in the cabin was the rush of their breathing and the brush of his palms on her blouse.

How could his heart not be in his caress, his kiss? No one could be as passionate as Asheris without possessing deep feelings to fire his embraces. He simply couldn't recognize that he loved her just as deeply as she loved him.

"Asheris," she whispered, her skin tingling as he kissed her neck. Her body was crying out for his touch and for the feel of his naked skin against hers. She reached for the buttons of his crisp shirt.

"If we start this, I will not wish to stop," he said, his voice husky. "It is not my desire to hold back."

"No one is asking you to hold back."

She looked into his face and saw Asheris's mouth slanting upward in his dazzling slow smile.

TEN

Karissa pulled his shirt out of his pants and caressed his torso as a faint growl rolled up his throat. She slipped the shirt off his shoulders and down his arms. It fell on the floor behind him. Then she pressed a kiss in the center of his chest and hugged him, filling her soul with the glory of his warm skin against her cheek and the pounding of his heart in her ear. This was what she wanted more than anything in the world—to make love with Asheris, to hold him in her arms, to cherish him.

He eased her back, unbuttoned her blouse, and drew it off. He kissed her and unhooked the fastener of her bra. This, too, he peeled off to release her breasts. She looked up to see his face was flushed.

"You are beautiful," he whispered in awe, and he kissed her between her breasts, just as she had done to him.

Her nipples hardened with desire. She closed her eyes and sighed with pleasure as his hand swept down from her shoulder and his palm passed over the firm peak of her breast.

"Asheris!" She gasped.

As if to torment her, he captured her left breast in his hand and surrounded her right nipple with his mouth. He suckled, lightly at first, until she plunged her hands into his hair to draw him closer. She wanted him to consume her breast, to take her into him as she wanted to take him into her body. Soon he was pulling on her nipple, half sucking and half biting, and she arched back to allow him more room, while short cries of pleasure burst from her lips.

Then Asheris tipped her into his arms, sweeping her off the ground. As he carried her to the bedroom, she clung to him and rolled her head onto his hot bare chest, highly aware of the way her hips brushed across the front of his trousers with every step he took.

He laid her down on the coverlet, and she sank back against the pillows. Asheris stood gazing at her as he unbuckled his belt. She returned his regard and reached for the button on her waistband, but he stopped her so he could be the one to unfasten it. Then he unzipped her pants and slowly dragged them off. Next came her underclothes and she was naked.

With a few quick movements, he stripped. His manhood jutted out, swollen and huge, and she felt a powerful stirring inside at the sight of him. When he knelt on the bed and straddled her, she reached out and stroked him, anxious to touch his hardened silken flesh.

"Ah!" he said, gritting his teeth.

"You are the beautiful one," she gasped, cupping the rest of his sensitive flesh.

He lowered his torso until his chest grazed her nipples and his shaft brushed her belly. He moved upward slightly, just enough to create an erotic friction between them. She moaned in his mouth.

He eased her legs open and moved in between them,

never once freeing her mouth. Her hands swept over his back and down his arms as she arched upward. With each brush of his body, she felt a throb of aching need blossoming deep within her. Nothing had prepared her for the hunger she felt for this man. When she rose up, he moved his hips forward, and his shaft came up against her. They both let out a ragged sigh.

Then, because they were molded to fit perfectly together, he found her entrance in a single stroke. Karissa gasped in ecstasy as he eased into her. She clasped the backs of his arms and sank into the coverlet, surrendering to him. He pushed farther inside her, filling her with his hard bluntness, and she smiled with joy at the sensation of taking him in. She had never wanted a man more, never wanted to be filled like this before, never felt such a rightness in lying beneath a man and accepting him. And she had never ever had this urge to grin.

Asheris kissed her smile. "You like this?" he whispered.

"Oh, yes!"

"It is beyond imagining."

"Yes!" She ran her hands down his back as he plunged deeper and deeper inside her until he pulled back with exquisite control.

"Please, Asheris," she whispered. "Don't stop."

"You want all of me, then?"

She knew what he meant. He wanted to pour himself into her but didn't know if she would accept him. The truth was, she longed for his seed to flood into her. It was a startling realization, coming from the glorious knowledge that she loved Asheris as she had never loved anyone else.

Karissa took his face in her hands and looked him in the eyes. "Yes, I want you," she said, "all of you."

Her words sent him into a frenzy. He plunged into her, rocking her until her breasts were bouncing between them and his skin was wet with sweat, and she was grabbing his buttocks and writhing beneath him, chanting his name over and over again, and then his seed was bursting out in a glorious rush, filling her, and she was wrapped around his body and wrapped around his manhood, squeezing him until he was spent and trembling and collapsing upon her, and she lay there rigid beneath him, grabbing the bedspread on either side as her body was racked by wave after wave of orgasm, pressing down on him, pushing him out.

Almost as soon as she sank back, breathless and shuddering, Asheris felt himself growing hard again. He had never before recovered so quickly with a woman. Giving her a few moments to catch her breath, Asheris kissed her breasts, her neck, and then her parted lips. Her eyes opened halfway as she regarded him with a sultry, sated expression that sent shafts of joy through him and made him surge anew inside her.

Her eyes fluttered open. For a long moment she gazed deeply into his eyes, a half smile on her lips. He could feel a similar smile on his own.

"And how would you do this if you were a panther?" she asked, raising one eyebrow to tease him. Her question inflamed him, for he had often fantasized about that very thing.

He paused for a moment, weighing the possibility that he might alarm her with the truth. But somehow he knew that Karissa would not be afraid of anything he did with her. He slipped out of her and grabbed her wrists.

He saw the look of surprise in her eyes as he twisted her onto her stomach. With a few more nudges, he urged her onto her knees and elbows. Then he took her from behind, his chest riding her back, his hands clutching her breasts, his body slamming against hers, his every thrust rocking her forward. She sank her forehead into the pillow and grabbed the edges of the pillowcase. He could see her knuckles growing white as he found his rhythm. This time he seemed to last forever, even through her cries of release. Then what began as a climax for him transformed into a state of oblivion, of a timeless coming, of a shattering shimmering joining that went on and on and on. He heard his own voice uttering a growling noise and then he closed his teeth upon the flesh at the base of her beautiful neck as he let himself go inside her in another deluge. He emptied himself completely, exquisitely, utterly.

For a moment they hung there together unmoving, as if neither of them could believe what had just passed between them. Then Asheris let out a long sigh and raised his head. Slowly Karissa melted onto the coverlet and he melted with her, both of them slick with sweat and his seed. He kissed her hot cheek, stroked her outstretched arms, and then eased his body away. She moved her arm to allow him room and Asheris lay down beside her, his leg across her calves, while both of them struggled to catch their breath.

As the wind rocked the ship, he lay there and spread his hand across her flank. He liked the way his hand looked on her, possessing her like that. His manhood had burst twice inside her, and the experience had been phenomenal. But as he lay there, he felt his heart bursting with love for her, and the feeling was indescribable. He loved this woman. He loved her beyond anything he had ever known. And he longed to reveal his feelings. But how fair would it be if he declared his love, knowing full well that he might never be able to give his heart completely?

He now knew he could never settle for less. He wanted everything with Karissa. Giving parts of himself would never be enough, not for him and not for her. It would have to be all or nothing, even if it meant never making love with her again. Anything less would be too frustrating, too painful.

Desperate with anguish and despair, he gathered Karissa into his arms and embraced her tightly. Unknowingly the priestesses of Sekhmet had reached across centuries to damn him again, for their curse was ruining his chance for love once more. What had he done to deserve such unhappiness? How could he bear it?

Suddenly the ship lurched so hard they were flung off

the bed. Asheris scrambled to his feet and reached for Karissa. He pulled her to her feet.

"What happened?" she cried.

"Perhaps we have hit something." Asheris released her and stepped to the porthole between the bed and the door to the bathroom. He looked out at the whitecaps in the river, whipped up by the severe wind. "I believe we have run aground."

She scampered up behind him and wrapped her arms around his torso. Before he could reach up to touch her, he heard the captain of the vessel make an urgent announcement over the intercom.

"All passengers and crew, report immediately to the upper deck. I repeat, report immediately to the upper deck."

Then the announcement was repeated quickly in a variety of other languages.

The ship gave out a loud metallic yawn, and listed again, and this time remained at an angle so severe that Asheris found it hard to keep his footing. He clutched Karissa's arm to keep her from falling. Her eyes were wide with fright.

"Asheris!" she cried. "Is the ship sinking?"

"It is probably taking on water. Hurry and dress," he said, briefly kissing her on the lips. "You must get up to the lifeboats."

"What about you?" she asked, reaching for her underwear.

"I must go below and see to the crate."

"No, Asheris!" She grabbed at him, but he slipped past her and snatched up his pile of clothing.

"It will be too dangerous," she cried. "You could be killed!"

"I must go. Hurry, now, Karissa!"

He yanked on his pants and left her calling to him to come back.

*   *   *

Asheris retraced his steps of a few hours ago, only this time the path was made much more difficult by the listing ship. By the time he reached the lower deck, he had to wade through water shin-deep in places. That meant the hold was probably submerged. He pulled open the door that led to the companionway interior. Fortunately the door was on the high side of the listing ship, which allowed him a view of the watery expanse of the hold. Most of the freight the ship carried was too heavy to float. But a few barrels and crates bobbed on the surface in the dark. Asheris narrowed his eyes, searching in the gloom for one particular wooden box. He spotted it about fifteen meters away, near a cluster of barrels.

Without a second thought, Asheris ran down the stairs and plunged into the cold water, praying the ship wouldn't roll before he could get to the crate. He feared being entombed in the watery depths of the Nile and wondered vaguely what would happen to the spirit panther, should it be trapped underwater as well.

A few minutes later he grabbed the rope handle of Senefret's crate and turned to tow it back to the stairs. The ship screamed again, louder this time, as the iron and steel superstructure twisted under the weight of the huge vessel. The hold tilted and the water covered up the last of the small portholes near the ceiling. Asheris pushed himself to swim harder, faster, but the weight of the wooden box dragged behind him. He thought of Karissa and pressed on.

At last he felt the railing of the stairs and pulled himself up toward the angled door. He found the submerged stairs and used them for leverage as he hoisted the crate up the flooded companionway. The doorway proved a tight fit for the crate, but he managed to wedge it through. He slid the crate up the corridor toward the next door, pushed it through, and then struggled up the next set of stairs, walking half on the wall and half on the stair treads. The water dripping from his hair soon turned to sweat, both from the effort of dragging the box and the pressing need to get off the ship before it sank in the storm.

Finally he got to the upper deck, only to find the crew still struggling with the lifeboats. Due to the angle of the deck, they had fouled the pulley systems on many of the boats, and the passengers and crew were panicking all around him, running back and forth from the suspended useless lifeboats to the railing. The ship shuddered beneath his bare feet and lurched sideways. Asheris grabbed hold of the brass rail near the door and watched in horror as most of the others careened across the deck and plunged screaming into the choppy waters of the Nile. In the deepening dusk, Asheris saw crocodiles slide down the far bank and slip into the river. Frantic, he glanced around. Where was Karissa in the melee? He couldn't see her anywhere.

"Karissa!" he yelled into the gale. He wiped his hair from his forehead and called again as a terrible feeling spread in the pit of his stomach. Had she fallen into the river with the rest of them? "Karissa!"

Uttering an oath, he let go of the crate and stumbled to the rail. The crate slipped across the deck, hit the railing, and bounced end over end, sailing through the air and hitting the water with a smack. Asheris saw it disappear and then bob to the surface a few meters away. Luckily it hadn't hit anyone. The surface of the river was churning with flailing people and floating debris. Behind them he could see the nearly indistinguishable bumps of the crocodiles as they swam inexorably closer.

Then he saw Karissa. She was vainly trying to reach a barrel, but was continually thrown back by the waves in the water. Though she was fighting to stay afloat, from all appearances Karissa didn't know how to swim. Soon she would tire and the crocodiles would take her under.

Asheris looked back at the crate, which was quietly floating downriver. He must make a choice and make it immediately. Either Karissa would die in the river or he would lose Senefret's body forever. He only took a moment to consider, for he knew where his heart truly belonged. Though he might never be free from the ancient curse, he knew without a doubt that he loved Karissa Spencer and would give up his own life, his own hopes and dreams, and even Senefret's afterlife to save her.

Bracing himself against the raging wind, he climbed onto the railing and jumped off.

He hit the surface of the water cleanly and went under. Up through the cold black water he swam, praying he would not be too late. He broke the surface with a gasp and looked around as water streamed into his eyes and a wave struck him in the face. Off to his right he glimpsed Karissa, just as she was sinking beneath the waves.

"No!" he yelled. He lunged forward and grabbed a handful of her hair as she disappeared in the current. Desperately, he threw his left arm around her and took off for the shore with swift sure strokes, knowing within minutes the crocodiles would be upon them. Already he heard the terrified cries of the less fortunate as they were snatched by the reptiles.

He prayed to the gods that he would make it to shore in time, not only to escape the crocodiles but also to outrun the setting sun. Once he transformed into the panther, he would be no help to Karissa. She was limp in his grip, and he wondered if she might not make it. Distraught, he forced his arms and legs far beyond their usual limits, until his muscles screamed in agony. Still he pressed onward, concentrating on the dim lights of the shoreline and telling himself that he was nearly there.

Nearly there. Nearly there. Nearly there.

At last he felt the temperature of the water change, become warmer, and then the smell of mud and reeds filled his nostrils. His free hand struck sand. He had made it! Asheris dragged himself to his feet, clutched Karissa under her arms, and hauled her out of the water.

His knees were buckling even before he made it all the way to the warm sand. Gasping for breath, he eased Karissa onto her stomach, made certain she was breathing, and then collapsed on the strip of beach beside her.

After he recovered somewhat, he looked around, thankful that no crocodiles lounged on this small spit of sand. Then he checked Karissa to make certain she was comfortable. A pang of happiness washed over him. He had saved Karissa, and perhaps Senefret would one day understand the choice he'd had to make. Asheris reached out and lightly caressed Karissa's hair as he gazed at her delicate profile. He knew he would never tire of filling his eyes with her.

But there was nothing else he could do for her. His energy was completely drained. All he could do was pull her into his arms and wrap himself around her drenched body. He was tired beyond endurance. He couldn't walk another step. Perhaps a rescue crew would find them. Asheris laid his head on his arm. Then all went black as he lost consciousness.

He slept through the rest of the storm, the rest of the night, and didn't wake up until sunrise, when the sound of barking dogs startled him awake. Asheris jerked up, grimacing in pain at the stiffness in his muscles. He glanced at the sky, which was blue and clear, with no sign of the storm of the previous night. Then he glanced down at Karissa, still lying in the sand beside him, her cloud of black hair tangled around her shoulders.

He suddenly realized he was still dressed in his pants. He never returned from his forays as a panther with clothes on. In fact, he had learned to remove his clothing at dusk, to keep it from being ruined or lost during the transformations. Why hadn't he lost the pants last night? Perplexed, Asheris glanced around at the sand. He couldn't see a single panther track. There was no evidence whatsoever that he had been a panther the night before. In fact, he had awakened still wrapped around

Karissa in the exact position he had assumed before falling asleep.

What could it possibly mean? Had he remained a man the entire night? But how could that have occurred? The only way the curse could be lifted was by the hand of a woman who truly loved him, but he had always assumed his destiny was linked to Senefret. He stared at Karissa. Yesterday afternoon she had said she loved him, but he hadn't connected her confession to the curse. Could it really be true? Was he no longer cursed?

Just then the reeds above him parted and a dog's head poked through the blades. It yapped and growled, waking Karissa. An instant later, Jamal's face appeared directly above them.

"Mr. Asher!" he exclaimed with a huge grin. "Praise Allah! We have found you!"

Just after noon, Karissa stood at the side of the Land Rover while a manservant put a small bag containing her scant wardrobe and toiletries in the back. Then she walked into the house to see if Asheris had finished his telephone conversation. She wanted to say good-bye to him in the garden and not at the busy airport in full view of strangers.

She said her good-byes to Eisha and then turned as Asheris walked up, dressed in white. He looked radiantly handsome.

"You really are going?" he said in greeting, taking her hands in his tan ones. "A way cannot be found to change your mind?"

"I wish I could stay. But all the arrangements have been made. I can't turn my back on my business. Surely you understand that."

"Yes." He smiled sadly. "I understand. Still, I wish it were not so." He pulled her closer and she nestled against him, feeling as she had felt from the very first that their bodies had been molded to fit together as one. He gazed down at her and smiled, which was highly infectious. She knew she was grinning back, unable to control the joy she felt in his arms. He had sacrificed a great deal to save her life, and his sacrifice meant the world to her.

"I'll come back," she promised. "As soon as I can."

"Tomorrow?" he urged, kissing her with longing and passion. She smiled beneath the kiss and he raised up from her mouth. "How can I endure the hours until you are back in my arms?"

"I promise it won't be long."

"Good. Because you are part of me, Karissa. And I will miss you."

She gazed up at him. It was true. A strong bond bound them together, unspoken, unbroken, undeniable. Only one thing marred the joy of the moment. Though Asher had saved her life and given up Senefret's crate, he still had not admitted that he loved her.

She touched his cheek. "Asheris, why don't you just come with me?"

"I would, but for the call I just received."

"And?"

"It seems a fisherman has found my crate."

"Oh." Karissa felt a twinge of disquiet that she instantly pushed aside. If Asheris could countenance her leaving for the interview, she could countenance his efforts to give Senefret a proper burial. She tried to smile. "You'll phone me, won't you, once you find out what's in that little cedar box?"

"Of course. I will call you every day, just to hear your voice."

He kissed her again, embracing her until the manservant appeared and discreetly suggested that they leave for the airport.

"Just a moment," Asheris said, stepping back but keeping her hand in his. "There is something I wish to do while you are still here."

"Yes?" Karissa glanced up at him in surprise.

"I have been thinking about personal freedom very much lately."

"Yes?" She still didn't comprehend what he was getting at.

Asheris walked to the nearest bird cage and lifted the latch on the door. "At one time I thought these birds were beautiful and fascinating to watch. But now I see them only as hostages."

Karissa's heart swelled anew with love for Asheris as she looked at the falcons sitting on the perch. She knew very well why he had been fascinated with birds. He was part cat in his soul. The only thing she didn't understand was why his fascination for birds should suddenly change.

"I thought I was protecting them," he continued, "when all the time I have been keeping them from living their natural lives."

"Safety isn't what makes life worth living," she replied. "I've learned that lesson well enough."

He glanced down at her. "That's why I thought you might like to see the birds set free before you go."

"I would," Karissa said, as tears came to her eyes. Asheris had set her free of her past, of her guilt. And she would always love him for it.

Asheris opened door after door and the birds took wing, soaring over the garden like angels spiraling to the sun. One of the falcons rose up above their heads and circled the garden, crying out a haunting *scree, scree*.

Karissa shaded her eyes and watched the birds as Asheris came to stand behind her and wrapped his arms around her.

"They shall come back to my garden," he said softly into her hair, "of their own free will. I am certain of it."

She nodded and rested her head against his chest, reveling in his wonderful combination of strength and sensitivity. Just like the birds, she would return to Asheris, too, back to his garden and the man she had come to love with all her heart.

EPILOGUE

Baltimore, Maryland

Karissa heard a sound in the back of the gallery and put aside her wineglass. She was quite certain she was the only person remaining after the film crew had left. Even Josh had waved good-bye and left to have a drink with one of the blond makeup artists.

"Who's there?" Karissa called, tiredly rising up from the chair where she had been interviewed. The filming had taken two days and she was exhausted. But her spirits were dragging more than her body, for Asheris had not called her once since she had flown back to Baltimore. Something had happened to him or he had decided to forget her. Either possibility was devastating.

She walked toward the rear of the room. "Who's there?" she called again.

No one answered.

She peered into the darkness and then she saw

them—two golden eyes gazing at her from out of the gloom. Her voice caught in her throat and her heart began to pound furiously.

"Ebony," a low voice rumbled near the back door. "If you carve a cat in ebony, you will find satisfaction."

She couldn't believe her eyes or her ears.

"Asheris?"

He stepped out from behind a wooden crate and held out his arms. He was dressed in his long black coat and gloves, and she knew she had never seen a more beautiful sight in her entire life. With a cry of joy she vaulted into his embrace.

After a long hug and an even longer kiss, Asheris pulled away from her mouth. "Look what I have brought for you," he said, pushing aside the lid of the crate.

Karissa glanced at the contents of the box. In the shadows, she could see nothing but a dark lump. "What is it?"

"Ebony," he declared proudly. "For your next and assuredly best sculpture."

"How can you be so sure? I haven't been successful yet in capturing the spirit of the panther."

"Ah, but this time you will."

"Why do you say that?"

Asheris held her close. "Because the panther spirit is no longer trapped within me. It is free to be captured by your hands and brought to life in the wood I have brought you."

"Asheris!" Karissa pulled back. "What are you saying? You are no longer under the curse?"

"No. Your love has freed me, Karissa." He smiled, his teeth flashing in the darkness. "I am a new man!"

"But why didn't you say so before? Before I left Egypt?"

"I was not certain then. I had to see if the night belonged to the panther or to me. And I was reluctant to mention it to you in case my hopes were unfounded. When I was certain, I longed to tell you in person, not on the telephone."

His silence of the last two days was instantly forgiven. She grinned and hugged him tightly, wondering what it could mean for the two of them. Was he whole now, whole enough to give himself completely to her? Or did part of him still belong to Senefret?

"There is more, Karissa," he said, stroking her hair.

"Yes?"

"I barely know how to begin." He laughed and looked down at her, and his face was full of joy. She had never heard him laugh before, and the sound nearly brought tears to her eyes.

"Come and sit down," she urged, pulling him by the hand to the interview set. She sat down on the upholstered chair, but he remained on his feet and paced back and forth in front of her.

"Well?" Karissa asked, dying of curiosity.

He glanced at her and smiled again. Then he pulled off his gloves and stuffed them into the pockets of his overcoat.

"You recall the small cedar box?" he inquired.

"Of course."

He reached into the inner pocket of his coat and drew out a folded paper. "Inside the box was this letter to me. From Senefret."

"What?" Karissa thought she hadn't heard him correctly.

"Yes. Senefret was the one who broke into the tomb, left the box, and then resealed the entrance."

"Senefret?"

Asheris nodded, his eyes alight.

"But I thought it was her tomb, her mummy!"

Asheris nodded again. "As we were all led to believe. But in fact, the mummy was the body of a young priestess who had died of a wasting disease at the same time Senefret was to be executed. The woman was entombed in place of Senefret."

"Why?"

"To fool the head priestess. For you see, Senefret

escaped the temple of Sekhmet, leaving the lesser priestesses empty-handed and in a great deal of trouble should their leader ever learn of the escape."

"Senefret escaped?"

Asheris grinned. "Senefret was resourceful. She left the box there, hoping someday I would return from the war, break into her tomb, and find the letter she had written to me."

"So what ever happened to her?"

"She had fled to the outer provinces to raise our child."

"She had a child by you?"

"Yes. A girl." His eyes gleamed and he sat down next to Karissa. "How I wish I had known all of this. I have spent an eternity grieving for Senefret, when all the time she was never in the Valley of the Damned at all!"

Karissa stared at him in shock. Then she reached out a trembling hand. "May I see the letter?" she asked.

"It is a copy," he said, giving it to her, "that I have translated to English so that you may read it."

His thoughtfulness never ceased to amaze her. She scanned the text, which explained most of what he had already told her. At the bottom of the page, however, were words that tugged at her heart.

I know of no other way to contact you, my heart, for to be seen with you would mean certain death for both of us, and I could never put your life in danger. I only hope that someday you will come to know that I live for you, if not in this lifetime, then through our daughter, and her daughter after her, for a love such as ours was meant to endure.

Karissa looked up from the letter to find Asheris studying her intently. She frowned. "How do you know this is genuine?" she asked. "How do you know it wasn't a cruel joke and that the mummy really was Senefret?"

"There was one way to find out," Asher replied grimly. "Senefret had a peculiar mark on her neck. When I unwrapped the mummy, I found no such mark. Had it been there, it should have been evident, even after thousands of years."

A chill coursed through Karissa. "What kind of mark was it, exactly?"

"A red spot in the shape of a cat, to identify that she was the chosen one of the temple of Sekhmet."

Karissa was so shocked she dropped the letter. It fluttered to the floor, but she took no notice.

"Karissa, what is wrong?" Asheris stood up.

"I have such a mark," Karissa whispered, slowly rising to her feet. "So did some of the other women in my family."

"A mark in the shape of a cat?"

"Yes."

"Where?"

"Here." Karissa pulled back her hair into a ponytail and lifted it off her neck while she turned her back to Asheris. "See there at the base of my hairline?"

He stepped closer. "I do not believe it!" he exclaimed.

"I was told it's a family birthmark."

She felt Asheris's warm touch on her neck as he outlined the shape of the tiny cat with his index finger. Then he slowly turned her around and regarded her, his eyes dark and probing.

"You never mentioned your mark."

"There was no reason to." She stared up at him, realizing the impact this had on both of them. Could she belong to the same family as Senefret? Could she be genetically linked to the beautiful queen-to-be who had captured Asheris's heart? Could she possibly be the very same essence of woman as the Senefret of long ago?

"Oh, God, Asheris! Am I—"

"Yes!" he exclaimed, squeezing the tops of her arms. "You are of her lineage! That explains everything—the way I was drawn to you, the reason your voice freed me in the sphinx, the way I've been in love with you from the very first."

"You're in love with me?"

"Of course, but I could never tell you. I was not whole. I was half panther, half man, and half devoted to a woman I thought long dead. Never could we have spent a night together without the ancient curse preventing my love for you." He laughed and squeezed her again. "But Senefret is in you as surely as you are standing here!"

"You love me!"

"I love you as surely as the sun rises in the east!" He embraced her, crushing her in joy. "Ah, Karissa, I love you boundlessly, hopelessly, and eternally!"

She felt her heart blossoming with happiness, the likes of which she had never known. In that moment she knew why she had the mark, why the land of the Nile had always called to her, and why this man had become part of her heart in so many ways in such a short time. Her blood was the blood of a queen, flowing through eternity toward Lord Azhur just as the Nile had flowed to the sea since time began.

"Then I come from an ancient line," she murmured near his ear. "I'd like to explore that heritage."

"The only way to do that is to come back to Egypt," he replied, "and employ the services of an expert."

"And who might that be?" she teased.

"Though I dislike braggarts," he said, "I must admit I am well-qualified."

"Yes, you are." She hugged him tightly.

"And if you can be persuaded to travel with me again, I have two tickets for luxury accommodations on the *Cairo Queen* leaving New York in four days."

"Another ship?" she asked, cocking her eyebrow.

"I rather enjoyed the other voyage before we hit the sandbar." Asheris kissed the tip of her nose. "And I thought you might like a longer trip this time."

"As long as we don't have any crates to worry about."

"No more crates, my love," he replied. "I have learned

enough from the past to know that all I want is the future with you."

"A little bit of here and now wouldn't be so bad." She pulled him down to her mouth.

"Mmmm," he mumbled, drawing her against his body.

"Are you sure you are no longer a panther," she asked, kissing his cheek, "not even a tiny bit?"

"What proof do you require?"

She whispered her request in his ear.

He growled.

Patricia Simpson received a B.A. degree from the University of Washington, where she works as a graphic designer. She lives near Seattle.

AUTHOR'S NOTE

During the research for this story, I turned up some fascinating facts about ancient and modern Egypt, including a new theory regarding construction techniques of the pyramids and the mystery surrounding the sphinx. Some experts now believe that the sphinx is much older than previously thought and that hidden chambers lie deep beneath the sand—chambers that have gone untouched and unseen for thousands of years. Was the sphinx simply a guardian figure? A temple of worship? An oracle? Or did it play a major role in ancient Egypt, with a purpose yet to be discovered?

Not being able to let such mysteries lie, I decided to write another book about the land of the Nile, in which I will explore the enigma of the sphinx while uncovering the startling secrets of the Spencer family. It will be called *The Lost Goddess*.

COMING NEXT MONTH

FLAME LILY by Candace Camp
Continuing the saga of the Tyrells begun in *Rain Lily*, another heart-tugging, passionate tale of love from bestselling author Candace Camp. Returning home after years at war, Confederate officer Hunter Tyrell only dreamed of marrying his sweetheart, Linette Sanders, and settling down. But when he discovered that Linette had wed another, he vowed to never love again—until he found out her heartbreaking secret.

ALL THAT GLITTERS by Ruth Ryan Langan
From a humble singing job in a Los Angeles bar, Alexandra Corday is discovered and propelled into stardom. Along the way her path crosses with that of rising young photographer Adam Montrose. When it seems that Alex will finally have it all—a man she loves, a home for herself and her brother, and the family she has always yearned for—buried secrets threaten to destroy her.

THE WIND CASTS NO SHADOW by Roslynn Griffith
With an incredibly deft had, Roslynn Griffith has combined Indian mythology and historical flavor in this compelling tale of love, betrayal, and murder deep in the heart of New Mexico territory.

UNQUIET HEARTS by Kathy Lynn Emerson
Tudor England comes back to life in this richly detailed historical romance. With the death of her mother, Thomasine Strangeways had no choice but to return to Catsholme Manor, her childhood home where her mother was once employed as governess. There she was reunited with Nick Carrier, her childhood hero who had become the manor's steward. Meeting now as adults, they found the attraction between them instant and undeniable, but they were both guarding dangerous secrets.

STOLEN TREASURE by Catriona Flynt
A madcap romantic adventure set in 19th-century Arizona gold country. Neel Blade was rich, handsome, lucky, and thoroughly bored, until he met Cate Stewart, a feisty chemist who was trying to hold her world together while her father was in prison. He instantly fell in love with her. But if only he could remember who he was . . .

WILD CARD by Nancy Hutchinson
It is a dream come true for writer Sarah MacDonald when movie idol Ian Wild miraculously appears on her doorstep. This just doesn't happen to a typical widow who lives a quiet, unexciting life in a small college town. But when Ian convinces Sarah to go with him to his remote Montana ranch, she comes face to face with not only a life and a love more exciting than anything in the pages of her novels, but a shocking murder.

Harper Monogram — **The Mark of Distinctive Women's Fiction**

I'M DEBBIE MACOMBER'S ADOPTED CAT, JAKE-O.

I'm two years old and I'm an orange-and-white spoiled tabby. My favorite toy is a bunched-up paper ball. My favorite food is whatever is on your plate. And I only drink water from the kitchen sink. Debbie's daughter, Jody, is the one who waits on me hand and foot. I reward her by sitting in her lap while I purr, and allowing her to occupy the same house. While I may act like a dog, I know I'm the top cat in my household!

MY NAME IS TRISKET MILLER.

My owners, Linda Lael Miller and her daughter, Wendy, found me in a pet shop five years ago and were taken with my coloring (a sort of gray calico) and my abundant panache (I was standing on another kitten's head). They purchased me for the bargain sum of $9.95 and have revered and adored me ever since. (They are fairly intelligent as humans go.)

What kind of animal companion would live with paranormal author Patricia Simpson? Why, me—a black cat, of course! **MY NAME IS MIDNIGHT** and as well as being an object of beauty and a paragon of good manners, I proudly served as the inspiration for the panther in LORD OF THE NILE. Lending a touch of regal aloofness to the Simpson residence, I keep my favorite author company during her long nights of writing. When there's such a handsome cat like me around the house, who needs those other cover models. Hmmm?